SEASON OF SKULLS

ALSO BY CHARLES STROSS

Singularity Sky
Iron Sunrise
Accelerando
Glasshouse
Halting State
Saturn's Children
Rule 34
Scratch Monkey
The Rapture of the Nerds
(with Cory Doctorow)
Neptune's Brood

THE MERCHANT PRINCES

The Bloodline Feud
(comprising *The Family Trade* and *The Hidden Family*)
The Traders' War
(comprising *The Clan Corporate* and *The Merchants' War*)
The Revolution Trade
(comprising *The Revolution Business* and *The Trade of Queens*)
Empire Games
Dark State
Invisible Sun

THE LAUNDRY FILES

The Atrocity Archives
The Jennifer Morgue
The Fuller Memorandum
The Apocalypse Codex
The Rhesus Chart
The Annihilation Score
The Nightmare Stacks
The Delirium Brief
The Labyrinth Index
Dead Lies Dreaming
Quantum of Nightmares
Escape from Yokai Land

STORY COLLECTIONS

Toast
Wireless

CHARLES STROSS

SEASON OF SKULLS

TOR DOT COM

TOR PUBLISHING GROUP
NEW YORK

SEASON OF SKULLS

A Tordotcom Book
Published by Tom Doherty Associates / Tor Publishing Group
120 Broadway
New York, NY 10271

www.tor.com

The Library of Congress Cataloging-in-Publication Data
is available upon request.

ISBN 978-1-250-83939-8 (hardcover)
ISBN 978-1-250-83940-4 (ebook)

Our books may be purchased in bulk for promotional, educational, or business use. Please contact your local bookseller or the Macmillan Corporate and Premium Sales Department at 1-800-221-7945, extension 5442, or by email at MacmillanSpecialMarkets@macmillan.com.

First Edition: 2023

Printed in the United States of America

0 9 8 7 6 5 4 3 2 1

For Caitlin

SEASON OF SKULLS

UNWANTED COMPLICATIONS

It was a bright, cold morning in Hyde Park, and a detachment of Household Cavalry was riding along North Carriage Drive in parade dress, escorting a tumbril of condemned prisoners to Marble Arch.

Imp—Jeremy Starkey, also known as the Impresario—paused beside the Peter Pan statue to watch. A tall, skinny man in his early twenties, with swept-back hair and a narrow, intense face, Imp might have been a grown-up Pan himself: a Peter Pan who'd lost his wings and grown up hard and cynical under the aegis of the New Management. He tugged his scarf with unease, then checked his counterfeit Mickey Mouse watch. He wasn't going to be late to the meeting with his sister and her lawyer if he took an extra ten minutes, he decided. Nevertheless, he drew his disreputable duster tight and hunched his shoulders. A chill wind was blowing, as if practicing to set the cartful of fettered felons swinging once they danced the Tyburn tango. It was 2017, yet some things in Bloody England never changed.

Albeit not *quite* everything.

Cavalry soldiers in polished silver cuirasses riding huge animals through the park were nothing new. But beside their cuirasses and high-plumed helmets these riders wore polished steel plate that covered them from head to foot, with wireless headsets and grenade launchers, quadrotor observation drones whining overhead. Their faces were blank behind curves of bulletproof mirror glass. Their horselike steeds had sickle-bladed claws on either side of their hooves: their heads bore fanged maws and the front-pointing eyes of predators. Someone was clearly concerned about rescue attempts.

Imp shuddered and looked away from the dour procession. The distant noise of the crowd gathering around Marble Arch to watch the execution hurt his ears. He didn't want to hear the taunts of idiot rubberneckers who couldn't imagine that one day it might be them.

"Not my circus, not my monkeys," Imp muttered under his breath. *Not my holiday, not my hanging,* he meant. He brought his roll-up to his lips and began to inhale, but the joint had burned out, and besides, it was down to the roach. He walked across to the dog-waste bin and dumped it, then continued on his way.

It wouldn't do to keep Eve and her solicitor waiting, even though he feared the coming meeting almost as much as his own personal execution.

▸◂▸◂▸◂

There's a fine line between love and hate, Eve reflected, as she watched her brother explain his mistake to the solicitor. *Will she testify against me if I murder him?* Eve asked herself. *Is provocation a defense?*

Like her brother, Eve was tall and lanky, but there the resemblance ended. She'd carefully curated her image as a blue-eyed ice queen in a designer suit. A penchant for sudden-death downsizings and the warm and friendly disposition of an angry wasp went with the territory. It had been utterly essential while she'd been Rupert's executive assistant. But now she wondered if the weight of armor she wore was worth the cost: even the lawyer seemed leery of her.

The solicitor cleared her throat, glanced at Eve for permission, then addressed Imp. "Let me get this straight, Mr. Starkey.

You didn't ask your sister to confirm that she was undergoing a security clearance background check. You did not seek professional advice before initialing every page of the, um, 'nondisclosure agreement,' and the witness statement attached to it. You didn't read pages two through twenty-six. You did not ask for a translation of section thirteen, paragraphs four through six, even though it was written in medieval Norman French. Nor did you read section fourteen, the special license, which was drafted in fourteenth-century Church Latin, or the codicil stating that the contract—most of which you didn't read—was subject to adjudication under the laws of Skaro—an island in the English Channel with its own unique legal code—and that by signing you ceded your right to redress in any other jurisdiction. At no point did the messenger offer you any payment or inducement for your signature. Is that right?"

Imp nodded sheepishly. "I was *very* stoned. We'd just buried Dad."

Eve's cheek twitched, but her expression remained as coldly impassive as the north face of a glacier.

The solicitor clearly found it a struggle to maintain her facade of professional sympathy. "Well then. To summarize, you signed an affidavit certifying that you were the oldest living male relative of your sister, Evelyn Starkey"—the lawyer sent Eve a tiny nod that might have passed for feminine sympathy—"and signed a binding agreement to marriage by proxy, solemnized under special license as permitted by the Barony of Skaro, where the messenger acted as the representative of the groom, Lord—"

"Baron," Eve corrected automatically, then bit her tongue.

"Baron Rupert de Montfort Bigge, Lord of Skaro." The solicitor sent Eve another coded look. "Is that your understanding, too, Ms. Starkey? Or should that be Mrs. de Montfort Bigge?"

Fuck. A very expensive crunch announced the demise of the Montegrappa Extra Otto Sapphirus Eve held clenched in her fist. She dropped the wrecked fountain pen on her blotter and flexed her aching fingers. The writing instrument, carved by hand from solid lapis lazuli, was one of the most expensive pens on sale anywhere: it had come from Rupert's desk. The body might be repairable but the converter, siphon, and nib were a write-off. Emerald ink bled across the absorbent paper like green-eyed anger.

"I go by Starkey," she said, ruthlessly strangling a scream of rage in its crib. "So, what are my prospects for an annulment?"

The solicitor switched off her voice recorder and restacked the papers. "I'll need to do some research, I'm afraid. Skaroese law is a *very* esoteric speciality and I can't offer you a professional opinion without further work, but this is my supposition: in general a proxy marriage contracted in a jurisdiction where it is legal—the *lex loci celebrationis*—is recognized as binding in England and Wales. Assuming this contract is properly drafted—and there would have been *no point* in obtaining your brother's signature if it was not—an annulment would have to be carried out under that legal system, which means . . . ," she trailed off, side-eying Eve's brother.

Imp looked up, his expression hangdog. Unlike any canine he knew exactly what he'd done wrong.

"Jeremy." Eve pointed at the door. "Scram."

"Aw—" Whatever protest he'd been forming died unvoiced when he looked at her: Eve's expression was deathly. He uncoiled from his visitor's chair and slouched doorward, shoulders hunched. "I'll just be in the staff break room."

Eve waited for the door to shut. "*Finally.*" She congratulated herself for her restraint in not strangling him as she rubbed her forehead, heedless of her foundation. The viciously tight bun she'd put her hair into in anticipation of this confrontation was giving her a headache. "How bad is it? Really?"

"Well." The solicitor slid her folio sideways, out of Eve's direct line of sight. "If your hus—if Baron de Montfort Bigge is dead, and if you can obtain a death certificate, then you're off the hook. Once you obtain a death certificate it's all done and dusted and you can remarry if that's what you want to do."

"Assume he's not dead, just missing. No body, but no proof he's alive either."

"Then you need to either provide proof that he died or run down the clock. You can apply for a declaration of presumed death after seven years in the UK, and Skaroese law probably says the same—I will confirm that later—so, six years and nine months from now. In the meantime, if he's missing, his continued existence is not an impediment to you unless you wish to marry someone else—" The solicitor raised her eyebrow. "Or is it?"

Eve's cheek twitched again. "The law takes no account of magic. Or aliens and time travel, for that matter."

"Magic—" The solicitor was momentarily nonplussed. Eve hoped she wasn't one of the materialist holdouts. The arrival of the New Management (not to mention an elven armored brigade rampaging through the Yorkshire Dales, vampires taking their seats in the House of Lords, and superheroes breaking the sound barrier as they sped to intercept airliners) had sent many people into reality-denying madness. They called the casualties of the Alfär invasion crisis actors and used elaborate conspiracy theories to explain the Prime Minister's penumbral darkling and appetite for human souls. It was all a Russian disinformation scheme, a viral pandemic that induced delirious hallucinations, or a conspiracy of (((cosmopolitans))). "Seriously?"

"Contracts have implications for ritual magic." Eve let her smile slip, allowing her feral desperation to shine through. "If he's not dead then as long as the marriage is legally binding, I'm—" She shook her head. "Let's not go there."

Rupert had imposed a geas on her—an obedience compulsion—as one of the initial conditions of her employment. She'd thought it contemptibly weak at the time, and he'd never tried to use it, so she'd never tried to break it. He ensured her compliance through traditional means—gaslighting and blackmail—and she was completely taken in by his pantomime of sorcerous incompetence. When she finally discovered the proxy marriage certificate after his disappearance, it became clear that he'd known *exactly* what he was doing with the geas: the bumbling was a malevolent act.

Skaroese law was based on medieval Norman law, but hadn't been updated much since the fourteenth century. The Reformation had passed it by, and it still embodied archaic Catholic assumptions. Skaroese marriage recognized the status of *feme covert*: a married woman was legally of one flesh with her husband, a mere appendage with no more right to own property or express an opinion in court than his dressing table or his horse. A geas given additional strength by such a marriage contract was only distinguishable from chattel slavery because the rights it granted her husband were nontransferable.

Since discovering the document, Eve had awakened in a bath of cold sweat at least three times a week, stricken by the conviction that her scheme to rid the world of Rupert had failed.

The solicitor continued to lay out the dimensions of her prison. "As the marriage was contracted under Skaroese law, you should apply for an annulment in that jurisdiction." (*And I can bill for more hours,* Eve mentally added, a trifle unfairly.) "You'll need to obtain a decree of nullity from the diocese, essentially a declaration that the marriage never existed. That'd be the diocese of Skaro, which is the first stop. Have you spoken to your priest?"

"Ah, there might be a problem with that." Skaro had been taken over by the Cult of the Mute Poet a generation ago. The worshippers of Ppilimtec, god of wine and poetry, did not play well with other religions—and Rupert was its bishop. There had been no other church on Skaro for decades. "I might be able to get one, though." *If I offer to cover the repair bills, pay for the exorcism and reconsecration, and fund a stipend for the priest and his bodyguards, surely the Catholic Church would assign someone?* It wasn't as if she was a believer herself, but her mother had dragged her through baptism and confirmation in her childhood, so no loophole there. As for the bodyguards, Ppilimtec was a jealous deity. Annulment was going to be expensive, but as she had effective control of the Bigge Organization, money was the one thing she was *not* short of.

"Then that brings me to another question." The solicitor paused apprehensively. She tugged at her jacket, brushed imaginary lint from her lapel, screwed up her courage, and asked, very quickly, "In *strictest confidence,* Ms. Starkey, have you ever engaged in sexual intercourse with Baron Skaro? Either before or after the proxy marriage?"

Eve shook her head. "No, I never had sex with—" She paused for a double take. "Does telephone sex count?"

"Tele—" The solicitor gave her a blank look. "Could you clarify that?"

No, Eve thought, but her mouth answered regardless. "Rupert would phone me at any hour of the day or night—I was his executive assistant *and* PA, both hats at the same time—and treat me like a phone-sex worker. The only way to get him to shut up was to tell him a pornographic bedtime story until he finished wanking." She could feel her cheeks glowing. "It was workplace sexual harassment, but I couldn't quit the job—"

Eve felt something cold and moist on the back of her left hand. She glanced down with carefully concealed distaste. The solicitor had laid a hand on her wrist: the woman wore an expression of heartfelt sympathy. "I understand completely," she said. *Show me where the bad man touched you.* "I'm pretty certain the Catholic Church doesn't count coerced telephone sex as intercourse for purposes of obtaining an annulment." She smiled apologetically.

"In general, the three requirements for a valid marriage in canon law are that the couple married freely and without reservation, that they love and honor each other, and they accept children lovingly from God. None of those apply to you. I see absolutely no way that these papers"—she tapped her folio—"can be construed as anything other than an attempt to bypass the intent if not the letter of the law, so I think it ought to be possible to convince a parish priest to petition the diocese tribunal for an annulment on your behalf. It normally takes eighteen months or so to obtain one, with the right supporting documents. But as I said, I need to research the minutiae of Skaroese law." She rose. "Is that everything you wanted me to cover?"

Eve suppressed a brief impulse to bang her head on the table. *Eighteen months.* Eighteen months of maximum vulnerability, eighteen months of night terrors, eighteen months of uncertainty and paradox. "It'll have to do," she said tightly. "If there's anything I can do to speed the process up—*anything*, whatever the cost—be sure to let me know." She stood and led the lawyer to the door of her office. "Day or night," she emphasized, showing her out.

▸◂▸◂▸◂

Rupert de Montfort Bigge, Baron Skaro, had been missing for nearly three months, lost in the dream roads that connected other lands, times, and universes. He'd been trying to retrieve a cursed tome that Eve had procured on his behalf, and creatively mislaid.

If he was still alive, Rupert would be in his late thirties but appear a decade older. He'd chosen his grandparents well: born to a birthright of privilege and wealth, he'd had the freedom to squander everything fate handed him and to write it off as a learning experience.

After schooling at Eton he'd studied Philosophy, Politics, and Economics at Oxford. While at university he'd joined the Oxford Union, a debating society and the usual first step toward a Conservative junior minister's post. He'd also joined other, less savory clubs, and a particularly damning video shot at a boisterous underground dining club had surfaced when his name was put forward for a parliamentary seat. Bestiality was a crime, necrophilia was a crime . . . bestial necrophilia in white tie and tails fell into a *Twilight Zone* loophole that Parliament had failed to criminalize, but the candidate selection committee nevertheless felt it best to err on the side of caution. (Questions about his vulnerability to blackmail had been raised.) Rejected by politics Rupert sulkily slouched off to the City, apparently intent on dedicating the rest of his life to the pursuit of drugs, depravity, and wealth beyond the dreams of avarice.

Had Rupert been just another chinless wonder with a penchant for Bolivian nose candy, high finance, and the English vice, his subsequent trajectory would have been undistinguished and short. But somewhere along the way Rupert conceived a plan. The precise details were obscure—he fully confided in no one after the Dead Pig Affair—but this much was clear: Rupert still harbored political ambitions, but not parliamentary ones. His new path to power centered on the secret cult he had joined before he was sent down.

Strange faiths that practiced unspeakable rites were springing up everywhere these days, growing in numbers and spreading like clumps of horrifyingly poisonous toadstools as the power of magic waxed. Rupert ascended rapidly through the priesthood of the Mute Poet, using their sacramental rites to obtain investment guidance from his unholy patron. And he made use of every available edge, from option trades to obsidian sacrificial axes, to bloat his fortunes and selectively evangelize the faith.

The Cult of the Mute Poet presented itself to the public as a somewhat eccentric Christian sect: the Church of Saint David, patron of poets. Its inner circle, however, worshipped Our Lord the Undying King, Saint Ppilimtec the Tongueless, who sits at the right hand of Our Lord the Smoking Mirror. Fifteenth-century conquistadores in the New World had witnessed the rites performed by Nahua priests and been impressed by the results: so they had copied their practices and applied them to their own corrupted saints. When you recited the right phrases and made sacrifice appropriately, *things* that dwelt in other realms might listen and lend their will to your ends—even if they were not the beings toward which your pleas were directed. And it wasn't as if the Catholic Church wasn't syncretistic by design—it was right there in the name—so what if it required a little human sacrifice to energize the power of prayer?

The Church of the Mute Poet was not the worst of the sanguinary cults that festered beneath the aegis of the Inquisition. Most of the most gruesome offenders were stamped out before the return of magic. In any case, all were overshadowed by the New Management, the government of the Black Pharaoh—N'yar Lat-Hotep—the Crawling Chaos Reborn. But the followers of Ppilimtec the Tongueless survived, alongside certain others. They thrived under Rupert's Machiavellian leadership, building congregations and attracting converts, and with every victim sacrificed and each service of worship conducted, Rupert funneled power to his Lord.

In return he received the benefits accrued by a high priest.

But to what end?

Eve neither knew nor truly cared. She just wanted to be free of his demands. She'd risen to a position of power almost absentmindedly, unaware of the proxy marriage that made her his magically enslaved minion (and, inadvertently, his heir). Discovering that as his wife or his widow she controlled his hedge fund and web of offshore investment vehicles was a pleasant bonus, but in truth, Eve hadn't tried to kill him for the money.

Eve had ambitions of her own. She was bent on revenge against another cult, the Golden Promise Ministries, who had taken the life of her father and the mind of her mother. Unfortunately, cleaning up the mess Rupert had left behind—his followers had been up to their eyeballs in foul schemes—was sucking all the air out of the boardroom and leaving Eve no time for her own plans.

Then, as if that wasn't bad enough, she'd come to the attention of very important people.

▸◂▸◂▸◂

Two weeks into the new year—four weeks after she led her security team to Castle Skaro and interrupted her husband's followers, who had been attempting to sacrifice a family of superpowered children in order to summon Rupert's shade from wherever he'd been banished to—Eve received a visit that she had been both expecting and dreading for some time.

Taking control of Rupert's business empire in his absence was one thing (she'd already deputized for him over a period of years). But his occult empire was another matter entirely. His followers were numerous and murderously devoted to their Lord. He'd sent them instructions via an after-death email delivery service: Eve dared not read her incoming messages without first subjecting them to three layers of filtering, just in case he tried to Renfield her from beyond the grave.

At least she'd cleaned house in the security subsidiary. She'd had to, after a failed assassination attempt. Sergeant Gunderson had proven to be trustworthy, although she hadn't managed to extract any useful intelligence from Eve's would-be killer before he choked himself to death on his own tongue. And Eve's own basement den was safe, although she used Rupert's ostentatious luxury suite upstairs for receiving visitors.

She was reviewing the quarterly figures from the Bigge Organization's defense procurement subsidiary when her earpiece buzzed. "Starkey," she snapped irritably. "I'm on do not disturb for a reason. Is the building is on fire?"

"Ma'am, you have a visitor waiting in reception," said the

receptionist who'd interrupted her spreadsheet-minded musing. Something in her tone put Eve on notice that perhaps the building *was* on fire, figuratively speaking. "She's from the House of Lords and she's asking for you by name."

Eve shuddered: this was *absolutely* a metaphorical house fire. "I'll be right with you," she said, much more politely, and hung up.

Eve secured her laptop then pulled her heels on and checked her makeup, clearing the decks for action. Those people—the House of Lords—didn't exactly pay house calls: they had minions to do that sort of thing. And a mere minion wouldn't turn up unheralded and expect to see the boss. So, while it might be something minor—a social call on Baron Skaro's widow, for instance, an invitation to discuss Rupert's tax returns, a request for a cup of sugar—Eve was fairly certain that it *wasn't* minor. And that meant she had to get her game face on. After all, the sequel to the curse *may you live in interesting times* was *may you come to the attention of very important people.* And they didn't come much more important than the New Management of Prime Minister Fabian Everyman.

Under the New Management, the House of Lords wasn't just a sleepy debating club for aristocratic coffin dodgers. In 2007 the House had been reconstituted as a serious, albeit unelected, revising chamber that handled a lot of lawmaking and committee work on behalf of the government. Then when the New Management arrived, it had been given executive responsibilities as well. In particular, matters of thaumaturgy, necromancy, and demonology now fell within the ambit of what had once been known as the Invisible College, a secretive body originally established under the governance of the Star Chamber.

Eve was not one to overindulge in *Star Wars* references, but as she entered the ground-floor lobby area she sensed a disturbance in the Force. It felt as if a thunderstorm was about to break: the doorman, the receptionist, and the duty security guard had frozen like rabbits before a hungry fox, all of them paralyzed and unable to look away from a woman of indeterminate age. Her glossy black hair was as tightly controlled as her bearing, and her suit was vintage Chanel, Eve guessed. At her shoulder stood a man whom she recognized immediately as ex-military, quite likely ex–special forces.

"You must be the Ms. Starkey I've been hearing so much about." (Eve felt a treacherous flash of relief at her visitor's use of her real name. *Way to make a good first impression.*) The woman smiled as she extended her gloved hand. "Johnny, introduce me," she told her bodyguard.

"Yes, Du—Your Grace." Despite being a mountain of muscle in a suit of sufficiently generous cut to conceal a small arsenal, and despite having a vestigial Scottish burr, the bodyguard showed dangerous signs of sentience. "Ms. Starkey, please allow me to introduce Her Grace, Baroness Persephone Hazard. Her Grace is the Deputy Minister for External Assets."

"Please, call me Seph," said the baroness. "I think it's long past time we had a little talk, don't you agree?" She met Eve's eyes, smiled, and gazed deep into her soul.

Eve's brain froze as words failed her. She had an apprehension that she was in the presence of a great predator: perhaps a triumphant witch-queen, or the viceroy of Tash the Inexorable in a broken Narnia where Aslan had been crucified before the sacrificed corpses of the Pevensie children. But then the ward she wore on a charm bracelet around her left wrist grew hot, the sense of imminent damnation began to recede, and she blinked, broke eye contact, and regained self-control. A hot prickling flush of embarrassment and anger spread across her skin. Baroness Hazard was not only a practitioner but a really strong one: stronger than Eve, stronger than her father, stronger than Rupert. And Persephone had just rolled Eve, spearing through her defenses before she realized she was at risk.

But Eve was still alive. Which meant the baroness wanted

something from her, not just her skull on a spike. So the situation was probably still salvageable? The gridlock behind her larynx broke. "Follow me," she said hoarsely, then turned and retreated downstairs to her office. She heard footsteps following her: the baroness's heels and Johnny's heavier tread.

Eve's office was much smaller than Rupert's, but it was less prone to interruption and Eve had ensured it was secure. She sat and waved at the seats opposite. The visiting sorceress sat, while her bodyguard stepped inside and closed the door, then took up position beside it. He stood at parade rest, his unblinking gaze fixed on a spot a meter behind Eve's forehead. Eve raised an eyebrow at the baroness. "Is he . . . ?"

Seph nodded. "Johnny has my back," she said with complete assurance.

"Always," he rumbled, a hint of warning coloring his voice.

Eve fought the impulse to hunch her shoulders. "I'm sure your time is very valuable," she said, smiling but keeping her teeth hidden. "How may I help you?"

Seph crossed her legs, smirked, and asked, "What do you know about the Cult of the Mute Poet?"

Eve felt as if her life ought to be flashing across her vision at that moment. It didn't happen in real life, but *if it did* this was the right time for it to happen, wasn't it? The baroness was clearly not asking her to read back the Wikipedia article on the god Ppilimtec, Prince of Poetry and Song. There was another game in play.

She took a deep breath, then very carefully said, "I am obedient to His Majesty the Black Pharaoh, N'yar Lat-Hotep, wearer of the Crown of Chaos. I will swear any oath required of me to confirm my loyalty. Is that why you're here?"

The baroness cocked her head to one side. In the distance, Eve felt rather than heard the rumble of the breaking storm. "That is an acceptable start, but I fear I was insufficiently precise. Let me amend my question. What is *your* connection with the Cult of the Mute Poet?"

Eve licked her desert-dry lips, then began to explain everything: from her mother's fall into a decaying orbit around the black hole of the Golden Promise Ministries to her own vow of revenge, to her recruitment by Rupert, the subsequent degradation and depravity, the proxy marriage she had only found out about the previous month, and finally her discovery that Rupert was in fact not only an organized-crime kingpin but the cult's bishop or high priest and that she was, in the eyes of Skaroese law, of one flesh with him. Midway through her confession her phone rang. She muted it and carried on. The baroness nodded when she enumerated her visits to Skaro and to the church in Chickentown, described the bloody carnage in the conference room and the underground chapel, then confessed her own desperate anxiety about the question of Rupert's existence. It was, she felt, as if she had lost control of her own tongue—but that was impossible, wasn't it? Rupert's office was thoroughly warded, she herself was warded, she'd know if—

Finally, the baroness spoke.

"I find it interesting that your former employer"—Eve felt a stab of gratitude that she said *former*: it implied a certain distance—"left werewolves in your security detachment. And even more interesting that the survivor suicided."

"Werewolves?"

"Not *actual* shape-shifters, skinwalkers don't exist, you can trust me on that! I mean undercover loyalists with orders to conduct assassination or terror operations on behalf of their absent leadership. It's something you usually only see with State-Level Actors." Seph paused, then looked thoughtful. "Was Rupert an SLA? In your opinion."

"Not on the same level as His Majesty, but"—she recalled the paperwork from his office, under the battlements of a Norman fortress—"obviously he has his own jurisdiction, doesn't he? Held *in feu* as a vassal of the Duke of Normandy." Unless somehow one of Her Majesty's ancestors' law clerks had fucked up and—*no, don't go there,* Eve thought, *don't even* think *that thought.* "He had a surprising number of heavily armed goons, connections to shady arms dealers, annual revenue measured in the billions of euros, and his own cult, so yes, I think you *could* reasonably make a case that he was a State-Level Actor. Or at least that he fancied himself as a kind of occult Ernst Stavro Blofeld." (The kind of necromantic Bond villain who liked to relax by hunting clones of himself on a private island, or extorting trillion-dollar ransoms from the United Nations in return for not repopulating New York with dinosaurs.) "But then he died"—*hopes and prayers*—"and his mess landed in my lap."

"Jolly good, Ms. Starkey."

Persephone's smile flickered like heat lightning, liminal and deadly, and Eve had a sense of barely constrained magic aching for explosive release. The baroness was clearly of human origin, but sorcerers of such power rarely stayed human for long. Either the Metahuman Associated Dementia cored them from the inside out, or they made a pact with the deadly v-symbionts that thrived in the darkness. Or they transcended their humanity in some other arcane manner: it mattered not. What mattered was that whichever path they chose, they trod the Earth like human-shaped novae and left blackened footsteps in the molten rock, until they finally burned out and collapsed into some incomprehensible stellar remnant of proximate godhood. Persephone was still human for the time being, but Eve uneasily apprehended that she was sharing her office with a polite but not entirely tame nuclear weapon.

"Understand that I speak now as the mouthpiece of the New Management. *It pleases His Majesty,*" Persephone continued, and there was an echo in her voice as if a god was taking note of her words and nodding along gravely, "*for you to do as you wish in the matter of the Church of the Mute Poet.*" Which, Eve interpreted, meant she'd just been handed enough rope to hang herself with—and not a centimeter more.

Then Persephone continued, in more human tones, "But are you absolutely certain that Rupert de Montfort Bigge is permanently dead?"

Eve froze. "I sincerely hope so!" she burst out.

"You didn't actually see his corpse, did you?" Persephone had the effrontery to look sympathetic, damn her eyes.

"I didn't," Eve confessed. "But I don't see any way he could have survived if he followed my directions. And he had no reason not to." She flinched as an entire herd of black cats padded across her open grave.

"Well." The distant shining darkness entered Persephone's gaze again. "*Let it be understood by all that Rupert de Montfort Bigge, Baron Skaro, is hereby de-emphasized by order of the New Management. Should he set foot on these isles again, he shall find no sanctuary in the House of the Black Pharaoh. He is outside the law, and though he may live or die, none shall give him aid and comfort. Furthermore, the New Management decrees that pursuant to the marriage contract executed by the outlaw Baron Skaro in her absence, being his lawful wife, Evelyn Starkey is recognized as his sole heir and assignee.*"

Persephone paused. It was just as well: Eve was on the verge of hyperventilating and needed an entire minute to regain control once more. Eventually the black fuzz at the edges of her vision receded.

"I, uh, I . . ." Eve couldn't continue.

Persephone continued, back to speaking in her own voice, "You are summoned to attend the Court of the Black Pharaoh within the next three months—you will receive instructions by post in due course—at which time you will swear allegiance to His Dread Majesty." *Or else* was a given. "At that time His Majesty may choose to leave you be or dispose of you in accordance with his wishes." Eve found it hard not to flinch again.

"That's not necessarily detrimental to you—the government has numerous executive posts to fill and a shortage of competent vassals. If you play your cards right you may prosper, never mind merely survive. But. Terms and conditions apply, as they say. Your complete submission is a nonnegotiable and *absolute* requirement of the New Management: no ifs, no buts."

Translation: *You're drafted!* Eve steeled herself and nodded. "What else?" she asked.

"As heir to Baron Skaro's properties, rights, and duties, His Majesty holds you responsible for any future transgressions by the Cult of the Mute Poet. The buck, as they say, stops here." The baroness pointed a shapely finger at the desktop in front of Eve. "But the New Management is not hanging you out to dry. You are welcome to call on me for advice and guidance, and if at any time you feel you really can't cope, you can petition to be relieved of your responsibilities. That's a card you can play only once, but it's better than ending up with your head on a spike."

Eve translated mentally: *We're taking over your operation but we're keeping you on as Corporate Vice President for Cannibal Club Poetry Slams, unless you fuck up so badly we decide to execute you.* She nodded, her mouth dry. "Is that all?" she asked.

"Not quite!" Baroness Hazard beamed at her. "There's one last thing. His Majesty appreciates tribute, as a gesture of submission on the part of new vassals. In view of the uncertainty surrounding the postulated death of your husband, and in order to prove beyond reasonable doubt that he is dead, I would strongly advise you—and I am sure this aligns perfectly with your own preferences—to gift His Majesty with the head of the outlaw Rupert de Montfort Bigge when you are presented at court. It would be a perfect addition to His Majesty's cranial collection, and it would be one less thing for everyone to worry about—both His Majesty and yourself, if you follow my drift."

With that, she rose. "Welcome to the team, Evelyn. I look forward to working with you in future. Goodbye!"

The year is 2017, and in a few months' time it will be the second anniversary of the arrival of the New Management.

Welcome to the sunlit uplands of the twenty-first century!

One Britain, One Nation! *Juche* Britannia!

Long live Prime Minister Fabian Everyman! Long live the Black Pharaoh!

Iä! Iä!

(Now *that's* the spirit of the age, eh what?)

Magic, in abeyance since the dog days of the Victorian era, has been gradually slithering back into the realm of the possible since the 1950s. Wartime work on digital computation—the works of Alan Turing and John von Neumann in particular, the codification of the dark theorems that allowed direct manipulation of the structure of reality—turn any suitably configured general-purpose computing device into a tool of hermetic power. Cold War agencies played deep and frightening head games with demons at the same time their colleagues in rocketry and nuclear physics reached for the stars and split the atom. Old dynasties of sorcerers and ritual magicians—those who practiced magic as an intuitive art rather than methodical science—have gradually regained their skills and rediscovered their family secrets.

The onslaught of microelectronics cannot be described as anything less than catastrophic. For five decades, Moore's Law has driven a relentless exponential increase in performance per dollar, as circuits grow smaller and engineers cram more transistors onto each semiconductor wafer. Minicomputers the size of a chest freezer, costing as much as a light plane, arrived in the 1960s. They rapidly gave way to microcomputers the size of a typewriter, costing no more than a family car. Speeding up and shrinking continuously, they became cheap and ubiquitous. Now everybody has a smartphone as powerful as a 2004 supercomputer. And while most people use them to watch cat videos and send each other selfies, a small minority—mere millions of sorcerous software engineers, worldwide—use them for occult ends.

More brains in the world, and more computers, mean more magic: and the more magic there is, the easier the practice of magic becomes. It threatens us with an exponentially worsening explosion of magic, a sorcerous singularity. When it was first hypothesized in the 1970s, this possibility seemed so threatening that the security services gave it a code name (CASE NIGHTMARE GREEN) and considered it a worse threat than global climate change. Then the floodgates opened, and in the tumultuous wake of a major incursion that killed tens of thousands, the security services made a very explicit pact with a lesser demiurge. They pledged their support to a strong political leader who understands the nature of the crisis, and who has promised us that He *will* save the nation—for dessert, at least.

Long live Prime Minister Fabian Everyman!

Long may the Black Pharaoh reign!

Iä! Iä! N'yar Lat-Hotep!

H. P. Lovecraft[1] misspelled His name and libelously misconstrued His intentions. Egyptologists questioned his very existence. Nevertheless, N'yar Lat-Hotep is very real: an ancient being worshipped as a god for thousands of years who takes a whimsical and deadly interest in human affairs. For a period of centuries, perhaps millennia, He absented himself: but then, not so long ago in cosmic terms, He squeezed one of His pseudopodia through the walls of our world and installed Himself in a nameless, faceless human vessel. A cypher, a sorcerer overwhelmed, or one who

1. Racist, bigot, and author of numerous fictions of the occult that are as accurate a guide to the starry wisdom as the recipes for explosives in *The Anarchist Cookbook*.

made a pact with a force beyond his understanding: it makes no difference how it began, only how it ends.

Having obtained a toehold, He applied himself to the challenge of taking over a small and fractious landmass on the edge of Europe, a nation with an overinflated regard for itself, a fallen imperial hub not yet reconciled to its own loss of primacy. Its complacent rulers were easy prey for this canny and ancient predator. He took over the ruling party in the summer of 2015 and declared Himself Prime Minister for Life, to the unanimous acclaim of Parliament, the royal family—for the PM approves their civil-list payments—and the media—or at least those editors who value their lives. (Nobody bothered to ask the public their opinion: the Little People don't count.)

Since 2015, the New Management has made some changes.

His Dread Majesty is nothing if not a traditionalist, and also a stickler for the proper forms. By appointing His minions to the House of Lords He has brought the foremost occult practitioners of the land into His court—those who are willing to swear obeisance to Him, of course: there are certain followers of rival gods who are unwilling to bend their necks, and consequently run the risk of bills of attainder and execution warrants being laid against them. But there is a silver lining to His rule! He has very limited tolerance for corruption among those He entrusts with the business of government in His name. He prizes efficiency over humanity, consistency over mercy, permanence over progress. It is possible to thrive and grow wealthy in His service, but only as long as one's loyalty is above reproach and one strives tirelessly to build the Temple of the Black Pharaoh. The old oafish ways of bumbling inefficiency and furtive old-school handshakes passing envelopes stuffed with banknotes are banished forever! And the nation is healthier for all that.

It should be clear by now that worshippers of the Red Skull Cult, members of the Church of the Mute Poet, and devotees of mystery cults devoted to gods and monsters that claim to be His rivals are not, to put it mildly, likely to flourish under His Dark Majesty's eye. Which is why Eve's summons to pay court to the Prime Minister is such a big deal. As a high priest of Ppilimtec—the Mute Poet—Rupert was swimming against a riptide: but the Prime Minister is nothing if not strategically generous, and He has granted Eve an opportunity to kiss the ring, bend her neck, and distance herself from her missing-presumed-dead master.

At a price, of course.

▸◂▸◂▸◂

"Tuesday, March seventh," Wendy Deere spoke into her voice recorder. "Castle Skaro, Bailiwick of Skaro, ABLE ARCHER on assignment for Ms. Starkey, Chief Operations Officer, de Montfort Bigge Holdings. Investigation of tunnels continuing."

It was a cold spring morning on Skaro, a craggy island in the English Channel, close to the Normandy coast. Skaro was a lump of rock with perhaps two square kilometers of usable land area, bounded by cliffs at one side and a slope down to a village clustered around the sheltered harbor at the other: the top of the island was dominated by Castle Skaro, a stone-faced example of medieval military architecture.

Wendy had arrived at the castle with Imp the previous evening, flying in on the company helicopter. Her stuffy guest room resembled a failed hotel conversion from the 1950s, and at Imp's suggestion she ate supper in her room. ("You don't want to risk the dining room," he warned her. "The staff will insist we wear evening dress while they stare at us disapprovingly, and the food's shite.") Now it was morning, and after an unappetizing buffet breakfast in the grand hall she'd marched down to the dungeon to get started.

Not for the first time she asked herself what the hell she was doing here. Bad enough that it meant spending time with Imp, who was charming if chaotic, not to say supervillain adjacent. His sister was cut from an altogether darker cloth, and Eve's missing boss—the subject of Wendy's extended investigation—was an absolute horror show. *Lie down with dogs, get up with fleas,* she thought with a shudder. *Or rabies.*

The tunnels under Castle Skaro had gotten a lot of use over the centuries. The feudal lords who'd ruled the rock in times gone by had stashed assorted criminals, casks of wine, pirates, contraband, hostages, inconvenient relatives, and barrels of gunpowder in the cellars. They'd also served as a refuge for outlawed Catholic clergy on their way into exile on the Continent, which perhaps explained the old chapel, before it had been reconsecrated and put to horrifying sacrificial use by the Cult of the Mute Poet.

There were other tunnels dug into the opposite flank of the cliffs—excavated by Nazi slave labor, with reinforced concrete gun platforms on top. According to the very incomplete maps that existed the Nazi tunnels didn't connect to the castle cellars, although Eve had her doubts. Wendy could understand why: piracy and smuggling were the main reasons why Skaro had been settled in the first place. It certainly wasn't for the sandy beaches, sunbathing, and fine dining.

Wendy shouldered her day pack and trudged down the first flight of stairs. The scene-of-crime people had done their thing and the cleanup crew had been and gone. The dehumidifiers and air purifiers had taken the clammy chill out of the air, which now felt no worse than any other deep-dug cellar. Nevertheless, she shuddered as she passed the cells (their doors chained open to display freshly painted walls and floors). People had been imprisoned here and murdered in the chapel next door. Rupert had disemboweled his most recent victims just before Christmas, removing their organs then weighing and inspecting them in a carefully scribed sorcerous energy-containment grid. His success as a private-equity investor was based on haruspicy, the reading of entrails: his profits were drenched in entirely unmetaphorical blood.

"C'mon, Imp, where *are* you?" Wendy muttered. They were supposed to map at least one more tunnel today, and if possible make a start on the third level. But there was no way in hell Wendy would risk exploring these abandoned tunnels on her own—if you slipped and broke an ankle down here it might be years before anyone found your remains.

"Yo! Sorry I'm late!"

Imp bounded through the door behind her, like a greyhound eager to share his latest mud bath with anyone who'd stand still for it. He was tall and lanky—long-boned, Wendy's dad would have said—and wore an antique tweed greatcoat over drainpipe jeans and a ruffled shirt. He could have been the walking personification of the word "louche." And indeed, he *was* an art-school dropout and would-be filmmaker. But he was also a supervillain of sorts and Wendy was still an ex-cop, even if she was working for his sister these days. Which, she supposed, made her the feline counterpart to his mutt.

"Mr. Starkey." She tilted her chin and narrowed her eyes at him. "You're late. What time do you call this?"

"I call it boyfriend-drama o'clock." Imp was brazenly unrepentant. "Do you have any idea how hard it is to get a signal on this godforsaken lump of rock? I had to go all the way down to the castle gates to call Doc! He was texting me all night—he keeps complaining that I'm only here so I can skip washing-up duty, but if I'm not there and not making any dirty dishes why should I wash his plates for him?"

Wendy gave his complaint precisely the weight it deserved (none) and instead got to work. She tapped her voice recorder. "Second passage, exploration starting." She opened the door and shone her headlight down a low-roofed tunnel that looked as if ancient hands had clawed it out of the living rock with their fingernails. She glanced round. "Coming?" she asked.

"If you insist." Imp's grumble was pro forma. He complained whenever anyone asked him to do something that might be mistaken for work. He did it as a point of principle: Imp was one of those people who'd never take an honest job that paid twenty pounds if there was a dishonest one that paid ten pounds instead. "What do you expect to find?"

"No idea." She switched on her GoPro. The tunnel stretched ahead, sloping gently downward. Shallow steps were cut into the rock at roughly one-meter intervals. At the end she could just discern dark openings to either side.

Actually, Wendy had some vague expectations. Somewhere in this warren the old lords of the isle would have built an emergency escape route—probably to the underwater caverns used by the smugglers. The cultists must have taken the bodies of their victims somewhere, and that would be a good bet for where to look for a chamber full of nightmares. The door they'd entered by was too new and too well maintained for this tunnel to lead to a dead end.

"What's that ahead?" Imp asked as she approached the far end.

"Looks like a crossroads chamber. You've done more of this live-action dungeon-crawling shit than I have." The opening swallowed the beam of her headlight, leaving just a dim puddle of light to spill across the floor of the room. "Wait—" Something gleamed in the darkness. "Well, that's different. Voice memo, there's a gated fence down here in chamber, uh, tunnel two, chamber one past the chapel vestry." She leaned close, inspecting the lock. "Looks to be quite recent." Padlocks went *way* back, but bike chains with plastic jackets were signs of modernity. "Imp?"

"What?"

"Witness." Wendy willed an imaginary pry bar into existence between her hands.

"What is it with you and gates?" he asked, as she slid the tip of the bar into the first link of the chain.

"Shut up and give me a hand." Wendy sidestepped to let Imp get close. Her illusions had heft and solidity but only lasted as long as she maintained physical contact with whatever she'd created: a couple of seconds after she let go they faded out. "Put your hand here and help me *pull—*"

Imp grunted, adding weight. The chain link came apart on the welded steam: it was made from poor-quality steel. "Okay." She unlooped the chain. "Voice memo, forced the padlock, entering the gated chamber. There is another tunnel. Proceeding along it."

"First it was that charnel house in the graveyard, now it's a dungeon. You and your chains, Wendy, it's not healthy!"

Wendy tuned his whining out. The new passage was cold and dank. The walls narrowed and Imp had to duck to avoid scraping his head on the ceiling. It descended more steeply, with deeper steps cut into the rock at close intervals. "How much farther do we have to go?" Imp asked.

"I don't—*stop!*"

Wendy stumbled to a halt and braced, but Imp managed to avoid trampling her. "Why did you—"

"Look." Wendy reached into her shoulder bag and pulled out a much larger flashlight. "Voice memo: corridor ends in a natural cave. Floor is flooded with, I think—" She knelt. "—it's seawater. Which means—"

"Look over there," Imp said, his voice hushed. His torch beam illuminated a patch of rock that rose above the lapping water.

"Where—oh. Oh, right. Is that a rowboat?" It was upside down on the narrow quay. Some of its overlapping planks appeared to have rotted through, and a filthy tarpaulin covered one end.

"Look past it." Imp guided his beam sideways to illuminate more of the quay, a narrow rim of dry path surrounding the underground pool. The dark mouth of an open doorway gaped at them. "There's another chamber!"

"Okay, going there. Voice memo: going left around the edge of the flooded cave."

Wendy paused by the overturned boat. It was indeed half-rotted away: nobody was going to go fishing in it, let alone smuggling spirits or guns or sacrificial victims—whatever the denizens of Castle Skaro felt the need to bring in and out by dead of night. "This looks really old," she noted. "I wonder how long it's been here?" The door beyond was ajar, hanging by a hinge that had corroded in the damp, briny air.

"Voice memo, open door in semiflooded cave. Behind it—"

Imp gasped as her headlight illuminated the next chamber, flickering across the rotting hulk of a much larger wooden ship. It leaned against the wall of a dry dock: it had clearly been abandoned a very long time ago.

"What the hell?"

Kensington Palace, overlooking Kensington Gardens, is one of the most exclusive residences in London. Built in 1605, it has been continuously extended and repurposed as a crash pad for second-tier members of the royal family and their friends and houseguests. Currently there are four dukes and a princess rusticating there ostentatiously, greeting official visitors and dining in state beneath portraits of their ancestors. For privacy they retreat to cottages in the palace grounds. The public areas of the great house are sometimes open for guided tours: tourists pay an entrance fee to walk through the State Apartments and gape at their rococo decor and the works of art from the royal collection.

Imp lives next door.

On the other side of the back wall of Kensington Palace there is a quiet side street called Kensington Palace Gardens. It is lined with eighteenth- and nineteenth-century town houses built by up-and-coming members of the beau monde, the cream of society: those who had the blunt to live next door to the younger, wilder royal offspring. These houses are smaller, cheaper, meaner, and less accessible to the public than the royal palace and its outbuildings. They are also in a parlous state of neglect. Overgrown hedges and crumbling walls shield their cracked windows and rotten roofs from the public gaze. Their lawns are rewilded jungles, an urban paradise for feral cats and the rodents they stalk. Rusty camera enclosures stare blindly at their facades, and prominent notices warn of patrolling security guards, but the buildings are far gone in decay—in some cases the joists have collapsed, and during heavy rainfall water cascades down the mildewed carpets of the grand staircases.

The houses in Kensington Palace Gardens do not rot because they are worthless. On the contrary: this is some of the most expensive real estate on the planet, second only to the grounds of the Imperial Palace in Tokyo. None of these derelicts are worth less than fifty million pounds on the open market. Almost all of them are held as investments by private-equity organizations and sovereign-wealth funds. The owners don't care about the physical structure—rebuilding a collapsed house would cost mere single-digit millions. Meanwhile the London property market glows white-hot, like a Wolf-Rayet star getting ready to throw its supernova retirement party. Tenants are not acceptable, lest through some arcane legal sleight of hand they acquire squatter's rights to the dwelling. So they are left to subside, empty and neglected. Except for one:

Imp and Eve's ancestral home.

To unaided eyes it's no less derelict than its neighbors. But if viewed with a thermal camera, it glows, and a peek in the microwave spectrum would reveal a residence rotten with Wi-Fi and cellular data. Imp lives here these days and plays host to housemates: his boyfriend, Doc Depression; their associate Game

Boy; and the occasional visit from their teammate, the irascible Deliverator, and her girlfriend, Wendy.

Imp and Eve's great-to-the-nth-grandfather had purchased the town house during the first flush of family wealth in the nineteenth century. At that time the London property market was merely expensive rather than insane. Great-to-the-grandpa was a ritual magician—more precisely, an oneiromancer: one who works sorcery in dreams. He made arcane alterations to the top floor before he passed the dwelling on to his children and grandchildren. Over the decades, the Starkey family created a dreamworld maze of imaginary bedrooms and kitchens and corridors and stairwells and sculleries. The labyrinth opened off a closet door in the attic, forming a concrete representation of the Starkey dynasty's spells in the shape of a reified memory palace, shared by the entire family.

When magic went into eclipse in the early twentieth century the Starkey family fell upon hard times. Their spells fell dormant: the family lost most of their power. Their immediate grandfather had to sell the family home. His son in turn eked out a living as an accountant, their mother a computer programmer turned housewife. The house of dreams passed from hand to hand, eventually running aground on the shoals of a foreign investment vehicle's balance sheet. There it rotted, unoccupied and unloved for over a decade.

It was during this period of neglect that Imp broke the lock on the gate, redirected the unwatched CCTV cameras, and turned it into a discreet squat for feral artistic supervillains. Then, three months ago, Eve arranged for one of the Bigge Organization's subsidiaries to indirectly fund her acquisition of the deed to the house. And she hired Imp as her live-in janitor.

But Eve had not spent the thick end of sixty million quid merely to regularize her younger brother's living arrangements.

Last December, Rupert decided to get his hands on a long-lost book of arcane lore. He'd given Eve orders to obtain it by any means necessary, so she'd hired her brother and his team for the retrieval. Whoever had stolen the manuscript had stored it in a nightmarish dream of a past that never was, and she needed Imp's help to break into the dream roads upstairs.

The imaginary, liminal spaces behind the closet door on the top floor gave access to rooms that didn't actually exist—rooms decorated and furnished in the styles of bygone decades. The dream roads were a sorcerous network of paths that connected different places and times, both those that were real and others that were less so.

Venturing past the burned umber wallpaper, shag carpet, and music centers of the 1970s, the intrepid explorer might find bathrooms furnished with avocado-green ceramics. Farther inside they might discover white porcelain toilets, encaustic tiled floors, kitchens plumbed for town gas and fitted with hand-cranked mangles and wooden washboards, pantries with cold slabs and iceboxes. Beyond the pre-war era, the dim filament bulbs gave way to hissing gas mantles and soot-smeared windows that opened onto a view of damp Victorian cobblestones. Doc and Game Boy had opened an outside door leading into the years of the Great War and heard the wail of the zeppelin-raid sirens. And as a group, they'd once visited the Whitechapel slums of the 1880s, where Imp and Eve's ancestor had hidden the tome from which he had gained his power—at a terrible price.

It was a fitting tomb for a concordance bound in human skin, a malignant document that had been misfiled more than a century ago in a charnel library belonging to a sorcerous secret society. The book was cursed: anyone who came into possession of it without permission from its lawful owner would die horribly, and ownership descended down the family line.

Rupert had neglected to be sufficiently precise in his instructions to Eve, and she had taken full advantage of his free rein: although she'd used his corporate accounts to pay for it, she'd laundered the funds creatively enough to bamboozle a nineteenth-century thaumaturgist's intent-based spell. When she finally returned to the realm of the real and met Rupert coming to take possession, she verbally resigned from his employment—then directed him to where the book lay waiting, like a bloodthirsty sentient mantrap.

Now Eve needed to maintain control of her ancestor's memory palace. In this age of resurgent magic, the spells encoded in it were becoming alarmingly active. In return for signing over co-ownership of the house and a salary as part-time janitor, she'd given her brother one overriding, urgent duty. Imp was to prevent unwelcome visitors from emerging via the dream roads, by any means necessary.

After Rupert vanished, Imp had nailed the closet door shut then painted over it. He and his friends lived downstairs like dwellers on the slopes of a dormant volcano, doing their best to ignore the sleeping death beneath whose shadow they existed.

But sometimes even long-dormant volcanoes may erupt without warning.

BONES AND NIGHTMARES

Immediately after Baroness Hazard's visit, Eve booked herself a three-hour one-on-one etiquette-training session. She was looking forward to her court presentation about as much as root-canal surgery—with or without anesthesia—but doing it without preparation was an obvious no-no.

Eve had grown up in the middle-class suburban wilderness of Croydon, not rubbing shoulders with the elite. As Rupert's assistant she'd taken a strictly supporting role: always the servant, never the master. But there was no way to avoid stepping into the spotlight when her summons arrived. Hopefully Lady DeVere could at least prepare her for the worst pitfalls. But as the metaphorical drill bit whined and grated against her second molar, preparing her for the operation to come, she was having second thoughts.

"Tell me again, in your own terms, what it is you want to accomplish," Mary said breathily. "I'm sure this must be very exciting for you! What do you look forward to most about your first presentation?"

Eve's cheeks froze. "I hope not to end up with my skull on a spike down Tyburn Way."

Mrs. DeVere's answering smile was strained. "Please don't pull faces, dear, it's unflattering. The unwritten number-one rule of this sort of event is, everyone is happy to be there! It's a *good* life! Nobody likes a misery face, do they? So best to put your happy face on: we can't help but *feel* cheerful when we *look* cheerful and it makes the time fly by so much faster, so give it your best old school try, what?"

Eve forcibly defrosted her facial muscles and took stock of Mrs. DeVere, whose own smile was now teetering just on the right side of simpering. Her tutor was turned out in classic Sloane-dowager style—a Jaeger twinset and pearl necklace—the sort of outfit Diana Spencer might have worn had she failed to launch and instead married a minor earl with an estate in the home counties. (Which wasn't far from the truth, in Mary's case: she'd started her etiquette consultancy to round out her alimony payments and make useful contacts in preparation for her twin daughters' debut.)

"Remember, happy thoughts only!" Mary twinkled. "Otherwise the cornfield awaits!"

"I shall try to remember that," Eve conceded. *Old money,* she reminded herself. *Let me tell you about the very rich. They are different from you and me.* Things were different again for those to the manor born, whose wealth was measured in centuries and pedigree rather than dollars and derivatives. "It's not going to be easy." Eve was not known for her sunny disposition, especially after half a decade carrying water for Rupert. "I'm afraid of putting my foot in it by accident and saying something . . ." She rolled her right wrist.

"Well, we'll just have to work on your internal censor then, won't we? Can you talk me through your situation again?"

"I've been invited"—a white lie, there had been no RSVP on the card: it was an unambiguous summons—"to be presented before His Dread Majesty in the Long Gallery at Lancaster House. It's to happen next Tuesday, six P.M. for a seven P.M. start, dinner at eight P.M. Dress code is white tie." The appropriate level of formality for a royal reception: Eve had blown the price of a midrange Porsche on a court gown she would only wear the one time. "A plus-one is permitted but not encouraged. In my case, I'm going stag." She forced a brittle smile. "So it's a royal reception with the Black Pharaoh, not the Windsors. Have you met him yourself?"

Mrs. DeVere wilted slightly. "Yes, well, sometimes life hands us mildewed fruit and we're still expected to make lemonade. . . ."

Eve deduced that Sally DeVere had not been *personally* introduced to N'yar Lat-Hotep, Crown Prince of Chaos and Despair, Master of the Ineffable Void, and current Prime Minister of the United Kingdom of Great Britain and Northern Ireland. Otherwise her reaction would likely have been more emphatic.

Mary added, "I've had tea with his chief of staff—Mrs. Carpenter—and she said he's a firm believer in tradition, if that's any help? I've seen him once or twice—at a distance, of course. But I would hardly call myself an *intimate*—"

Eve let her teeth show. "I do not believe *intimacy* is a desirable outcome on the occasion of one's introduction to the living avatar of an ancient supernatural horror. But setting that aside for the moment, can you walk me through what 'firm believer in tradition' normally means in terms of royal etiquette?"

"*That* I can certainly do!" Once back on familiar turf, Mary brightened perceptibly. She launched into a dissertation on the protocol to be observed at royal events—and indeed any upper-class shindig—that lasted nearly two hours and was sufficiently comprehensive that it overloaded even Eve's detail-oriented brain. She demonstrated (on slightly creaky knees) the precise degrees of curtsey due to different levels of nobility, the mandatory requirement to *never* turn one's back on the monarch (whether they were the Queen of England—living in seclusion, or, some might say, house arrest at Balmoral—or the Black Pharaoh himself). Small details that had eluded Eve received Mary's laser-sharp focus. For example, this was technically her court debut, but because she had absentmindedly acquired her title through marriage rather than inheritance, her dress and headpiece did not have to be white. (Not that there was sufficient time to procure an appropriate replacement.) "Moreover, because your husband is not confirmed dead you are not required to wear mourning colors! Isn't that ever so *convenient*?" she trilled.

Eventually Eve reached her limit. "This makes no sense! A baron's spouse, or a female baron, is a baroness, a duke's equivalent is a duchess, but an earl's wife is a *countess*? Which means you, I assume? But there's also a viscount, and a viscount's wife is a viscountess? And the rule about what color your gloves are depends on the time of year, unless it's a ball: I mean, *why*? Where does it all come from, who invented this stuff? How am I supposed to remember it all?"

"I—" Mrs. DeVere gave Eve a most peculiar look. "You know, I never thought of it that way. A moment, if you please?" She fell silent for a minute or so, and when she resumed talking she sounded quietly reflective. "Etiquette is all about communication, and in this case it's like learning irregular verbs, I think. Irregular verbs don't make sense, they just *are,* but we have to learn them if we are to speak the language correctly. You can't just go around conjugating 'I am/you am/they am' unless you are willing to be taken for an oaf, or a foreigner." It was perfectly obvious, which Mrs. DeVere considered worse. "It's just how things are, and the general consensus among people who matter is that if you don't know that, you're not fit to participate in polite society." Mary paused again. "You must think I'm awfully—" She flapped a hand as she searched for words.

"Specialized?" Eve offered, after a suitable silence.

Mrs. DeVere nodded gratefully. "You're right: these details are obvious to me because I grew up with them," she said, in a tone of voice that suggested she was discovering something not entirely forgivable about herself. "But I'm sure you acquired some sort of equivalent knowledge in your youth—family recipes for social success, if you like." Eve thought back to her father's lessons in sorcery and sacrifice, and held her tongue. "Let's go back to first principles."

Mary paused, then continued slowly and carefully. "The aristocracy are, above all else, about keeping land and blood in the family. Some of them hold estates that go back centuries, all the way to the Norman conquest or even Saxon times, passed down through the family line—eldest sons inherit, second sons fought in the Crusades or built an empire, third sons joined the clergy. The daughters' duty was to make a suitable marriage, either marrying up, or, if their parents were in financial embarrassment, marrying for *money*." Her moue of distaste caught Eve's eye. "The upper crust marry as a business arrangement—not for love, unless they're very lucky. Daughters provide heirs and manage the lord's household. So . . ."

She leaned forward again. "The points of etiquette I've been discussing, the details of a lady's introduction to society—these customs are the prerequisites for closing the biggest financial deal of a young lady's life, one on which her future prosperity and the prosperity of her children depend absolutely. Well, maybe less so in the past couple of centuries—we have so many more opportunities than our ancestors!—but land endures, and the ingrained customs of the land-owning gentry die slowly. A debutante still has to impress her mother-in-law-to-be, and *her* mother. Obeying the rules, even if they seem quaint and dated, signals one's willingness to conform to the really important requirement, which is to keep the family estate intact and pass it on to the next generation. Remember, it's all about blood and soil."

The furrow between Eve's brow had been deepening for some time. She finally reached the ends of her self-restraint. "But why should this matter to the Prime Minister? He's not even human!"

"But he's the Black Pharaoh, our lord and master, and rulers *always* require absolute obedience. The closer to the Crown one approaches, the more important one's obedience becomes. Conforming to the expectations of polite society shows that you've got skin in the game—the game of land and family, passing it down the generations. Which in turn reassures His Majesty that you're not going to turn all bolshie on him, doesn't it? You can't pass your land and title on to your firstborn if you go to the guillotine. Loyalty to the standards of the establishment implies loyalty to the monarch who leads it. And *that* is why it's important for you to mute your smartphone, smile, and always accept a gentleman's offer to dance."

▸◂▸◂▸◂

When she'd been Rupert de Montfort Bigge's PA, Eve had rated a windowless basement office for a workspace. But as the acting CEO of the Bigge Organization she was now entitled to use the CEO's office, not to mention the numerous homes (and one castle) he owned around the world. She hadn't been able to bring herself to move into Rupert's den full time: it was grotesquely jammed with eighteenth-century rococo furniture, and besides, the paintings were a crime against good taste. But playing *who's got the biggest desk* was as much a part of the job as playing *who spent more on their bespoke suit,* and during the week following Baroness Hazard's visit she'd called in Security to sweep for bugs and clean house, in anticipation of the inevitable repeat intrusion.

Which had finally come.

"Good morning," she said, shaking Persephone's hand. "Sorry about the decor—I haven't had time to fully redecorate yet." She'd replaced Rupert's Bond-villain lounger with an Aeron just so she wouldn't have to sit where his buttocks had rested, but replacing the dogs-playing-poker-grade paintings would be a time-consuming chore.

Her visitor glanced around. "I imagine you had bigger things on your plate." She nodded at the broken cuckoo clock on the wall and added, "Black Forest? *Really?*"

"It's bolted to the front of his personal safe." Eve walked

around the desk and waited for her visitor to seat herself. "I have no idea why, I mean it's almost as much a cliché as hiding it behind the artwork, isn't it? But never mind. What can I do for you?"

Her Grace Persephone Hazard—Baroness Hazard, Deputy Minister for External Assets, and all-around scary operator in the service of His Dread Majesty—smirked. "How about some refreshments? We might be here awhile."

Eve nodded and tapped her earpiece. "Starkey here. Order for Caffè Nero: I'll have my regular, plus a soy mocha grande with ristretto doppio and nonsugar sweeteners on the side. Deliver to the first-floor office." She made eye contact. "That's your preference, isn't it?"

Persephone nodded. "I see you did your homework."

"After your last visit, yes." Eve's smile went Botox-tight. "I got the message." It was clear to Eve that her position was precarious. The clock was ticking, the calendar entry saved. This second visit, though, had to be about something else. "And, ah, the tribute you suggested." Mary had confirmed that the Prime Minister was keen on symbolic demonstrations and gifts as tokens of submission.

"Yes, that." Persephone's smile faded. "You found it, I hope?"

"Yes, well, I *think* so." Eve hesitated. "I mean, I'm pretty sure it's the right one, but there are disturbing anomalies."

"Yes, so I gather. That's why I'm here—we wouldn't want to disappoint Him, would we? Do you mind if I examine it?"

Eve bit her lip. "To be honest, I was hoping you'd be able to authenticate it, but I didn't want to presume." She pushed her chair back and stood again. "It's an ugly thing. I didn't know if I should tidy it up—have it cleaned—so it's just as it came. I'd better show you."

The office door opened and a Gammon entered, bearing the coffee. She nodded at the sideboard. "Leave them there." The

Gammon departed, and Eve waited until the door closed again before she walked over to the broken cuckoo clock. There was no point putting anything in her stomach right before handling the gift for His Dread Majesty.

"Excuse me, but would you mind turning your back for a moment?" she asked.

"Really?" Persephone sounded amused but closed her eyes anyway.

"I make no apologies for good security practice."

"Carry on," Persephone said dismissively. "Practice on me all you like."

Eve stood before the clock and opened her mind's eye. She flexed her mental muscles, projecting an imaginary arm between the broken doors where once a wooden bird flew. She was not a powerful telekinetic—she could lift heavier weights by hand than by willpower—but the safe was booby-trapped, and she was quite certain she did not wish to experience wrist-reattachment surgery.

Picking locks by mind required intense focus even when she wasn't being watched—and judged—by the baroness. But Eve had opened the safe a few times now, and she only fumbled and had to restart the process twice. By the time it clicked open, a thin slime of perspiration glued her silk blouse to the small of her back. She tugged the edge of the clock, swung the wall panel open, then palmed a tissue and mopped her brow while Persephone was distracted by the shelves and recesses within.

When Eve had first cracked the safe she'd found a royal ransom in gems and jewelry in its shallow drawers, beneath a shelf lined with bulging ring binders. The files were worth more than their weight in platinum. The baubles remained in the safe, albeit itemized, bagged, and tagged—Eve intended to wear three of the fancier pieces to the reception—but she'd sanitized the contents of the files, shredding the most incriminating documents and delivering certain others to the baroness as a gesture of good faith. Now half the file shelf was occupied by an antique black leather hatbox, secured with a tarnished lock.

Eve carried the box to her desk and concentrated until the lock clicked open. Then she pulled on a pair of white cotton gloves, raised the lid, and removed the object within. It was about the size of a bowling ball and weighed about a kilogram. At sometime in the distant past the front had been tarred and wrapped in strips of linen rags, but a few hanks of straggly, brittle hair still clung to the back and sides. The lower mandible hung loose but was held in place by more tarred linen strips, stained with streaks of rust from the iron cage. The vertebrae were entirely missing.

"This is he."

She placed the mummified head carefully on her desk blotter, then turned it to face Persephone.

"This is the skull of Rupert de Montfort Bigge, hanged for piracy on August thirty-second, 1816, according to the notice attached to his gibbet cage."

The baroness's expression mirrored Eve's baffled skepticism. "You're *certain* of that?"

Eve reached into the hatbox and lifted out a water-damaged wooden tablet. Someone had used a hot iron poker to burn the words into it. "I agree that the date makes no sense, but the dental records match," she said. "I don't have any DNA samples to crossmatch, unfortunately. I'd *like* to think it's him, but—"

Persephone held up her hand, then extended an index finger toward the skull. "Let me see." Eve felt a prickling as of invisible spiders running up and down the skin of her arms: with it came a sense of numinous dread, of a great and musty emptiness, as if she somehow stood on the threshold of eternity. She swallowed. It was hard to draw breath. "Echoes of dying last longest," said the baroness. There was a sense of falling helplessly. "Yes, definitely hanged and gibbeted."

Persephone withdrew her finger. "You can put it away." She nodded to herself. "It might not be exactly what His Majesty is expecting, but he won't be displeased by it." Eve placed the plaque and the skull back in their box. "But maybe get a nicer presentation package? Or gift wrap it. He likes unwrapping presents, He says it makes Him feel festive." She shrugged. "Paper, gold foil, human skin, they're all the same to Him."

Eve lowered the lid and locked it back in place. "What do you think He'll do with it?" she asked, the follow-up queuing on her tongue: *Will it help me get a speedy annulment?*

"I expect he'll add it to his collection." The baroness smiled. "You can ask Him when you see him next week! Sorry, I've got to run now, meeting at Admiralty House, must dash, good luck." Then she departed, leaving Eve alone with the mummified skull of her husband.

▸◂▸◂▸◂

The following Monday morning found Wendy waiting in Reception at the Bigge Organization's head office.

She and Imp had flown home from Skaro on Thursday night. She'd spent Friday working from home, writing up her report on the tunnel system. She'd racked up quite a few billable hours on the sofa in sweatpants and fleece, which she found vastly preferable to skulking around a dungeon with a flashlight and a voice recorder.

Wendy hadn't delivered her report yet. She and Imp had agreed (it had taken very few threats on her part, which was a surprise) that it was best to deliver news of a two-hundred-year-old double-masted brig in the basement in person. It turned out that Imp could do a decent enough Shaggy impersonation, creepy castle explorations included: All they needed were a Daphne, a Fred, a mutt, and a bad guy in a rubber mask, and they could have filmed a live-action Scooby-Doo episode. He was not the most reliable fellow on the planet, but he had a weak spot for his sister, so Wendy gave it a better-than-even chance that he wouldn't blab to anyone. And what they'd found in the tunnels was potentially a game changer.

She'd spent Sunday chilling with her girlfriend Rebecca—the Deliverator—and Wendy felt centered as she started the new week. She even felt good about the upcoming meeting. Her manager at HiveCo Security's Transhuman Investigations Branch, Mr. Gibson, had gracefully accepted the Bigge Organization's bid for a month of her time. He had a handful of new hires to supervise, and as a newly promoted principal investigator Wendy was best kept in the field as much as possible, maximizing her billable hours. Even if in practice it meant chilling in the client's reception area while Eve waited for her nail varnish to dry.

Wendy tugged the strap of her handbag up and glanced at her phone for the nth time. Nothing had changed in the past five minutes. Uncle Greg was still forwarding insensitive jokes from Facebook. Del was still looking forward to the pursuit-driving course Gibson had promised her. Eve was now sixteen minutes late—

"Good morning, Wendy! I'm sorry I kept you waiting."

Wendy shoved her phone in her bag hastily and stood up. *Who are you and what have you done with Eve Starkey?* she wondered. The person facing her *looked* like Eve, but the Eve she knew—Imp's sister—was as apologetic as an out-of-control bulldozer, as warm and cuddly as the Ross Ice Shelf. Eve shook Wendy's hand—*She's shaking my hand! What's* wrong *with her?*—prompting Wendy to ask, "Is everything okay?"

Eve's forehead wrinkled minutely. "No, actually, it's—" She caught her tongue. "—not your problem." She offered up a blinding smile as false as a breast implant. "Come along, we'll use the office upstairs."

Wendy followed Eve up the main staircase, hustling to keep up. How Eve managed it in sky-high heels and a pencil skirt was a mystery to Wendy: Wendy wore a suit for work, but it was cut to conceal her arm muscles rather than flatter her figure, and her footwear ran toward steel-toe-capped boots rather than stilettos. Eve was blond, with sharp cheekbones and hair scraped back into a face-tightening bun: she dressed at the femme end of the Boardroom Barbie spectrum, but something about her presentation struck Wendy as trying too hard. What did she have to be anxious about?

They arrived in the boss's office, which was still saturated with Rupert's tasteless glitz. Wendy closed the door as Eve headed for her seat. "Are you *sure* everything's okay?" Wendy asked. "Is there anything I can do to help?"

"No, there's—" Now Eve caught herself *again,* and this time she changed course. "Maybe, but it's not why we're here. I'm forgetting my manners: can I offer you a coffee? Tea? Water?"

"A coffee would be great." *Will she make it herself, or was that a one-off?* (Imp had told Wendy about his sister's slightly terrifying coffee-making talent.)

"Yes, of course." Eve tapped her headset, then disappointed Wendy by saying, "Please send out to Caffè Nero, coffee for two in the CEO's office. My regular and, how do you take it?" Wendy told her. "A drip coffee with cream, sugar on the side," she added. Evidently there was to be no fancy display of telekinesis and pyrokinesis today. Eve tapped her headset again to end the call. "There, all set. So, how were the tunnels? And did my brother get up to any wickedness while you were there?"

"Imp mostly behaved himself." He'd smoked a joint before bedtime every night (he said the castle gave him the heebie-jeebies, which apparently were a variant of the collywobbles that Impresarios were prone to). But he hadn't trashed the guest bedroom, stolen the silverware, insulted the staff, or done anything to outrage Wendy's ex-cop sensibilities.[1] "I was *quite* disappointed."

Eve had given her carte blanche to slap him in irons and ship him home if he provoked her. As the lawful head of the government of the dependent territory, Eve could actually do that. But Wendy hadn't needed to. "He was actually *helpful*: he makes a pretty good flashlight stand when he forgets to slack off."

"Shocking. I shan't tell him, he'd be mortified." They shared a smirk.

It was time to cut to the chase. "Why did you saddle me with him, really?" Wendy waited patiently, imagining them sitting on opposite sides of the desk with all the decoration gone, as if they were in the interview suite of a police station.

"I have no idea what you're suggesting."

"He's your brother. You trust him not to screw you over." *At least when he's not stoned.* "Given his highly specialized skills"—robbing banks, making movies, and convincing people that everything he said was true—"I assume you wanted him to keep an eye on me in case I found something?"

Eve finally gave her a tell. It was a faint twitch at the corner of her mouth, coupled with a brief glance to one side. Wendy gave herself a mental high five. "Yes," Eve said. "What *did* you find in the tunnels?"

This is going to be good. "A cave with a pirate ship in it."

Eve managed to avoid a spit take, but it was a near thing. "*Excuse* me?"

Just as Wendy began to wonder if she'd made a mistake, someone knocked on the door. Eve called, "Come in," raising a hand in Wendy's direction. "Hold the story."

The door opened, and an ashen-faced Gammon poked his

1. Skaroese law was so outdated that the only statutes referring to cannabis concerned the taxable value of hemp ropes on sailing ships.

head inside. "Two coffees as ordered, ma'am," he reported. "And"—he sounded scared—"there's a body bag on a rail?"

"A—" Eve paused. "Oh, okay. Put the coffee over there and bring the bag in."

"Yes'm." The Gammon disappeared for a minute then reappeared, pushing a wheeled wardrobe rail over which hung a dress carrier.

"What are you looking at?" Eve demanded.

He hung his head. "Nuthing, ma'am. Thought it was a body bag, but it's too light to be full an' too heavy to be empty. Izzat all?"

"Get out," Eve said tiredly, then waited until he closed the door. She glared at the carelessly hung dress carrier and muttered something that sounded disturbingly like "Skin just *one* arms-dealing terrorist and that's *all* they ever talk about." She continued: "Can't get the help these days . . . Wendy, could you give me a hand with this?" Together they extended the rail to its full height so that Eve could hang it properly.

"That's a gown." Wendy was perplexed, but not so much that she blabbed her next thought which was *That's* so *not your style*. Eve was all about sharp suits, not dresses.

"Yes, it is," Eve agreed, sliding the carrier off its contents. "But you were telling me about a pirate ship before we were interrupted. Pray continue," she added, a little acid leaking into her tone.

"Okay." Wendy collected her thoughts, trying to pay no attention to the sight of Eve shaking out a voluminous mass of pink. It did not suit her, to put it mildly. (In Wendy's opinion Eve's natural colors were black and yellow stripes, just like a murder hornet.) "The short version is: Jeremy and I did a preliminary recon of the tunnel system beyond the chapel. It's very old and largely unmodernized. On the second level I found a gate leading to a much older tunnel with stairs down to a flooded cavern. You were right that it links up with the smugglers' caves.

More to the point, we found a bigger chamber that had been drained and turned into a dry dock with a sailing ship laid up in it."

"Well." Eve stopped fussing with the formalwear and sat down again. She glanced at the sideboard: the two coffees lifted into the air and floated across to the desk. One hovered in front of Wendy, who took it nervously. "Go on, drink, it's not poisoned. What kind of ship? How did it get there?"

"Wooden, about thirty meters long. Two masts beside it on the floor, gunports for cannon. I didn't see any, though. It was rotted enough that they could have fallen through the deck." She took a sip of her coffee. "The seaward end of the cave had been walled off. There might have been some kind of lock gate, I don't know enough. You need to send a naval architect or a historian. We didn't want to get too close to it, it was big and smelly and looked likely to give way under our feet if we climbed aboard." She took another sip. "It's been there a pretty long time. I don't think there'll be anything important left behind."

"You're probably right, but it still needs to be checked out." Eve looked mildly put out. "I'd already arranged for a survey team to go out on Wednesday to map the tunnels—are you willing to go with them? It's just a day trip. The ship sounds like it calls for another visit and a different team, but it'll take a while to arrange. In the meantime if you can record video of it and get some idea of its measurements, that would help. Was there a name on its bow? Anything to identify it?"

"The paint had all faded or peeled off, but there was a figurehead." Wendy pulled out her print of the report. "I photographed it. It's the usual big-breasted mermaid chick—an old sailor's wank fantasy." She leafed through the file and opened it at a page of photos. "There was also an embossed name plaque, which is why Imp and I agreed I should tell you in person. I enhanced it, here—"

Eve glanced at the pictures. "'Prince of Poets'? Well, I *never*."

Her eyes narrowed. "I'll still need to hire an expert, but that's a smoking gun." It was clearly a reference to Ppilimtec, the cult demiurge whose followers Rupert had led.

While Eve sat in thought, Wendy looked at the dress rack. "So what's that about?" she asked, tilting her head.

Eve's smile was sour. "Cinderella has been invited to a royal ball—well, a reception—tomorrow evening: attendance is mandatory. White tie. There will be gift-giving and hands to be squeezed."

"The royal ball? Which royals—the Old Firm or the New Management?"

"New, of course." Eve's lip curled. "What do you think?"

"Heh." Wendy chuckled weakly. "It's—" A momentary pause. "—much pink, very ruffled, wow." It featured layers of silk and chiffon, with enough lace and ribbon to suffocate a Disney princess.

"Did you just doge-meme me?"

"I didn't mean to—"

A snort. "Yes, you did, but you're right, it's going to make me look like an extra in a costume drama. Maybe a Jane Austen adaptation. As I paid a dress agent to handle it for me so I didn't have to waste brain cells, I've only got myself to blame." Wendy reflected that Eve was as laser-focused on making money as most women of her apparent wealth were on spending it: she wasn't prone to retail therapy. "I told her *white-tie reception at Lancaster House, the PM will be attending,* many measurement sessions eventuated, and then she delivered *this*. And I can't tell if she's taking the piss or deadly serious because I failed my GCSE Girl exams when I was sixteen. So what do *you* think?"

"Seriously? You're asking me? A butch ex-cop whose idea of dressing up is a pair of DMs with daisies painted on them?"

Eve's face fell. "I have no actual friends," she confessed. "No girlfriends, no boyfriends, either, I mean, no friends, *period.* I was too busy to socialize when I was at university, then working for Rupert was . . . not good for me. I imagine when he was young he was the sort of kid who enjoyed pulling the wings off flies then gluing them back on so he could do it all over again. Anyway, isolation meant safety, and now it turns out my social radar is broken: it only works in business settings."

"That's a—" Wendy leaned back in her chair. This was more Eve than she was paid to handle. "That's a shame."

"So, eh, you're on the clock." Eve had enough grace to look embarrassed. "Do you think you can be my paid-for bestie for ten minutes and tell me what you think?"

Wow. Too much. "I can try." Wendy stood up. *Be my friend, I can pay? Really?* "Look here." Covering her unease, she picked up the dress and offered it to Eve. "Hold this in front of you. If it fits properly, it'll make you look—" She hmm'd. "Royals. Doesn't matter whether it's the Old Firm or truly ancient, they're all about cosplaying the good old days, back when kings were kings, queens were queens, and peasants like us worked in the fields. So this is about two hundred years out of date, which I'd say puts you right on the mark? A little bit modern?" Mentally she crossed her fingers, but outwardly she merely raised an eyebrow. "Accessories?"

Eve indicated a bag dangling at one end of the rack. "There's a list."

Wendy took the list clipped to the bag and gave it a quick glance. "Shoes, evening gloves, bag—no, *reticule*: yes, Lady Bridgerton, you are indeed equipped for the ball. What's a tessen—do I want to know? Well, have you booked your pumpkin and enchanted your mouse coachmen?"

"*Snarl*," said Eve. She returned the dress to the rack with quick, overcontrolled movements.

"You'll have to fill me in on the court gossip later," Wendy couldn't resist needling. But then she sobered up. There was an opportunity here, and if she didn't take the chance she'd be kicking herself later. "But afterward, how about you, me, and

Becca go out for—when was the last time you had a night on the town?" Eve's deer-in-the-headlights expression spoke volumes. "The first rule of getting your girl card reinstated is that you have to make time to let your hair down and get plastered with friends at least once a month. So this Friday night you're going to back away from the keyboard and we're going to show you what you've been missing, okay? Who knows, you might even enjoy it!"

▸◂▸◂▸◂

As Big Ben struck six the next evening, Eve stepped out of her armored SUV onto the gravel footpath leading to Lancaster House, leaving behind her escort of heavily armed mercenaries. She was trailed at a discreet distance by Sally Gunderson, wearing a well-tailored tux; the head of her close-protection squad carried a gift-wrapped and beribboned box. Eve paused at the steps, and Sally handed her the box under the watchful gaze of the SCO19 cops standing guard duty.

The cops wore armor. Their fluted gothic steel was polished to silvery brightness and updated with Velcro fasteners, VR headsets, and 360-degree cameras. They bore Basilisk guns: weapons that resembled a bullpup rifle with a cluster of cameras instead of a barrel and receiver. Only the most intimidating toys for those guarding the Black Pharaoh.

Sergeant Gunderson marched back to the car, leaving Eve to present herself to the silver-haired majordomo waiting on the front steps. "Evelyn Starkey," she said. "I'm on the list." She looked past the guards. "Where do I put this?"

"Please follow me, ma'am." The majordomo escorted her to an X-ray machine tucked behind the grand staircase to the ballroom. An arch like a metal detector stood beside it, if airport metal-detector arches were wrought-iron cages holding human bones. Her skin crawled as she stepped between the undead pillars[2]: the arch scanned her and confirmed that she did not, in fact, intend harm to His Dread Majesty. Meanwhile the X-ray belt and explosive detector hummed and spat out her reticule and the gift-wrapped box. "You may proceed, my Lady."

Eve allowed herself to be relieved of her coat and led to the staircase. A liveried attendant trailed after her with the gift. The top of the stairs brought her to the piano nobile, the level with the reception room and rooms of state. The cavernous central hall rose three stories high and was capped by a vaulted roof with inset skylights. A balcony surrounded the main level, and pillared porticos fronted the long gallery on one side and the main ballroom on the other. Every available stretch of wall bore a painting. For the most part they were portraits of supercilious-looking ladies and gentlemen in eighteenth-century court finery. Eve fancied that if they'd been alive they'd have been aghast that someone of her low birth could ever be allowed in here. *Good.*

Though Eve was early she was not alone. Discreet waiters hurried in and out of side doors bearing platters of drinks and canapés. Other attendants hovered to take new arrivals' overcoats (should they have any) and offer help (if any were needed). Guests in formal attire barely changed since the nineteenth century—men in white tie and tailcoats, women in gowns, tiaras, and long gloves—stood in small clusters, chattering brightly, smiles nailed to their faces. Everyone seemed intent on maintaining the illusion that they were here of their own accord rather than attending at His Dread Majesty's command. She recognized some of them: here stood an MP bloviating at a banker, while over there a cluster of last decade's wilted Britpop superstars posed, desperately pretending this was an industry awards ceremony rather than a ghastly occult remake of *The Weakest Link*.

Eve found waiting on her own boring, but not as boring as

2. Necrotechnology was another of the miraculous innovations the New Management had brought in: why should felons cease paying their debt to society just because they'd been executed?

trading content-free small talk with the other victims. This sort of affair was Rupert's forte: she generally liked to stay out of the limelight. She briefly wondered if she should have dragged Imp along as her plus-one: it would have been educational for the boy. But then she contemplated the possible failure modes of an encounter between her brother and the Prime Minister and reconsidered. (She wasn't sure if lèse majesté was once more a capital offense, but if it wasn't, Imp was exactly the person to get that changed in a hurry.)

Guests kept drifting in and after half an hour the long gallery was overheated, not to mention overflowing with dreadful people—less the cream of British society than the rancid scum floating on the top. As a conventionally pretty blonde, Eve was used to keeping her back to the wall, fanning herself defensively, and maintaining her distance. A few idiots who should have had PREDATOR tattooed on their foreheads attempted to engage her in conversation, but she was in a blessedly business-free zone and had no compunction about cutting them dead. She was trying to deflect the attentions of an incredibly tedious professor of computational metaphysics (there being no computer bore like a *sorcerous* computer bore) when someone waved a hand under her nose.

"Hello?" It was Baroness Hazard, wearing a vintage Dior gown and a barely not-vulgar quantity of diamonds. "You look absolutely lovely, Eve! So glad you could join us tonight!" Her voice dropped ten decibels. "The boss will see you now. Did you bring the tribute?"

Eve beckoned to her attendant. "After you," she told Persephone as she tugged her satin gloves up, her palms greasy with cold sweat.

Persephone turned on her towering heels and swept out of the gallery, leading Eve through a succession of ever smaller and more elaborately decorated sitting rooms and reception areas.

They passed between another pair of police in chromed

armor guarding a doorway, and arrived in a room that resembled the ladies' loo of a very upmarket hotel. It was furnished with marble-topped occasional tables, spindly Louis XIV chairs, and a bucolic eighteenth-century landscape painting that looked vaguely familiar. *Is that a Stubbs?*

"Package on the table," said Persephone, snapping her fingers. The attendant placed the gift-wrapped skull precisely where she pointed, bowed deeply, and fled. He hadn't uttered a single word the entire time, Eve realized. *Tongueless, magically muted, or just terrified?*

"Now we wait."

"What—" Eve began.

Persephone touched a finger to her high-gloss lips. "No chatter, please. We serve at His Majesty's pleasure."

Eve wanted to say, "This is ridiculous," but then the door to the toilet cubicles opened and the august person formerly known as Fabian Everyman, MP, came out and she felt time slow down, as if she was steering into a skid in anticipation of a coming car crash.

Record scratch.

Later, if anyone had asked her, Eve might have said that her brain froze. But that would have been a misstatement, an attempt to frame an utterly alien experience in familiar human terms. And human terms didn't quite fit the situation, because His Majesty was not a human being. As it was, Eve only managed to retain trivia, the minor details: they swirled around a blind spot in her memory, a human-shaped hole that was occupied by His Arcane Majesty the Black Pharaoh, N'yar Lat-Hotep.

It suited His Majesty to play dress-up as a human politician, although His suit was woven from skin and bones and sinew, the clothing a mere outer integument. Subsequently, Eve couldn't recall His face. She *did* remember afterward that he wore immaculate formalwear, his shoes polished to perfect mirror-bright blackness, his kidskin gloves made of leather as fine as the foreskin of a virgin sacrifice. Across his chest he wore a kingfisher-blue sash bearing the star of the Order of the Garter. Beside it hung other medals and medallions that bespoke membership of various chivalric and arcane orders. But despite all the half-glimpsed details, her eyes refused to focus on His face. Not that she was actually trying: she had an uneasy feeling that once seen, his visage could not thereafter be forgotten.

Baroness Hazard curtseyed deeply, eyes downcast, and Eve copied her. Refusal was unthinkable, part and parcel of the dreadful realization that the only reason she continued to breathe in His presence was because it did not suit His needs for her to suffocate right now.

"Good evening, Baroness." His resonant voice conveyed sardonic amusement. "And *you* must be the Evelyn Starkey I've been hearing so much about recently. Or should I say, Evelyn de Montfort Bigge, Baroness Skaro?"

Eve tried to swallow and found her salivary glands had gone on strike.

"You may rise," he added, and her knees responded of their own accord. "I gather you brought me a gift."

Eve tried to swallow again and this time she succeeded, although her throat was parched. "Yes," she finally managed to say. "May I . . . ?"

"*Of course* you may show me," said the Black Pharaoh. "I do so *love* receiving presents!"

Eve watched her hands as they fluttered around the gift box like captive doves. She felt as if they belonged to someone else, and she found herself involuntarily repositioning her body, swaying obligingly aside to afford Him the best viewing angle. She saw her fingers tug the ends of the bow, unraveling the knot and laying the ribbon aside: the gift wrap was Hermès silk, carefully folded by an origami expert. It opened without a hitch to reveal the antique leather hatbox, which she had paid to have restored as best as could be managed at short notice. The lock—the key was still missing, despite her best efforts to source a replacement—clicked open without her intervention. Clearly the PM was impatient to see His offering.

Eve lifted the lid. "This is attested to be the head of Rupert de Montfort Bigge," she said uncertainly, "although there are some anomalies."

She lifted the linen-wrapped cranium and displayed it before Him. Her evening gloves were a comfort, insulating her from direct contact with the grisly relic. "It was found in a gibbet cage in the dungeons beneath Castle Skaro, bearing the plaque you see at the bottom of the box."

She watched the Prime Minister inspect the skull. She could not tell the color of His eyes, although his gaze seemed as penetrating as X-rays. He was silent for several seconds, as if lost in thought. Finally He spoke.

"History repeats itself: first as tragedy, then as farce." He gave a softly theatrical sigh. "Madam, this is *indeed* the skull of Rupert de Montfort Bigge—and so you have discharged the letter of your obligation to the Crown. But it is not the *correct* skull that We desired for Our collection, and so We are presented with a dilemma."

Eve's knees threatened to give way out of sheer terror at the idea of displeasing Him.

After an unnerving pause, the Prime Minister continued. "We accept your tribute in the spirit in which it was intended. We recognize that it was an honest mistake, and difficult to avoid under the circumstances. You are not at fault in this matter, and We agree in principle to accept your oath of fealty—later. No punishment or imputation of negligence attaches to you. However, as a sorcerer like yourself must appreciate, time travel fucks *everything* up. Ah, the memories it brings back! We swear We've been here before." He chuckled at His little joke.

He paused, and Eve watched her puppet hands return the

skull to its box. She was not in control of her own limbs: she felt herself to be a marionette dancing to the tune of His will. (Which was distantly terrifying, for Eve was a practitioner of no small capability herself, and she wore powerful wards about her person. She had failed to notice His creeping usurpation of her bodily autonomy: if He had not also numbed her adrenal glands and amygdala she would probably be in the grip of a screaming panic attack. And Eve did not panic lightly.)

"Where was I? Ah yes—as I was saying, it would not be appropriate to accept your oath of fealty right now, but perhaps once you have retrieved the *correct* skull We will be able to proceed. It's entirely up to you, Ms. Starkey—or should I call you Baroness Skaro? No pressure. The ball, as they say, is in your court. Should you choose to decline the honor We shall not punish you. But until We see proof that Rupert de Montfort Bigge is permanently deceased, We will be unable to swear you to Our service as his lawful heir, and to extend such protection as that oath provides. So you will never be completely certain that you are safe under Our eyes." His voice dropped slightly. "Persephone, please remove *that*"—a finger waggled vaguely in the direction of the box—"and add it to the next consignment for Marble Arch. Tier two, rod K, I think. There is a suitable niche waiting for it." The unblinking gaze settled back on Eve. "This audience is at an end. It has been a great pleasure to meet you, Ms. Starkey. Can We express Our hope that you will choose to linger in the long gallery? A first-class buffet will be served in half an hour, and there will be after-dinner entertainment and dancing. You might enjoy the chance to practice your waltz: you never know when it might come in handy!"

▸◂▸◂▸◂

Eve stayed for the buffet—it was marginally less ghastly than the rubber conference chicken she had grown to despise over the years—and the *extremely* good single-malt Scotch that followed. But the music was not to her taste. She'd been hoping that the rumors were true and His Dread Majesty had reanimated Freddie Mercury for the ultimate royal command performance: but instead there was a classical string quartet playing weirdly atonal waltzes and polkas on ivory-hued instruments that gave her an uneasy feeling they were watching the audience hungrily. The guests might not have been consciously aware of the surveillance but they responded anyway, displaying the forced levity of concentration-camp inmates drafted to perform in a costume extravaganza filmed under the eyes of SS guards. There was raucous laughter, but some of the dancers seemed to be dead, or perhaps soul-drained and not yet smelling.

Eve eventually shook off the attentions of a private-equity investor—she was unclear whether he wanted to hire her as a cryptocurrency consultant or a dominatrix, but either way he made her skin crawl—and summoned up the *mana* to energize a ward she wore concealed inside one of her gloves. She hadn't brought an invisibility spell (their drain grew exponentially the more people they had to mislead—one that would work in a public event this size could only be sustained by mass human sacrifice). But a mistaken-identity glamour was nearly as good when it came to covering her retreat: anybody seeing her would mistake her for an uninteresting stranger. Once englamoured she successfully made her way down the main staircase, but she was so out of sorts that it took her five minutes to remember to cancel the ward in order to get the cloakroom attendants' attention. Once she'd retrieved her coat, Eve texted Sally to bring the car around. Then she stepped outside to wait.

It was past eleven o'clock when the car dropped her back at HQ. The daytime reception staff had long since given way to the graveyard shift. A solitary bullet-headed Gammon slumped behind the security desk, playing with his phone: at least he wasn't sleeping on the job. *Why do I bother?* Eve asked herself.

The evening had left her in a foul mood, and the last thing she needed right now was a reminder of Rupert's predilection for flash over function and size over substance. She'd been meaning to downsize the bloated security staff to Sally's team, who were competent if expensive: she saw no reason to pay for a battalion of human traffic cones just because Rupert liked to walk around with a meat shield.

"Ma'am!" The Gammon noticed her and sat bolt upright, his face ashen. He attempted to hide his phone, unsuccessfully.

"As you were," she said coolly. She walked toward the lift. "Any visitors? Is everything as it should be?"

"Yeah—I mean, yes, ma'am!" He was glassy-eyed from fear or professional embarrassment. Eve decided to let it slide for now. There'd be plenty of time to fire him tomorrow if his HR file confirmed her impression of bone-idle fecklessness. Meanwhile the lift arrived. She stepped inside and rode it down to the subbasement, intending to catch up on emails in her office: a necessary post-event cooldown.

Eve slept (when she slept) in the Victorian housekeeper's bedroom in the attic and spent most of her working hours in her windowless lair, deep underground. Since Rupert's disappearance she'd had it swept for cameras and listening devices, then splashed out on upgrades. She'd added a comfy chair for reading, a multiscreen Bloomberg terminal for business intelligence, and a dartboard for practicing her telekinesis. It was getting a little bit crowded—cluttered, even—but it was *hers*. Unlike in Rupert's office, she could hide inside and lock out the world whenever the pressure of performing in public became overwhelming. *Like a seal in a designer suit,* she thought, *always balancing a ball on my head.*

Her office wasn't the only room below ground level. Like other London-based oligarchs, Rupert had expanded his dwelling downward and outward, tunneling under his garden. What had started as a modest eighteenth-century town house now had a basement and two sublevels. There was an underground swimming pool, a cinema room that would have been right at home in a large multiplex, a religious chapel dedicated to rites Eve shuddered to contemplate, barracks rooms and panic rooms and a bomb shelter for the troops, and finally a rough tunnel cut into the clay and chalk under London, lined with ominous niches covered with cement. She was absolutely certain, beyond a shadow of a doubt, that ghosts did not exist: if ghosts were real she'd have been unable to answer the phone without being drowned out by the moans and entreaties of Rupert's victims.

Eve sat down, pulled off her gloves, and sighed. Her scalp itched, but if she started pulling out hairpins she'd never stop, and there'd be epic bed head tomorrow. So by way of relaxation she logged in to her secure email account and checked for new mail.

There was mail, as usual: rust never slept, and neither did the far-flung arms of the Bigge Organization. But one name leapt out at her, making her blink in surprise:

From: Rupert
Subject: Inactive account reminder

"Shit," she said aloud, momentarily worried. Like Google, the corporate mail system provided an inactive-account watchdog system. Staff could leave messages that would be automatically delivered to select recipients a set time after they last logged in. Rupert had disappeared almost exactly three months ago. Of course she'd ruthlessly blocked everything matching his name and had Support go through the mail spool nuking anything that matched, every day. She also had a couple of assistants who double-checked her inbox for hidden booby traps. But they'd left earlier in the evening, and if a delayed—

Record scratch.

Eve found herself blinking suddenly sore eyes at a blank screen. "What?" she said aloud, her voice creaky. *Am I coming down with something?* Her stomach grumbled and she felt cold and stiff, as if she'd been sitting in the same position for too long. *Did I just zone out?*

She touched the trackpad and her screen came back to life. The clock in the task bar said it was a quarter past two in the morning. Nearly three hours had been snipped out of her memory as if they'd never happened. Her extremities were freezing. She squeezed her feet back into unforgiving shoes, pulled on her gloves for warmth, and chafed her upper arms. "What was I just doing?" She was hyperventilating, she realized shakily. She felt the first signs of a panic attack coming on—something she hadn't experienced since the last terrible night with her father, going through the motions of CPR as she waited desperately for the ambulance to arrive.

The phone on her desk rang.

Eve answered it automatically. (It was dead of night in London, but a quarter past ten in Tokyo: it *might* be urgent.) "Yes?"

"Good *morning,* Eve," purred a voice she'd hoped never to hear again. "My office. *Now.*"

As if in a terrible dream from which she could not wake—as if in a replay of her earlier audience with the Black Pharaoh himself—Eve rose from her chair. She took her reticule and made her way to the lift. The screaming inside her head was distant and muffled but continuous. The lift rose: one story, then two, finally coming to rest on the first floor above ground level. Her sore feet carried her to the threshold of Rupert's office. She tried to stop them, struggling against her own disloyal muscle and bone, but a nightmarish sense of inevitability swamped her will. Resistance was not only futile, it was as hopeless as an act of treason against the universe itself. She tried to stop herself again, but failed.

The door opened to reveal Rupert's livid, gloating face. "Hello, *wife*." He chuckled glutinously. "Kneel. I say, dammit, get on your knees, bitch! It's been too long."

The ghost roads had not been kind to Rupert. He wore the same evening attire, white tie and tails, as he had on the fateful night when he followed the lost boys (and Eve) through the door to the dream roads in the Kensington Palace Gardens house. The reticulations behind the sealed portal led back into a mist-shrouded memory of 1888, where the cursed tome Rupert sought had been hidden for safekeeping by a forgotten Starkey family ancestor.

But he had disappeared months ago. His outfit was filthy and ripped, the trouser hems frayed and the elbows shiny with dirt, as if he'd worn nothing else for the intervening time. And it was in prime condition compared to its wearer. Rupert de Montfort Bigge was not merely filthy and worn down; Rupert looked as if he'd died and been sent to harrow a coal-fired hell as a reward for his crimes: then, having failed to find it, he had returned to haunt the land of the living.

"It wasn't there," he snarled. "I searched everywhere and found its trail but *it wasn't there*!"

Eve forced words past her fear-dried tongue. *Play dumb. . . .* "What wasn't there?"

"The book, *wife*. Speak only when spoken to," he added offhand, and her larynx seized. He chuckled again, a darkly knowing sound. "Did you discover the marriage contract? Nod or shake your head."

Words were inaccessible, but resistance was impossible: Eve nodded mutely.

"I knew you'd betray me if I pushed hard enough, and you did, didn't you? Even though you played along so well. Jumping eagerly to obey whenever I called. Told me bedtime stories on demand." (Eve shuddered.) "But you're a bitch and all bitches bite the feeding hand sooner or later. I made you deal with the arms dealer and design the waste-disposal machines to keep you distracted. (Oh, and I enjoyed the snuff videos afterward.) But do you remember the geas you consented to during your onboarding? You thought it was weak and you could break it whenever you wanted to, didn't you? Well, you're not as smart as you think! I had you in the palm of my hand right from the start! A little nudge here and a little push there and soon enough I had you where I wanted you. You didn't even notice yourself doing things for me that you'd never have contemplated of your own free will, did you? Did you!"

Rupert's voice rose as he inched toward her, but Eve's feet were frozen in place and she was unable to flee. He was so close that she could feel the fine spray of his spittle. It bore a rank note of decay, of fecal corruption. Rupert was dead, though his body still walked and ranted: she couldn't move or speak but she could *see,* and Rupert's body was as soul-dead as the walking corpses in the royal reception earlier in the evening. He just hadn't fallen over and rotted yet.

Decay starts when the gut bacteria and flora keep on growing after the human tissues stop metabolizing and their cell membranes rupture in apoptosis. Bacteria and fungi invade the dying cells lining the intestines, divide and replicate and ferment anaerobically, breaking down membranes and migrating into the other organs. Merrily pumping out methane and carbon dioxide as the host body putrefies.

Whatever force had killed Rupert was metaphysical rather than biological, and it had swung the reaper's scythe cleanly through human tissues and unicellular passengers alike. There was nothing left alive to start the decay process, not even gut bacteria. His body kept moving, but it was powered by a necromantic metabolism and mobilized by telekinesis. Bits of his cadaver kept breaking—his cheeks were rosy with rupturing capillaries, his eyes cloudy—but it wasn't *normal* decay. Eve had read up on vampires—PHANGs, as the New Management called them—and was fairly sure Rupert was something else, some sort of nightmarish lich animated by the will of his master, Saint Ppilimtec.

"I know what you tried to do! You messed up the chain of ownership so that the curse bound to the manuscript would kill me if I took it! But I'm smarter than you! Death spells don't work if you're already dead! I locked my soul up somewhere safe and secret years ago so it couldn't kill me. Left a reminder in Outlook that would send you an email and trigger the geas if I was gone too long. The manuscript ran and hid and I need it to take back my body—or the original *Necronomicon*—and it's lost in the dream roads! But there was more than one copy of the book, and I'm going to get one by hook or by crook! And when I've got it I'll fucking show you who's boss!"

There was a lot more spittle and ranting after that. Eve forced herself to swallow her pride and nod every so often. She encouraged him to continue because she was afraid that when the ranting stopped the shouty corpse would assault her.

"You want to know how I did it, don't you?" Rupert asked, grasping for any excuse to gloat some more. "You're my *wife*, married by proxy under the law of Skaro, so by the doctrine of coverture you are an extension of my body—we are one flesh and one blood. The geas is reinforced by your marriage vows, so you are no more able to disobey me than my fingers are." He held up his clenched right fist and simpered, then brought it to his face and kissed it. "Such a little thing, and so much more powerful once the marriage contract was signed!"

The semblance of humor abruptly faded. "Now listen closely, *wife*. From now on you will obey my instructions without hesitation or resistance. You will not attempt to free yourself from our marriage, and if anyone tries to free you, you will kill them.

You will always and only act in my best interests. You will obey the wedding vows. When I come to impregnate you, you will submit to me enthusiastically, make no attempt to avoid conception, and protect my child. You will not disclose my orders without my express permission. Oh, and don't try to kill yourself either, you're not getting out of it *that* easily. Do you understand? You may speak now."

Eve shuddered uncontrollably, unable to acknowledge the enormity of what he'd just done to her. She'd expected physical abuse, but this dreadful anticipation—combined with the total destruction of her free will—was worse. Suddenly every act he'd forbidden was painful to contemplate. *I'll have to cancel the solicitor's session tomorrow morning,* she realized. *Make an appointment to get my coil removed.* She knew—she had an abstract awareness—that this was *wrong* and not what she wanted, but it was pointless to pursue an annulment now. If presented with the papers tomorrow, she'd tear them up. If Imp tried to make her go through with it, she'd have to kill him—*wait, really?*

A creeping dread swept over her. "What now?" she asked.

"What now, *master,*" Rupert sneered. "That's how you will address me from now on. Well?"

"What now, *master?*" Eve tried again, gagging on the word. Through a foggy haze of dismay, it occurred to her that there was something his orders required her to ask, whether or not she wanted to know the answer. "If you want me to serve your best interests, shouldn't you tell me what they are? You've obviously got a plan but I can't work toward it if I don't know what it is."

She actually felt *better* after confessing her ignorance to her master, which simultaneously felt deeply wrong and completely right. The geas was clearly at work.

"Oh, that's easy enough." Rupert walked behind her—no, behind *his*—desk and sat, then frowned. "Visitor's chair," he said, pointing. Evidently he wanted to make eye contact. Gloating down at her as she knelt beside the desk was in some wise unsatisfactory. Eve went and sat in the indicated chair. As Rupert gathered his thoughts she frantically iterated through possibilities: *Can I kill myself by arranging an accident?* she wondered. But no, any contrived situation she could imagine would arise from her own disobedience, so—

"Did you copy those orders from Asimov?" she asked. "Like, the three laws of robotics, a 'me robot, you human' kind of thing?" Asimov's robots were perfect slaves, after all.

"I have no idea what you're talking about." Rupert snorted. "No, I came up with them myself. Visionary imagination, y'know." His smug gaze drilled into her, seeking out the recesses of her soul and marking her private parts for deletion. "Vision and boldness are what it takes!"

"*What* takes?" Rupert's ego was no less irritating for being undead.

"The plan." Rupert chuckled again. This time it sounded as if his lungs were liquefying. "*My* plan—the plan to save humanity."

▸◂▸◂▸◂

Rupert's Monologue (Abridged, Without the Ranting, Repetition, and Preening):

Did you ever wonder why the magic went away? Or why it's coming back? Or why *He* swept in and took over the government, and we're suddenly knee-deep in vampires and elves and fucking *tentacle monsters,* and the police carry guns that turn people into red-hot pumice stone, and you and your waster brother have regained the powers your great-grandfather lost?

Magic is computational. Magic is transactional. And the arrow of time is not always unidirectional.

In periods when too much magic happens, the arrow of causality becomes prone to random reversals, until temporal paradoxes smooth the underlying line of history into a state where time travel doesn't occur—usually because the magic that permits it has once again become inaccessible. This has happened before, and sooner or later magic reemerges—usually because somebody powerful discovers a need for it, or forgets why it was banished in the first place.

Over the centuries there have been many organizations tasked with employing magic for the defense of the realm. Sir John Dee, Queen Elizabeth's astrologer, was in it up to the eyeballs. Another group, the Invisible College, conducted occult warfare during the French Revolution and Napoleonic wars. During the early 1940s a branch of SOE—the wartime Special Operations Executive—worked out of rooms above a Chinese laundry in Soho.

There have also been organizations charged with suppressing magic when it wasn't wanted. In Europe from the late fifteenth to early nineteenth century, the Inquisition didn't just make life miserable and short for secret Jews and Muslims in Spain, or suppress Protestantism in the Netherlands. From the 1830s to 1860s, certain self-proclaimed rationalists decided that it was part of the civilizing mission of the Victorian empire—an empire that saw itself as the pinnacle of civilization—to suppress the magic of its conquered subjects. They did so ruthlessly. The mass observation campaigns of the 1920s and 1930s nailed the lid down on consensus reality like a mad lepidopterist impaling butterflies in a cabinet. Each time it was about crushing variant realities, threats to the Crown, rivals to the rightful hierarchy.

There is a balance of power, a seesaw between too much magic and too much effort going into the *suppression* of magic. And it has been going on for centuries, perhaps even millennia.

I mentioned SOE, didn't I? They and their colleagues at GCHQ really fucked things up. In the 1940s magic was in abeyance until the development of digital computers. Computers provide sorcerers with a tremendously powerful tool, but nobody back then really understood the synergies between electronics and eldritch power. The inexorable progression of semiconductor miniaturization means that we now have computers in headphones, wristwatches, light bulbs. Computers in hotel doorknobs. Computers more powerful than the biggest mainframes available to the magical boffins of the civil service in the 1960s! They cost pennies and they're in the hands of utter idiots everywhere. Instead of a handful of PhDs with top-secret clearance who have studied for years and are sworn to secrecy, we've got hordes of children running demon-summoning JavaScript in your web browser for their own amusement. Not malware but *Malleus Maleficarum*–ware.

The more magic there is, the lower the activation threshold gets—it becomes easier to perform magic. I used to have an edge, thanks to the patronage of the Mute Poet himself, Saint Ppilimtec. But then that fucking travesty of a Prime Minister came along and didn't even bother fighting an election campaign, he just walked into 10 Downing Street and took over the government—I ask you!—and of course He disapproves of rivals, such as my Lord of Poetry and Song. Meanwhile every two-bit private-equity outfit is trying to front-run reality by selling credit-default options to Mephistopheles, who is so far out of his depth it isn't even funny: the devil lost his shirt gambling on the cryptocurrency markets, Cthulhu's insane on the blockchain.

There is *too much magic,* and it's snowballing. Magic attracts magical parasites, eaters and feeders in night, demons and sentient parasitic fungi and things that core your brain from the inside out. Not to mention hedge-wizards and tricksters and hackers and fools who think they're superheroes.

None of this is good for business—if it goes unchecked they're going to destabilize reality so badly we drown in a sea of chaos! It's worse than global warming, it's *global randomization*. So I'm going to take action, Eve, I'm going to *do something* about it, which is more than I can say for our current government, that useless shower—I'm going to make most of the magic go away! Think of it as sorcerous geoengineering to get rid of the excess thaum flux in the environment.

I admit my pursuit of the book in 1888 was premature and led me down a blind alley for far too long, but now I know better! My preparations are well under way back in 1816, and soon I will have everything I need to start the great wreaking and bring Lord Ppilimtec fully into our world! I set everything in place before I came back here, oh yes I did, I just had a few loose ends to tidy up in the here and now—like you, *wife*. I'm going back now, and then I'll have *all* the magic, and there won't be any computers or mad gods in Downing Street or hedge-wizards because I'll have *eaten* them.

What I said about magic destabilizing time until paradoxes edit them out? You can still get to the unstable regions via the dream roads, but once history flips from one metastable state to the next, things settle down. He who controls the past controls the future, as Orwell put it: and *I* intend to be the pilot of history, steering humanity across this strange new ocean.

Once my plan comes to fruition only the Priesthood of Ppilimtec will remain. I'll downsize the population to something our planet can sustain—for thousands of years, hundreds of thousands if necessary—something our lifeboat Earth can ferry through the perilous cosmos while the stars are right and the Elder Gods walk among us. (I am not needlessly cruel, however: I shall simply ensure that the teeming billions of the twentieth and twenty-first centuries were never born.)

It'll be a simpler, safer world when I'm done making changes. A world where everyone knows their rightful place in the great chain of being: the lord in his castle, the serf toiling in his field. All watched over by the loving grace of the Mute Poet, and I, his right hand, will be the undying Pope-Emperor of Earth.

Yes, a lot of people will have to go away. But you can't make an omelette—or a utopia—without breaking eggs or taking skulls, can you? Nobody else seems willing to even *try,* so I suppose it's all down to good old Rupert, *once again,* to roll up his shirtsleeves and save the universe.

And like it or not you're going to help me, *wife.*

▸◂▸◂▸◂

Eve watched helplessly as Rupert looted the office wall safe. He stuffed his pockets with velvet bags of cut gemstones and bullion, cardboard tubes of antique coins, a snub-nosed revolver, a box of cartridges. All the while he kept up his self-serving soliloquy, his tones unctuous, punctuating it with instructions for Eve to put his affairs in order once he took his leave. "I will be gone for an indeterminate duration," he told her. "Time travel through the dream roads is uncertain. I want things to run smoothly in my absence. While I'm away you should see everything carries on as usual. If anyone asks, I'm on a retreat and don't want to be contacted: I'm not missing."

Carry on as usual, Eve thought bitterly, unable even to nod without permission. The air in the office was thick with the stench of money and decay, as if Rupert's character had translated directly into his bouquet. He rummaged in a desk drawer, then pulled out a fat leather wallet. Eve recognized it as a haruspex's toolkit: full of sharp tools for sacrifice, bloodletting, and dissection. "All good," he said. "I think that's everything. Follow me." He headed for the lift.

Eve helplessly accompanied him to the second subbasement of the town house. It was perpetually unfinished: the roof was low and uneven, pipes dangled from the ceiling, power cables were stapled into rough trenches in the walls, and there was a constant hum of ventilation fans.

Rupert descended a short flight of steps into an even lower tunnel, illuminated by an LED strip that shed a dim bluish glow. They passed a side passage leading to a niche where a miniexcavator was interred too deeply to be extracted, then turned a corner. Eve's stomach clenched. This final tunnel dead-ended in London's ancient clay. The floor here was uneven, dotted with oval patches of smooth cement roughly a meter long. Niches like the shelves in a Roman catacomb were dug into the rock to either side. Some of them were plastered over: others were still vacant, gaping maws waiting to receive the bodies of Rupert's next victims from the chapel upstairs.

Eve swallowed bile. She'd helped Rupert, she'd organized the construction of this tunnel. She'd even arranged some of the burials here. *Enemies,* he'd called them, a peculiar euphemism for the residuum of human sacrifice. She'd gone along with his demands because she had a pressing long-term goal to work toward, and besides, they were already dead, and besides-besides, it came to her now that she had not been entirely in her right mind.

This particular late-night trip down memory lane felt different. At the end of the tunnel a pair of pits lay waiting. One of them held a mound of still-damp cement, poured from a compact electric mixer. Rusty splatter marks surrounded the grave, as if Rupert hadn't bothered to tidy up after his latest atrocity. The other pit was still empty. The dead end of the tunnel was covered by an elaborate summoning grid—a magic circle drawn in conductive ink, overlaid with logic diagrams and taped-down contacts. Wires trailed across the floor to a glass demijohn full of half-clotted blood.

"Take this," said Rupert, handing her the gallon jug. "I need to adjust the gain." He knelt close to the summoning grid and made a minute adjustment to one arc, using a Sharpie that bled conductive silver ink. "Right-o, I'm off to 1816 to start things properly this time, book or *no* book, now I know what I'm doing. . . . This should power up the ghost roads in the house you stole from me. Stand here for at least half an hour and do *not* let the wires lose contact with the blood. After that I should be gone: make sure everything is sorted before I return. And I *will* come for you, make no mistake. It may be a few months, or a few minutes, but cometh the hour, cometh the man." He smiled malevolently. "Be seeing you." He gave her an odd salute then turned and slithered back down the charnel passage, toward the sleeping twenty-first-century city beyond.

Eve stood for a timeless period in mute despair, holding the glass jug with gradually cramping hands. *He's gone,* a traitor part of her mind—the greater part—wailed: gone back in time to retrieve the mad sorcerer's cookbook or carry out some frightful rite that would end the world as she knew it, leaving her helpless to await his return. Presumably she—as a sorcerer entangled in his affairs—would retain her memories, but anyone not part of his vile scheme, anyone who didn't walk the ghost roads, might never exist.

But Eve had more immediate worries. The door on the top floor of the mansion in Kensington Palace Gardens might have been painted over and nailed shut, but that wouldn't keep Rupert out. If Imp and Doc and Game Boy were in residence things might be much the worse for them, although Eve had no reason to think Rupert bore them any particular malice: at least no more than he bore towards anyone else. Their lives simply meant nothing to him. *Hopefully* they were out on the town, down the pub, visiting friends, doing something that would keep them out of Rupert's path of destruction. It was too late for her, but perhaps . . .

She began to explore the extent of her latitude, probing at his bindings with her mind like poking a sore tooth with her tongue. *Yes,* she thought, *that* might *work. He didn't order me* not *to*—With shaking hands she removed her smartphone from her reticule. There was no mobile signal down here, but she'd flood filled the basement levels with Wi-Fi mesh routers: her phone had internet. "Siri, FaceTime Imp," she ordered. Then waited, and waited, itching with impatience.

Finally he answered. "'Lo, sis, what's up?"

"Are you at home?" she demanded. "If so, you need to get out *now,* you and everyone else."

"Hang on," he drawled, "what's—"

"Incoming hostiles!" she shouted. "Get out before it's too late!" Then she hung up, unable to answer his questions and simultaneously comply with Rupert's instructions. Surely it didn't conflict with Rupert's goal to warn her brother to get out, did it? It was obviously clearing an obstacle from Rupert's path, so . . .

She checked the time: ten to three in the morning. She took a deep breath. The tunnel air was musty despite the forced ventilation. Rupert's compulsion was fading, as if Rupert himself was receding down a long, dark tunnel. But he'd said "at least half an hour" and she didn't want to tempt fate, so she waited until her phone ticked over to show twenty past three. Then she carefully set down the jug of stagnant blood, picked up her skirts, and hurried to the lift.

Rupert was no longer present in the here and now: she'd felt the geas slackening as he walked into the past, then abruptly vanish as he traveled back before the year of her birth. He couldn't update his orders now, and she had a window of opportunity *right now* in which she could take action, as long as it didn't violate his instructions. But if he returned with the book he'd be able to enslave her again—this time, for the rest of her life—and who knew what his plan to alter history would accomplish, if it eventuated?

Rupert's office was as she'd last seen it, the safe door hanging open. Eve had previously taken inventory of the contents.

Now she yanked open the flat jewelry drawers and pulled out a velvet-lined box containing a thick rope of pearls. She wrapped it around her neck, clipped it shut, then added a ward—a defensive charm—on a fine silver chain. She looped a second, smaller rope of pearls around her right wrist, dumped a third into her bag, then added a couple of brooches and antique earrings. In addition to her grasp of ritual magical practice, her natural gifts included telekinesis: she could throw a bullet-sized projectile hard enough to cause injury.

Rupert had taken most of the old money, but she managed to find a handful of shillings and a couple of gold sovereigns to put in her reticule. And she still had her folding fan—a modern update of the classic samurai's tessen, a war fan of golden orb spider silk wrapped around ceramic razor blades. She'd commissioned it herself via one of Rupert's more eccentric arms-dealer associates. It was a rare personal indulgence: she'd taken to carrying it everywhere after the distasteful business with the assassins embedded in her security team.

It took her five minutes to grab everything she needed, then she headed downstairs. The guard on the front desk was missing and Eve didn't waste time looking: she simply pulled her coat tight and stepped out into the wintry night.

Kensington Palace Gardens was only a few streets away from Bigge HQ. Eve covered the distance in under ten minutes, although the damp pavement made her regret not changing into more practical footwear. Eventually she reached the row of decaying town houses. Imp's residence was dark and appeared to be deserted, although the front door was ajar. As she ghosted up the overgrown drive she checked her phone for text messages.

All safe at Del's, whassup?

She replied, immensely relieved when the geas, temporarily in abeyance, allowed her to do so:

Rupert's back. Avoid contact at all costs. He was heading upstairs at yours: I'm following him. A moment's thought, and she found herself able to add: He tried to pwn me. If I can say this, he's gone for now and it didn't stick. I'm going after him.

Almost instantly, Imp sent back: Don't go.

Must. The PM told me to bring him Rupert's head. If I fail I'm dead meat. If Rupert came back she'd be dead meat anyway. It was all just peachy.

Eve switched her phone off then swept up the tenebrous stairs two at a time. Rupert's odor lingered, combining the miasma of foul blood with the sick-sweet stench of diarrhea. She tried to breathe through her mouth as she ascended, heart pounding.

Finally she reached the attic. There were four rooms here, and a fifth door that had been painted over when Imp and his friends moved in—initially they had mistaken it for a shallow cupboard. Imp and Doc had nailed it shut and boarded it over, but tonight it had been flung open by a power sufficiently overbearing that the hinges and lock had shattered. The door itself lay halfway across the landing: beyond the gaping frame a corridor stood empty, waiting for her. The only illumination was a bare filament bulb, lighting the way into the dream of history that her ancestors had hidden away behind the door to their oneiromantic memory palace.

Am I ready? she asked, then reminded herself: *It doesn't matter.* Ready or not, she had to go. Rupert's geas had lost its power to compel her obedience once he receded before her date of birth. As long as one or both of them existed in the past, prior to the date of the proxy marriage, the geas was unreinforced. He'd said it might be months, but she couldn't count on that. She had to go *right now,* travel as close as she could to his target date, pray that she arrived before he did, and hope that a 2011 marriage certificate didn't serve to reinforce a geas once they were both in the nineteenth century. What was the last order he'd given her in his office? Oh yes: *Follow me*. She could work with that.

Eve took a deep breath, stepped into a passageway lined with bedrooms dating to the late 1970s, and followed the scent of decay all the way back into history.

"YOU ARE NUMBER SIX"

Subjective hours passed and Eve's calves burned: she'd walked through several kilometers of passages, hallways, and stairwells, and was still in the dream roads.

The top floor of the town house extended well outside the boundaries of its real-world footprint on street level, and as she traveled steadily farther from her starting point, the decor became increasingly archaic. Filament bulbs dimmed then gave way to fizzing gas mantles. Eventually she was forced to pause and waste time blundering around in darkened bedrooms until she found a lamp with a reservoir of foul, fishy-smelling oil.

Then she walked some more.

She passed the drained indoor swimming pool on the top floor, then the library full of books printed before 1908 that Imp and his gang had found. There was a roof garden full of dead rosebushes that formed a protective maze around a cluster of pathetic gravestones—markers for all the Starkey babes struck down by the family curse—aunts and uncles Eve had never known. Then a servants' staircase that led down to a scullery and a stone-flagged kitchen with an exit into a dream of the First World War, or perhaps a Wellsian Martian invasion.

But Eve marched ever onward. Her eyes were dry and sore, and her legs ached from walking in court shoes. (At least her heels were modest.) She didn't wear a watch and her phone was switched off, but it must be close to five o'clock in the morning by now and she hadn't slept for twenty-four hours. But she didn't dare make use of one of the bedrooms en route: the dream roads were not safe. She kept herself awake by humming tunelessly, improvising fresh lyrics to yesteryear's hits. When that became monotonous she invented new and imaginative ways to murder Rupert once she caught up with him. After all, it was what he'd taught her to do.

A vaguely familiar corridor was the first sign that she'd looped back into spaces she'd already traversed. The geometry was familiar but the furnishings were different. The wallpaper and carpet had changed, and there were candleholders at intervals along the walls in place of gas mantles or electric uplighters, but the corridor was *definitely* familiar: she could feel it in her aching bones. And now there was a short flight of three steps leading up to another passage, and then a door. She opened it and found she was back in an attic, but not the exact same version as the one she'd come from. The dimensions, door, and window placements were the same, but there were no light bulbs, no carpet or wallpaper. The walls were raw plaster and the doors barring access to the bedrooms were warped. The bare boards of a servant's staircase led down to the second floor. Eve paused a moment, just long enough to take in a faint and plaintive wheezing from behind one of the doors. It was unreasonably cold in the attic, and the night breeze moaned past the boards nailed to the joists. She shivered, then raised her lamp and descended the uncarpeted stairs as quietly as possible, taking care not to trip on her hem. It belatedly occurred to her that perhaps she should have procured period-appropriate attire before attempting emergency time travel. Her red-carpet gown was self-consciously retro in 2017 but would probably seem outlandish and unfashionable wherever she was now. Although this wasn't the real nineteenth century but a hallucination created from the leaking *mana* of a sorcerous dynasty's memory palace: a family of oneiromancers, dream manipulators. *Maybe I could claim to be a stranded foreigner?* she considered, but it seemed too clichéd for words, so she shelved the idea.

The second floor—third, to continental eyes—was where members of the household had their bedrooms. Again, the layout was familiar. This was Imp's room: that was the bathroom, there was a guest bedroom, here was a room that the lost boys had filled with random junk and rails of theatrical costumes. But the wallpaper was wrong and the pattern of the carpet was unfamiliar. (It was also, oddly, far cleaner that the dirty, damp-spoiled treads she'd traversed at the start of her journey). *I'm definitely not in 2017 anymore,* she noted. A side table with a polished granite top bore a silenced clock draped with a black crepe wreath and the paintings punctuating the stretches of wall between the closed bedroom doors were shrouded in black muslin. Eve picked up her pace. If there were servants they'd be about their morning chores soon, and she didn't want to be mistaken for a burglar.

She found the drawing room and dining room on the first floor. This being a town house, there was a compact library but no ballroom. The library door was ajar and there were no signs of life, so Eve stepped inside. Dust sheets covered the furniture and the fireplace was empty and cold. Perhaps her fear of servants was misplaced, although the memory of the sleeping presence in the attic lingered.

Eve took a deep breath then exhaled, her breath steaming in the chilly air. She'd been running on adrenaline since the previous evening, fear and uncertainty in the face of the Black Pharaoh giving way to gut-liquefying terror when Rupert popped up like a nightmare jack-in-the-box. She'd seized a narrow window of opportunity and fled without proper preparation, grabbing whatever came to hand before hotfooting it out of his lair. But now, contemplating her options in the dust-sheeted library, she realized her failure to plan for this situation was a terrible weakness. *What year is it?* she wondered. *Who lives here?*

There were no newspapers, only dust sheets protecting shelves of leather-bound ledgers, and she'd go blind if she tried to puzzle out their copperplate handwriting by lamplight. Nevertheless she pulled a fat volume down from one end of a shelf. She opened it to the last page. It contained a list of receipts and outgoings, but the only date she could make out was "33/2/15," which was singularly uninformative (other than to remind her that she'd come here via the dream roads and nothing could be trusted).

Flipping to the inside front cover she found a brief gloss: "Marsden estates, entailments, 1814"—which was much better. It meant she'd come down sometime after 1814 (and probably after 1815, if the date on the last page could be trusted): the house presumably belonged to someone called Marsden, but that was all she could infer. Without a copy of *Debrett's Peerage* it wasn't terribly useful to know, and she didn't have an offline copy of Wikipedia on her phone. Or a solar-powered phone charger, for that matter. Her report card should have read, "Planning for time travel: C-minus, could do better." She silently chastised herself, put the book back where she'd found it, then tiptoed onto the landing. Then she descended the final flight of stairs.

The ground floor was fronted by a hall and a sitting room for receiving guests. A narrow passage behind the main staircase led to the kitchen, butler's pantry, scullery, and other service facilities. *Best avoided,* she decided. In a final, futile search for information Eve opened the sitting-room door. The room was overfurnished and fussily decorated, displaying the owner's wealth to best advantage. Porcelain plates sat atop a picture rail from which dangled numerous paintings, all of them draped in black. The chaise, occasional table, and other furniture were dust-sheeted, except for a single wingback chair that faced the street window. It was still dark outside, with an oppressive quality that had largely been banished by the invention of streetlights.

"Ooh, my Lady! You gave me a funny turn! I didn't think any of you was up yet! Begging yer pardon, but 'is Lordship the Earl doesn't tell us who to expect from one day to the next."

Eve managed not to flinch at the bright chatter from the housekeeper standing in the doorway behind her. She gave the woman a tight little smile. "I hadn't gone to bed yet," she remarked lightly, mentally crossing her fingers. *Earl . . . of Marsden?* Aristocrats tended to be night owls, didn't they? They owned all the candles, after all. Aside from the short flickering stub held by the servant, obviously. "I couldn't sleep."

The servant—a tiny woman, bird-boned and with a pronounced stoop—bobbed a belated curtsey. "Yes, m'lady, let me light the candelabra and send Annie in to set the fire for you." She darted inside and whipped a sheet off the small sofa, snapping it to shake the dust on the floor. It stank of coal ashes but helped cover the rank note of sewage that hung in the cold air like a stale fart. (Eve vaguely recalled that the London sewer system wouldn't even be planned for another fifty years.) "I can send for a pot o' tea as well?"

"Tea would be good." Eve sank gratefully onto the sofa and placed her lamp on the small table beside her, giving silent thanks that the servants had obviously been expecting houseguests. She flicked a stray soot smut off her sleeve. "Don't let me keep you." She tried hard to achieve the exact note of disdain that would be in character for a well-off and slightly scandalous lady visiting her friends about town. She wished she'd brought Imp along: his peculiar talent for persuading people to believe whatever he wanted would have made this much easier.

She tucked her aching feet beneath her as the housekeeper bustled over to the candelabra and lit four of the sixteen tapers. "I'll be back with tea in two ticks, ma'am," she said, then scurried off. It was hard to be certain in the twilight but Eve thought she saw a black ribbon trailing from the woman's upper arm. Another sign of mourning. Eve yawned cavernously—it had been a long night—and debated what to do: flee at the crack of dawn, or throw herself on the mercy of the household with some cock-and-bull story about being abandoned and stranded in an unfamiliar city? *I could fake being an American,* she thought, in the sort of half-amused hypnagogic state that came from being half past tired. *Not many Americans in London at this end of the nineteenth century,* not when sailing ships often took ten weeks to make the Atlantic crossing and suffered a 5 to 10 percent attrition rate.

A mousy teenager scurried in, hastily placed tinder, kindling, and coals in the fireplace, messed around with a flint and steel until it caught alight, then scurried out again. Eve concentrated on keeping her eyes open, trying to concoct a sufficiently convincing damsel-in-distress narrative. But thinking was hard. She was so tired. There was some very aromatic tinder in the fireplace, heavy and rich and sweet-smelling—*no, it's the candles,* she realized. The scent overpowered the acrid wood smoke and the dank miasma of drains, curls of blue vapor rising and swirling in the air. *What on Earth are they burning?* she wondered. Whatever it was, it wrapped around her aching temples and brought sweet relief. She yawned again, unable to stay awake. *I've smelled this before,* she thought vaguely. *I wonder where my tea's gotten to?* She supposed she ought to get up and ask, but she couldn't muster up the energy to move. She felt a pleasant lassitude flooding through her limbs, like a syrupy bath of warm relief from her every ache and pain. *Opium,* that's *what this smells like—*

Eve's eyelids slid shut and she lay back against the back of the sofa, breathing softly.

A minute later the housekeeper returned and snuffed out the candles. She wore a leather plague doctor's mask, its snout stuffed with charcoal, and she held her breath until the candles ceased smoldering. She crossed to the sash window and opened a small brass louver set in the wall beneath it. The frigid night air soon displaced the fumes. Finally she returned to the doorway and pulled a discreet bell rope. Shadowy figures gathered in the hall outside the door. "She's all yours," the housekeeper told them. Then she retreated to the kitchen, leaving Eve alone with the men dressed as undertakers.

▸◂▸◂▸◂

Eve realized she'd fallen asleep. *Funny.* She must have been more tired than she thought: her head felt as if it was stuffed with cotton wool, her mouth was desert-dry, and she seemed to be lying on—no, *in*—an unfamiliar bed. And her feet felt *so* good. *No shoes.* She tried to wiggle her toes, then realized she was lying on her side with her face buried in a pillow. She brought her hand up to rub her eyes as she yawned, and that was the precise moment she realized she was wearing a cotton nightgown. Not a garment she owned, and not the garment she'd gone to sleep in.

I was drugged! The flash of indignation prompted Eve to struggle upright, and she fought her way out from under a pile of blankets and a counterpane. *What the hell?* Her head was fuzzy, but not too fuzzy to realize that you don't drug houseguests, and equally you don't tuck burglars and trespassers up in bed. Her eyes were sticky and itched and there was wan daylight. *I must have slept for hours.* It was winter and dawn had still been hours away when she entered the morning room. She blinked furiously and looked around.

She had awakened in a canopy bed piled high with embroidered pillows. Brocade curtains were tied back at each corner. Beyond them she could make out a low-ceilinged bedroom with whitewashed walls and a rug-strewn stone floor. The windows and door were arched, and the upper halves of the panes were hung with plain curtains. The effect was simultaneously cozy and airy, almost Mediterranean in style. Going by the quality of the light it was early morning. She'd been asleep for at least a couple of hours. It was equally possible she'd slept around the clock.

She yawned, then pushed her legs over the side of the bed and forced herself to stand. The air on her face was bracingly chilly, but she still felt sluggish: her head spun and she needed the bathroom. There was a dresser beside the bed with a bowl of lukewarm water sitting atop it, towels folded neatly beside. She looked down. Sitting on the floor was a lidded bowl of unmistakable function. *You have got to be kidding me.* Well, it was the early nineteenth century: flushing toilets were a bit much to expect. Resigning herself, Eve hiked up her nightgown and made use of the chamber pot, then washed her hands. Did they have servants whose job was to empty the things? She certainly hoped so.

Once relieved Eve took stock of the furnishings. The room had a fireplace (cold and unlit), a wardrobe, and a small sitting area with a chaise and chair and side tables. It was laid out almost like a hotel suite, albeit electricity-free and lacking a bathroom. She took stock of herself next, fighting off an unfamiliar heaviness that still fuzzed her head—a lingering effect of whatever drug her captors had used to keep her sedated. A pile of fabric stacked atop a bedside table turned out to be a costume fit for a period drama. It mostly consisted of a fine cotton morning gown and assorted underpinnings. A pair of sturdy leather boots waited on the floor, and a bonnet and heavy coat-like garment hung by the entrance. Her reticule sat on top of the costume, along with her pearls and her neatly folded gloves.

The longer she thought about it, the more peculiar Eve found her circumstances. It was disturbing enough that she hadn't been robbed of her jewelry and coin. Her necklaces and bracelet were not cheap, even in a time when cultured pearls were commonplace (and this was emphatically not such an age). Worse, the ward she had worn on her necklace was conspicuously absent—and *that* was particularly damning, because it didn't look valuable to unschooled eyes. It meant her abductors didn't care about her wealth and knew how to identify and neutralize magical defenses. Which meant—*don't panic,* she told herself—they (whoever they were) had considerable resources and some awareness of thaumaturgy. But they hadn't thrown her in a dungeon, which must mean something. So: *orient, observe, decide, then act,* as Sergeant Gunderson said. *And don't assume the lack of manacles means they're friendly.*

She shuffled to the window and raised a curtain corner. There were glass panes in the door, rippled and bubbled with a bullseye distortion. She squinted through them at the irregular courtyard outside. It was framed by crumbling brick walls overgrown with ivy. The doors and windows opposite were arched, almost gothic in style. One end of the courtyard was open, falling away in a flight of steps down to a steep cobbled street, and beyond the stone wall on the far side of the road Eve glimpsed a beautifully manicured lawn. Something about it was inexplicably familiar, as if she'd been here on a family vacation when she was four or five years old, or seen it in a TV documentary. And yet, equally certainly, she'd never been here before in her life. It snagged annoyingly in her mind like a loose thread of memory that threatened to unravel.

Eve wrestled with the unfamiliar costume. It took some time to figure out the buttons and laces: she resolved to invent the zip fastener as soon as possible if she was stuck here. Then, before she could lose her nerve, she opened the front door and stepped outside.

A striking variety of Italianate architecture was on display, from the charming cottages surrounding the courtyard to the bell tower rising from the top end of the cobbled street. Wherever she was, it was far more hilly than central London. Motion caught her eye: a dark figure stood at the top of the bell tower, their hooded face tilted toward her. *I have questions and you're going to answer them,* Eve thought, and she hiked up her skirt and ran toward the steps. But by the time she reached the top—red-faced, with burning thighs from the mad dash up six flights—the viewing platform was deserted.

Eve panted for breath, disgusted by her own lack of stamina. Her breath steamed in the chilly air. *I must spend more time in the gym,* she resolved. (If they had gyms in the here and now.) But as she leaned on the wall and looked out across the drop-off she paused, struck by the tableau on display below her vantage. Footpaths wove between painted and porticoed buildings, although the wan daylight did nothing to bring out their best appearance. The sky was a solid dome of gray cloud from horizon to horizon, and though the sun must have risen she couldn't work out where it was. The lawn she'd glimpsed earlier stretched between flower beds and footpaths, with a bandstand at one end. White buildings opposite the bandstand surrounded another courtyard. In another direction, a larger building loomed over the green. It was fronted by a row of pillars and flanked by a pair of statues that screamed "town hall." The seaside village was beyond pretty, well down the road to charming. If only her presence here wasn't so inexplicable!

Once she'd caught her breath Eve realized she was cold. Hanging around up here was a bad idea: she'd left the gloves on her dresser and neglected the cape and bonnet entirely. The air was frigid. *Dammit,* she scolded herself, *be more prepared next time!* Whatever "be prepared" and "next time" meant. She descended the stairs and walked past the cottage she'd awakened in, down the slope to the lawn with the flower beds. Someone was moving furniture about on a patio in front of one of the buildings and Eve made her way toward them. She found a maidservant wrestling with a furled parasol that she was positioning over a table. Given the weather it was a nonsensical waste of time, but the maid carried on as if she expected the clouds to part and admit a scorching burst of light from the daystar at any moment. She wore a long black dress edged with white piping in a design that, again, felt vaguely, inexplicably familiar.

As Eve approached she looked up. "We'll open in a minute!" she said apologetically.

"What is this?" Eve's gesture took in the entirety of the formal garden, not just the terrace, but the woman clearly misunderstood her.

"This is the café! We'll be open in a minute. You're new here, aren't you?"

Was it that obvious? "Where?" Eve asked warily.

The maid finished with the parasol and turned to go back inside, then paused. "Would you like breakfast?" she asked hopefully.

"Where is this?" Eve repeated, biting back the impulse to intimidate. The serving staff weren't responsible for her predicament, although she'd welcome the chance to direct some choice words at whoever was in charge.

"This is the Village, ma'am," the maid offered, with the uncertainty due an unpredictable animal or a small child on the edge of a tantrum. "Would you like a cup of tea?"

The Village. For a moment Eve's head swam. *No, it can't be!* Memories danced in her mind's eye as she realized why it was familiar—she'd seen it all before, watching reruns of the classic psychological thriller series on the sofa with Daddy when she was little. She'd come here via the dream roads, hadn't she? Was she stuck in someone else's story and expected to take on a role? "Where's the police station?" she demanded.

The maid's smile became fixed. "I don't know what that is, ma'am."

What was the next line . . . ? Eve racked her brain. "Can I use your phone?"

The maid began to back away. "The town hall can help you!" she said, a note of desperation in her voice. "I've got to go! We open in a minute!" She spun round and dashed through the café's front door, slamming it behind her hard enough to rattle the windows.

"Well!" Eve huffed to herself. She looked around. Now that she had the context—and the key to the dream—bits and pieces fell into place, except everything was slightly askew. *Portmeirion*—the village setting of the show—*was built in the 1920s, wasn't it?* It certainly hadn't been around in 1815 or 1816! The TV show had a very 1960s sensibility—150 years out from Rupert's destination, totally at odds with the maid's costume and her own, although the black uniform with white edging was on point for *The Prisoner*. So this wasn't an *exact* re-creation of the surreal luxury prison camp for retired agents, but a confabulation coughed up by the dream roads for some arcane reason. The sky was a fuzzily opaque mass, like the swirling mists of the dream London she'd chased Imp and his gang through when they went hunting the missing magical tome: but this seemed somehow more stable, more *solid* than that manifestation of chaos. A lot of *mana* had gone into building this re-creation of Portmeirion. The buildings were subtly wrong, incorrectly positioned, and the paths were flagstoned or cobbled, and there was no sign of the neat tarmac she remembered Number Six dashing along as he tried to escape from the Village and its omnipresent CCTV cameras, but it didn't feel as if it would evaporate if she looked away.

The town hall, Eve decided, would be her next port of call.

Turning the corner just past the café Eve found a public noticeboard beneath a tiled awning facing the street. There was a map on the board. A bell dangled on a chain beside it, and as she reached for the bellpull she heard the sound of shod hooves on cobblestones. She glanced round. A two-wheeled cabriolet was approaching slowly, pulled by a tired-looking horse. As it drew up, the coachman tapped the brim of his hat in salute. "*Où désirez-vous aller?*"

Eve paused. "Do you speak English?" she asked.

"Of course, ma'am. Most people here prefer French, that's all. Where would you like to go?"

"Take me to the town hall, please." She climbed into the passenger seat below his bench. "What is this place called?"

"I thought you might be French. Or perhaps Prussian." He cracked his whip, and his mare slowly lumbered forward.

Out of his line of sight, Eve rolled her eyes. Just her luck to discover that particular species of cabbie existed in all times and places. "Why would I be French or German?"

"Oh, we get all sorts here. Especially since Waterloo." He spat phlegmatically in the direction of a flower bed. "Walk on," he told his nag, then clicked his tongue. "We'll be there in a jiffy," he added, then fell silent, leaving Eve to stew in her imagination.

▸◂▸◂▸◂

The cab came to a stop outside a baroque building fronted by an ornamental portico beneath a green domed roof. The effect was only slightly spoiled by its small size, for it was a town hall precisely proportioned to match a village. "*Deux sous, s'il vous plaits, madame,*" said the jarvie.

"Oh, I haven't got . . ." Eve began to apologize as she stepped down.

"Don't worry, pay me next time. Be seeing you!" he replied, making an odd finger-gesture of salute.

"I will," she promised.

She considered her next move as she slowly climbed the town-hall steps. The imposing doors bore no knocker, but an iron bellpull hung beside them. When Eve pulled the handle a gong sounded somewhere deep inside the building. As the note died away the door opened. Eve was confronted with a very short butler in eighteenth-century attire: a striped brown tailcoat, knee breeches, a powdered wig, and slightly grubby white stockings. "Number Two is expecting you." The fellow's face was stiff with disapproval at he stared up at her. "*This* way, madam." He turned and retreated toward a pair of white double doors at the far side of the vestibule.

"Stick to the script," Eve muttered under her breath as she followed the butler. She had a nagging feeling that she'd missed something, some vital step in the Number-Six-awakens-in-the-Village sequence. But it was so long since she'd watched the TV series with Dad! And what was a re-creation of a 1920s resort, famous for hosting a surreal 1960s spy show, doing in the 18-teens anyway?

The doors swung open to reveal a circular morning room. Tall French windows at the far end flooded it with washed-out daylight, and the bed of coals in the fireplace to her right barely took the edge off the morning chill. There were sofas and spindly Louis XV chairs, and an unlit chandelier dangling from the middle of the ceiling. And on the opposite side from the fireplace, standing in front of a chair drawn up behind a leather-topped pedestal desk, waited a smiling man without a face.

"The sleeper awakens at last! Delighted to see you," said the fellow. Eve almost recoiled in horror before she caught herself: it wouldn't do to show fear. *Is that . . . no,* she realized, *it can't be Him, surely!* But it was the same trick. The Prime Minister's face was impossible to perceive because one subconsciously recognized that to do so was to risk a long drop into a void of madness. *This* man's face was merely blurred because he was a sorcerer of considerable skill who did not wish to be recognized. (It was probably a variant of her mistaken-identity ward.) His accent was not dissimilar to that of the Prime Minister, Fabian Everyman, the living incarnation of the Black Pharaoh—but neither was it identical. The Prime Minister was the human aspect of a god, but this was still a man, or perhaps the premonition of something terrible that had not yet been reborn into this world. If he *was* the one who would live to become the avatar of N'yar Lat-Hotep, he was as yet two centuries removed from his destiny.

Eve forced a smile. "Number Two, I presume?" She walked across the carpet toward him, but stopped when he bowed, stiffly, from the waist, and waited. *Oh*: she remembered after a moment to curtsey. "Why am I here?" she asked, deciding to forego the inevitable polite lies and go for the throat.

"I thought *you* might be able to tell *me* why you're here." Number Two's invisible smile turned chilly, and she suppressed another shudder, reminding herself that he certainly wasn't the PM. Aside from the concealing glamour Number Two wore breeches and an elaborately embroidered tailcoat, the high points of his shirt collar protruding over a ridiculously knotted cravat. He was short enough that Eve could look him in the eye even without heels. He wore no wig—that fashion was apparently on the way out—but his hair was long and tied back in a plait secured by an extravagant bow. He should have seemed faintly ridiculous, but for all his harmless appearance she sensed that she was cast in the role of a vixen who had unwarily triggered a spring-loaded trap and was now held immobile for the gamekeeper's inspection.

"Would you care for a seat, madam?" He directed her toward the armchair closest to the fireplace. Eve allowed herself to be steered: she was quite cold from her coatless perambulations. After she sat down Number Two took the chair to her right, just outside arm's reach. "A pot of tea, Number Forty-Nine," he called.

"Yes, sir." The butler faded through the double doors, closing them silently behind him. Eve was instantly on guard, for the closed doors and lack of a chaperone sent a worrying message about her status here. In this period it was simply *not done* for an unmarried lady to be left alone with a strange man, however harmless he might appear. "Tea and civilization," sighed Number Two. "One has to work hard to keep up appearances, what?"

Eve faked a smile and nodded, reflecting that appearances were often deceptive and frequently lethal in her line of work. "What *is* this place?" she asked. "And who are you?"

Number Two's shoulders hunched inward minutely. "This is the *Village*," he told her. "And while you are here, you will answer to Number Six—or, in social situations, hmm . . . what is your preferred name, madam? I assume from your accent that you are English."

"Evelyn Starkey at your service." She crossed her arms defensively. "Why the numbers?"

"True names have power, as I'm sure you know. Ah. That *wasn't* your true name by any chance was it? Oh *dear*."

Name-based attribution was so old-school that Eve nearly rolled her eyes: there were defenses against it, defenses her father had drilled into her before she was a teenager. "Does it really matter, if I'm to be called Number Six?"

Although why she'd given him the name she secretly detested . . . that was worrying. *Is he using a truth compulsion?* she wondered, shifting uneasily in her chair but not quite certain whether she was under siege.

"Maybe: maybe not." Number Two relaxed slightly. "I think for now you had best be . . . ah, yes. You can be Lady Evelyn de Montfort, oldest of the two daughters of the late Earl de Montfort. Your brother inherited, your sister Elizabeth married the Marquis of Bath, but you are unattached." *An old maid,* Eve translated. "There's an up-to-date Debrett's in the library: be sure to do your homework."

He made a complex gesture with his hand, and a strangler's knot of lies tightened around Eve's throat. *Fuck, there* is *a compulsion ward under the carpet!* For the second time in less than a month she'd been rolled by a practitioner with a truth binding: it was infuriating! Worse, the Persian rug beneath their chairs might conceal other esoteric booby traps. But if she betrayed any understanding—

"What have you done to me?" she asked tightly.

"A binding to ensure your silence outside this room—it's for your own good. We do this to everyone in the Village, mm-hmm, as soon as they arrive. Confidences are frequently exchanged in here, and it would not do to allow gossip to spread freely." Number Two waited as Eve worked her way through a fit of near strangulation before he continued. "While you remain here you will not use the name you gave me, but will represent yourself as Number Six to similarly enumerated individuals, and as Lady Evelyn de Montfort to everybody else. Nor will you disclose your true background to anyone but me."

"But what if I meet the *real* Evelyn de Montfort?" she choked out.

"You won't." Number Two's expression was smugly knowing. "She succumbed to a very public fit of hysterical derangement during her season. It caused quite a fuss, so her parents sent her to live in a country house where she is well cared for and receives no visitors who might upset her."

"You mean an asylum."

"My, you don't mince words, do you?" Number Two shook his head. "My dear, you should be aware that indirection and subterfuge are a way of life in the Village. We so enjoy our little games, don't we? And I suggest you take the opportunity to make the most of your stay here: it's not every day that a commoner receives an invitation to live like a lady with a portion and prospects! (Even though the family estates are entailed for the next sixteen generations and your notional brother has a regrettable weakness for whist and horses.)"

The doors behind them opened and the butler—Number Forty-Nine—sedately wheeled in a tea trolley loaded with porcelain crockery and a gently steaming pot. He positioned the trolley between their chairs, poured two cups (milk first, then tea), and retreated.

"I imagine you have questions," said Number Two, sipping delicately.

"I—" Eve paused. "You kidnapped me and brought me here. May I ask why?"

"You may ask anything you like, my dear, but I am under no compulsion to answer. Suffice to say that the manner of your arrival in the Earl of Marsden's morning room suggests that you are either a spy, a sorcerer, or both. As you are clearly an Englishwoman I am giving you the benefit of the doubt *for now,* but the information in your head is undoubtedly priceless. I don't think you realize what a valuable property you are! A lady like yourself is worth a great deal to certain factions. Members of whom are represented among our peaceful community in the Village."

"Yes, but what *is* the—"

"The Village is a village!" Number Two interrupted tetchily. "A spa, resort, or sanctuary for fugitives and guests of the Crown, you might say. Our residents include exiled Bourbon loyalists—mostly members of the second estate—spies fallen out of favor with the emperor, members of the colonial Illuminati, Dutch alchemists, Prussian cryptozoologists—we have *quite* the collection, best kept under a bell jar where they can do no harm!—and anyone else the Service deems it useful to keep an eye on. We also collect unidentifiable persons of interest, yourself included, *Lady de Montfort.* A lot of people are profoundly interested in getting to know you, oh yes, they are."

Well, fuck, Eve thought, a new and unfamiliar sense of dread worming its way through her stomach. The dream roads had certainly taken her to the destination year Rupert had indicated, but in so doing they'd also landed her in a preposterous oubliette from which, if fiction was any guide, there was little or no hope of escape.

"I have to get back to London," she said tightly.

"I'm sure you do, my dear, but all of us want things we can't have." Number Two sipped his tea placidly, pinkie finger extended. "Who are you working for, really? Fouché? Metternich? The Grand Turk? Cabal the Necromancer?"

"Nobody you've ever heard of," Eve said stonily, then took a defiantly indelicate gulp from her cup. Her throat burned, but she refused to give him the satisfaction of seeing her wince. "I'm not from around these—parts."

Number Two nodded. "Well, personally I believe your story. I *do* think you're telling the truth. But what I think doesn't count, does it? One has to be sure about these things."

Eve glowered at him. "And that gives you the right to detain me here and poke your nose into my private business?"

"Please, my dear! You must agree that it's my job to check your motives. A few details might have been missed."

"Bah." Eve put her cup and saucer down and stood. "I don't care: I'm leaving."

"Feel free to attempt to do so." She sensed rather than saw Number Two's smile. It was not a particularly friendly expression. "Better men than you—and even a woman or two—have tried. There's no way out. Alternatively, perhaps you'd like to spend some time here? Get to know the people, as it were, make new friends, that sort of thing. Please, think of it as a house party, and yourself as a guest! Relax, enjoy yourself, and everything will sort itself out."

"I don't think so." Eve stalked toward the doors, which opened before her arrival as if powered by a concealed motor.

"Be seeing you!" called Number Two.

Eve stalked away in high dudgeon, and remained in that state all the way back to her cottage. How dare Number Two gag her like that! He might have the right to detain her for questioning if he was indeed in service to the government—as her confinement in the Village implied—but she had no intention of telling him anything useful. (Could she accidentally create a temporal paradox if she did so? The very idea gave her the collywobbles.) She had every intention of escaping as soon as she found out where (or when) Rupert had ended up. And being stripped of her name also rankled, although she couldn't articulate precisely why. But it was the high-handed manner of his instruction that offended her the most: his unthinking assumption that as a woman she could be ordered about, caged in, forced to answer to an impudent number. She'd had enough of that from Rupert to last her a lifetime.

By the time she got home her teeth were chattering with cold and barely suppressed rage. The weather was decidedly autumnal, her dress wasn't terribly warm, and she'd worked herself up into a fine fit of paranoia. So when she flung open the door and surprised a maid in the act of sweeping up the coal dust around the fireplace, she was primed to explode. But the maid was clearly determined not to give her any cause to do so, for she leapt to her feet and curtseyed. "Your Ladyship! Begging your pardon but Housekeep said to tell you that your luggage is in the wardrobe, and proper laundered after the coaching wreck. Also that lunch is served at one o'clock at the café every day, an' dinner's at eight in the dining room at the big house." (She'd already relaid fresh kindling in place of the cinders.)

She bobbed again, positively quivering with enthusiasm to impart her messages. Eve peered at her suspiciously, then called on a spell she'd come to use so frequently she'd recorded it as a macro, triggered by an almost invisible finger-twitch. Tendrils of light wrapped around the woman's head, revealing the telltale traces of ensorcellment: her mind was not her own. "Do you want me to help you with your hair and dinner dress, my

Lady? If you need me, just ring." The maid helpfully pointed at a bellpull by the door.

Eve forced herself to smile and nod. Polite society in the early nineteenth century was stuffy and unforgiving of social deviation, and it would be best not to defy expectations if she wanted her chamber pot emptied and hot baths on demand. "I'll be certain to do that." She grabbed her gloves, then reached for the bonnet and pelisse on the coatrack. The latter was of heavily embroidered silk and trimmed with fur, which suggested something about the real Lady de Montfort's wealth. She pulled them on, grateful for the extra insulation. "I'm going for lunch now. By the way, what is the date today?"

"Oh, it's the eighth, my Lady! Monday the eighth of July."

"Of what year?" Eve raised an eyebrow and waited.

The maid looked puzzled. "Of 1816, of course! When else might it be?" She smiled uncertainly.

"I have no idea," Eve said drily. She stepped outside and screwed her eyes shut while clenching her fists and counting to a hundred. It was better than screaming at the poor woman, who had done nothing to deserve Eve's ire except to tell her that she'd arrived six months out.

The café (and just the name alone was a suspicious anachronism, in Eve's opinion) was serving lunch when she got there. A couple of gentlemen—she *thought* they were gentlemen, although their behavior left a lot to be desired—were seated at the outdoor table, drinking scrumpy from pewter mugs and hooting about something. One of them tried to cop a feel as she swept past, but she dodged his wandering hand and made it into the safety of the café lobby, where the maître d'hôtel directed her toward a side room. "The ladies' dining room," he sniffily informed her.

Eve paused on the threshold. "Who were those men?" she demanded.

"That's the Comte d'Auberge and Sir Lawrence Hackmanworth." The head waiter gave her an arch look. "May I have your number? Otherwise it will be difficult to serve you."

"I'm told you may call me Number Six." Eve gave him a coquettish smile—although judging from his reaction she looked more like Harley Quinn. "And I'm hungry enough to eat the chef! What do you have for me today?"

"I'll send the maid to see to you." The waiter withdrew hastily, pretending he hadn't heard her question.

The ladies' room was completely dominated by a circular dining table. Eve found herself sandwiched between Number Eighteen, who grandly declared herself to be the Dowager Countess of Ealing (and had the years to back it up), and a nervous woman of wan complexion and uncertain age who timidly glanced at the doorway between tiny sips of murky brown soup. "I've never been so cold in July in my life! It's an utter disgrace. Don't you agree, Flora?" the countess demanded.

Flora the Uncertain murmured something indistinct to her soup, so the countess turned her bulldog interrogation on Eve. "Summer will never arrive this year!" she announced, then stared at Eve expectantly. It was clearly an invitation to a fight, although it was obvious that the countess would simply pull rank and declare herself the victor.

Eve nodded. "I expect you're right," she said. *It's July, it's overcast, and it's so cold I'm wearing a fur coat. Wasn't there an eruption or something?*

Being agreed with so easily quite set the countess back on her heels, but before she could object to Eve's agreement they were interrupted by the serving maid, who slid an unappetizing bowl in front of Eve. "Today's special is Brown Windsor soup, ma'am," said the maid, who bobbed a curtsey, then fled.

Eve picked up her spoon and took an experimental sip. She forced herself to swallow, then put her spoon down: she was hungry, but not *that* hungry. Meanwhile the countess regrouped.

"Don't you think it's suspicious?" the countess asked. "No sooner is the Corsican devil shipped off to rot on a new island hell than the weather turns horrible, what? Do you suppose another of Boney's mad scientists is to blame?"

"Er." In desperation Eve took another sip of the dreadful soup. It was almost worth it to avoid being sucked into a conversation that could only lead in one direction. She decided honesty was probably the least damaging option: at least her opinion would be defensible. "No, not really. There could be any number of reasons for the unseasonable weather. Why blame sorcerers or conspiracies when volcanoes erupt all the time?"

"Nonsense!" The dowager fixed her with a gimlet eye. "I fail to see how a volcano erupting could bring us to a state of Fimbulwinter. Whereas an attack by ice giants—" The countess launched into a long and deranged tirade about the perils of trusting the Aesir with, well, anything.

I'm in hell, Eve thought, wishing for a glass of something, anything, to rinse the horrid taste of the soup out of her mouth.

Flora sighed disconsolately and put her spoon down, her bowl almost full even though she seemed to be half-starved. Eve turned to her for escape. "How do you do?" she asked. "I'm new here, but I'm told to call myself Number Six. May I ask your number, please?"

Flora turned a haunted expression on her. "They're all dead," she whispered. (She had a faint French accent.) "*All* of them."

"I'm sorry?" Eve peered at her warily.

"I wouldn't bother if I were you!" the dowager trumpeted. "She sees the dead everywhere, that's all she goes on about—"

The serving maid reappeared and removed the full soup bowls from Eve's and Flora's settings, but the dowager defended her plate with the ferocity of a mastiff guarding a marrowbone. It was weighed down by a slice of burned-looking brisket and a pile of boiled potatoes swimming in a gravy that didn't bear thinking about.

"Excuse me, is any of the main course left?" Eve asked, but the maid bustled away, leaving Eve to stare at her empty table setting.

"Dead," whispered Flora. "Men, women, children, animals. All dead and buried in the fields under inches of ash. Fish floating belly-up in the lakes and rivers. Poison falls from the sky: Sanggar is ended, all the crops destroyed, roofs stove in."

Eve's skin crawled. She brought up her revelatory macro: when she looked at Flora she saw not a geas or some other compulsion, but a numinous glow. The woman's head was surrounded by a nebulous swarm of tiny, mindless eaters. They were attracted by the flavor of her power, whatever it was—some sort of oracular sight, apparently. Without protection she'd be consumed by the extradimensional parasites as they chewed a latticework of tiny holes in her brain. Metahuman Associated Dementia had turned Eve's mother into a husk after a cultist church had gotten its claws into her. Eve cautiously cut back on her own power—it wouldn't do to attract that kind of attention while she was unwarded—then a thought struck her. "Do you have a pencil and paper I could borrow?" Eve asked.

Flora barely responded, but the dowager sent her a guarded stare. "Why?"

"I want to help." She nodded at Flora. "She needs it."

The dowager sniffed. "Are you a forger?" she demanded archly.

What? Eve shook her head. "I'm a—I like to draw," she extemporized. "I'd like to sketch for Flora, that's all."

"Well, I *suppose* that's not illegal—"

The serving maid returned with plates for Eve and Flora. It was not quite as terrible as Eve had expected, but still unappetizing: much the same as the countess's platter, only hers was accompanied by boiled cabbage, boiled carrots, and boiled peas. Eve stared at it, hoping she was missing something. "It's all boiled," she said. "Is this normal here?"

"It's normal for this year," the countess pointed out. "Been unnatural cold so the fruit's all died on the trees and the crops rained flat in the fields. It will be a *terrible* year for wine, you mark my words. And there's no olive oil to be had!"

("A hard rain falling from beyond the sky," Flora whispered.)

"Well." Eve concentrated on her knife and fork for a few minutes. The food didn't taste quite as awful as it looked, probably because she hadn't eaten since yesterday evening (assuming she'd been brought here from the London town house without delay). "I might have been preoccupied," she said vaguely. *Wasn't there a worldwide famine in 1816?* "About that pencil and paper . . . do you think I could borrow them after lunch? I'd be ever so grateful, and so would Flora."

"I suppose so," the countess said condescendingly. She rapped on the table until the serving maid stuck her head inside. "Have my footman fetch my writing box at once," she said, then moderated her tone slightly. "There'll be half a sou in it for you."

"Yes, ma'am," said the maid, ducking her head.

Eve doggedly finished the main course, then forced down a desert of figgy pudding—the ancestor of the modern Christmas pudding. It sat in her stomach much as a cannonball sat atop a brass monkey: the hot posset that followed it wouldn't have caused her to fire the chef if she was back home. She then spent another half hour using the countess's writing supplies to sketch and energize three hasty wards. Such trivial scribblings wouldn't do much good against an attack by a real practitioner, but they'd keep the magical brain leeches at bay for a while. "You should fold this into a small muslin bag and wear it around your neck," she advised the countess. "It will keep bad dreams at bay." She smiled encouragingly. "And you, too," she told Flora, wrapping the woman's unresisting fingers around it.

Flora startled as her hand closed, and her expression cleared. "Who are you and what did you just do to me?" she asked.

"Just being a good neighbor. You need to keep hold of this"—the scrap of paper was glowing faintly—"until you can put it in a pouch around your neck. It's important. Do you know what it is?"

Flora shook herself. "It's. It's." Her eyes widened. "Protective?" she asked.

Gotcha, thought Eve. *It takes one to know one.* "Your mind's been wandering, hasn't it? I'm Eve—I'm told to call myself Number Six here. What should I call you?"

"I'm Flora, of course! Flora St. John. Number Sixty-Two." She rubbed her forehead. "Oh, I feel so much better! Did you know you have a *very small* number? They assign rank based on innate strength, you know—that or how suspicious they are of you. Have you met Number Two?"

"I really couldn't say." Eve spared a glance for the countess, who was watching them with the intensity of someone absolutely determined to collect all the juiciest gossip. "Thank you for the use of your writing slope, Your Ladyship. May I say I hope we meet again?"

"Oh, absolutely." The countess rose without a by-your-leave—as she clearly outranked Eve and Miss St. John, it was her right to do so. "Be seeing you!" she trilled over her shoulder as she sailed through the door, leaving Eve alone with Flora.

"So," said Flora, "I suppose you're new here. Would you like to see the Village?"

▸◂▸◂▸◂

Flora gave Eve a guided tour of the Village over the course of an afternoon.

The Village was very similar to the Portmeirion of Eve's own era: an Italianate baroque resort sitting on a rocky stretch of the Welsh coastline. Like Portmeirion, it nestled behind a gentle arc of sandy beach curving away to a rocky headland. Like Portmeirion, the Village was surrounded by craggy rock faces and impassable cliffs. There was no obvious way in or out by land. And there were plenty of smaller differences. Portmeirion hadn't been built until the 1920s: macadam road construction hadn't been invented in 1816, and the Village was too out of the way to benefit from the new Telford model. Instead the footpaths crisscrossing the hilly slope above the seafront were paved in flat setts, and the steeper paths were either cobbled or left as bare dirt tracks, the former uneven and uncomfortable to walk on, the latter treacherous and slippery when it rained. Eve became increasingly convinced that the Village was either a copy of her own time's Portmeirion—or, more disturbing, the true original, which had been erased from the history books, leaving her own time's version as a reconstruction. Why did it even exist? And who had built it?

"How do new guests arrive here?" Eve asked, as they cautiously descended a path by an ornamental rose garden, its bushes left skeletal and bare by a late spring frost. "What about food?"

"Guests just appear," Flora said vaguely. "I think it has something to do with ley lines. Food and coal come in at the cove past the beach. There's a pier, you know."

"A pier?" Eve tried to sound bright and spontaneous but achieved only questionable success. She'd purposely avoided grilling Flora about her own arrival lest it provoke her into lying. (Lies would not serve Eve's purpose: worse, unless Flora was a glib-tongued spy, the need to tell untruths would make her uneasy and likely to clam up completely.) "Who uses it?"

"There's a ship. I think it sails from Bristol. Anyway, it puts in every week or so to land supplies—but it doesn't linger, and the servants bring the cargo in by cart after it puts out to sea again. Nobody goes down to the pier while it's here."

"Nobody?"

"Rover doesn't like it." Her guide scuffed her shoe meditatively on a loose patch of gravel. "Don't try to escape, I implore you, it always ends badly."

"Does anybody ever leave? Officially, I mean?"

"Oh, I suppose so," Flora said carelessly.

"Have you been here long?" Eve tucked her hand under the other woman's arm, taking advantage of the cold to bring her closer.

"I think a, a year—I'm not sure? Two years, perhaps?" Flora didn't pull away, but she was shivering, and not from the chill in the air. "There was a coaching accident? Or maybe the war. And they're all dead, you know."

Fiona's hand was slipping. Eve repositioned it around the paper ward. Such a small thing—an inscribed spell, a logic diagram in an inhuman language—but Fiona's grip tightened once more, her gaze sharpening. "Thank you. The visions came first, then the leeches." This time it wasn't a shiver but a full-blown shudder. "They make my soul fade."

"I know." Eve led her gently toward a row of cottages set against the hillside. Below them, at the intersection of the hillside path and a steep road, a two-wheeled trap was slowly passing by. "You need to be very careful not to summon too many of them or they'll eat you faster than you can heal. You won't come back from that."

"You seem to know a lot."

"They took my mother," Eve admitted.

"Are you one of them? A practitioner?"

"I might be." Eve looked away so that Flora wouldn't see her face. *Liar, liar, pants on fire: you are* totally *a practitioner.* Not just any practitioner, either, but the eldest child of the Starkey line, oneiromancers since at least the 1880s and quite possibly as far back as this remote time. "I should make you a better ward, or at least a more substantial one. Once I can procure the correct materials." Encouraging dependency seemed like a fast track to obtaining Fiona's help, although the transactional approach left Eve feeling slightly soiled. This wasn't a business negotiation, after all: Flora was an innocent afflicted by an unwanted surfeit of seerdom, and manipulating her was a poor reward for her confidence. "When people leave do you know where they go? Or why?"

"I suppose Number One orders them released when he decides they're not a threat to the Crown." She gave a nervous giggle. "Or perhaps they try to run away and Rover eats them."

In the TV show she remembered, spies and prisoners who tried to flee the Village were chased down and dealt with by a thing called Rover, a cheesy 1960s special effect provided by a weather balloon and sinister mood music. But Eve was conscious that she'd come here by means of the dream roads, and if this Village was in some sense entangled with a 1960s TV show, she had no intention of coming face-to-face with an occult guardian that would almost certainly *not* turn out to be a weather balloon. Number Two's willingness to employ coercive bindings reminded her of the New Management, and his casual threats and blandishments—and barefaced references to foreign sorcerers incarcerated in the Village—were all the more menacing in that light. As for Number One, to make an educated guess: they would turn out to be someone from her own time, too, and a *Prisoner* fan at that. (Which didn't narrow the field much: it still had a cult following decades after the closing credits rolled for the last time, much like *The X-Files*. There'd even been a cable TV remake.)

They proceeded downhill and turned into another street. "Here's the old people's home," Flora told her, pointing to a low, sprawling building with a ramp for bath chairs. "Not that you have to be *old* to live there, but it helps. Most of them are in their forties and fifties, but senile. It strikes practitioners early."

MAD for sure, Eve thought. A concentration camp full of ritual magicians must be a hot zone for cases of infection with magical neurophages. She wondered if Flora realized how close she was to joining them. "Over there, what's that?" she asked, by way of distraction.

"Oh! That's the chessboard. When the weather's good, Number Two and the countess play living chess."

"And what's that?"

"That's the bowling green."

In such manner they perambulated around the Village for almost two hours. Eve took in all the sights. There was a sailing ship permanently beached upon the shore—or rather, a folly of stone in the shape of a ship, for there was no hull below the waterline. On its mast it flew flags. Eve recognized the Tricolour and the Jolly Roger, but drew a blank on some of the other, more arcane symbols. "It's for the children to play on, bless them," Flora explained, which rather puzzled Eve, who had not seen a single child so far.

Flora pointed out the Assembly Rooms, whatever they were (closed today); a Subscription Library (also closed: apparently it was a local holiday); the Post Office ("they don't take letters, though"); a row of shops selling sausages, candles, household knickknacks, and general supplies; and finally a tailor next door to a modiste.

"You'll need a gown for the ball," Flora told her.

"What ball?"

"There's always a ball whenever anybody new arrives," Flora said vaguely. "The countess insists."

"How am I supposed to pay for a gown?"

"If you have an allowance, you can collect it from the Post Office."

"And if I don't?"

Fiona's cheek's pinked. "There are ways to get money if you need it badly enough, I'm sure—not that I know about such things!" She cleared her throat. "Oh, look, it's the parson!" She waved at a paunchy, white-haired fellow in a tricorn hat who was hobbling along the street toward a much younger buck in a heavily embroidered coat of vaguely military cut. "Coo-ee! Over here, sir! We have a new neighbor, you'll never guess her number!"

Eve resigned herself to constant scrutiny for the next few days. The Village was a closed community and it quickly became apparent from conversations with the locals—both the English residents like the dowager and Parson Richards, and the foreign ones, such as the Comte de Castres and the Baron Von Francken-stein of Hesse-Darmstadt—that any arrival was a novelty: Eve *would* be introduced to and examined by absolutely everyone. This was the age of Jeremy Bentham and the Village was a perfect panopticon, in practice if not in architecture. For her part, she kept her inner eye open. About half the residents appeared to have some degree of empowerment. However, Number Two was the only one who tried to sink his claws into her, and she gradually began to relax. Role-playing Lady Evelyn de Montfort, sister of an earl, was not significantly more challenging than role-playing Eve Starkey, Chief Operations Officer of the Bigge Organization: it called for a different costume, but a jewel-polished smile and upright carriage would work for both identities.

It was almost too easy, she thought warily.

And she was right.

Eve visited the Post Office the following morning, where she was sniffily informed that the money order for her monthly allowance needed her signature before payment could be released. Accordingly she signed, and in return accepted the princely (or perhaps ladylike) sum of five hundred sous—rather than the eighty-seven guineas written on the note. (The Village apparently ran on an entirely artificial company scrip, to make it harder for the inmates to escape.) It was in any case a significant sum: perhaps twenty thousand pounds in 2017 money. Being an earl's daughter came with perks.

Eve noted that apparently her real signature was acceptable for money orders received from outside the Village. Where

Number Two had gotten it from, and how it had been linked to the real Lady Evelyn's accounts, were questions she filed away for future research: her list was growing rapidly.

She spent the rest of the morning in the Library, memorizing her fictional family tree for the past five generations, then met up with Flora and the dowager for lunch.

"You *will* come to dinner at the Assembly Rooms, my dear?" the dowager asked over pudding. The Assembly Rooms were apparently the social hub of the Village's polite society, the site of a dinner buffet and dance held once a month. The next event was three days hence. "Everyone's dying to meet you!"

Eve forced herself to smile amiably. "I'm sure they are," she agreed. She expected the ball to be as much fun as pulling her own teeth out with pliers: the local noblemen ran the gamut from boring to bestial, the ladies from snobbish to superficial. But as an unmarried lady, Eve wasn't allowed to approach strange men without an introduction. Asking after Rupert—or Baron Skaro—had so far produced no reactions save for a couple of knowing smirks. She had to do better, so she needed an introduction to what passed for society in this backwater. "I look forward to it and of course I'll attend," she assured the dowager. Then after lunch she allowed Flora to escort her to the modiste's.

Buying clothing in 1816 was a strange experience for Eve. The department store had only just been invented in London: the Village was much too small to support such an emporium. There were no sales here, nor were there off-the-rack clothes and standardized sizing. The only choices were secondhand or bespoke, which meant made-to-measure by a high-end dressmaker. She was led to understand that it was unthinkable for an earl's daughter to wear someone else's castoffs, but everything bespoke was beyond expensive. Not to mention slow. The sewing machine wouldn't be invented for another half century. At least seamstresses were cheap. The fabric selection was limited, the styles fussy and demanding (lots of lace and ribbon was mandatory, along with fasteners that required the assistance of a maid, to signal her wealth). It was, in Eve's efficiency-focused opinion, an utter nuisance.

It took Flora considerable effort to talk her in to spending two-thirds of her month's allowance on a silk ball gown and the necessary accessories—new kidskin gloves and headdress—along with a couple of day and evening dresses fit for a lady of her rank. She tried not to wince at the cost, which would have fed a family of twelve for a year. It was like driving a posh car instead of an economy model, she rationalized: an outward sign that she was rich and therefore to be taken seriously. Eve was always eager to be taken seriously, because in her experience it meant less time was wasted due to being ignored. The sooner she caught up with Rupert the better.

"When will the evening gown be ready?" she asked Madame Heloise (who spoke with a broad West Ridings accent).

"If tha'd come in fer't'fittin' on Thursday it'd be ready by countess' ball?" Madame speculated, sucking her ill-fitting teeth. "Might be scant o' t'trim, mind, but us can finish't later." Eve mentally translated this into *just-in-time-manufacturing, Regency-style,* and relaxed somewhat. She'd been half-afraid Madame was going to swallow her tongue and choke to death.

After visiting the dressmaker Eve pled exhaustion and slunk back to her cottage. She was expected to pay for coal and maid service and it was another wintry day, but she bolted the door and lit the fire anyway (thanking her fates for blessing her with a minor talent for pyrokinesis). She lit a candle as well, although it smoked appallingly and stank of beef dripping. (The good beeswax tapers were insultingly expensive.) She pulled the curtains shut, dragged the quilt off the bed, and huddled in front of the fire, brooding over her fate.

Experience had taught her that it was disturbingly easy to lose sight of the big picture. But if she had one thing going for her, it was her dogged, bloody-minded determination to avenge her parents—which in turn meant securing the helm of de Montfort Bigge Holdings, which *in turn* meant stopping Rupert from taking back control, thereby protecting herself and propitiating the PM. Eyes on the prize: the PM wanted Rupert's skull on a stick and she wanted to keep her own head firmly attached. So it followed that locating Rupert (or the missing book) had to be her priority.

However, living in a Jane Austen setting turned out to be more problematic than any number of starry-eyed fans assumed, and Eve was never starry-eyed at the best of times. It wasn't just that there were gibbets on the hilltops, highwaymen behind every bush, and bloody-handed aristocrats and sorcerers living large and taking the piss—she could find all of those things within a kilometer of her front door in 2017. But she also felt acutely exposed by the gaping holes in her cognitive map: the unknown unknowns started with Rupert (was he even here?) and expanded from there.

"How did I get here?" she asked herself, increasingly frustrated and baffled. (*This is not your beautiful house. . . .*) She'd been drugged in London, fallen asleep, and awakened in the Village. Which actually suggested this dream-roads version of 1816—very unlikely to be the real thing—was a snare and a deception. Most likely it was a pinched-off fistula of false history reconstructed from the memories of an earlier traveler. Just as Imp's expedition to 1888 Whitechapel had almost ended up in the lap of a Jack the Ripper confabulation, this one followed in the footsteps of an earlier explorer who had clearly watched *The Prisoner* one time too many and re-created it out of its own time for some reason or other. But why? Was Rupert somehow obsessed with the show? If so, he hadn't mentioned it to her. (Some people had certainly pointed to occult symbolism in its story line: and she could see how the cultlike secret society of spies surrounding the mysteriously absent Number One might appeal to Rupert.)

Assuming this version of the Village's location was the same as her own time's Portmeirion, London was some hundreds of miles away—and there were no planes, trains, or automobiles. Eve inferred she'd been carried hither by occult means, either a ghost road or a ley line. Number One (whoever he was) would want rapid access to his prisoners, so that made sense. But ley-line end points were choke points, tightly constrained and guarded, not to mention hidden from the locals. Food and cloth and coal came by sea, so presumably the ley line was too constricted to supply the Village. "If I was going to guard something from an internment camp full of sorcerers and spies, I'd either ward it or bind a demon to it," she mused aloud. "Maybe both. And I'd put it somewhere inaccessible. In the back of Number Two's closet, maybe?"

She grumped and moved another lump of coal onto the fitfully sputtering fire with her imaginary fingers. It was finally beginning to cast off a faint warmth.

"I should have thought this through better," she admitted to herself. Although Rupert might have returned before she made her escape, if she'd taken the time to prepare properly.

I could hide out here, she realized. The geas wasn't broken but it appeared to be suspended or weakened once she left the present. Semantics mattered in spellcraft, and the date on her marriage certificate said 2011, which meant she wasn't married to Rupert in 1816. *I could go native.* Cut a deal with Number Two and make herself useful, perhaps. But she had no reason to believe Number Two would be any less ruthless than Rupert—his sorcery's resemblance to the PM was disturbing.

If she could escape from the Village maybe she could go underground and change her name, seeking employment as a poor but respectable gentlewoman fallen on hard times. She could be a governess or paid companion. But then she'd be stranded in an age without the germ theory of disease, antibiotics, anesthesia, dentistry, underground sewers, and civil rights for women. There'd be no TV or movies, no recorded music, no telephones, no electricity, not even any trains for a couple of decades. What did they even use instead of tampons here? She'd find out by and by, after her contraceptive implant failed. Hitting her sixties in the 1850s wasn't terribly appealing, assuming she even lived that long in a period when smallpox and dental abscesses killed people all the time.

She could get used to it if she had to, she supposed, but it'd be a life of grinding poverty unless she somehow found and married a wealthy man, which was pretty much the fate she was fleeing from in the first place. Well, leaving aside the bit about Rupert being the blood-drenched priest of a nightmare god, not to mention a nasty little shit. The idea of selling herself into legal subordination stuck in her throat, but she absolutely had to consider all the angles. *I could go husband hunting,* she thought pragmatically. *Find and marry a dim-witted but basically decent toff.* She could certainly devise a halfway-sticky love glamour if she set her hand to it. But the correct term for someone who used a love spell to trap an otherwise unwilling partner was *rapist,* and Eve's conscience rebelled at the idea.

I may have killed in self-defense, but the only time I tortured *anyone Rupert was pulling my strings,* she remembered, and was dismayed by how long it had taken her to realize this. It shed a new light on certain experiences she'd had since she began to work for him. The thing with the arms dealer had been gruesome, although she'd gone through with it without a second thought at the time. Some people didn't deserve to live, she firmly believed that. But what she'd done under the influence of Rupert's geas, subtly reinforced by the proxy-marriage contract, went far beyond anything necessary. It had damaged her, and now she knew *why* it had happened she realized she couldn't manipulate someone else the same way.

Am I less ruthless than I thought? Eve wondered. It was a disturbing insight to have at this point, especially as she was alone and isolated with only her own bad-assery to fall back on. She didn't believe in redemption narratives: repentance wouldn't save her. There was too much blood on her hands, even if she had been under Rupert's influence when she shed it. Being less ruthless meant that she was weak—prone to squeamish fits of conscience while on death ground, vulnerable to hesitation. Which might get her killed. She *had* to be tough, otherwise Rupert would destroy her. But what if she wasn't tough enough?

She swore bitterly, then donned her outdoor layers and headed for the Library to ask what day the newssheets arrived. Any activity was better than sitting in front of the fire wrestling with her doubts.

It was late at night and Imp was deeply asleep, his dreams a confusion of sunken pirate ships and squirrels with cutlasses, when his phone rang. It was the ringtone he'd assigned to his sister, in honor of her reappearance after a five-year absence from his life: unmistakable, raucous, and intensely annoying because she never called at reasonable times.

As it happened he was alone in bed—Doc was off somewhere doing Doc things (he'd muttered something about visiting his parents the day before, then somehow absented himself without Imp noticing his departure). He rolled over, yawned, and sat up.

"'Lo, sis, what's up?"

"Are you at home?" Eve demanded. "If so, you need to get out *now*, you and everyone else."

The panic in his sister's voice shook the sleep right out of his head. "Hang on," he drawled, "what's—"

"Incoming danger!" Eve sounded—there was no other word for it—hysterical. "Get out before it's too late!"

Huh? Imp rubbed his eyes. "Wait a moment, what kind of—" She'd ended the call. "Shit."

He blinked at the ancient bedside alarm radio, its green digits a blur behind the scratched-up plastic window. It was a quarter to three in the morning. *Incoming danger.* "Shit," he repeated, then rolled out of bed, shoved his feet into his boots, and bolted for the door.

"Game Boy! Del, Wendy, Doc, kitchen mice, everyone! Get out *now*!" He banged Doc's bedroom door open, stuck his head inside to confirm his boyfriend's absence, then pelted downstairs. He grabbed his overcoat in the hall then shoved inside the door of what had once been the dining room. "Game Boy! It's a raid! Fire in the hole!"

"Whu?" GeeBee didn't have the benefit of Imp's air-raid siren ringtone to yank him into wakefulness, so Imp flicked on his light and loomed at him over the back of a rat king of cable-tangled games consoles. Game Boy slept in a sleeping-bag nest beneath a row of monitors and an office desk covered in controllers and keyboards. He blinked sleepily up at Imp. "Whassup?"

"Get dressed, we've got to get out," Imp insisted. "Is anyone else here?"

"Whut. Issit fire?" At least Game Boy was sitting up, shoving his fringe back, wearing a tee shirt in the sleeping bag—Imp hunted around on the floor for his lucky trainers and thrust them at him.

"Eve says we've got hostiles incoming."

Game Boy's eyes widened. "*Shit!*" He scrambled to get his feet in his shoes, then grabbed a suspiciously bulging day sack from beside the door. "Let's go."

Thirty seconds later they scrambled through the kitchen door and took shelter among the shadows in the overgrown garden. It was a chilly spring night, with dew on the ground and a lazy breeze blowing that sliced through Imp's coat. It came to him that he wasn't wearing any trousers and his heart was pounding fit to burst.

"This had better be good," Game Boy warned, his voice squeaking slightly.

"Eve said incom—" Imp fell silent. A crack of light flickered as something or someone passed in front of it on the other side of the back door. The flicker came again, with the cadence of human footsteps. Just one intruder, not like last time, *good*—then Imp realized it was very *not* good, for a single intruder could only mean a *confident* intruder. And the Starkey residence was mainly of interest to sorcerers.

Last time they'd been raided it had been an omnishambles; they'd been elsewhere and elsewhen when the Transnistrian mafia made a forced entry, followed by Rupert's pet assassin, and then Rupert himself, which had been an immense stroke of good fortune, for all of those intruders had been armed to the teeth and more than willing to kill each other. As it was, Imp and his mates were still cleaning up the mess months later. (Or, more accurately, pushing the wreckage around and shirking any actual cleaning wherever possible.)

Game Boy tapped Imp on the shoulder.

Yes? Imp mouthed at him.

Follow me. Game Boy took Imp's wrist and did his thing that involved walking between the blades of grass and rays of moonlight. Imp allowed himself to be led, and a minute later he realized they'd somehow bypassed a high brick wall surmounted with broken glass set in cement and were somehow in the royal park beyond the garden.

"I'm not decent," Imp warned. He'd only had time to grab boots, tee shirt, boxers, and a disreputable tweed coat pulled tight around his shoulders: he looked like a flasher.

"Tough," Game Boy chirped. He dumped his backpack on the grass and yanked out a pair of joggers, which he pulled on—Imp had a good forty centimeters on him, they'd never fit. "Who that?"

"She didn't say." Imp shuddered. Eve was most afraid of one person. The government wouldn't have given her enough advance notice to warn anyone, but Rupert liked to gloat—

"Not *him*."

"Yes, him. I mean, probably. It would be just our luck, right?"

"What are we gonna *do*?"

Imp took a deep breath and regretted it. *I'm going to catch my death of cold,* he realized. Dawn wasn't due for three or four hours. He had his phone, he had his wallet, he had a company credit card—for expenses, Eve had told him—but if it was Rupert it was Rupert's company *and don't go there*.

"Righty ho, looks like we're squatting next door," he told Game Boy. "We can camp out in the back room until morning, then see what the damage looks like. Meanwhile I'll tell the others to avoid the house until we know it's safe to go inside, or Eve calls to give me the all clear." He pushed a note of cheerful confidence into his voice, to forestall Game Boy's near-inevitable panic attack: the kid was strung tighter than a crossbow. "If it *is* you-know-who he'll only be heading upstairs, so once he's out of the picture we can figure out what to do. . . ."

LIFE IN THE VILLAGE

The weekend came, the weekend went, the phase of the moon changed, and Eve was haunted by the panicky apprehension that time was slipping away from her. Certainly time in the Village seemed to be measured by the day, not the hour or the minute or the microsecond as Eve was accustomed to. Her loss of control was a maddening itch: not merely her loss of control over her circumstances, or her deadly vulnerability to Rupert's magic, but her lack of understanding. Why was the Village *here,* in a dream of the early nineteenth century? It didn't belong! She didn't belong! She especially didn't belong in this place, and she wanted answers—and also the return of her own identity.

There was a church service on Sunday that she shirked, claiming a headache. On Monday the Village band sat on the bandstand and played vigorously enough to fend off the cold for a while, and on Tuesday night the supply ship put in at the pier and off-loaded the coming week's supplies, including the news-sheets Eve had ordered. Alas, she was not awake in the small hours, so she missed the opportunity to witness the vessel's arrival in person—much less sneak on board and stow away. But perhaps this was for the best, in view of what happened on Wednesday.

She was walking around the central square late in the morning, trying to work up an appetite before lunch. The community at large seemed to be taking advantage of a warm front that had passed over in the night, bringing lighter cloud cover and respite from the cold. A six-piece brass band sat on the bandstand, resplendent in red-and-white uniforms of military cut: the martial air they were playing put a spring in her step. She wasn't the only resident enjoying a preprandial walk. There went the parson, portentously chuntering at an elderly fellow in a periwig who she only knew as the barrister. On the other side of the lawn, the Dowager Countess of Ealing was taking the air with a companion who was *not* Lady St. John—Eve had not yet deciphered Fiona's status—and there went Madame de Vosges with *her* companion. (It seemed to be a status marker for ladies of high rank to be attended by not-exactly-servants who were nevertheless not their social equals.) There were other ladies and gentlemen about, to whom Eve had not yet been introduced. But then she spotted Number Two. He was marching at a fast pace, not exactly trotting but not dallying either. He strode rapidly across the lawn toward a plinth with a statue. In his hand he clutched a brass speaking horn, and even though Eve couldn't distinguish his features his posture conveyed a terrible determination.

Across the square, the clock in the tower began to strike noon. As its chimes reached a cacophonous climax Number Two clambered onto the plinth, where he stood before a statue of Atlas supporting a featureless white ball. He raised his trumpet and cleared his throat. "Good morning, ladies and gentlemen! It's a beautiful day, isn't it? Your attention, please. Here are two announcements. Ice cream is now on sale in the café for your enjoyment! The flavor of the day is strawberry."

A ripple of excitement ran through his audience: Number Two had gotten their undivided attention. In the absence of refrigeration ice cream was an exotic luxury, and in the current climate so were strawberries: combining the two made for a doubly exotic treat in the year without a summer. *How did he manage that?* Eve wondered.

But then Number Two continued. "Next, would you be so good

as to give a warm Village welcome for our latest resident, Lady Evelyn de Montfort, oldest sister of Earl de Montfort!" Polite applause broke out. Eve's head swiveled defensively: everywhere she looked strangers were staring at her with barely concealed interest. "She's very new here and hasn't quite settled, but I'm sure with your help she will! She will! Just as everybody settles here after a time, they move in and they don't move out."

Eve snorted in quiet disgust. "In your dreams," she muttered quietly—then cringed in shock as her words echoed back at her from all quarters, ringing out as if picked up and amplified by a hidden microphone. A trick of acoustics seemed unlikely, which meant magic—

"They had a choice!" Number Two chortled. "Wait for it! Wait!"

Everyone in the Village square came to a halt, freezing in place. The band downed their instruments and doffed their hats. Number Two gesticulated frantically at Eve. "Be still!"

The statue of Atlas shivered, an infinitesimal tension entering the great marble shoulders that bent beneath the weight of the white orb. Then the orb rippled. No longer a globe, it bloated and wobbled horribly as if inflating from some underground reservoir deep below the statue. It emitted a sinister chitter, echoing across the square. Eve twitched her fingers to invoke her perception macro. To her magically enhanced eyes the orb glowed a sickly nacreous green, flashing and flaring with sinister intent.

"Be still!" Number Two exhorted everyone, and it seemed for a moment that the Village held its breath. But then a young man at the opposite side of the square cried out in terror and bolted toward the path down to the shoreline. "Stop! Don't do it!" Number Two called, an odd tone of insincere expectation entering his voice that was quite at odds with his words. "Turn back before it's too late, I implore you!"

But the man kept running. Atlas shrugged: then the white

ball rippled down from his shoulders and rolled across the lawn, showing every sign of sentient malevolence. *This can't be happening,* Eve thought, a prickly hot sweat springing out across her brow. Occult power rippled from the thing in waves. It oscillated between a perfectly spherical mass and a pancake, repeatedly stretching out a single determined pseudopod then sucking its body into the distal tip in a headlong rush downhill: amoeba-like, but a billion times larger and motivated by spite, hate, and hunger.

"Come back, Oskar! You can't outrun Rover!" Number Two called. But Oskar clearly had no intention of stopping. The white blobby mass rippled so powerfully that it briefly became airborne as it crossed the footpath, bouncing in increasingly implausible leaps after the fleeing inmate.

Oskar screamed once, then the ball ran him down and stopped dead, pulsing rhythmically. It had swollen to at least twice its original diameter, Eve saw, and there was a dark man-shaped shadow moving inside it, pushing against its inner surface with increasingly feeble motions. It was both horrifying and fascinating, and Eve studied it avidly. *So* that's *how a shoggoth feeds.* She'd read about them but never seen one in real life. Rover settled atop its prey, surface rippling, and began to shrink back down toward its original size. *Juvenile specimen, no sign of reproductive buds,* Eve noted. *Well, that explains the ice cream, if not the strawberries.* Shoggoths were at home in subfreezing conditions, which made them extremely rare in England, for which Eve was profoundly grateful. As nightmare fuel went they were in a dead heat with unicorns. And now it seemed she was trapped in a pocket universe with one courtesy of the dream roads, drawing on the mythic archetype of a surreal spy thriller for its power: she definitely remembered this scene, although not from the inside. It had been one of the most powerful sequences of the pilot episode, and it was a very bad omen for her desire to escape.

Without any warning the band raised their instruments and struck up a jaunty march, just slightly off-key at the start. Eve almost jumped out of her skin when everyone around the square resumed their activities, although their chatter was slightly too loud and their laughter bright and forced. Number Two climbed down from the plinth and crossed the lawn toward her, giving her no way to flee without being pathetically obvious about it. The megaphone dangled from his hand like an executioner's discarded mask. "Well, my Lady, did you enjoy our little diversion?" he asked.

"I thought it was in terribly poor taste." Eve glared at him, clenching her fists so that they wouldn't betray her by shaking. "Did he know it was going to happen?"

"That would be cruel, my Lady! Besides, if he hadn't run he wouldn't have paid the price."

Eve took a second to compose herself. "What if the price of staying was even higher?"

"What indeed?" Number Two smiled behind his horrid glamour. "Will you be at the ball on Friday?"

"I suppose so." Eve gave him a lethal stink eye: Regency society balls were another goddamn archetype, she supposed. "It's not as if I have anywhere else to be, is it?"

"Indeed not!" Number Two doffed his hat with false bonhomie. "Be seeing you!"

▸◂▸◂▸◂

That night, Eve dreamed of Rupert.

This, in itself, was unusual. Eve was descended from a long line of oneiromancers—scryers of dreams—and in her opinion it was best not to subject herself to potentially lethal portents. So she and her brother had been trained from an early age not to dream trivially or accidentally. She usually slept soundly and retained no memory of her hypnogogic adventures unless she had first performed certain rituals her father taught her: anointing her wrists and forehead with essential oils, meditating on her desired outcome, then sleeping in a bed surrounded by a protective ward.

She was therefore slightly alarmed to find herself standing beneath a blazing red sun at the top of a stepped pyramid. The smell of dust and stench of metallic blood hung heavy on the air, as heavy as the collar of jade and gold clamped around her neck. She was dressed in a skirt of flayed human skin and a chest piece wired together from finger bones: her head was heavy beneath her headdress, a skull-like crown held in place by her braided hair woven through its eye sockets. She raised a black glass knife to the sky as she chanted pentametric prayers to the Mute Poet, verses in a language she did not understand that nevertheless rang with power and drew the satisfied regard of the tongueless horror they praised.

A queue of men, women, and children stretched down to the base of the pyramid below her, guided by soldiers standing to either side. Their eyes were dull and their faces placid as they took their turn to lie down upon the altar and bare their breastbones. They were pale-skinned, sometimes sunburned, often older and in poor physical condition: desk jockeys and day traders and vicars and doctors and estate agents and housewives and airline executives, all destined to feed the newly risen—and voracious—god. Despite the geases binding them it took four priests to hold their arms and legs still when Eve brought the knife down upon their stomachs. (The soul might be enslaved but the skeletal muscles twitched toward life and freedom regardless.) When she pulled—it was hard work, and sweaty, and her arms ached—she cut through muscles and diaphragm and up under the ribs to reach the still-beating heart and sever the major blood vessels. Blood squirted and pulsed in an endless arterial stream. Hearts went in one basket, livers in another, before the gutted bodies rolled carelessly down the far side of the pyramid to the reapers of skulls. Rivulets of carmine dribbled down the steps to one side, and all the while the sonorous chant of praise to the Lord of Poetry and Song continued, the insatiable hunger squatting in the back of her head to remind her that Saint Ppilimtec needed *more*—

—She and the other priests and priestesses had sent so many souls to his stomach, yet still he was running on empty—

—By order of her lord and master Rupert, whom she served helplessly, screaming inside her skull behind lips unable to do aught else but join in the chant—

And then she was somewhere else, and if this was a lucid dream she would have felt a pathetic sense of gratitude at no longer being in thrall to Rupert's sanguinary rituals, even though she was still a helpless captive in *something*.

Eve found herself walking the halls of a great house beneath gothic vaulted ceilings pierced by skylights, passing splintered wooden doors to either side and tapestries on the walls half-eaten by dream moths that glowed like rotting toadstools. She knew that she was pursued, that her pursuers weren't human, had never been human. That she had to find the library before something awful happened. *Library?* she dreamed of asking: she was wearing the same evening gown she'd worn to the Black Pharaoh's reception, but also manacles and an iron collar that sat upon her collarbone like the ritual breastplate she'd worn as a priestess. There was something *important* in the library that she had to find before the things behind her caught up. Things with too many limbs clicking busily along the flagstones, not stiletto heels but the legs of something like a monstrous land-dwelling lobster, and she knew that if she turned round and looked she'd see—

"You didn't imagine you could get away that easily, did you?" Rupert smiled over her as she lay on the altar, squinting into the red sun and the dust. The priests didn't hold her, but the manacles at wrist and ankle were locked to rings set in the altar, as was her iron collar. "How naive," Rupert commented. He wore the same tattered monkey suit he'd returned from the dream lands in, and his hollow eyes glinted with a light like sunlight glancing off bleached bones on desert sands. On his head sat a strange headdress made from a gemstone-encrusted human skull. "Remember, I'll always find you in the end, *wife*!" And he raised the obsidian blade.

▸◂▸◂▸◂

By Friday morning the weather had turned chilly again. There was no frost, but a cold overnight rain had brought a miasma of dank misery to the Village, and the slate-gray clouds overhead painted everything in drab, washed-out tones.

Eve spent the morning in the Library, scouring more newssheets for any hint of Rupert, both by name and by every alias she could imagine him stooping to. (Baron Skaro, Rupert Bigge, Rupert de Montfort Bigge, and variations thereof. He wasn't one to willingly hide his light under a bushel.) The cost was not inconsiderable, for the Subscription Library charged a fee per loan that varied according to the price of the item. Newspapers were taxed heavily, and her weekly reading list cost more than her lunch. But the ghastly dream—thankfully, unrepeated—had put the fear of an alien god into her, and giving up on the search was unthinkable.

Rupert wasn't mentioned in the society pages of *The Times*. He wasn't in last week's issues of *The Observer* or the Dundee *Courier and Argus,* and he was entirely absent from *The Spectator.* She became frantically excited for a few minutes when, scanning the previous week's run of *Lloyd's List,* she ran across a report of pirate activity in the Bay of Biscay. However, it turned out to be the work of Barbary privateers, which didn't sound remotely like Rupert. Any nautical moneymaking scams he engaged in were more likely to involve barratry and a complicated reinsurance policy, possibly backed up by magic: not that Rupert objected to violence, but he preferred to give his victims no opportunity to fight back. Chain shot and boarding actions with pistol and cutlass—in the face of extremely peeved sailors armed with boat hooks and blunderbusses—was a game too rich for his taste.

After lunch Eve returned to her rooms and discovered that Madame Heloise's girl had finally dropped off the gown she'd commissioned, along with a note of apology. The embroidery around the hem and bodice was unfinished. Madame was very sorry, and she would be happy to complete it after the ball. Eve normally couldn't have cared less about such fussy detail work—her taste tended toward austerely tailored business suits—but apparently a lady was expected to wear enough ribbon and lace to strangle a giraffe just to signal her wealth. *Well, at least I still have my jewelry.* She made up her mind: *I shall wear bling,* all *the bling.* She'd brought it along as ammunition—pearls made excellent bullets if you were telekinetic—and also as a source of ready cash at the nearest pawnbroker, but in this situation it'd work as a different sort of broadside. She pulled the bell cord, and waited impatiently for Mary the maidservant. "You called, my Lady?"

"I need you to help me dress for the ball."

"And put up your hair?"

"Exactly."

Getting ready involved interminable hours of primping and not a little poking with pins, but at least the early nineteenth century went light on makeup. (Although Eve had to reject the white lead face powder twice before Mary dropped the matter.) Her maid complained repeatedly about the length of Eve's hair, which was too short to yank into the fashionable French styles, even though to Eve's way of thinking this was no bad thing. The dress itself proved to be more of a headache than she'd expected. Her everyday outfits were simple enough that she could dress without assistance, but the ball gown was held together with ribbons and worn over a corset tight enough to make eating a questionable proposition. Despite the fittings it wasn't quite right: more pin-sticking ensued.

By early evening she was almost presentable, correctly accessorized, headdress pinned in place, oddly bulky gloves and reticule in hand, tessen dangling from her wrist, and throat and ears dripping with pearls. She shook her head in exasperation. *And I thought the dress code for the PM's reception was annoying!*

"What is it, my Lady? Is something the matter?" Mary wrung her hands.

"No, it's perfectly fine. If . . . after the ball, will you help me undress?"

"Yes, my Lady!" Mary dipped a nervous curtsey. "I'll stay here, shall I?"

"That would be best. I don't expect to be out too late," Eve added. "You can call the carriage for me now."

The Assembly Rooms were the nearest thing the Village had to a social hub. They boasted a large dining room and a public dance hall, with gaming rooms to one side. It was sad and dingy compared to Lancaster House, but far grander than the Village café: if the town hall was where administrative events took place, the Assembly Rooms were the beating heart of the community. The carriage—it had four wheels, unlike the regular two-wheeled cabs, and the jarvie wore a high hat—dropped her at the Village taxi rank, conveniently close to the Assembly Rooms' entrance. Number Forty-Nine, Number Two's Oddjob, was waiting on the door. He bowed her through and announced her arrival for anyone in the lobby area who needed to know.

Dinner was served early. Or perhaps Eve had lost track of time and was slightly on the late side of fashionable: either way, shortly after she arrived Number Forty-Nine started announcing pairs of numbers. At first Eve wondered if she'd wandered into a bingo contest, but then she saw that he was pairing up couples to enter the room together. "Number Seven and Number Six!" called the butler. Number Seven was a hunk, not so much beefcake as prime Kobe steak in painted-on breeches and a midnight-black evening coat. Eve tried not to drool too obviously. *He's gorgeous,* she thought appreciatively. *Why haven't I seen him around?* He also seemed vaguely familiar, as if Eve *had* seen him somewhere—after a moment's thought she realized that he resembled one of the portraits in the gallery at Lancaster House. But he seemed preoccupied and totally uninterested in small talk: all she got out of him was a name, Lord Ruthven, which she took to be a transparent ruse. After delivering her to her seat he excused himself and vanished. *Tall, dark, and sexy but he just isn't that into you, unlike the handsy creep at the café,* Eve told herself disgustedly. *Absolutely typical!*

A raised platform at one end was reserved for the Village elite. The parson was already seated there, chattering amiably at the dowager, as were a couple of other titled ladies and gentlemen whose status and wealth was clearly higher than Eve's (she was, after all, merely the spinster sister of a near-bankrupt earl). There were cards with names and numbers at every seat. Eve found herself relegated to a side table, sandwiched between a stranger and an unwelcome neighbor: Sir Lawrence of the wandering hands, who was unnumbered. Opposite her was a card for a Lady Sutherland who had not yet arrived. To her right was an unfamiliar man, and opposite him sat a boy who struck Eve as being very much on the young side for a dinner party, never mind a ball.

"How do you do," she said politely to her neighbor, ignoring Sir Lawrence's gross throat-clearing. She side-eyed her neighbor's name card. Number Seventy-Five, Viktor, Baron of Hesse-Darmstadt, wherever that was—somewhere that would later become part of Germany, she supposed. "I'm very pleased to meet your acquaintance, my Lord. Is he your ward?" She nodded at the lad, who was staring at the table as if he could coerce food into appearing before himself by force of will.

"*Jah, mein*—I mean, my Lady? I have not the pleasure of your introduction?" The baron was of indeterminate pre–middle age, somewhere between his late twenties and late thirties, with a receding hairline, prominent muttonchops, and kindly eyes surrounded by crow's feet. His coat had clearly seen a lot of use, although whether he kept it through poverty or force of habit was unclear. He looked at her card. "I see you are the new arrival, no?"

"I am." Eve dipped her chin. "Let's not stand on ceremony, though."

"*Jah, genau.* I am very pleased to meet you, my, no, Your Ladyship! And this is my boy. Say hello to Her Ladyship, François. François?"

The lad looked up and fixed Eve with a stare as sharp as a diamond tipped-drill. He had deep-set eyes of a gray or gray-blue hue, delicate features, and dark reddish-brown hair: his skin was sallow, and he struck Eve as looking rather sickly. He raised a hand and waved languidly.

"François, what have I told you?"

François sighed. "Yes, Papa." He had an indeterminate accent, bridging French with Spanish, or perhaps Italian. To Eve: "I am pel—no, I am pleased to meet you." He spoke softly. "Staying here has been most educational, wouldn't you agree, Papa?"

The baron sighed, not unaffectionately. "Yes, son." There was something more than slightly off about the nature of their relationship, Eve decided: as if they were playing the role of widower and son, rather than actually being related by blood.

"How old is he?" asked Eve.

"He will be—"

"Six—"

"*Twelve* in October." The baron spoke over François's interruption, at which point the lad pursed his lips rebelliously. "Isn't that right, *son*?"

"It is always twelve, why can't I be six, like a normal boy?"

She blinked, unsure what she'd heard. But at that moment Sir

Lawrence chortled heartily and blatted in her ear. "Well *hello*, dolly! It *was* you at the café last week, wasn't it?"

Eve's cheek muscles froze as if she'd dunked her face in a bucket of liquid nitrogen. It was a learned reflex, a habit ingrained from years of dealing with Rupert. She palmed her dessert fork as she turned to Sir Lawrence. "I don't believe we've been introduced, sir," she said blandly, then pointedly turned her attention back to François. Under cover of the table cloth she transferred the fork to her right hand. It was a precaution, but experience of dealing with Rupert's drinking chums from his Bullingdon days had taught her that it was a necessary one.

". . . we could be in Brest by now," the boy was earnestly telling the baron, until he noticed Eve had rejoined them. "My Lady?"

"Don't mind me."

Eve smiled at the boy and prepared to join in the conversation (*why Brest?* she wondered), but Sir Lawrence cleared his throat peremptorily and gassed meatily in her ear. "It says on your card you're Lady Evelyn de Montfort, and it says on my card that I'm Captain Sir Lawrence Hackmanworth, RN, Retired, so I think you can take us as jolly well introduced, what? So what's a girl like you doing in"—his hand languidly described an ellipse, and Eve realized he had a very large and nearly empty glass of brandy at his side—"the *Library* every day? Are you studying for your bluestocking come-out? Come on, you can tell me."

Eve's lip curled as she glanced at him: he was both drunk and deliberately obnoxious, and she needed to shut him down lest he get the idea that she was easy game. "I *really* don't think we've been introduced, *sir.*" She kept her tone icily polite. "Furthermore, I don't believe an introduction would work *at all.* Your name will inevitably slip my mind." She turned away from him again.

"Oh, don't be like that! I mistook you for a new kitchen maid the other day, simple mistake, anyone would have done the same if you keep going around dressed like that. I must say—"

"Shut up," Eve snapped repressively, shocking him with her forthright response. She tightened her grip on the fork in case he tried to get handsy again: it sounded as if he genuinely thought his excuse was valid, that everything was fine as long as he reserved his unwelcome attentions for the serving staff and left ladies of higher social standing alone. She needed a distraction. "Oh, look, is that the soup?" Waiters were walking among the tables, dispensing bowls and ladling some sort of green broth into them from a tureen.

There was a disturbance across the table from her. François was on his feet, pulling the empty chair beside him out and bowing as a rosy-cheeked woman—evidently Lady Sutherland—swept in to fill the last vacant seat at the table. The baron, Viktor, had given up on Eve and was already engaging with his neighbor on the opposite side, which meant nobody was paying any attention to the way Hackmanworth was braying at her. His type was much the same from one century to the next: subtlety never worked. "Soup!" he barked, raising his brandy glass with his right hand as he transferred his left to her kneecap under the table. "I need a refill here, and the same for the lovely lady—"

Eve poked the tines of her fork against the inside of his thigh. "Sir Lawrence, just to be clear: *you will unhand me at once.*" Sir Lawrence froze. She spoke quietly, but with an authoritative tone she usually reserved for the stupidest of minions: years as Rupert's amanuensis had taught her to speak psychopath with a native accent. "What is it they said about Lord Byron—'mad, bad, and dangerous to know'? Well, you might want to ponder the matter of me being unwed at my age, and ask yourself whether you really *do* want to get to know me better. I promise you won't enjoy the experience." She jabbed him with the fork, not quite violently enough to break the skin, but sufficiently to make her point. "Leave me alone"—*Harley Quinn smile*—"or I *will* maim you."

But she'd miscalculated. As she let up the pressure, Sir Lawrence chortled. "I love a fiery lass!" And instead of removing his wandering hand, he squeezed her kneecap painfully. "It's going to be fun changing your mind!"

"I don't bluff," Eve said, and stabbed him as hard as the blunt fork permitted.

Sir Lawrence froze. After a few seconds, his hand withdrew: but the look he gave her promised retribution. Apparently he didn't enjoy losing. "Whore," he said, quietly and coldly.

"I don't play games," she told him. "Leave me alone." Then, to prevent further conversational gambits, she pointed her face at the baron and pretended to be listening politely while he lectured the boy about galvanism and cellular division.

Dinner was a trial bordering on a torment. The food was barely better than the everyday fare served in the café and dining rooms, and everything was made worse by Eve's unfortunate neighbors. Sir Lawrence was a brooding presence (his earlier good-humored bullying had given way to a sullen glower after the Affair of the Dessert Fork), Baron V seemed to think the table a lecture theater and the boy François his student (and his lesson in natural philosophy was so full of errors and elisions that Eve's teeth ached from keeping her mouth shut), and Lady Sutherland was obsessed to the point of mania with the price of Belgian lace. Eve's other tablemates, including the taciturn hunk Number Seven, were too distant to provide succor. As for the boy, he was mainly attentive to his guardian—*who is* definitely *not his father,* Eve decided—but showed a canny interest in those around him, in a way quite at odds with his youth (whether he was twelve, as Baron V insisted, or six, as he seemed to believe). He had the manner of a late teenager who had skipped the sulking-in-the-bedroom-listening-to-emo-music stage, combined with the ominously neat and attentive demeanor of a lad yearning for a scholarship to a military academy.

After a couple of hours the meal fizzled out in a puddle of second-rate sherry trifle. The dowager rose and thanked everybody for attending in stentorian tones, then announced that tea would be served in the blue room. The women all rose, and as Eve followed them she couldn't help noticing—resentfully—that the waiters were bringing out cigars, port, and brandy for the men.

Eve found the drawing-room conversation largely inaccessible, for her knowledge of the niceties of nineteenth-century couture was minimal, as was her acquaintance with eligible titled bachelors: so she adopted a fixed smile and nodded whenever it was expected of her. All her evenings spent studying instead of zoning out watching period dramas on the TV were catching up with her. Eventually the dowager led the ladies in procession to the ballroom, where a not terribly proficient string quartet was murdering Haydn. The dim lighting—only a quarter of the sockets in the chandelier bore candles—cast deep shadows behind the pillars. It gave everything a murky tint, like a tropical fish tank that had gone too long between cleanings.

Eve nursed a flute of lemonade and lurked grumpily on the margins, watching from between the drapes screening the windows. At least playing the wallflower was undemanding. It was a bit like turning up at a school dance when you'd only transferred the previous term and didn't know anyone. A school dance where she'd arrived unfashionably early, so that the dance floor was empty and the air was too cold. It was in every respect a second-rate imitation of the Prime Minister's reception at Lancaster House, right down to the faceless éminence grise presiding over it: the only respect in which it was an improvement was that Number Two was less terrifying than N'yar Lat-Hotep.

This is awful, Eve thought the second time she turned down an invitation to dance. She was picking up some odd glances: it wasn't the done thing for single ladies to reject invitations. But faux pas or not, she was more familiar with Krav than quadrille, let alone racy new styles like the Viennese waltz. Her moves would be *totally* wrong, and the only fellow she actually wanted to send arse over tit was Sir Lawrence. The game simply wasn't worth the candle until she'd arranged for some discreet lessons.

"Oh, hello, I say! New girl. Coo-ee!"

Eve looked round. It was Tiggy the Head Prefect, or her skinny blond nineteenth-century counterpart. The kind who was all smiles and sunbeams for the teachers but lurked in ambush behind the bike rack with her homies and their hockey sticks, waiting for the class victim to try and go home. Eve knew her kind well: she saw the type specimen every morning in the mirror—she'd practiced for years to turn herself into one, in unconscious obedience to Rupert's nudging.

"Hello!" Eve flicked her fan open and waved an experimental greeting at Bitchy Ball-gown Buffy. Ceramic razor blades concealed in silk and lace were the *best* razor blades. "May I have the pleasure of your name?"

"Theophania Ffoulkes-Ward at your service!" Buffy—no, Tiggy—no, she was *actually* a Tiffany, for realz—gave her a slow once-over (*is she checking me out?* Eve wondered interestedly), then simpered and ducked a very abbreviated curtsey. "Of the House of Ward." (*Odd, why does that ring a bell?*) "My daddy is a baronet! He was created one for services to the Crown."

"Charmed, I'm sure." Eve smiled and curtseyed, unsure what message Tiffy was trying to convey with her blatant title-dropping, and hoping like hell she was getting the etiquette right. A quick glance with her inner eye revealed the woman was positively dripping with sorcerous mojo, *mana* staining her aura with an ominous sunset glow. She was completely free of parasites: clearly either she knew how to ward herself or her emotional-support tarantulas had eaten them. And now the penny dropped as Eve remembered where she'd heard the name. The Wards had been a famous family of mages around the time the Starkeys had first risen to prominence, although Eve couldn't remember for the life of her what had become of them during the century-long magical drought. "Are you an aficionado of the arts?" Eve asked.

"I might be." Tiffy coyly covered her mouth with her fan. "I saw you having trouble with the Beast," she whispered, barely audible over the music. "Watch out for that one: be sure to bolt your door at night."

"He has a poor reputation?" Eve raised an eyebrow.

"He's a creature of unruly impulses. I've not seen him go after a member of society before but he's an unholy terror to the maids. And he doesn't seem to like you very much. Or rather, he likes you in entirely the wrong way: fortune hunter, y'know, too many of that kind here."

"I can't imagine why," Eve remarked drily, and poured the dregs of her lemonade down her suddenly parched throat. *Great, I have my very own stalker.* "Why are you telling me this, Lady Ffoulkes-Ward—may I call you Theophania?"

"I answer to Tiffy." She nodded. "Lady de Montfort."

"Eve."

Tiffy glanced round to reassure herself they were not being overheard. "My Number is Twelve. Yours? Six, I believe. That's powerful—very low. Why are you here?"

"A . . . misunderstanding," Eve said carefully. "I was in the wrong place at the wrong time, and I think they took me for someone else." That was the absolute truth, and if Tiffy was an interrogator working for Number Two her occult lie detector would tell her as much. "How about you?"

"Oh, I'm sure it was just a mistake! Me, too," Tiffy confided, dropping her voice until Eve had to lean close to hear her. "I *swear* I didn't mean to tread on his toes but my mama was *so* furious she threatened to send me back to Saint Hilda's Institution for Young Ladies until I learned to behave properly this time"—Eve's eyebrows rose—"right after I called the Earl of Arundel's heir a philandering rake—"

Eve couldn't resist. "Well, is he?"

Tiffy rolled her eyes. "*Of course* he is, they all are, but that's not the point, I simply had to stop her marrying me off to the first meat-headed meal ticket that came along. It would have simply ruined all my plans. *All* of them! So I set out to make a scene and perhaps I slightly overegged the pudding, but anyway," she continued, sliding her arm through Eve's and dragging her toward a side door, "I woke up here, under Fabian's eye"—Eve startled at the name—"rather than back in Saint Hilda's with the doctors this time. Perhaps the quacks refused to take me because of the business with the chapel. Even though they've had time to reconsecrate it by now. But the Village is *such* a bore, isn't it?"

"I wouldn't know, I've barely arrived." Eve allowed herself to be steered along a servant's passageway tucked behind a panel concealed in the wainscoting, then through another door that led into a snug library fitted with floor-to-ceiling bookcases. It was dimly lit by a small overhead chandelier. The centerpiece of the room appeared to be a snooker table, but then she got a good look at the design etched in silver on the baize. "What the—"

Tiffy spun to face her. "We have about five minutes before anybody notices we're missing," she announced, dropping the flibbertigibbet pose. "Quickly. Are you with the Invisible College, Metternich's people, or the Silver Sisterhood?"

Eve crossed her arms defensively. "If I was with any of them, whoever they are, why do you think I should tell *you*?" She nodded at the table. "And what's *that*?"

It was a fake-out, but Theophania seemed to fall for it. Or at least her exasperated sigh of disappointment was proficient. "It's a summoning grid—an occult tool for communing with spirits." With leather wrist and ankle restraints neatly tucked away inside the drop pockets, and a blood gutter at neck level, Eve noted: evidently Tiffy didn't realize Eve could see through the glamour concealing the grisly trappings. "The billiard club is a cover for the League of Necromancers, meeting on alternate Tuesday and Thursday evenings. So, College or Illuminati or Orbis Tertius, who are you really, *Evelyn*?" She raised her hands. "And don't say you're Lady Evelyn de Montfort because the real Evie's about six inches shorter than you and faints if a man notices her, never mind stabbing him with a dessert fork. For which, I grant you full credit: Sir Lawrence completely deserved it."

Oh, for fuck's sake, is everyone in this place a player? Eve shook her head. "Believe me, when I said wrong place, wrong time, I was telling *nothing* but the truth." Her instinct was to go all *Doctor Who* on Number Twelve and say *Tiffy, I am from your far future,* but somehow she couldn't make her lips go there: *Number Two's geas strikes again.* "I can't say any more. Number Two, you know."

Theophania rolled her eyes. "You will," she warned Eve. "Everyone talks eventually. It's what they bring us here for. They want *information,*" she spat. Then she crossed to the side door, turned, and gave Eve the usual stylized two-fingered salute. "Be seeing you."

Eve leaned dizzily against the sacrificial altar for a few seconds. She fanned herself as she stitched the shreds of her composure back into place, even though she wasn't perspiring. *Is everyone in this place mad?* Quite possibly the answer was "yes." What she'd learned of her fellow residents suggested the Village had started as an internment camp for sorcerers captured during the Napoleonic wars, a genteel Georgian version of Camp X-Ray at Guantanamo. And ritual mages were usually a few screws short of a full set, even if they didn't succumb to full-on Metahuman Associated Dementia.

While she regained her composure, Eve inspected the books on the shelves. The handsome oxblood spines and edging appeared to be the product of a single bookbinder. There were titles embossed on the spines, but when she focused on the gilt lettering her eyes began to swim. *It's another illusion, isn't it?* She reached for one of the books but her ward warmed up suddenly and began to vibrate. *Well, maybe I* shouldn't *touch that.* She pulled her hand back, then ran one finger along the shelf, just in front of the row of books, until her ward stopped stinging her. *Interesting,* she thought, reaching out to pull the unenchanted volume for inspection—and the whole section of bookcase vanished as if it had never been there to reveal a small watcher's niche equipped with a wooden stool.

A spy hole, Eve realized delightedly. *This is what they used before CCTV!* A scuff of shoe leather from outside warned her that someone was approaching through the servants' corridor, so she ducked inside the secret room, right before her ward vibrated again. From inside the niche, the illusory bookshelves formed a transparent, wavering surface that she could see through as easily as a half-silvered mirror. The door opened fully, and Baron V entered, followed by the boy François.

"Wait here," the baron told his young charge sternly. François nodded sullenly. "I will return presently. *Don't* wander off or it will be the worse for you, *Your Majesty.*" He pronounced the unexpected honorific with a contemptuous sneer, as if it were intended as a slur. "It would not do for Number Eleven to find you here, do you understand?"

François nodded. The baron left, closing the servants' door

quietly. *I'm trapped!* Eve realized. *This is all Tiffy's fault!* Trapped in a glorified confessional by a tween-aged boy whose guardian called him "Your Majesty." It was annoying, but short of setting up a glamour and bluffing her way out—improvised, and without the usual materials—she was stuck until the baron returned for his ward.

François was searching the shelves for something specific. Finding a book, he withdrew it and opened it on the table, an expression of fascination on his face. He was clearly planning to be here for some time. Eve stepped back and gathered in her skirts to sit on the wooden watcher's chair, then froze as it groaned loudly beneath her. *Oops, busted.*

François turned and stared directly at her. "Mademoiselle de Montfort? What are you doing in there?"

"I was avoiding Sir Lawrence." It was the first thought that crossed her mind. "Curious, isn't it? What are you and your guardian doing here?" *And how can you see me? Are you an adept?*

François looked at her as if she was stupid. "I am reading this book, it is a translation. Monsieur *le* Baron is preparing our escape."

"Splendid!" Eve beamed. "And what is the book you are reading?" she asked.

François picked it up and held it to his chest. "It is titled *The Book of War* by Master Sun. It is a very famous text from China. I have read Monsieur Amiot's translation, of course, but this is a new one by the English missionary—" His expression closed up. "You are a lady, you would not understand its importance."

Eve forced herself to smile. "Reading for its own sake is improving, I say, even though not all books are for all readers. Where are you going when you are free?"

"To Paris, to retake my throne." Not since Eve had been in secondary school had she been on the receiving end of such a supercilious stare from a twelve-year-old boy. "You can't come, though. I have no need for a mistress at this time."

That stung. But before Eve could respond the door opened. The baron beckoned to François. "Here, boy." He passed the lad a cape and a satchel. "These are yours." The corridor outside was shadowy but Eve saw that the baron was dressed for a walk in the cold. "Hurry up now! There's no time to lose!" The glamour on the hidden room seemed to block his view of Eve, which worried her. Why could François see through it, but not Von Franckenstein? (The baron was older, uglier, and ruder than his fictional counterpart, a corner of her mind noted irrelevantly.) She held her breath until the door swung shut behind the boy, then waited just a few seconds longer before she followed the pair out into the passage. She wasn't ready to leave the Village just yet—not until she had a better idea of Rupert's whereabouts, or that of the book he was hunting—but if the baron knew of a way out, she absolutely had to shadow him.

Eve stealthily trailed the baron and his ward through darkened passages and crooked stairways. In a silk ball gown and slippers rather than a traveling outfit and sturdy boots she wasn't ready for an escape attempt, but needs must. She'd had no hint that the baron was planning a breakout tonight, but when she considered the matter it seemed like as good a time as any. Many people would still be shaken by Oskar's demise, and the baron was probably counting on the guards relaxing, secure in the knowledge that their prisoners wouldn't be tempted to risk the young man's fate. Anyway, who ever tried to break out of jail after a five-course dinner followed by ballroom dancing? It was absolutely ridiculous—so of course it was the perfect moment.

If only she'd had advance notice in order to ready herself!

And some idea of how the baron planned to make his break would have been helpful, too, come to think of it.

Eve had established that the Village was surrounded by mountainous crags on all the inland sides, apart from two steep paths that traversed exposed hillsides with no shelter from observation. To the seaward side there was the beach, the pier, the stone ship on the waterfront: and of course Rover. So which route was the baron taking—land or sea?

Neither, as it happened.

Eve paused periodically to get a sense of where the baron was leading her. Near the end of one passage she found a servants' staircase, and by the creaking of warped boards she realized he was ascending. She followed as fast as she dared, stepping lightly and relying on her lesser weight and the baron's preoccupation with his escape to cover for her. The stairs were unlit, so she felt her way in darkness to the second landing. Here the weak moonlight from a window gave her the impression of a narrow passage lined with doors. Judging by their tight spacing they were servants' bedrooms. An even narrower staircase continued steeply upward from the end of the passageway, and by the huffing and creaking coming from it she deduced it was the way forward. But this gave her pause for thought: *What's he doing on the roof?* It was increasingly cold as she left the function rooms below. The steps chilled her feet through the soles of her thin slippers, her breath steamed in the air, and her dinner sat in her stomach like a small cannonball. But she was near the top now, and she heard voices—the baron's gruff bass and François's unbroken piping.

"Here, give me the carboy and regulator." It was the baron. "Stand over there, boy. Yes, right there. Ensure the rope is fastened properly, we can afford no mistakes lest we set the canopy ablaze."

Eve tiptoed closer to the open doorway onto the roof. She was struck by how little light there was, even with a nearly full moon. Streetlights running on coal gas had only arrived in London in 1807, and didn't take off outside the metropolis for some years. The Village still relied on candles and oil lamps in windows. Away from public buildings, the landscape was shrouded in darkness.

". . . the basket," the baron was telling his ward. "Once the Montgolfier begins to expand, you must bolt the door before you join me inside." There were noises that sounded suspiciously like steel striking flint, and a flash of sparks, then a steady flame that grew brighter by the second, and a faint sizzling sound. "*Gut, sehr gut . . .*"

"Is it working?" piped François.

"Patience, child!" Eve crouched behind the door as the baron bustled around, adjusting something that rustled like the dowager's voluminous skirts. "It takes time, as you can see. But a cold night is best for an ascent, yes? The cold air is denser so the hot gas is more efficient."

Eve peeped around the door and froze, mouth open in astonishment as she took in the rooftop tableau laid out before her.

It was a dark night, and by rights the flare from the baron's gas burner should have lit up the entire Village square. Such a beacon should even have illuminated the cliffs above. But the rooftop of the Assembly Rooms, despite having a steep pitch around the edges, was flat on top, providing an apron surrounded on all sides by a slate-clad ridgeline. The baron was evidently preparing to make his escape in a hot-air balloon of the Mongolfier pattern, inflated by gas from an incandescent fuel brazier burning high-grade coal. The flames coming out of his brazier were distinctly bluish, the products of incomplete combustion. *Carbon monoxide for heat and excess hydrogen to augment lift,* Eve speculated. It was a dangerous strategy—carbon monoxide was poisonous, and hydrogen mixed with hot air made for an explosive mixture—but it was much more efficient as a lifting gas than hot air alone. *Where did he get the fabric to make the balloon?* she wondered. It had to be lightweight, probably silk, and specially treated, which would make it phenomenally expensive.

As Eve watched, the dome of the balloon began to rise. Soon it loomed over the roof. It was a cold night but the burner threw off so much heat that perspiration beaded her brow. And now she saw the baron fussily plumbing together a series of glazed earthenware carboys, draining one after another into the burner between scoops of coal. "This is the blue water gas," Baron Von Franckenstein lectured François as he pumped and shoveled, sweat gleaming on his forehead. "The alternating carburetor turns the water to steam and injects it through the furnace bed, creating the hot producer gas which we burn in the upper Venturi device, here. It is *most* efficient," he added with satisfaction. Any other villain would make it the occasion of a monologue: the baron made it the occasion of a chemistry lecture. "Boy, are you paying attention? I said, boy!"

François startled. "*Oui,* monsieur?"

"Is the rope ready to cast off?" the gentleman scientist asked his charge. "We shall begin our ascent shortly—look how high the envelope rises, she is eager to flee the bonds of Earth and take to the skies, we must wait only until she is sufficiently buoyant to cross the mountains inland when we release our ballast—"

This has gone far enough, Eve thought, and gathered herself to step out onto the roof and give him a piece of her mind. What did the baron think he was doing, risking the lad's life on a nighttime flight over mountainous terrain beneath an untested and likely explosive gas bag? But as she pushed on the door someone grabbed her around the waist, pinioning her arms before she could resist. She inhaled but before she could protest a hand clamped across her mouth. Furious and frightened, Eve raised a foot and stomped on her assailant's instep, but her dancing slippers were no match for boots. So she bit him as hard as she could, bitterly regretting her lack of venom glands.

"Fuck!" Hot breath blew against her neck. "Will you stop that?" her assailant demanded. His voice was like velvet dipped in brandy, shockingly intimate in her ear. "Do you *want* Rover to get you?"

Eve stilled, and allowed her jaw muscles to relax. It was Number Seven, tall, dark, and handsome—and, very irritatingly, no longer ignoring her.

"He doesn't have the lift to take you in the balloon," her captor added. He sounded both intelligent and civilized, unlike Sir Lawrence, which worried Eve considerably: intelligent opponents were far more dangerous. "Not as well as François, and the boy is his meal ticket. If I take my hand from your mouth will you refrain from screaming? All it will do is make everything worse. Nudge me with your right foot if you agree."

Eve stomped on his right toe as hard as she could. It probably hurt her more than it hurt him, but it got the message across. A second later the hand covering her face loosened.

"Jolly good," whispered her captor. "Now let's watch."

Infuriating. She briefly considered stabbing him, but decided that now was not (yet) the time: mirroring his de-escalation seemed prudent, at least until she knew who she was dealing with. Besides, she was very aware of the press of his broad chest against her spine, warm and delicious. "Rover." She swallowed. "Will it kill them?"

"Probably not, they're too valuable. Oskar was both troublesome and essentially disposable, that's why Number Two made an example of him." A pause. "You should return to the ballroom: this is not a suitable place for a lady. If you were to be seen here—"

"Yes, yes I know, it would be a scandal, my reputation would be besmirched." Eve didn't bother to dilute her acid tone. "But as the only person who has seen me here so far is you, whoever you are—"

"I'm wounded that you don't recognize me, my Lady! Number Seven at your service, although you may call me George—"

"*Unhand me,* Number Seven." The arm curled around her chest—did he think he was being reassuringly protective?—disappeared without even a token grope. So, points to Number Seven (aka Lord Ruthven, aka George) for not being a piratical asshole like Sir Lawrence Hackmanworth, but no points at all for being a controlling ass who thought it was all right to grab women from behind for their own protection.

"Thank you." She shrugged, repressing a shiver at the sudden chill—his embrace would have been more than pleasant under other circumstances—but kept her back turned. To look round would be a sign of weakness. "What makes you think the baron's not going to make it?"

Outside the doorway the balloon continued to inflate. The brazier's flame-throated bellow was oddly muffled, and by the tingling in her fingertips Eve sensed magic at work. He'd probably begged, borrowed, or stolen some sort of antisound amulet: they were expensive devices, bespoke constructs that were far less reliable than the cheap microelectronic gadgets of her own time. (Invisibility was even worse, but at least this period had plenty of public executions if one absolutely *had* to obtain a hand of glory.)

George snorted. "D'you think the baron is the first inmate to attempt to escape by Montgolfier? Or that his departure from the ball went unnoticed?"

"Now that you mention it . . ."

"It's about to get very messy up here, my Lady, and unless you enjoy washing bloodstains out of silk you should leave. Chalk it up to learning the ropes." She felt Number Seven shift on his feet and heard the hissing rasp of steel sliding from a scabbard. "Be seeing you." It was a warning as much as a farewell.

"All right, going now," she said, and stepped aside as George—all broad shoulders and throbbing muscles in tailcoat and skin-tight breeches, now that she could see him properly in the moonlight—swept toward the balloon, leading with the point of his smallsword. *Well, there's a sight,* she thought dizzily. *Heroic archetype ahoy!* The baron shouted something angrily and she decided that if Number Seven was right about the bloodstains she really didn't need to be here. So she rushed down the pitch-black stairwell as fast as she could, trying to ignore the distracting ring of steel on steel. Which perhaps explained why she didn't realize she had company until she ran headlong into Captain Sir Lawrence Hackmanworth, Retired.

▸◂▸◂▸◂

"Tell me what happened, in your own words." Number Two give her what she surmised was meant to be a meaningful stare—his face was as thoroughly masked as ever. "I recognize this is distasteful, my dear, but it really *is* important that you tell me the truth."

The guards had brought Eve to the town hall—Number Two's residence—and down a winding spiral staircase to a darkened room she hadn't seen before. The basement chamber was windowless, circular, shaped not unlike a dissection theater. Brass periscopes hanging from a ceiling rose projected views of the Village and its surroundings onto the walls of the chamber, dim and upside down. It was a camera obscura, a panopticon observatory from which the entire community could be surveilled by means of mirrors and prisms tucked away in rooftop viewing turrets. In the middle of the room two men in fusty black servants' uniforms sat facing the walls astride a seesaw, slowly oscillating between fixed binocular viewing stations at various heights as they manipulated focusing dials and levers. A meticulously hand-painted depiction of the zodiac circled the room below the cornice work, but there was something strangely distorted about the shapes of the constellations, as if it was a snapshot of the night sky in another eon, the stars warped out of place.

Number Two was seated in a banker's chair on a podium at the back of the room. The guards had politely but firmly escorted Eve to a rococo Louis XV armchair beside him, then equally politely manacled her to the armrests. "Merely a precaution," Number Two had explained. "You should consider it a tribute to the skill with which you defended your virtue." By which he presumably meant Sir Lawrence's bloodstains, which were indeed going to be an abominable nuisance to get out of the silk. She would probably have to dye the gown black after they released her. Which was not going to happen without some fast talking. She was pretty sure she could unlock the shackles, and she might be able to take down one or both of the guards, but tackling Number Two and the goons on the seesaw as well seemed like excessive optimism, a step too far.

"I followed the baron and his son up to the roof because I was curious." Eve shrugged diffidently, then decided not to repeat the gesture—her fichu had been the first casualty of her collision with Sir Lawrence. "The ball was tedious and I confess I do not like to dance."

"Tell me what you found in the library."

"The library?" She considered dissembling, but discovered her tongue was reluctant to be still. The truth geas in Number Two's office extended below ground level as well. "I was looking for clues, anything really, that might lead me to the location of what I'm seeking. It was fruitless, but in the process I discovered a priest's hole. While I was there, Baron Von Franckenstein and his ward entered. The baron told François to wait, then when he returned to fetch the lad I simply followed. When they reached the rooftop I watched from the stairwell."

She recounted her meeting with Number Seven—George—and his suggestion that she should leave.

"And then?" Number Two waited.

Dammit. "The stairs were very dark and I was hurrying, so I didn't see Hackmanworth in time to stop. He grabbed me, and gloated—he made an unmentionable pest of himself during dinner, did I mention that? So I made good on my promise."

Sir Lawrence had actually snarled, "My turn, now," shoved her against the wall, grabbed her left breast painfully hard—she was sure she had bruises—then tried to stick his tongue down her throat. Which was a strategic blunder on his part. He was big and physically overbearing and clearly had only one thing on his mind: but Eve was freakishly tall by the feminine standards of 1816, had taken classes in Krav Maga for self-defense, and was still keyed up from her confrontation with Number Seven. She'd bitten half through his lower lip and tried to knee him in the balls—a hard target that she hadn't quite hit—then he'd struck her across the face hard enough to bounce her head off the wall. By the time she recovered he was yanking her skirts up, clearly intent on raping her. But the lanyard of her fan was still looped around her wrist and he didn't register her unfurling it until she slashed its razor edge across his wrist and then his cheek. "Should have aimed for his throat but I wasn't thinking clearly," she heard her traitor tongue confess.

"Number Ninety-Four, where is the fan?" Number Two asked somebody behind her.

"Here, sir."

"Jolly good." Looking back at Eve, Number Two might have raised an unseeable eyebrow. "Are you certain you didn't misunderstand Sir Lawrence's intentions? He can be overenthusiastic at times, but I'm sure he didn't mean any real harm—"

Eve resisted the impulse to set Number Two's hair on fire: it wouldn't get the answers she needed and he was probably warded against such attacks. "*In case you hadn't noticed,* I am here as an unmarried spinster of good breeding with a modest income, and he's a fortune hunter"—and a serial rapist known as "the Beast" to the servants—"and also a brute." Her tongue betrayed her careful attempt not to fill in the details, and Number Two frowned furiously at her description. "If he ruined me he could offer for my hand and my legal guardian would probably take him up on it to avoid a duel." Eve glowered at Number Two. "Or maybe he would consign me to an asylum for fallen women, or something equally barbaric." Her tongue carried on regardless of common sense and decency. "If I see him again I will kill him, and it will be self-defense because you can be sure *he* now means to kill *me*."

"Well, we can't have that." Number Two's lips were pursed with prissy distaste. "I'm afraid you leave me no option but to send him away."

"You could send me away instead," Eve said hopefully. "I mean, wouldn't that solve both our problems?"

"No, I don't think so. Hackmanworth is only here for the seaside air: he was due some rest and recuperation after his last posting. His welcome can be withdrawn temporarily." Number Two flicked imaginary lint from his sleeve dismissively. "You, however, are here because you have been entrusted to my care. You need not marry him, but you have made a dangerous enemy."

"Hackmanworth? Dangerous? I'd never have guessed."

"No, I meant the baron. Or the boy, or Number Twelve—you can never be certain who has the knives out for who, eh? Not Number Seven, though, he seems quite taken with you, even spoke in your defense: he must be touched in the head, ha ha." Number Two leaned toward her, oozing genteel disapproval. "I shall put your shrewish disposition this evening down to an attack of hysteria, but please be very clear that it must not be repeated: otherwise privileges can be withdrawn. Perhaps it would be best if you spent the rest of the night in the hospital just in case." To the guards: "Take Number Six away."

"What? No! I am not a number! I'm a free woman!" Eve tensed as they lifted her to her feet. "What are you doing?"

"It's for your own good, I advise you to cooperate. The doctor will see you in the morning. If he finds you are well you can return to your apartment once Sir Lawrence has departed."

Eve fulminated all the way to the hospital. It was more of a cottage clinic than a real hospital, with half a dozen sparsely furnished cells rather than a ward with multiple beds. If Hackmanworth was still at large perhaps a night in a room with bars on the windows and locks on the doors might not be such a bad thing—it was surely safer than returning to her own rooms—but being treated as a perpetrator rather than the victim of a crime grated on her. Meanwhile her head ached fiercely, her most expensive gown was a wreck, she'd missed her flight out of the Village, *and* she'd lost her favorite fan.

It did not escape her attention that Number Two hadn't mentioned the baron's or François's recapture. He wasn't the type to admit failure: he took every opportunity to remind her the Village was escape-proof. Nor did she fail to notice that he hadn't said anything about the fate of Number Seven—the mysterious George, who bore arms and seemed determined to protect her from inadvisable adventures.

So what have we learned tonight? Eve asked as she lay on the lumpy hospital cot. *Start with who we've met: Number Seven, polite hunk who seems to work for Number Two. Number Twelve, scheming minx, loyalties unclear—the Silver Sisterhood, maybe? Baron Von F, the one who got away, classic mad scientist only not obviously deranged. François, creepy boy,* Your Majesty. *Sir Lawrence,* definitely *dangerous but not my problem anymore.* But now she began to shake as she remembered how close he'd come, and the thought had her on her knees, spitting into the chamber pot to get the taste of his blood out of her mouth. *I really* would *have killed him,* she realized bleakly: *and then they'd have hanged me.* Because in this here and now they always believed the man, even more so than in her own time. Women had fewer rights in early-nineteenth-century

England than in early-twenty-first-century Saudi Arabia. *But he's not my problem anymore,* she repeated to herself, hoping it would sink in eventually.

Just like its TV archetype, the Village—a phantasm supported by the willing suspension of disbelief of millions of viewers—was riddled with spy holes and spies, not to mention scheming asshats. It was also rife with sorcerers who could enchant anti-sound amulets and superefficient town-gas reformers that spat out hot hydrogen to inflate implausibly nonleaky balloons, because that made more sense than Baron Von Franckenstein being half a century ahead of the state of the art in chemistry. A freak like her should fit right in, if not for the whole being-a-woman angle. But Rupert *wasn't* here. Nor was he creating waves in the newssheets.

Where could he be? she wondered.

Well, let's see: she'd found what appeared to be Rupert's remains in a gibbet cage in the Channel Islands, but they belonged to the Wrong Rupert, according to the Prime Minister. But then, he'd made two trips into the dream roads, hadn't he? And the second was still in progress. At a guess he would try once more to retrieve the book and return to the twenty-first century, which meant *either* via the ghost roads in the attic of the Earl of Marsden's town house *or* the tunnels under his headquarters *or* those under Castle Skaro. He'd already burned the one-time summoning grid left under his headquarters, which Eve had been compelled to activate by the dead hand command he'd left behind. Skaro was isolated and hard to get to . . . but if he was trying to retrieve a copy of the manuscript from somewhere overseas, it would be easier to smuggle it into Skaro than London. Assuming finding the manuscript was still an objective, of course.

I need to get to London, Eve decided. It would be easier to gather intelligence and learn of Rupert's whereabouts in London anyway. Every day she spent in the Village meant Rupert was a day closer to his goal. Besides, lingering here in the ghost roads was a really bad idea. The clock was ticking: and the longer she lingered, the harder it would ultimately be to return to the present day.

▸◂▸◂▸◂

Four uncomfortable, cold, paranoid hours later, and Imp figured he finally had things under control. An hour into their impromptu housebreaking exercise next door he'd wheedled Game Boy into returning to the Starkey house to retrieve his clothes. GeeBee had been resistant at first, and the headache resulting from nudging him hard enough to override his sense of self-preservation was absolutely *killing* Imp—but at least now he wasn't at risk of being lifted for indecent exposure. Game Boy hadn't noticed any signs of intrusion apart from the front door, which had been ajar. He'd sneaked in, grabbed Imp's discarded trousers and shirt, and sneaked out again: but he hadn't conducted a proper search, much less checked the door on the top floor. So now they were waiting for Wendy in the big Greggs on the high street, eating sausage rolls and wrapping their hands around cups of coffee to get warm.

While Game Boy had been raiding Imp had texted Eve, but the message status came back as undelivered. They'd given each other permission to locate their sibling's phone, except Eve's wasn't showing up. When Imp bit the bullet and tried to call her it went straight to voice mail. And at that point he realized that, yes, it was serious. Eve was no more likely to leave a phone unanswered than she was to join a cult or elope with a random stranger.

Group chat was a wonderful thing, and Wendy working on assignment for Eve didn't hurt either. So Imp was only on his second coffee when Wendy walked in the door. She took one look at him—and at Game Boy, who was into his third filter coffee and beginning to twitch—and sat down opposite. She was wearing her cop boots and a business suit, more corporate than dapper. "Tell me everything," she said sternly, and Imp brought her up to speed without demur.

Wendy was a good listener, only interrupting to nudge Imp back on topic when he veered into the long grass; then she extracted Game Boy's version of events. Finally she offered up her own opinion. "Right. Well, first we're going to visit Bigge HQ and see if we can find Eve there—"

"But she said—"

"Yes, but we're going to do this *properly*, and that means verifying everything. Did she say what the threat was?" Wendy gave Imp a hard stare—an opportunity to wedge his foot farther down his throat. "No? Didn't think so. So first, we're going to make sure she didn't just have a bad dream. Then we're going to pull Sally Gunderson in on the loop before we go back to the house, or were you planning on checking it for axe maniacs and gangsters yourself?" She stood up. "Finish your coffees, we're going."

The office was only a twenty-minute walk away, but two hours later they were still there. This time sitting in a cramped security office while one of Sergeant Gunderson's men scrubbed back and forth through video footage captured by a variety of cameras in the building the night before.

"That—that nails it." Sally did not sound pleased as she pointed at the shadowy figure in the middle screen. "The boss man is back."

Game Boy squeaked unhappily.

"At the stroke of midnight, as well." Wendy seemed calmer than any of them. "Where did he come from?"

"Let me backscroll for you, ma'am." The video cowboy reversed rapidly, skipping between cameras. "He came up in the lift. From . . . second subbasement level? There are no cameras down there, something about security reasons."

Wendy nodded. "No windows, no back exits. So he just appeared?"

"So it seems." Gunderson's tone was grim. "That's not supposed to be possible."

"And then . . ."

She shrugged. "At two twenty-six he meets up with Eve Starkey in his office. She was working downstairs." A sober-faced nod in Imp's direction, subtext: *my condolences*. "They take the elevator back down. At two thirty-seven he comes back up the lift and leaves through the front door. There . . . there's no night watchman on duty, there's *always* a man on the door overnight. Anyway, at two fifty-one, Eve enters the lift in the subbasement and comes up, then she leaves via the front door as well."

Wendy nodded again. "Has anyone been down to the sub-subbasement yet? Because I think we should take a look."

Sally looked grim. "After you."

It took a while, but they found the steps down to the lowest level, the tunnels with rough walls and suspicious patches on the floor, then finally the inscribed ritual diagram and the jug of bright red liquid.

"Is that . . . ?" Game Boy asked, not quite able to finish the sentence.

Imp nodded. "Let me look," he said, leaning closer to the ward on the end wall. "It's some kind of summoning grid, but I can't figure out what for," he complained. "*That*"—he pointed at the still-uncoagulated jug—"is from the sacrifice that powered it." His gaze trailed to the freshly filled niche in the floor. "And this whole tunnel is . . ." He shivered, eyes wide and scared. "It's one for the murder squad, all right? If there still *is* a murder squad these days. Much Fred West, very let's get the fuck out of here."

It took them another hour to be sure, but by late morning Wendy had assembled a time line that was beyond contention. Rupert de Montfort Bigge had—however improbably—reappeared in the basement of his own headquarters. He'd had an after-midnight meeting with Eve (who, going by the video evidence, was not happy to see him), led her down to the cellar, then left the building. Sometime later Eve had phoned Imp to warn him, then she, too, had left. The night watchman's absence was barely noted. (There was a suspiciously fresh patch of concrete in the sub-subbasement tunnel: *sic transit gloria minion,* in all likelihood.)

"But where did they both go?" asked Sergeant Gunderson. "The same place? Or . . ."

"I think we know." Wendy gave Imp a stern look, and he hunched inside his coat.

"Can't make me go there," he said sullenly. "Not without an escort."

"Relax, you're getting an escort." Wendy looked at Gunderson. "Eve told Imp to evacuate the house on Kensington Palace Gardens. Can you get a team round there and clear it, bottom to top? I doubt we'll find either of them, but they might have left us a clue."

"On it." Sally left.

Wendy turned to Imp. "Your sister's a survivor," she told him quietly. "And it's only been about eight hours."

"But what if—" He trailed off. It didn't really matter.

"We'll find her," Wendy promised him. "One way or the other. We'll find him, too," she added, quellingly. "And I know who to call about the cellar, too. They'll have *questions* for him." If he'd been preying on the de-emphasized the police might not take any action afterward, but Wendy was willing to bet that now the New Management had their eye on Eve, things would go less than swimmingly for Rupert. Investigations always had a way of shining a spotlight where the government of the day wanted it shone.

"They went through the door to the dream roads," Game Boy predicted dolefully. "If they went to our house, they're in the dream roads." But Imp and Wendy both pretended not to hear, for their own reasons.

AN UNSUITABLE BOY

Eve slept uneasily and awakened around dawn with a raft of new fears. Yes, she could defend herself against the likes of Sir Lawrence—she didn't even need the fan: at nose-to-nose range she could purée his gray matter with her telekinetic talent—but she couldn't fight off a determined band of guards. She'd seen the lurking footmen, detected the wards they hid under the high collars of their black-and-white uniforms. Number Two could outescalate her, overwhelm her with bodies, or set Rover on her. Overt defiance was a very bad idea. So this morning she was willing to lie through her teeth to persuade the doctor she was safe to release.

Shortly after her awakening Eve was visited by a jailer in a nurse's uniform who rousted her out of bed, bundled her into a shapeless smock, and summoned the doctor to inspect her. Dr. Jakes was a ruddy-faced ex-Navy sawbones with rum on his breath even though it wasn't past eight in the morning. He had rough manners, even rougher muttonchops, and she was pretty sure he'd last washed his hands before the French Revolution. But Eve bit her tongue and dialed her charm up to eleven, 1816-style—simpering high femme with a side order of histrionic sighs and a passing threat of swooning. Which act apparently sufficed to convince Jakes that the cause of last night's shrewish fit was her uterus going walkabout, and that it was back where it jolly well belonged now.

It was humiliating to play the fainting-female card, but

considerably less humiliating than the treatments on offer on the locked ward, which included leeches, cupping, waterboarding, and nonconsensual genital massage. *When I conquer the world of 1816 I shall order my minions to invent modern medicine immediately,* Eve resolved as she slunk back to her apartment and barricaded herself inside.

Women in this time didn't vote, open bank accounts, mostly couldn't own property, and didn't have formal access to education. There were few roles open to them, none of which Eve found tolerable. This was the era that had given the English language the word "bluestocking" as a term of derision. If she violated the expectations of polite society she'd lose whatever freedom—however minimal—she had as a benefit of her false identity. She would have been enraged, if she had allowed herself the luxury of anger. Instead, she patiently laid her plans and waited. And waited.

Sometime in midafternoon, a folded sheet of paper slid under her door. She paused to read it.

> *Your overenthusiastic suitor departed on the 1pm stage: it is now safe for you to show your face in public again.*
>
> —*No.* 2

"Aha." *Showtime.* Eve pushed her lunch—a cold collation—aside, and headed straight to the wardrobe. She'd purchased a mobcap, and now she shoveled her remaining food into it. A bread roll, a couple of slices of boiled ham, and a sausage wouldn't get her far, but it was a start. Then she tucked the bundle under her pillow, pulled on her pelisse and bonnet, and set out for the Library.

Over the past week the villagers and the librarian had grown used to Eve's voracious reading habits. She saw no reason to disappoint them today. She ploughed through *Lloyd's Register* looking for news of letters of marque or reports of piracy in the Bay of Biscay, combed the society pages in *The Times* for Rupert's known aliases, and even read the classified advertisements. As usual she found no sign of him. But this time she made sure to memorize certain important numbers—for in the age of sail, tide charts were of crucial importance to the traveler.

After the Library she visited the Post Office and asked for the addresses of her solicitor and banker. She kicked up a fuss about her ruined evening gown, and explained that it was absolutely essential that she write to them for an advance on her allowance in order to pay for a replacement. The stony-faced clerk silently wrote down their details and sold her the paper and quill for a couple of letters. (Of course, she was not about to write begging letters here, much less post them: anything she mailed from the Village would certainly be intercepted by Number Two. But rule number one of any escape plan was to have a plausible excuse for any suspicious preparations you might be making. And having names and addresses for a bank and a lawyer seemed prudent, even without any other uses she might have for a stash of writing paper.)

Next she gathered up her wits, visited the town hall, and summoned up a bright, brittle smile. "Is Number Two in residence?" she asked the butler sweetly. "I mislaid my fan last night, and I believe he might know of its whereabouts."

"Please take a seat, m'lady." Number Forty-Nine sniffed pointedly and disappeared into the back of the building. A minute later he reappeared, bearing her fan on a silver tray. "Number Two sends his best regards and expresses the fond hope that you will sleep better tonight—but find no need to unfold your device." He bowed briefly then waited for her to leave.

Eve walked back to her apartment with a spring in her step that lasted until, back indoors, she tried to flick her tessen open. It stayed stubbornly closed. She tried again, then furiously flung it at the floor, where it bounced—and stayed closed. He'd glued the slats shut. Eve fumed, then set to work. It took her over an hour to warm and weaken the glue by subtle application of her pyromancy—a delicate touch was required to release the ceramic bones without burning the silk covering. Eventually she got the fan to open again, although it was stained and tattered, and she had acquired a vicious headache. It was, she thought, a powerful metaphor for life in the Village: unasked for, sticky, and a vexatious nuisance.

When evening arrived Eve summoned the maid and requested a more substantial cold collation. She ate lightly, consuming only the most perishable items. The rest she added to the bundle in her cap along with certain other papers she'd written, her reticule, and a string of pearls. (It wouldn't do to wear all her jewelry in public. This was a lawless time and she'd risk robbery or worse.) She layered up in boots, bonnet, and coat for an evening walk, then tucked the bundle under her skirt and set out for a leisurely after-dinner stroll.

It was time to leave.

▸◂▸◂▸◂

Eve didn't know where she was going to find Rupert or the book he was hunting, but she knew neither of them were *here*. (He might not even be *now*.) He'd left no traces of his presence in the periodicals and chronicles she'd read in the library. It followed that she needed to continue her search elsewhere. She had some ideas for starting points: he might be in London, where he could have used his oracular powers to raise funds and work toward his goals—whether locating the manuscript, or some revised objective. She also knew that someone bearing his name was executed for piracy on Skaro later in the year, at least in some previous version of the time line. It might not actually be him, but it was worth checking out.

But before she could do anything, she had to escape.

The Village was an open prison guarded by mountains, sea, and monsters, but Eve had an edge her jailers were unaware of. She had grown up in the 1990s rather than the early nineteenth century, and as a child of the video age she had an instinctive grasp of camera angles that exceeded anyone now living who wasn't a formally trained artist. And she'd been paying attention in Number Two's underground panopticon lair.

The Village's camera obscura system was impressive and doubtless seemed supernaturally efficient to people who grew up during the Napoleonic wars. All the obvious paths out of the Village were surveilled, the better to keep inmates from escaping over the cliff or along the beach to the pier. She'd noticed a periscope covering the Village green from atop the bandstand, another monitoring the approach to the town hall, and one in the vicinity of the Assembly Rooms. But it provided only a limited number of viewpoints, and they weren't mobile. At best, they could traverse and elevate, and perhaps add some simple magnification. But even with sorcerous light amplification they couldn't work in complete darkness. It was a daytime-only monitoring system. More critically, the apparatus in the basement of Number Two's headquarters permitted only a limited number of observers—two, patrolling constantly around the ring of eyepieces using the seesaw contraption.

Eve theorized that the panopticon was a decoy. The periscopes permitted Number Two to keep a pair of eyes on the approaches and sustain a mystical appearance of omniscience, but he must rely on other defenses to prevent serious escape attempts. There was probably some sort of wide-area ward around the Village that would ring a bell in the panopticon if someone stepped across the perimeter. The observers could then release Rover or some other defensive automaton. So it followed that Eve needed a distraction when she made her move.

Obviously human eyeballs were a scarce commodity, so certain areas weren't monitored. Sheer cliff faces and the doorless and windowless rear aspects of houses didn't warrant a periscope. But they'd still be within the Village boundary ward. So Eve summoned up her magic visualization macro and concentrated on feeding power to it as she strolled up the hillside lane.

There. A glowing ribbon of mist swooped through the craggy jumble of rocks on the cliffside to her left, just beyond the point where the path curved around and turned downhill, back toward the Village. Eve walked around the loop and stopped at its highest point. She looked back down the slope, taking in the array of buildings spread out below her: the crescent of the beach stretching into the distance, the gray waves of the incoming tide capped with lacy white spume. A laser-speckle of *mana* glinting on the rooftops showed her the location of the sorcerously enhanced periscopes. *Three, four . . .* She took a count, then went back and counted them again for good measure. Only eight had coverage on this side of the Village. If the periscope eyepieces in the panopticon room were distributed around the compass in accordance with the direction of the periscope prisms, the ones she could see would only be useable by one observer at a time. So a mere 12.5 percent of them were watched at any given moment. *Good odds: I'll take them.* She turned her back on the watchers and set to work.

Reaching into her stash, Eve pulled out a paper and her fan. The paper already bore a painstakingly drawn ritual diagram. She spread her fan, then carefully sliced a shallow cut along the edge of her hand. Next, she dipped a fresh quill in her own blood, chanting quiet imprecations and commands in a language unsuited to human vocal cords. Sketching rapidly, she connected the final lines. She'd drafted the enchantment in her room, pretending to write a letter. Once she activated it she placed it on the ground under a conveniently sized rock just inside the boundary of the perimeter ward. Her bloody arrow pointed due northeast across the perimeter, and she hastily drew a matching symbol on the back of her left hand. Her skin tingled and her toes throbbed with pins and needles, a warning sign that eaters were converging on her: she'd dropped her personal defenses to match this spell to the one surrounding the Village, and she'd expended more than enough *mana* to attract more parasites. She walked back down toward the Village green, then along the seafront past the stone ship.

Dusk was falling as she returned to her room and sat down to wait.

Once full dark arrived, the Village tended to fall silent. Candles were expensive: nobody wanted to move after midnight. Eve waited for quiet, then slipped out and made her way to the beach. Again, she noted the location of the periscopes. Only two faced in this direction, and at night her drab cloak would be almost invisible. She looked toward the pier. Was it her imagination or was there a light near the horizon? A biting onshore breeze sucked the warmth from every inch of exposed skin. *Time to go,* she decided. She raised her left hand, squinted at the bloody sigil she'd drawn on it, and uttered a command. There was a momentary sting of pain as the flecks of blood combusted: then a matching spark on the hillside, and a brilliant flare of *mana* as her decoy triggered the perimeter ward. After a few seconds two of the periscopes turned to focus on the hillside; she hurried down to the beach while the watchers were distracted.

The pier at the far end of the cove lay beyond the edge of the broken ward. As she'd surmised, the ward formed a simple loop. The flare of power from her decoy highlighted the point of first rupture where she'd broken the perimeter. Nothing happened as she stepped across the perimeter onto the beach: there were no separate alarm zones here, no sophisticated countermeasures. Where the cliff rose steeply by the end of the beach it was undercut by a natural cave. Enterprising hands had hollowed it out, digging into the rock and lining it with wooden shelves. They were mostly empty at the moment, awaiting the arrival of a new week's delivery of provisions.

One row near the bottom held items awaiting uplift, including a couple of travelers' trunks.

The approaching ship had two masts, with lamps burning fore and aft and to either side. Right now she couldn't see much in the gloom, but faint voices carried across the water, along with the clattering noises of a boat being winched over the side.

Eve crouched by the shelves and extended her senses, running her imaginary fingers along the inside of the biggest leather- and brass-bound trunk. She found it half-empty, the bottom lined with fabric. She closed her eyes and focused on the padlock. Opening it, she lifted the lid to find wool and cotton scraps and water-damaged roll ends. Apparently it was leftovers from the dressmaker, heading back to wherever the Village got its supplies.

Eve dragged a double armful of offcuts out of the shipping trunk and carried them to the back of the cave. Then she climbed in, pulled her knees up—she was going to be awfully stiff if this took more than a couple of hours—and pulled the lid down. A moment later she remembered the padlock. Reaching out with her imaginary fingers she fumbled it back into place, then turned the tumblers inside the lock, trembling and prickling with stress perspiration. In the distance the bosun called orders across the water. The chest was musty and smelled faintly of mildew. She tried to take shallow breaths, forcing herself not to sneeze by sheer effort of will. The lid was loose enough that she was in no danger of suffocating, although if they dropped her in the sea by accident—*they won't do that,* she told herself forcefully. Think of something less unpleasant: *I hope they don't put me at the bottom of a pile in the hold.* She hunkered down to wait, still wondering if she was making a terrible mistake.

Eve learned that time passed painfully slowly when you were hiding in a trunk. The ship took forever to tie up at the pier.

Then there was much grunting and bumping of sacks, wicker hampers, and other luggage as the sailors unloaded supplies and loaded the outgoing cargo. Her box was kicked more than once, which she found terrifying. Then unseen hands roughly picked her up and for a heart-stopping moment she felt the chest hang in midair. She wondered again if they were going to drop her in the sea, where she would drown if she couldn't open the padlock in time—but then they lowered her, and kept lowering until she hit the bottom of the hold with a tooth-jarring thump. More sacks and small items thudded down on top of her, then the timbers of the ship began to creak and sway gently. The stuffy air in the chest combined with the gentle rocking of the ship to lull Eve into a shallow doze.

Sometime later she shuddered awake, surfacing from a suffocating near nightmare to discover that it was not a dream at all. Her back and knees were burning, there wasn't enough air, and she had no idea which way was up. Icy terror made her panic for a few seconds until she remembered how she'd gotten here. *I'm on the ship and we're under way,* she realized. She reached out with her imaginary fingers. Above her, she felt a sack full of rags. Behind her head, a wooden wall, then water flowing by steadily. She groped around until her head ached fiercely but at last she found the padlock, twirled the tumblers, and flicked it open. She no longer cared whether the sailors discovered her: she simply had to get out of the box. She pushed at the lid, discovered her telekinesis was nowhere near strong enough to shift the heavy sack, then heaved with her shoulder. Nothing moved. Now the panic returned and redoubled, and she thumped the walls of the chest as hard as she could. She was nerving herself to cry for help when there came a slithering thud from the sack, and somebody raised the lid.

She sat up stiffly. The hold was in near-complete darkness, broken by a single dim lantern at the far end. She felt rather than saw someone leaning over her, so she reached out and grabbed a handful of heavy fabric—a coat. Her rescuer recoiled but, tellingly, they didn't cry out. "*Who are you?*" she hissed.

"Mademoiselle?"

She recognized the high-pitched voice instantly. "François? What are you doing here?" She kept her voice down. As her eyes adapted she could see dim shapes around her in the hold, but nothing at the end of her arm. "Why can't I see you?"

"I have a, you say, *un main de gloire*?" A horrible fusty smell tickled her nostrils. François blew out a long breath, and she finally saw him crouched before her. He was holding a bizarre candle shaped like a withered hand, the fingertips still smoldering. "Why are you in the chest, mademoiselle?"

"I imagine for the same reason you are in the hold. I'm escaping." Eve peered at him. "Where's the baron?"

"He is in a very small cabin where Monsieur *le* Captain put him."

Eve was instantly on the alert. "You'd better explain."

François beckoned her toward a darker corner of the hold. "The balloon, she is a distraction. Monsieur *le* Baron's real plan is to pay Monsieur *le* Captain for passage? While the guards chase the balloon, we use the *main de gloire* to escape by stealth and hide under the pier. The baron, he offers to suborn the captain, say he can pay, he tells Monsieur *le* Captain he has funds in *Londres*. So Monsieur *le* Captain, he say he will take the baron back to the Village if he does not pay when we arrive, but for now, 'e takes him *en voyage*. The baron is in the captain's room? But me they do not care so much for, so they put me down here. This is still better than the Village, is it?"

"They picked me up from the pier," Eve said slowly. "Just like you, I used a distraction. So we're on our way somewhere. Do you know where the baron is trying to go?"

"There is a town called Lever-pull? I hear him talk of it. From there, by stage to *Londres*?"

Liverpool. He means Liverpool. Eve forced herself to nod

silently, then count to twenty in base three before she spoke. "Liverpool is in the northwest, about four hundred kilometers from London." Which made sense if the Village was on the Welsh coast near the site of her own time's Portmeirion. "Do you know how long it will take to get there? To Liverpool, I mean?"

"I hear the captain say, it is to sail south and then west around Angle-sea? Then northeast. Perhaps a day or two, if the wind and tide are with us."

"That seems rather—" *slow*, Eve was about to say, but then she realized all her instincts about sailing times were wrong. She was used to car ferries, container ships, and Rupert's pals' VIP yachts that zipped along at forty kilometers per hour. This was an early-nineteenth-century sailing ship, a mass of leaky wood encrusted with barnacles. It might have sails but it was nothing like a twenty-first-century yacht. Nor did she have no idea how long it would take to get to London by coach once they made landfall. Had passenger trains been invented yet? She added another item to her list of things to do if she wound up marooned in the nineteenth century: *Invent the railway company (hire James Watt and Isambard Kingdom Brunel as engineers—if they've been born yet).*

For the first time since approximately never she mentally kicked herself for goofing off in history classes. (She'd spent them dreaming up unworkable and ethically dodgy love spells to use on Kyle Wilson, until she went off him and transferred her stalkerish intentions onto Anabelle Blair.) Mind you, during her time in secondary school the education syllabus had been dictated by one of those ministers who had a bee in his bonnet about how history ought to be about teaching "Kings, Dates, and Battles" instead of actually *useful* social history like how people in 1816 went to the toilet and where to book a stagecoach seat. So, not much loss . . .

"Ma'am? Are you unwell?"

Eve shook herself and gave François a wan smile. "It's the sea," she said. "Are they feeding you?"

"*Oui.* Are you—"

"I bought food, but not enough for two days." A thought struck her. "Can you hide me? With your candle, if anyone comes?"

"Of course!" He thrust it at her. "I was fright—afraid at first when I hear the thumping chest, so I lit it. But this will get you off the ship when we make harbor, yes? Where do you go, then?"

François was so sober-serious he would take offense if treated as anything other than an adult, but by the same token he could be relied upon in some respects. Eve made up her mind. "I am going to London. I can pay my own way, but it may be easier if we all travel together." She had absolutely no doubt that the Village despot would be furious when he discovered they were missing. "The baron and I could pretend to be a family, and you our son." Instead of a single woman or a man and his ward, both of which the pursuers would be looking for. "Can you tell him, next time you see him?"

"Yes, I will tell the baron." François nodded very seriously. "It is a solid feint. Then we can plan our campaign together."

▸◂▸◂▸◂

It took two days and a night for the brig to claw its way out into the Irish Sea, make its way cautiously past the large island of Anglesea, then catch the incoming tide in the Mersey estuary. François left the hold thrice a day to receive a ration of food. Sailors descended into the hold a couple of times to remove casks of drinking water and return empties. Their arrival was heralded by the tolling of a bell, which gave Eve plenty of time to hide in a dark corner at the opposite end of the hold, clutching François's hand of glory (which she tried to keep unlit—it stank abominably of burning fingernail clippings and graveyard grease). They weren't at sea long enough to need the barrels of hard tack and bully beef the ship carried for emergencies: for which Eve was duly grateful, because from the second day she stealthily helped herself to the totally unappetizing minced corned beef and stale crackers (her own provisions having run out).

While she was undisturbed Eve occupied herself with exercises of the art. She practiced her intuitive talents (weak telekinesis, adequate pyrokinesis, and, close-up, the ability to feel through solid objects). She restrung her rope of pearls, moved a handful to her pocket for use as currency or ammunition, and strung the rest around her waist under her shift. She set up a target made from scraps of cloth, then practiced juggling and hurling pearls at the far end of the hold by force of will alone. Musket balls would serve better, but she'd have to buy some first; meanwhile, she might need to defend herself before she could pawn her jewelry.

This was a dangerous time. Starvation had skulked in through the door and was lounging in the parlor thanks to a disastrous harvest. Food was unaffordable for many, and unemployed soldiers home from the war resorted to banditry out of sheer desperation. There was little or no street lighting, and no constabulary in the modern sense. (She added to her list of options for being marooned in 1816: *Move to London, marry a lord with political ambitions, have him invent the police*. Except that would involve marriage 1816-style, which was again *not* on her bucket list.) Finally, after considering her options for getting off the ship, she inscribed a very specific ward on the lining of her chest.

When not practicing as a human fire lighter or preparing to smuggle herself ashore, Eve laboriously renewed her macros—the carefully memorized invocations she'd bound to mnemonic finger gestures. Some sorcerers could use binary notation to command an almost limitless repertoire of small spells, but Eve stuck to decimal and kept just nine committed to muscle memory. Best to be able to recall everything instantly: less was more, and she made sure to practice. The gestures were not unlike mudras. With her right hand she assigned *this* finger-crook to twirl the tumblers of a lock open or locked, *that* two-fingered twist-and-wiggle to pull a pearl (or other small item) from a pocket; another rapid circle of her left little pinkie was set to deflect unwanted attention. On her other hand, she had less frequently needed items: tag an item for tracking, apply the next macro triggered to someone or something else.[1] By the time they reached the Wirral peninsula at the mouth of the Mersey she'd gotten the sequence down to an almost instantaneous flicker-snap, like shaking the water from her just-washed hands. She hoped she'd never need to use some of them: in the here and now they hanged pickpockets.

During the afternoon of the second day at sea, François hurried down into the hold and knocked on Eve's chest—she'd taken to sleeping inside it with the lid lowered like a cut-price vampire. "We are coming inside the harbor!" he told her, quietly excited. "How are you to get ashore?"

"Does the ship dock?" she asked. "Or do they use boats?"

"There is a pier." But the boy looked uncertain.

"Well. Is the baron going to the coaching inn once he's ashore?" François nodded. "Tell him I'll meet him there this evening."

Landing in Liverpool was only marginally less uncomfortable than being winched aboard the ship in the first place. It involved a lot of waiting curled up inside the chest while sailors stomped about the hold, shouting incomprehensible instructions and lifting nets full of bulk cargo. Barrels clattered and thudded for a while, then strong hands lifted her and turfed her facedown

1. She took care to ensure her macros could not be conjugated to encode a Universal Turing Machine: accidentally summoning a demon while touch-typing was not on her bucket list either.

into a net of her own. She spun dizzyingly for a few seconds as the rope tightened, then the deck crew began to turn the capstan and she rose high in the air. Then she swung sickeningly sideways and landed with a tooth-rattling jolt. There were new noises: seagulls screeching, different men calling. Rough hands lifted the chest and loaded it onto a cart, where Eve had to endure another interminable wait. Clattering, banging, another jolting drop—and finally the slam of a door and the sounds of the harbor were muted.

Eve raised the lid of her box, pulled out the macabre relic François had given her, and willed the fingertips aflame. It threw off a choking miasma and a powerful fluxion of *mana,* but not much light. Eve gathered her small bundle of possessions and tiptoed toward the door of the warehouse.

Liverpool was as a rude shock after the manicured perfection of the Village. The skyline was dominated by sail-furled masts and rough warehouses. The stench of decaying fish and the angry shrieks of seagulls circling overhead battered her senses. The roads were unpaved, the piers filth-strewn and rickety. Men and women toiled on the piers, hauling handcarts and bales of goods between ships and storage, but nobody spared her a glance. The burning hand did its job of concealment well—too well for her purposes. Indeed, she had to step nimbly out of the way of more than one officious-looking customs officer or barely sober sailor. So she skulked into an alleyway and extinguished it before shoving it into her bag.

The docks in 1816 were a far cry from those of 1916 or 2016. The city already held over a hundred thousand people, but the pompous civil architecture of the Mercantile City and Baltic Triangle would not be built for a third of a century. The poverty and deprivation were palpable, and the docks were not a good place for a woman on her own. She barely made it a hundred meters before a grimy man in a shiny-elbowed coat catcalled her; another hundred meters and she'd been propositioned twice. *Docks,* she cursed. *Also pubs.* Or rather, gin palaces—or if not palaces, lean-tos. Something about her—either her forbidding expression, her relatively fine clothing, or her determined fast march forward—deterred her admirers from giving chase, but it was clear that the men hereabouts had two things on their mind, the other of which was gin. The local girls gave her flinty-eyed looks as she passed their doorways: best not to linger.

Things improved after she turned onto Lord Street. If nothing else there were fewer streetwalkers and johns in evidence. She passed a shop with the dangling balls of a pawnbroker but it looked too mean for her needs. She was limited by the handful of coins she'd brought with her. She didn't expect them to go very far: she really needed to find a proper jeweler's shop. As the shadows lengthened she grew increasingly worried, but finally found the entrance to Redcross Street, and thereafter the Crown Inn. Which, as advertised in the newspapers she'd spent far too much time reading in the Village Library, was a post-coach terminus.

As soon as she stepped inside the pub, Eve was assailed by the fug of stale beer and overcooked beef: also by the eyeballs of several males in states of dubious sobriety. She resisted the impulse to flinch, then began to move forward just as a barmaid accosted her. "'Ere, ducks, we ain't 'avin' your sort in—"

"I've come for my husband," Eve told her icily, not breaking step as she zeroed in on the baron, who had taken over a small table in one corner for himself and François. *Interesting,* she thought. Evidently the captain had soaked Viktor for most of his ready cash if he wasn't renting a private room.

"Ooh." The barmaid tried to keep up. "Din't realize you was with the gennelman. What'll you be 'avin'?"

Eve smirked. "A glass of your best red," she said, seating herself opposite the baron. Her mood was sour, her feet sore, and her belly empty. "Hello, *darling,*" she said sharply, eyeing the baron's half-empty pewter tankard. "I see you didn't wait for me."

Von Franckenstein turned tired eyes on her. He looked utterly exhausted, and a bit dispirited. "Mademoiselle Six . . ."

"Lady Evelyn de Montfort." Her smile didn't reach her eyes. "Or, considering we are traveling together, Lady Evelyn Von Franckenstein, presumably? To avoid any possibility of scandal."

"*Are* we traveling together?" he asked slowly.

"I certainly hope so. After all, we're traveling *from* the same place, and if your path takes you through London"—she nodded at François—"we're traveling *to* the same place. I can pay my own coaching fare," she added. "It's just more convenient for"—a single woman—"us to travel in company."

"And you believe it is less likely that a pursuer will ask after a married couple and their son than for a lone woman, or a father and son traveling together." Von Franckenstein nodded and took a mouthful of beer, then curled his upper lip. "Or so you told François."

Von Franckenstein sounded as if he had not made up his mind whether to allow her to accompany them. Eve decided to escalate. "There *will* be pursuers. Did you think escape would be as easy as walking away? But I have skills that you will benefit from if we are traveling together."

Abruptly, François, who had remained silent until this point, gave the baron a very adult look. "*Father,*" he said with curious emphasis, "I think we should bring her. She would lend us a—" He chewed his lip. "—a *tactical* advantage."

"Yes, my—" The baron wavered, then collapsed in the face of François's intensity. "—my boy." He regarded Eve. "You say you can contribute. Honesty forces me to admit that I am financially embarrassed. I cannot pay for seats inside the coach—or even on the roof. The captain of that ship is a cutpurse and a scoundrel! Not to mention a part-time smuggler. I can withdraw funds once I arrive in London, but for now . . ."

"I see." Eve gritted her teeth. "How much do the tickets cost?"

"It costs seven shillings to York on the Royal Flier, but there are only four seats inside. It leaves at five o'clock and arrives at nine. From York we can take a coach for London directly down the Great North Road. If you have the money I can enquire with the sales agent."

Eve silently counted out most of a pound in change. It was enough to live off for nearly a month if one was not extravagant. *Airline tickets,* she told herself. *First class, at that.* "I will need to pawn jewelry when we arrive in York," she told him. "But if we get there by nine there should be plenty of time—" The baron looked perturbed. "What?"

"It will take us sixteen hours riding posthaste to York, my Lady, I am quite sure the pawnbrokers will have shut for the night. Perhaps we could take the following day to recover before we embark on the next leg of our odyssey?"

Sixteen hours? But it's only a hundred miles away! Eve swallowed. And York was two hundred miles from London. "We'll be lucky to get there this week."

"I should say so! And we must be up before dawn tomorrow if we are to have a hope of arriving anywhere, so I shall go and reserve our seats and buy us a room for the night—if you have another sixpence?" He rose.

"Sixpence." Eve passed him the coin. "Get us a room together. Just remember, I'm not sharing the bed," she added. *Not with you: not with anyone.*

▸◂▸◂▸◂

The next twenty-four hours passed like a fever dream: a mostly waking nightmare from which Eve could not escape.

Von Franckenstein was true to his word. He used Eve's coin to pay for a room with a bed and a narrow cot. He and the lad stretched out on the bed, leaving the cot for Eve. Which was barely acceptable: something bit her repeatedly around the ankles and wrists in the night, and when she wasn't kept awake itching and swatting at her unseen bedmates, she was disturbed by the baron's oddly nasal snores. There was no privacy, no heat, no toilet—just a rank chamber pot—and the only items of clothing Eve dared remove were her bonnet and boots. Before bed the baron inflicted a strange headpiece on the lad: a metal skull cap, with electrodes that pressed against his forehead and neck and a leather chin strap to hold it in place. Eve watched but held her counsel. It seemed best to save her questions until she no longer needed the baron as an escort.

At an hour of the morning when she would normally have been awakened gently by her alarm (then collected a freshly brewed coffee on her way to the basement gym), a thunderous knocking on the door jolted her out of her stupor. "Time to rise, or we shall miss the coach!" Viktor declared, shoving his feet into his boots.

Eve bit her tongue and followed suit. They traipsed downstairs and out into the dank courtyard where a light drizzle was falling. A pair of coachmen and a hostler were harnessing four miserable-looking nags to a terrifyingly flimsy contraption by means of a collection of straps and buckles that appeared to have been stolen from a fetish club. "Yer in luck," said John Coachman, tapping his forehead with a grim expression. "Ain't nobody else travelin' to York today, and the weather should keep the tobymen at home." He handed Eve up to the coach—or rather, picked her up and shoved her into the rear-facing seat inside. François and the baron took the front-facing one. It was a tight fit, and the doors were as eggshell-thin as those of a utility helicopter. Rather than glass the windows had wooden shutters, so the interior was stuffy and dark, not to mention cold and drafty. The seat cushions had been pounded to the consistency of plywood by thousands of pairs of buttocks and gave little protection from the bouncing of the leaf springs, and the carriage stank of stale pipe tobacco and mildew. The two coachmen climbed on board, one behind and one on the bench up top, and then the coach began to move.

Eve was already exhausted and felt distinctly grimy from two days on the run with insufficient sleep. She was grateful that the baron seemed equally tired and disinclined to idle chatter. As for the boy, he spent most of the trip with his nose buried in a book—Machiavelli first, then a treatise on artillery. As the coach clattered and swayed out of the center of town he murmured to the baron, "I dreamed of her again—of Joséphine." But the baron simply nodded and closed his eyes.

In Eve's time the roads between Liverpool and York were motorways. But in 1816 macadam construction and steam engines barely existed, never mind modern concrete or internal-combustion automobiles. There were a few turnpikes with tollbooths to pay for their upkeep, but even the toll roads were mostly unpaved and seldom wide enough for two coaches to pass in opposite directions.

As their carriage climbed through the wooded foothills of the Pennines, rattling past hill farms and shabby villages with none of the picturesque cottages of Eve's day, they left civilization far behind. Occasionally they drove past the high stone walls that surrounded the private, wooded grounds of some noble family's mansion. More often they bumped along narrow lanes overhung by dripping, unhealthy-looking trees. The rain grew heavier, rattling off the roof of the carriage and chilling the air so that their breath steamed. After a while, Eve managed to wedge her head against one corner of the carriage so that she could snooze.

Eve dozed fitfully all the way to Preston—a small market town at this time—but when the coach stopped in Blackburn to change horses they took on three more passengers who'd paid to sit inside. (Blackburn, a mill town, was evidently prosperous enough this decade that people had reason to travel there.) Another handful of less well-endowed passengers perched precariously on the rooftop, which did absolutely nothing good for the coach springs. Eve was crammed up against one wall by a plump older lady and her abigail, and found herself forced to raise her knees to avoid the outstretched legs of a thuggish-looking fellow with a whisky-sweat hangover and a lasciviously wandering eye. She made sure to ask the baron—"husband, dearest"—if he could procure a pie at the next stop: Viktor gave her an odd look but nodded as they moved off. Eve closed her eyes again. It was impossible to sleep crammed into a corner of a bouncing coach, but at least she could avoid her fellow travelers.

Traveling by post coach in 1816 was the equivalent of business-class air travel in the twenty-first century: expensive and fast, albeit less private than traveling in the coach and livery of a rich aristocrat—the counterpart of an executive jet. Which is to say, it was tedious, cramped, and so uncomfortable it made Eve long for the luxury of an economy-class seat on an overcrowded Ryanair flight with blocked toilets, drunk football fans, and heavy turbulence. *I'm never going to complain about airliners ever again,* she resolved silently, although right now the prospect of returning to the age of heavier-than-air travel seemed hopelessly optimistic.

The coach rattled on through Lancashire then crossed into the West Riding of Yorkshire, pausing every couple of hours to change out the team and take on or drop off passengers. Blackburn gave way to Whalley, Clitheroe, Gisburn, Skipton, Otley, and finally Wetherby. They left the high ground behind, crossing a rolling landscape of hills and dales; passengers got on and off along the way. As the sun dipped close to the horizon—burning through the open shutter at Eve's shoulder, so that she was forced to screw her eyes shut—they crossed into the North Riding, then rolled across the low plain toward the cathedral city of York.

Much to her surprise Eve dropped off to sleep again during the final two-and-a-half-hour run from Wetherby. She awakened to the absence of motion, then a draft as the coach doors sprang open to admit the shouting of hostlers and stable boys. A mounting block rattled as it was shoved up against the side for the ladies to use—the ladies in question being an elder in widow's weeds, and herself. "Come along, *wife,*" the baron said snidely as he stretched his legs out and slid toward the exit. "You, too, boy, help your mother down."

They were in the courtyard of yet another pub. Pubs seemed to be the airport departure lounges of the age: overpriced public establishments full of exhausted, footloose travelers and those who preyed upon them. It reeked of horse manure, coal smoke, and body odor. Eve unkinked her complaining limbs and dizzily stepped down from the coach, shook her skirts out, then grabbed her bundle of belongings before one of the barefoot urchins made off with it. She yawned, then remembered to cover her mouth. "Another room for the night, *dear*?"

The interior of the Black Swan in Coney Street proved to be loud and smoky. It punched Eve in the sinuses with an entirely new set of foul smells: choking clouds of fresh pipe tobacco overlaying stale beer suds. Rooms were available, at a price. Eve passed her rapidly diminishing purse to the baron, who haggled irritably for a while before nodding to her. "We're to follow his boy," he said. "Come along now, Fran—er, Frankie. And wife." Eve followed them up a narrow staircase and into another cramped, dingy room. "We will stay here tomorrow night also," the baron declared. "In the meantime I must write to my banker. It becomes urgent."

Eve bit the bullet. "Get me to a respectable goldsmith or pawnbroker in the morning and I'll sell some jewelry," she told him. She shed her coat and sat on the narrow cot the landlord had provided for the boy. A wave of dizziness swamped her. "You can repay me when we get to London." Frankly she didn't care if Viktor stiffed her for the room and carriage fare, just as long as she had somewhere safe to sleep and a man and his ward willing to sustain the fiction that they were a family. Despite her fatigue it occurred to her that although Von Franckenstein had behaved honorably so far, a little reinforcement was a good idea. "Just as well I keep my jewelry warded against pickpockets and thieves. York has quite the reputation."

"I'm sure I don't understand your implication, madam."

Eve yawned. "I'm not implying anything," she demurred. "Just observing that they have several gallows here, and there must be a reason." They'd rattled past the one on the Knavesmire on their way into town, although it was empty at the moment.

"I"—Viktor drew himself up, aggrieved—"am going downstairs in search of supper and ale in *polite* company," he sniped. "François, come with me." He bowed stiffly in the doorway. "Be seeing you, *mein frau.*"

Eve waved tiredly and lay down. Her eyelids were so heavy that although her stomach was empty she couldn't summon the energy to follow him, let alone to apologize. Instead she gathered just enough focus to activate a protective macro that would awaken her if anyone approached, then swan-dived into the black depths of sleep.

Eve dreamed of Rupert again that night, but this time she wasn't present in body within the dream. It was more like a true divination. She was watching from above—almost like a disembodied CCTV camera, or one of Number Two's periscopes—looking down on a library or household office or gentleman's den in a club. There were windows, but it was night and there was little to see through them. Bookcases lined two walls. There were comfortable wingback reading chairs and side tables bearing unlit oil lamps, a sideboard by the window with a whisky decanter and glasses, and a chandelier overhead in which a goodly number of candles burned. A log was burning merrily in the fireplace, hissing and popping from time to time.

The sole occupant of the room crouched before one of the bookcases like a dusty black spider in human form, holding a candlestick as he searched the spines before him. It was Rupert. But here he was neither Priest of the Mute Poet nor walking corpse: merely a mortal man marooned out of his own time, wearing period costume and a haunted expression. "Must be in here somewhere," he muttered to himself, pulling a pair of thick clothbound volumes off the shelf. He had a pocket book and a stub of pencil, and as he leafed through the books he occasionally paused to scribble notes. His expression made her think of a man whose ship had sailed and who was now desperately trying to calculate the odds of it sinking.

"Where *is it*?" he hissed to himself, closing one of the books and fetching a different volume from the opposite corner of the room. "Where is the library? Damn her eyes, where is *she,* for that matter? *She'd* be able to find it, no question—"

He froze, then slowly looked round, scouring every corner of the room until his gaze came to focus on the corner Eve was watching from. Trapped, Eve was unable even to blink. A claustrophobic panicky sense of breathlessness began to steal over her as Rupert's lips curled in a humorless smirk. He straightened up, still watching her—

Then Rupert was gone, and so was the room. Indeed, so was almost everything. She hovered above a nearly featureless black plain: when she tried to look around she noticed a faint network of silvery tracks running hither and yon, so dim as to be almost impossible to see. The tracery faded out against a sharply drawn horizon that she instinctively knew to be incredibly distant. Overhead she saw a spray of stars that arched across the sky, surrounded by the faint luminescence of a distant spiral galaxy. It wasn't the Milky Way, for she was not seeing it edge on, but viewing it from a shallow angle, so that the lenticular shape and the whorl of spiraling arms were clearly visible—and there were far too few stars elsewhere in the sky.

This must be the far future or the remote past, Eve realized numbly. *Where* am *I?* She looked down again (her body seemingly invisible) and tried to focus on the silvery paths.

"Lost in the dream roads, sweetie?"

She should have startled at Persephone's words—her voice was unmistakable—but her body felt distant and unresponsive.

"Where are you?" she asked.

Baroness Hazard chuckled. "At home, searching for you because His Nibs has taken an unusual interest. Seems I've found you, after a fashion."

Eve tried again: "Where am *I,* then?"

"Good question." The sorceress paused. "Are you awake now?"

Eve took stock. "I was dreaming of Rupert," she said, "and then—yes, I, I'm awake." And stuck inside a lucid dream. She experimented with her orientation, discovered she could pan and tilt her disembodied viewpoint at will. "Oh. That's good. Right. What's happening?"

"It looks like I found you in time to block Rupert, for now. You should ward yourself when you sleep until you escape back to reality, otherwise it will feed on your *mana* until your soul rots, just like him. The dream realms are another kind of lucid dream after all, a shared one—and they feed on drama. Eve, His Majesty doesn't dabble arbitrarily but He doesn't always confide in His servants either. You should be worried, whatever you're involved in is more important to Him than just fetching some dusty manuscript or whacking a traitor. Don't go wandering into any other dream realms if you fetch up back here, and don't forget—don't forget—" Persephone trailed off.

"Don't forget what?" Eve demanded.

"I don't know. Looks like I, uh, forgot. Or someone overwrote that part of our common history while I wasn't remembering.

You're trapped in an unstable bubble of alternate history, like a metaphysical pitcher plant. Rupert inflated it but it's digesting his soul. If you stay too long it'll eat you as well. Eyes on the prize and don't dillydally. Can't stay—" The plain of silvery paths rippled. "Ciao, bella!"

Then Eve woke up.

The next morning Eve slept past dawn, for she was exhausted from travel and enervated by her portentous dream. Eventually she was dragged awake by shouting and banging outside the window as passengers boarded the coach for its return trip to Liverpool. Viktor, who had been snoring quietly, startled awake with a terrified gasp, then lay panting for a minute. Finally he announced, somewhat shakily, "Let us break our fast, *mein frau.*"

"Yes." The public rooms downstairs would be mostly empty once the stage had departed. Eve yawned as she sat up and looked around. "Where's François?"

"What—" The baron sprang out of bed like a jack-in-the-box, an expression of baffled fury on his face. "We must find him at once, else all is lost!" After a moment Eve recognized that his expression was not fury but terror.

"Ease up," she urged him as she forced her aching feet into stiff, cold boots. "He's a twelve-year-old boy, he's probably just off exploring."

"A *six-year-old* boy," the baron hissed, "who might get us hanged, drawn, and quartered in his eagerness to reclaim his rightful place." He sent her an unreadable look. "You are an accomplice," he added, "don't think to turn king's witness. We must search at once!" He pulled his shoes on and stood.

Accomplice to what? Eve wondered. "He might just be downstairs," she pointed out. "Let's go for breakfast and ask if anyone's seen my son before we start panicking."

"*Your* son—!"

"That's the story we're selling," she reminded him, and after a moment the baron nodded stiffly.

"I do not like your manners, madam, but I think you are correct. To breakfast."

Eve followed her ersatz husband downstairs to the lounge, where they found François cleaning out a bowl of porridge with apparent gusto. Eve hammed it up for the benefit of any early-morning travelers and late-night drunks who were paying attention, doing her best impersonation of an overprotective mother. "What have I told you before about going off without telling anybody? Foolish boy!" She grabbed him in a tight hug and fussed over him until the baron nodded approvingly and ordered a cooked breakfast for himself (and, after she kicked his ankle, one for her).

The breakfasts were an expensive indulgence—they each cost more than the night in a private room—but after sleeping for almost eight hours and eating a platter of fried food the size of her head Eve finally began to feel human. All she needed now was a bath and a change of clean clothes and she'd be on top of the world. But the bath and washerwoman would cost even more money, and she was acutely aware of how few coins she had left. "We need to find a jeweler," she told the baron, "and we need to do it *now*."

"Very well. What story do you propose to tell him?"

"I am your young English second wife—you are a widower—and we are temporarily distressed because—" Eve blinked. *Of course.* Her hair was dull, her dress crumpled and sweaty from three days' wear, and Von Franckenstein was no better—clearly unshaven and travel-worn. "How about—" She paused dramatically. "—a highwayman!" It fit the narrative requirements that the dream roads and this realm seemed intent on imposing on her.

"A—" The baron nodded slowly. "Yes, I think that is an explanation that will work."

"We came down the Great North Road by coach but a highwayman held us up in the vicinity of Durham. He took all your money and most of mine, but was scared off by a party of dragoons. I kept only some of my pearls, which I now need to pawn. If anybody asks, you sent your valet ahead to London to prepare rooms for our arrival, and my feckless abigail deserted us after the robbery—if indeed she was not in league with the villain!"

"*A* highwayman, or a party of three or four?" Viktor's tone was lightly amused, but he watched her intently.

"A party, I think, but it was near sunset and I didn't count them. Oh, and the dragoons—they *may* have been in the pay of the turnpike company since they were discharged, or they might have been a band of robbers themselves, for they hared off after the money when they discovered we'd already been relieved of our purses. Let's keep it vague."

He nodded slowly. "Yes, that will convince. You are very good as subterfuge, it seems. Wife?" He offered her his arm and she took it. "If you have a small piece you can wear, a bracelet perhaps, you should put it on now. I will guard you, of course, but stay close. François, follow us. Also, keep your eyes on *Fräulein Sechs,* in case of thieves."

As they walked Eve quietly asked, "Just what is the deal with François?" *Why are you so terrified of losing him?*

"Later." The baron was close-lipped, but she could feel the tensing of muscles in his arm when she raised the matter. "To be overheard means death."

No melodrama there, Eve thought, and shelved the matter until a more convenient time.

Unlike their previous stops, much of the center of York was familiar from Eve's last visit. In the twenty-first century it was a picturesque tourist destination, a Roman town that had thrived as a walled medieval cathedral city before being bypassed by the industrial revolution and pickled in aspic by the heritage industry. But in 1816 the railway (and tourists) had not yet arrived. It was a stinking, filthy, noisy place, with houses crammed together and leaning drunkenly toward each other across cobbled streets with gutters down the middle that served as open sewers. There were few vehicles, and those were mostly carts pulled at walking pace by mules, but Eve still came close to being run over by a flock of sheep on their way to market, and her coat and boots were splashed by foulness she didn't want to think about.

Finally Viktor paused. "I think this will do," he said tersely, head swiveling as he checked on François. "Stay close to us," he told the boy, then pulled a bell rope beside a door.

The painted sign above the entrance proclaimed it a jewelers' shop (a highly inappropriate name, for no Jews had lived in York since the Clifford's Tower massacre). But there was little on show behind the diamond-shaped windowpanes other than painted miniatures depicting necklaces and brooches, and a few cheaper pieces set far enough back to offer smash-and-grab thieves only a slashed hand for their trouble.

Once the shopkeeper answered the bell—he peered at them suspiciously for a while before admitting them to the cramped lobby area—Viktor embarked on Eve's script. "My good sir, I find I need to pawn some of my wife's jewelry to meet our immediate needs. We were waylaid by highwaymen on the road south. . . ."

Viktor's foreign accent clearly put the shopkeeper off his stride, but when Eve chipped in with a related account, and put her arm around her soi-disant son, he began to relent. "Show me the items you are willing to part with and I can at least give you an opinion. They'd better not be stolen, mind!" Which was as good a tell as any that they'd found the local fence.

"I hid these when we saw what was happening"—Eve gave

him a tight smile—"inside my clothes." She reached into her pocket, feigning reluctance, and pulled out her pearl earrings. "They took my necklaces and the rings from my fingers, but I kept these. . . ."

Fifteen minutes later Viktor and Eve left the shop, richer by almost ten pounds in coin. It was a substantial sum—five or six months' wages for a lady's maid, more than enough to see them to London in comfort—but she was absolutely certain that they'd been ripped off. "How much do you think they were really worth?" she asked Viktor.

"Twenty guineas at least," he bit out.

"I suppose it will have to do." She sighed heavily.

"I may post my letters, now?"

"Yes, but where—"

They were back at the inn. "Right here, when the next carriage comes. And then we shall eat lunch and you will tell me about the man you are searching for," he added quietly. "Your *real* husband, the man who is hunting you, yes?"

Meanwhile, two days earlier, in the Village Town Hall:

"You let them go *deliberately*?" Number Seven demanded incredulously.

Number Two smiled gnomically and steepled his fingers as he watched George from across the width of the morning room.

The clouds had parted for once. Morning sunlight spilled through the tall French windows, trickling in golden rivulets across the carpet toward Number Seven's feet. George stood to one side of the entrance, carefully avoiding the circle of power under the carpet. For his part, Number Two sat at his pedestal desk: but now he closed the card cover on a file he had been reading and put down his pen.

"The best way to flush game is often to let a caged bird fly and spread panic among their companions huddling in the undergrowth, don't you think?" Number Two's invisible smile widened.

"Well, now we have that idiot Hackmanworth rattling around, raising hell ashore instead of at sea. And you let the Baron of Hesse-Darmstadt *and* his ward escape at the same time! Isn't that damnably close to treason?" Number Seven spoke calmly, but the way he squeezed his tricorn hat between his hands made it clear that he was very upset. "*And* the witch?"

"Which witch?" Number Two blinked.

"Why, are there—you didn't! Tell me you didn't. . . ." Number Seven stared in disbelief. "You *did,*" he accused. "You let Number Six and Number Twelve fly the coop simultaneously? *Why?*"

Number Two examined his fingernails with evident satisfaction while he waited for Number Seven to come off the boil. "George, old chap, multiple plots abound. Come, have a seat." He waved at the chair beside his desk—not one of the seats positioned over the treacherous rug. Number Seven hesitated momentarily, then circled the room and sat down. "Number Twelve does as Number Twelve wants, as you know full well. She's too meddlesome to keep on a choke chain. This week she expressed a desire to retreat to the convent for a while, which I granted—conditionally. She is on her way back to Grantham with sealed orders, which are only to be opened pursuant to certain . . . events. She's going where she wants to go, I know where she is and have some degree of control, we're both happy. But you know, this isn't really *relevant* right now. As for Number Six, I expect her to run south in search of her mysterious husband. Grantham is on the Great North Road, the most direct inland route to London. Isn't that an interesting coincidence?"

"But the baron and his boy!"

"Will be back where they belong in good time, never fear." Number Two glanced at Number Seven and his expression hardened. "*I want them all,* George. All the boys! Including the ones Fouché packed off to the Portuguese court with their wet nurses, not just the prototype and his creator. At least this one is under observation, along with his maker: they made it onto the supply brig—Captain Fitzgerald is easily bribed but he knows which side of his bread is most reliably buttered—and even better, they're traveling in company with Number Six."

"You must arrest them," Number Seven demanded. "The boy and his guardian are too dangerous. The *woman* is too dangerous. Her alleged *husband*—a claim I don't for a minute believe—is even worse!"

"Dear fellow, just because he blundered into your town house and smashed all your carefully prepared wards—"

"He smashed the tea service, too! Not to mention killing—"

"Yes, but look what he accomplished for us! These are desperate times, Number Seven. Even though the Corsican's reign of terror is over, the Crown is in peril. We let too many genies out of the bottle when it looked as if all was lost: the baron and his boys—giving Number One all he asked for, for that matter. Cleaning everything up will take *years,* and that's assuming we don't all starve in the meantime. Anyway, while I recognize your concerns are entirely legitimate, I'll not go against Number One without good reason." Number Two leaned forward. "Our masters trust—trusted—him implicitly. But I still have questions: what caused his change of temperament on this most recent visit? What is he trying to achieve? And what is this hitherto-undeclared woman of his here for?" He tapped the blotter on his desk for emphasis as he continued. "She clearly bears him no love. Nor did he at any point allude to this marriage—which she denies vehemently—when he first arrived. Then there is the matter of his sudden reappearance and immediate disappearance six months ago. An adept of such flagrant puissance is no common thing, and it happened so soon after Waterloo. . . . Questions are being asked by the Invisible College. He was to be their latest initiate, did you know that? As the man himself is not here, I think we shall have to seek our answers from his past-and-future spouse.

"Which brings me to why I called for you."

Number Seven crossed his arms and waited stubbornly.

"Your next mission, should you choose to accept it," said Number Two, "is to follow the tracker I have placed on the boy François—"

"*The Napoleon*—" Number Seven interjected venomously.

"Yes, the cutting off the branch. The duplicate that Von Franckenstein grew in the womb of a beheaded witch kept alive by unclean means, a reproductive stump nurturing a graft created from the bodily fluids he stole from the emperor during the Congress of Erfurt, yes, yes, we know all that. We *will* get him back—and the other baby nightmares—in plenty of time to prevent an unpleasant repetition of the events of last summer. We shall not be overrun by an army of Napoleons—they will serve the Crown by hook or by crook, or they will be dealt with swiftly and silently. Consider it taken care of. Anyway, back to your mission: there is a tracking ward tattooed on the underside of the boy's left foot, and he is bound to silence about it by a very strong geas."

"Ah." Number Seven relaxed minutely. "A bellwether, then?"

"Yes. Number Six is traveling with the baron and his ward. It is logical that they will journey together toward London. But before they get there they will run the gauntlet of Number Twelve—and meanwhile, you will be close on their trail. The baron and his boy are your lodestone but your real objective is to find Number Six, gain her trust, and stay with her until Number One makes himself known to you. . . ."

▸◂▸◂▸◂

Back at the Starkey house, Wendy waited outside with Imp and Game Boy until one of Sally's team came to the front door to give them the all clear. "Nobody home, ma'am, but the door you mentioned on the top floor is broken." He looked a little spooked. "It's bigger on the inside than the outside. . . ."

They made their way up to the attic. The door to the dream roads lay against the wall opposite the first passage. Some force had yanked it from the doorframe, rupturing the layers of paint that had sealed it in and pulling the hinge screws right out of the wall. The mortise lock had been ripped right out of the door so forcefully that the dead bolt was warped.

"This is bad!" Game Boy complained.

"I'm going to stick my neck out and speculate here," Wendy said slowly, "but I read this as Rupert came back and blew the door off the dream roads, then Eve followed him. At a safe distance, of course."

"But where?" Imp scratched his head.

"A better question would be when." Wendy scrutinized the clutter in the side rooms, where Imp and his crew had dumped the wreckage left behind by the Transnistrian mafia invasion a few months earlier. "Assuming he's still after the book?"

"Swive. Clunge. *Fuck*." Imp's excursion into archaic cursing swiftly reverted to contemporaneity. "It could be *anywhere*. Eve said she dumped it in an elevator lobby somewhere below the present day."

"If he found it he wouldn't have gone back," Game Boy announced. "I mean, after he came back to now."

"And Eve's been gone for several hours." Wendy paused. "Last time, when we went through the door—the Whitechapel thing." (Game Boy shuddered.) "How long were we gone? Five hours? Six?"

"She's much farther away this time," Imp said with dismal certainty.

"That gibbet. The one with Rupert's body." They'd found it in the basement under Castle Skaro, when they'd gone in with Eve and Sergeant Gunderson's team to lance the festering cyst of Mute Poet cultists there. "What was the date on it, because that's an end point, she'll have gone back before then—"

"Why?"

"Because if she was following Rupert's trail she wouldn't have come out after he was dead, would she?" Game Boy finished.

"Right. Uh, I'll look it up." Wendy made a note on her phone. "Anything else?" She gave Imp a pointed look.

"I need to do something about that. . . ." Imp's gesture took in the shattered door and the open passage that it had occluded. The passage looked ordinary enough right now, if a little dated in decor and illuminated by dim incandescent light bulbs, but it made his skin crawl. It was *open,* and anything could come out—dreams, nightmares.

"Can you ward it?" Wendy asked. "You're the nearest thing to a practitioner we've got right now."

"I can—" Imp swallowed. "I can *try.* Might need to consult the library." The library was only a few corridors inside the dream roads, and while it was badly out-of-date the occult texts within it had been selected by his ancestors. "Or, you know, we could go back to Eve's office and see if she has any sorcerers on call? Like, locum wizards or something?"

The look Wendy gave him was distinctly unfriendly. "We could do that. But in the meantime I've got to call this in to my line manager—with your sister gone he's going to want to know who to invoice for my billable hours."

"Wait!" Game Boy's voice cracked. "Are you ditching us? Was it all about the—"

"No." Wendy shut him down. "I'm not dumping you." She glanced at the doorway. "If nothing else, I have no desire to see her ex-boss come back. It's just, I'm on an hourly rate and Mr. Gibson will be unhappy if I go haring off on a wild-goose chase without checking in. Recovering the client from an extradimensional void so she can sign off on my invoice isn't exactly normal business practice."

"Okay." Imp's shoulders slumped. "And then?"

"Wanting to rescue your sister isn't enough: we need a plan. And a destination," Wendy added.

"So we have to find out where and when she's gone?" asked Game Boy.

"Yes."

"And then—"

"Getting it all lined up is going to take time."

They fell silent as the enormity of their situation sank in.

STAND AND DELIVER!

The trouble with lies was that unless you were very good *and* very lucky they inevitably came back to bite you on the arse, Eve reflected. Not the little lies, like her successful plea of poverty due to highwaymen—mere background color that lulled any suspicion on the part of the jeweler that she and the baron might be thieves—but the *big* lies. Such as the one Number Two had locked her into with his geas.

Viktor Von Franckenstein was terrifyingly astute—as befitted a fellow who was evidently an occult researcher—and Eve found him increasingly frustrating to deal with. Most of the time he concealed it behind a blandly inoffensive facade. But it became clear that he'd learned that Eve was frantically searching for Rupert, and that he was her putative husband and a threat to her. When she asked how he knew he just smiled and changed the subject. (And he also changed the subject whenever she asked about François, about how he'd ended up in the Village, about why the boy's mere identity might be perilous to know—none of which were acceptable topics of polite conversation to the baron, any more than her precise relationship with Rupert was to Eve. None of which gave her the warm fuzzies.)

"Although we are traveling in company for safety I am unable to trust you with my most intimate secrets, madame—and I can't help noticing that you seem to feel likewise about me. Why don't we agree to keep our own counsel?"

Eve resisted the urge to roll her eyes. "If you insist," she conceded. "But I must continue to read the papers. Just in case." She *could* sketch a ward on the underside of the bedroom chair and compel him to honesty. But if she went that far it'd destroy whatever tenuous trust they had built, and she still needed a fake husband while she was on the road. Even if she hired an abigail—a temporary lady's maid—striking out for London on her own would be considerably harder. Viktor could open doors for her that were routinely barred to women, an infuriatingly common problem in this century.

They stayed at the Black Swan Inn for two more days. Eve paid the publican's daughter Rose to accompany her to the shops. She acquired a spare frock and was able to have her old one laundered and mended. She also bought some sundries: handkerchiefs, a detachable pocket to wear under her gown, a new bonnet. The pocket she enchanted to divert wandering fingers and confuse avaricious eyes. She paid for a bath and then to have her hair styled closer to current fashion, the better to attract as little attention as possible. Rose chattered cheerfully, emitting a constant stream of consciousness. Eve listened discreetly, taking note: the girl revealed far more than she realized, especially about the local perceptions of the slightly odd wife of the extremely odd German exile. And when the noise became too wearisome Eve sent Rose out with a sixpence to fetch the latest newssheets.

Rupert remained stubbornly elusive. It was almost as if he'd overshot by a couple of decades and changed his name to the Scarlet Pimpernel. (Wasn't the Pimpernel fictional? Eve was unsure.) Nevertheless she doggedly ploughed through the papers whenever a new one arrived from the printers.

Wednesday night finally rolled round, and a stagecoach from Darlington to Peterborough arrived in the inn's yard for its overnight stop. It would continue at the crack of dawn. Viktor haggled for three seats, and she paid off the irrepressible Rose. They packed their bags before bed and Eve resigned herself to another horrendous day on the Great North Road. Once they reached Peterborough they would pause for the weekend, then continue to London the following Tuesday. At least, that was the plan.

One stagecoach ride was much like another: Eve found them blurring together with exhaustion. Economy-class travelers sat on the roof, along with the armed guards. The cramped interiors were reserved for first-class fliers. All the seats were occupied, so Eve was crammed into a corner or sandwiched between strangers. She'd tried to find a book to read in York, but the choice of reading matter was extremely tame, not to say limited by the proximity of rubbernecking busybodies. She'd been force-fed a bellyful of turgid Victorian novels in secondary-school English classes: now, faced with a choice between collections of sermons or a farmer's almanac, she gave up and resigned herself to dozing as much as possible. At least *this* coach had glazed windows, and the coaching company boasted of their bulletproof panels (although she doubted they would defeat an angry sparrow, much less a musket ball). So she watched the world go by, answered the prying questions of a migratory parson in monosyllables, and ignored the sin-searching glower of a similarly nosy matron.

The coach made good time, for the Great North Road was well maintained, running arrow-straight for long stretches between high stone walls. The macadam surface was a vast improvement over the dirt tracks elsewhere. Less welcome were the periodic shakedowns for tips—"kicking the passengers," it was called—by coachman and guards. It happened at every stop and seemed likely to double the price of their tickets by the time they reached London. It was all terribly boring and nonnotable, and Eve found herself wishing for something, anything, to happen to break the monotony. Until she got her wish.

The coach ran on schedule between posting inns, changing out horses and coachmen periodically. By sunset they were almost eighty miles south of York, with another forty miles to go to Peterborough. Eve squinted through the uneven window glass and covered her mouth as she yawned. She was stiff from inactivity and her back and thighs ached from the constant vibration. The coach was slowing: once darkness arrived the coachman would have to proceed by lamplight. *Might get there in time for breakfast tomorrow,* she thought glumly. She felt like slapping her self of a day ago for subjecting her now-self to this torture. She'd once flown from London to Sydney in economy class, and that had been bad enough: this was infinitely worse. François bore up stoically, but even so, as the shadows lengthened, he felt compelled to ask the inevitable question: "Are we nearly there yet? Is it going to be much longer, Father?"

Full dark found them swaying slowly along a stretch of unfenced road through woodland around Gonerby Hill Foot (which only a flatlander would consider hilly). Suddenly the coach lurched as the driver hauled on the reins and yanked on the brakes. Steel wheel rims screeched, and François was thrown into Eve's lap. The baron managed to keep his seat but Eve's current neighbors—an elderly merchant and his wife—fell sideways on top of her, leaving her suffocating and bruised under their complaints.

"Get *off*—" she began, just as voices from outside bellowed, "Out of the coach! The taxmen've come for thy highway toll!"

Shrieks, wails, and cries of indignation ensued. The carriage rocked violently as passengers spilled off the roof, then there was a thunderous bang as one of the guards discharged his blunderbuss. A horse screamed, then there were further gunshots—black-powder pistols this time. Eve shuddered and flattened herself beneath the squawking merchant's wife.

"Oi! Enough o' that! Get over 'ere and hold your hands up high! Davey, get the door! You'll pay for that, you—" The shouting highwaymen were clearly angry.

The old merchant shuddered. "Ex-soldiers," he quavered. "God save us!"

Eve gritted her teeth. "You're kneeling on my back," she hissed. If she could get to her bundle, the hand of glory would hide her. And if she could get off her knees and draw a line of sight on them, a handful of pearl bullets would—no. If the highwaymen were army veterans discharged after Waterloo they'd return incoming fire with interest. Anyway—she mentally kicked herself—she was traveling by coach, *of course* they'd have to be waylaid by highwaymen. The gothic archetype she'd blundered into on the dream roads demanded it; the only question was how best to deal with them.

"Come out, come out, fat pullets one and all!" Cold air swirled into the carriage as the door was yanked open. Abruptly the weight on her back shifted as the merchant was dragged wailing from the carriage. "Oh, lawks, God save us," moaned his wife.

"Get *off* me." Eve finally managed to slither out from underneath the woman. Folds of fabric had fallen over her head, musty and smelling of wet dog. Gasping for breath, she shoved at the blanket and flailed around on the floor for her bag. Some instinct made her reach out with her invisible hand, ghost fingers fumbling for a memory of its texture. She latched onto a corner triumphantly just as strong hands tugged the blanket off her then grabbed her legs and *yanked*.

Eve fell face-first to the side of the road. It was a long drop from the coach and it knocked the wind out of her. She gasped, teetering on the edge of panic, as she heard moans and wails from the other passengers and the harsh, tense panting of a wounded man in too much pain to scream.

"Be quiet and pay up an' we'll be on our way the sooner!" shouted the spokesman for the bandits. "Wallets, purses, coin, and jewelry, come all and pay the turnpike toll and your souls will be lighter when it comes to getting in to heaven!" Rough laughter from at least two other throats.

"*What have we here?*" hissed a rough voice, far too close for comfort. Someone tried to roll Eve on her back. Her grip on the bag was tenuous and it felt as if her head was about to explode, but she tugged as hard as she could and it finally slid across the edge of the coach doorway and dropped to the ground beside her. "Hey, you're a pretty li'l thing!" She kept her eyes closed but silently recited the words of power she'd memorized for use in extreme peril. "What'll you pay your toll with, love, your money or your cunny?" He stank of sweat and stale gin. Behind him the other highwaymen were separating the passengers into smaller groups. The coachman and guards, if any still lived, had fled: there would be no aid from that quarter. With her mental fingers tingling and buzzing from the swarming eaters she'd unwillingly summoned, she fumbled inside her bag. Her mind skidded across the bony digits of the hand of glory and found the folded sticks of her fan while her personal highwayman yanked her skirt up. And with the fan on the grip of her will she finally ran out of fucks to give and surrendered to the killing rage.

"Get off me," Eve growled, *or I* will *kill you*: but the robber just chuckled horribly and held her down, so she ripped the fan straight through the thin fabric of her bag. It clacked open before her assailant could raise a hand, and she whipped the lace-covered ceramic razor blades through his throat. Hot blood sprayed out, catching her in the face: it squirted and gushed then the pulses slowed as he silently slumped across her and died.

Blinded and soaked to the skin, Eve reached for the hand of glory. A solid band of pain gripped her temples as she ignited the fingertips by sheer force of will.

She must have blacked out for a few seconds. When she regained her senses all sounds were muffled. Nobody was speaking, at least not any words she could recognize. Everything was blurred, she could barely see, and she held something horrible and waxy with her mind, something that felt like the left hand of death. Eve struggled to pull herself out from underneath the dead highwayman, rocking up on her elbows and shoving herself away from his body.

I killed him, she realized with a sinking sense of inevitability. There was no guilt as such—he'd meant to rob, rape, and probably murder her—but she dreaded discovery. If his comrades in arms found her with his corpse, covered in his blood, she was done for. *Why are they not coming for me?*

Once she had a hand free she was able to smear it across her face. Her eyes watered for a while and she teared up, but finally the red cleared and she could see again, albeit dimly. Head pounding, she crawled under the carriage and peered out. The clearing held a strange diorama. Lit by chilly moonlight, a gang of ragged men with guns and swords surrounded the other passengers. They were systematically stripping them of property and clothes. She took the hand of glory in her right hand—as she loosened her mental grip on it her headache eased—then was caught on the horns of an immediate dilemma: how to juggle the blood-drenched fan, the hand, and her bag? Eventually she hooked the bag strap with a toe and pulled it along behind her.

Crawling out on the far side of the carriage, Eve picked herself up and tiptoed away. She stood no chance against half a dozen armed highwaymen, even with this pallid invisibility. When they noticed their comrade's absence they'd come after her, and she could expect no mercy. She very much doubted that the baron and his young charge would put their lives on the line for her, certainly not if it jeopardized their mission (whatever it was): so she silently stumbled away into trees and the night.

▸◂▸◂▸◂

Eve trudged through the woods. She was despondent. Her sorcerous overexertion had brought on the visual distortions and pounding headache of a migraine, leaving her half-blind in the moonlight. She was sore and bruised, her hands stung, and her dress was torn and blood-soaked. Worse, she was haunted by her actions. She couldn't stop second-guessing herself: could she have handled things better? It was clearly pointless, but the question kept nagging at her conscience. Eve prided herself on her realism. She faced facts, and the facts right now were that happenstance had bloody well happened, and now she had to live with the consequences. But she couldn't reconcile herself to it. All she could do was keep walking, hope there was no pursuit, and keep worrying at the bloody sore until the cold light of tomorrow's dawn arrived.

At some point during her flight she stumbled and nearly fell. A while later she walked face-first into the trunk of an oak tree and, half-stunned, dropped the hand of glory. When she found it again it was obviously done for, its fingers burned down to bony stumps, so she kicked dirt over it and called it a grave. Then she carried on, a wary arm held before her face to fend off stray branches.

The moon set and the dark of night closed in. It began to rain, a light drizzle that soaked through clothing and drenched her more thoroughly than an ice bath. She began to shiver, and her teeth were chattering when she finally slipped and fell again. She'd stumbled on a shallow ditch, and although she hadn't quite gone in, her boots and hem were now waterlogged and freezing cold. Clambering up the opposite bank, she wrung her sodden skirts out then stumbled onto a track surfaced in crushed stone chips. She shoved her dripping hair out of her eyes and looked around. Shadows and gloom—not to mention the lingering effects of her postsorcery migraine—made it hard to be sure, but on the far side of the road (it was wide enough for a carriage) there was another ditch, then a stone wall that rose above head height. It curved away into the darkness an indeterminate distance ahead. She picked a direction and shuffled forward on numb feet. If she was lucky there'd be a gatehouse or a driveway, maybe shelter for the night. And if not, well, it wasn't a turnpike, so there'd be less risk of highwaymen: and it wasn't a forest after midnight, so there was less risk of tripping over a tree root and breaking her neck.

After ten minutes of stumbling along the road Eve could no longer feel her feet. Her hands burned with a dull ache, the shivers had become constant, and she vaguely realized she was becoming feverish. Then she fell over again. For a while she lay still, utterly exhausted and demoralized. The rain was beating down heavily now and it came to her that if she didn't start to move again she would succumb to hypothermia. That was, she supposed, a bad thing, although at least it would hurt less. *Do you want to let Rupert win?* Imp asked her—she was pretty sure he wasn't really there but that didn't stop him: he'd always been irritatingly persistent—*because* this *is how you let Rupert win.* That stung. "Go away, you're not here," she muttered, and pushed herself onto her side. It took some time but she confirmed that her arms and legs still worked and would support her. "You're wrong," she slurred, then lunged upright and began to shuffle drunkenly forward.

A light came into view around the curve of the wall. She blinked, wondering if she was delirious as well as feverish, but it stayed where it was: *a lamp,* she realized fuzzily. There was indeed a lamp, burning steadily in a lantern hanging from a post, then another, and another, forming a trail that led away from the road. It was a driveway. *Saved,* she told herself, *I'm saved,* and nearly burst into tears of joy.

The rain fell constantly. Eve shuffled forward blindly until she came to a gravel loop fronting a building. Steps and a pair of stone lions loomed out of the darkness to either side of a huge pair of doors. But no lights shone in the windows above the entrance. Was anybody home? She stumbled against the door. Fumbling in the shadows, she groped for a handle or door knocker: something, anything, that would get her inside. She finally felt something beside the door: a bellpull, which she proceeded to yank with all her remaining strength. There was some resistance, but it made no sound. The rain intensified yet again, falling in sheets against the front of the building and soaking her to the skin. She knew she should be feeling around with her mind's fingertips, hunting for a lock or a latch, but there seemed to be nothing there. She felt as if her inner eye had gone blind from overuse. *Or perhaps I'm sick,* she realized, as another convulsive shudder racked her rib cage. *Freezing.* Hypothermia was insidious. She yanked on the bellpull once more, and fell forward as the door she was leaning on was pulled open.

"Go away, we're closed—" the maidservant began, then stumbled over her tongue as Eve gasped, "H-highwaymen!" and collapsed at her feet, inconveniently blocking the threshold.

The next thing Eve noticed was that she was much, much colder—so cold, in fact, that she was shuddering and shivering and her teeth were clattering despite a red-glowing fireplace burning barely six feet in front of her. Random impressions made their way into her numb, uncomprehending brain. She was lying on her side on a cot in a smallish room with high, shuttered windows and a draft blowing, and there was a recently stoked fire in the grate. She was swaddled in blankets, and for a moment she was gripped by the fear that she was back in the coach, lying under the merchant's wife or the dead highwayman, and her escape had been a nightmare. But she didn't feel wet: indeed, the blankets seemed to be dry and didn't smell of wet dog. Someone had stripped her then put her in a nightdress and dropped a pile of bedding on top of her. *Rescued!* Eve rejoiced, and if she had been the crying or praying kind she'd have cried tears of thanks to her gods.

The storm had intensified while she was in her swoon. The wind soughed around the window casement and moaned down the chimney. Gusts raised swirling sparks in the fireplace and set the hissing flames to dancing and throwing out heat. The coals were burning down fast and there was no other source of light in the room. Eve was appallingly tired and disoriented, her mind adrift on a tide of exhaustion. And as the tide ebbed, it rocked her to sleep on a sea of uneasy dreams, with no inkling what might have become of her traveling companions.

▸◂▸◂▸◂

In her delirium Eve didn't dream about Rupert. But that was scant consolation, for after an interregnum of disturbingly disjointed random imagery she found herself in a lucid state. She'd dreamed her way back to her own time, sitting in a drawing room opposite the Prime Minister, who was sipping orange pekoe tea from a delicate porcelain cup. She knew she was dreaming because she *could* see His face, or at least had a sense of recognizing a face-like structure drawn in childish crayon on the front of a skull of disturbingly nonhuman lineage. Furthermore she was trapped in the lucid dream, for although she was fully awake and conscious, she was unable to flee His terrible smile, and whenever she blinked she forgot whatever it was about Him that was so bad, which somehow made everything worse.

The PM was immaculately turned out in a three-piece suit, tailored in the fashion of 2017. He sat in an armchair on the opposite side of a coffee table from her, and she realized she was wearing one of her regular work suits. For a moment she felt a stab of hope that she had been recalled to the present, but then she realized: *nope, still dreaming.* The green wallpaper and the tall bay windows filled with oddly thick glass panes put her in mind of an aquarium stocked with rare and deadly deep-sea predators, or perhaps a stuffy and self-consciously archaic luxury hotel. They looked out across the lawn, patio, and formal shrubbery of the back garden of Downing Street, which was lit as if by full daylight, but the sky wheeling overhead was pitch-black and dominated by the same isolated galaxy as the emptiness over the dream roads.

"Where am I?" she heard herself ask, and almost took fright at her own presumption: but the PM merely took another sip from His teacup and put it down, whereupon it had never existed.

"*You* are inside your own head, while *We* are in the green drawing room at Number Ten. We expect you have an update for Us." He smiled like a saint of hell. "How is your dream quest going?"

"I—" Her tongue stuck to the roof of her mouth for a moment. "Dream quest?"

"You *did* follow your quarry back through the dream roads, did you not?" The PM cocked His head too far to one side, His neck bending as unnaturally as a hanged man's. He was laughing silently, she realized. Laughing *at* her. "Chasing the odious Rupert de Montfort Bigge, *Mrs.* de Montfort Bigge—and that was most cleverly done of you, for you are not his chattel if he has not yet married you. Was that not your reasoning?" Eve nodded involuntarily, trying not to retch. When drafting magical contracts, as with legal agreements, it was essential to get the wording precisely right. Rupert's geas over her was still in force, but it only became absolute on the date on the marriage certificate. The PM's neck straightened with an almost silent *pop,* and was unbroken once more. "What have you learned?"

Eve managed not to gag. She took a cautious breath. "In my—our own—time there is a village called Portmeirion on the Welsh coast," she began, and described her adventure—a very sorry excuse for an adventure, more like a series of unfortunate narrative vignettes strung together in lieu of a plot—expecting to be reprimanded at any moment. But the PM simply listened, with a manner that, had He been human, she might have taken for sympathy. Being attended to so closely by an ancient horror should have been appalling, but Eve found it weirdly comforting: at least He was *interested*. It meant she hadn't chased Rupert down the rabbit hole for nothing. "Which brings me to *here,* wherever here is. Somewhere near Grantham with absolutely no clue about Rupert's whereabouts, but at least I haven't died of hypothermia or been eaten by a government shoggoth." She shuddered.

The PM inclined his head. "Things could always be worse," he said. "Grantham, you say? That's an interesting part of the world. There are ley lines there, you know. It was the site of facilities operated by the Invisible College and their successors until We downsized them."

"The Invisible what?" Rupert had mentioned them in his deranged rant, but made so little sense that Eve had ascribed it to his paranoia. But now she thought about it, hadn't Number Twelve also alluded to them?

"Come now! You've met Baroness Hazard: you've heard of them by other names, I'm sure. They were founded and initially led by Dr. John Dee, on the orders of Sir Francis Walsingham, spymaster to Queen Elizabeth. Later they became a sub-rosa select committee of the House of Lords. Most recently the upper tier—Mahogany Row, they call it—directed X Division, Special Operations Executive, a spin-off of the wartime secret services merged with the occult arm of GCHQ. As of the last cabinet office reorg they're DEATH, the Department of Existential Anthropic Threats to Humanity. That would be Us, by the way." He chuckled. "They move the chess pieces around the board at My direction. Pawns and rooks and queens, that is—We are the only king allowed in the game. If you have come to the house of dreams We expect you are about to encounter a countess—double knight's move, that piece—and if you survive you will cross a square to the other side of the board, and perhaps you will even become a queen? No, that's a different game. . . ."

The PM fell silent, then looked at her expectantly.

"What do you want me to do?" she asked.

"I want you to stop Rupert, of course." The PM hooked one leg over the arm of His chair. "You'll have to work out what happens next for yourself, One fears, but if you stop him We shall be pleased: it ties off a notable loose end left dangling since Bonaparte's expedition to Egypt. The great ritual sacrifice of the Terror provided the power that disturbed Our millennial sleep by interrupting the Age of Reason. Then the emperor's scholars opened My sarcophagus and awakened Me. But We were weak and Napoleon held the genius of empire, and he never liked Us anyway so We fled to England and spent the next two centuries recovering. But We digress!

"Suffice to say that if you address your marital situation in the dream roads you won't be enslaved by Rupert after your return. And it's fine to ask other pieces on the board for help."

"Other—" Eve blinked. "Who? Are we talking about the baron?" A thought struck her. "Did I miss the book? Was it in the library in the Village Assembly Rooms when I—"

"What? Of course not! If it was there We should have found it thirty years before you arrived. Nothing in the Village can be concealed from Us, only forgotten. And frankly, the *Necronomicon* is not a tool of great quality: We are more concerned with denying it to the one that Rupert serves.

"You'll find Rupert eventually—the dream roads run on archetypes and narrative logic—but you should probably not let the Invisible College know that you're looking for him. They take a dim view of meddlers. Also, you should take care not to get sucked into French postimperial politics." *Wait, what? Is He talking about the Baron and François?* But the PM was already moving on. "You must avoid the Silver Sisterhood and their countess if at all possible. And if you marry, have the good taste to pick someone who won't live into the twenty-first century, ha ha!" He raised his teacup and drained it, then made a now-familiar gesture with his fingers. "Be seeing you!"

She slept badly until morning.

▸◂▸◂▸◂

Number Seven—Lord George Ruthven, eldest living son of the Earl of Marsden—reined in his mount and cursed under his breath.

It was well into the early hours of the morning. His horse snorted and shifted uneasily. It was raining heavily, but not hard enough to completely wash away the stink of blood and ruptured guts.

"Sir?" Sergeant Benson asked quietly. He'd come to fetch George from his room in the inn not two hours earlier—disturbing his first rest after two days of hard riding, for he'd lost Number Six's trail in the North Riding and cast about almost as far afield as Hull, in case she'd taken ship for the Continent, before turning south. But then a patrol had reported back to the inn and gotten him up before he'd more than nodded off: they'd ridden back this way and discovered the coach that had been due in after nightfall had come to grief.

"Post guards," George said tiredly. "The robbers are long gone but it pays to be careful."

Benson nodded, then snapped a series of orders at his dragoons. He and George had served together during the Peninsula campaign and had a survivor's trust for one another's competence.

The coach blocked the road, doors hanging open and traces empty. The robbers had taken the team of horses as well as the baggage and, judging by the state of the victims, most of their clothes. An arm sprawled out from beneath the carriage, its limpness speaking of recent death—rigor had not yet set in.

Around Number Seven the dragoons dismounted and spread out, bayonets fixed and eyes wary. A wail went up from the distressed passengers huddled behind the stricken coach. They'd been tied up, half of them naked but for their smalls, and they were shivering with cold.

"Missed 'em by an hour," Benson reported grimly. "One coachman's dead, another's shot, so's a passenger, and one of the robbers's dead—'e's the one underneath, passengers say a woman passenger cut 'is throat an' ran away—"

George cursed. "Are they all here? Apart from the missing woman?"

"The passengers are, m'Lord—the guards also ran away. But I found the German and the boy you wanted."

George glanced back along the night-shrouded turnpike. "Send a man to fetch the wagon." He nudged his horse toward the sorry cluster of travelers.

The moon was still up, and in any case Number Seven had excellent night vision. He dismounted right in front of Von Franckenstein, who blinked dimly. "Who are you, sir? Are we rescued?"

"Where is she?" George demanded without preamble.

"I don't know who you speak of—" The scientist blinked again, then recoiled. "You!"

"Indeed, it is I. *Where is she?*"

"I know not! We were waylaid by bandits! Shots were fired, I feared for my life, and then—"

"*Papa.*" George glanced down. It was the boy François. Something about the lad's regard disturbed him: he had an unnaturally mature eye. It sat poorly on a youth of only ten or eleven years. "I told you, she went under the coach. Where the dead man met his end."

"Where is she now? Where did she go?" George asked the lad, trying to be calm lest he frighten him. But François seemed as cool as a cucumber, almost as if he was a veteran, victor of more than seventy battles.

"I think she ran into the woods," the lad said thoughtfully, "although I cannot say for sure: I was watching the robbers. She took the *main de gloire*—"

Von Franckenstein rounded on him. "You gave her that? You stupid brat! Don't you know what could—"

"If I had not, she would be dead!" François's shrill retort silenced his guardian. He addressed Number Seven directly. "It got her off the ship. Then she met us in Lever-pool and proposed we should travel together as a family, to London." Number Seven felt a stab of mild jealousy combined with admiration for the woman's prowess. She was magnificently effective, to say nothing of her feminine charms. Number Two was certainly right to worry about her. "It worked—nobody suspected anything in York—and if it hadn't been for these bandits—"

"But you lost her," George stated, carefully keeping his tone even. "Which leaves me with a problem."

"What will you do with us?" François asked, as the doctor said, "You must let me go! I am the only one who can make—"

"Sergeant," George called, "over here!" As Benson approached he made a curious gesture with the fingers of his left hand, holding it out of sight. "You, doctor, will go ahead with these soldiers. Sergeant, this gentleman and his son will ride in the cart to the inn. Feed them and buy them a room for the night and guard them well. I will meet you in a day or so when I've retrieved our runaway." The tips of his fingers were already itching. He moved them in a circle: the itch intensified unbearably for a moment, then faded. *Good.* "Sir, it will go the worse for you if you try to escape again. As for you, lad—" He gave François a hard stare. "I know who you think you are, and you can rely on the Department's protection for now, but you will *not* be allowed to escape this island without permission. There will be no ship to Asunción for you on my watch! Let alone to Saint Helena." To Von Franckenstein, he added quietly, "I keep an open mind, and if you took no liberties with the lady I see no reason to horsewhip you. But you'd better go back in your velvet-lined box willingly, or it will be the worse for you." The doctor nodded silently, then hung his head. "Now go with the soldiers."

"But our luggage! And the boy's headpiece—"

"Number Eighty-Six will make you another memory harness when you arrive back in the Village." George turned away, dismissing him. "Sergeant? Any last words?"

"No, m'Lord." Benson saluted.

"Good." George took his horse's reins and gently tugged. His steed snorted miserably but followed after him. The rain was intensifying, and the animal had already had a hard day. George walked toward the trees, careful not to twist an ankle or lead his horse astray. Riding through a coppice at night in bad weather would be reckless, but he had a feeling he'd need his mount and saddlebags on the morrow. Meanwhile his left index finger twitched and tingled, leading him away from the site of the robbery. His quarry had come this way on foot and alone. Sooner or later he'd overtake her—hopefully before she needed his protection from Number One, or one of the other hostile pieces arrayed against her on the chessboard.

▸◂▸◂▸◂

Eve awakened to daylight leaking through the cracks between the wooden shutters. The fire had gone out and the room was cold but she was no longer freezing. She yawned and stretched, then rubbed her eyes and looked around. The room *was* small and floored in bare boards: the walls and ceiling were painted white. Her cot was battered and as lumpy as the coaching-inn beds she'd learned to loathe over the past week, but there were plenty of blankets—gray, multiply patched things, but warm enough. A chamber pot and a rough table (supporting a water jug and bowl) completed the furnishings. And now she wasn't actually in danger of dying of hypothermia, Eve was struck by what she *didn't* see. Someone had taken the trouble to put her in a scratchy nightgown, but her coat, dress, bonnet, and boots were missing, as was her bag, purse, and jewelry.

Throwing off the pile of blankets, Eve approached the shutters. They hinged inward, revealing a glazed window. Its narrow panes were set behind wrought-iron bars: and when her eyes turned to the door, she saw that it had an inspection slot and no doorknob.

"Rescued," she swore under her breath. She'd jumped out of the frying pan but landed in the fireplace. The room was clearly a cell. It was a civilized one by nineteenth-century standards—there were no manacles in evidence—but nevertheless: it was a cell. "Crap."

She opened her inner eye and looked around, fighting off a wave of dizziness. She saw no wards or signs of eaters or other parasites, and she couldn't smell the sea. *I'm not back in the Village,* she told herself. Which had to count for something, didn't it? In *The Prisoner,* Number Six *always* awakened back in the Village, sooner or later. Clearly that part of the archetype hadn't kicked in—yet.

Eve leaned against the door and ran her imaginary fingers around the frame. It didn't take her long to find the hinges were riveted to iron bars bolted to the wood. And now she knew to look for locks on the opposite edge. There was a dead bolt and a rim lock on the back side of the door, which would have been trivially easy to pick if she was stronger. But the lock was a huge, crude thing and if she tried to brute-force it by will alone she'd end up with her brains leaking out through her nostrils. A wave of dizziness hit her like a hammer of delirium, and she staggered to the cot before she blacked out. She hadn't eaten for twenty-four hours, the back of her throat held a troublesome tickle, and antibiotics wouldn't be invented for another a century: just identifying the limits of her prison was exhausting.

She was sitting on the edge of the cot with her head in her hands when there was a rattle of keys and the door swung outward.

"Good morning, sister! How are you feeling this day?"

Rather than a prison orderly, Eve's visitor was a tiny, plump woman with twinkling eyes. She was bundled up in many layers, topped with a headscarf knotted tightly under her chin. If Eve stood she would barely come up to her shoulder. "Where am I?" Eve asked.

"Ye're in a place of refuge, sister! Are you well enough to eat?" The woman bustled in and held her palm to Eve's forehead, then pinched her cheeks. Eve, who would normally have gone ballistic over such an invasion of her personal space, was too tired to resist. "I'll just be seeing to the chars and pot, then I'll take you to the kitchen. Ye've missed breakfast but I'm sure Cook can find something to fill your stomach!"

"Ah." Eve tried to sit up. "That's very kind, I'm sure, but what *is* this place? My coach was held up—"

"Never you worry thy pretty little head about such things! We'll see you right as rain, be sure of it. This be Saint Hilda of Grantham's Home for Disgruntled Waifs and Strays, and you'll be safe here! May I ask your name, miss? I'm Hetty Baker, if it pleases you—"

Hetty dumped a shapeless gown on the cot then bustled about with an ashpan and coal scuttle, sweeping and relaying the fireplace. She tipped the ashes into the chamber pot and paused in the doorway, evidently expecting something.

"Lady Evelyn de Montfort," Eve said stiffly, managing to stand up again without wobbling. "Where is the kitchen? Where are—" She stopped herself before she got to "my things": all in good time.

"Let's be getting you decent first before you show your nose in public!" Hetty dragged the dress over Eve's head and laced her up, then led her along a corridor past more cell doors with hefty rim locks. They descended a steep flight of stairs and traipsed through a maze of service rooms, finally arriving in a kitchen with an open fireplace and a spit that looked big enough to roast an elephant. A taller woman (by 1816 standards: she was still shorter than Eve) bustled in from the pantry. Evidently this was Cook. "Is this the new arrival?" she asked Hetty, completely ignoring Eve.

"Miss de Montfort is a *paying guest,*" Hetty announced, with curious emphasis, "'oo arrived in the night, and she hasn't eaten since yesterday."

"Well." Cook set her platter down on the table in the middle of the room. "I'll see if there's a bit of cheese to go with the bread. She'll want something to drink, too, I expect."

"I—" Eve bit her tongue, swallowing her immediate angry impulse: *it's not her fault I'm hungry and irritable,* she reminded herself. "Yes, please."

Hetty bustled away while Eve was eating, and Cook left her alone. But the peace and quiet didn't last. Hetty came flapping back, wringing her hands. "Good goddess's morning to you, Miss de Montfort, and Matron says Dr. Clements will see you in the surgery as soon as you've broken your fast!"

Eve suppressed a shudder, for she had absolutely no desire to undergo another nineteenth-century medical examination. "There must be some mistake? There's nothing wrong with me—"

"Never mind your pretty little head about that, miss! Dr. Clements has to see all new arrivals! 'Tis to see they're well! Then Matron will be able to settle you."

"But I should be on my way. Where are my things?"

"Matron *will* be able to help you," Hetty reassured her, an inflexible note creeping into her voice. "She's with Dr. Clements now. Have you finished eating?"

Eve was still hungry, but the crust was so stale it threatened her dentistry. She stood up. "I'm ready," she announced in a resigned tone of voice.

Hetty hustled her through another passage, then across a wood-paneled hallway with shields and heraldic emblems nailed to the high picture rail, then up a staircase and along another corridor. They came to what had probably once been the boudoir of a wealthy lady. These days it served as a doctor's waiting room. The walls were hung with anatomical charts; a glass-fronted cabinet to one side held glass jars full of murky fluid that failed to conceal their disturbing, floating contents; and a fully articulated skeleton held together with wires hung from a miniature gallows beside the window casement. Eve half expected to see a baby crocodile dangling from the ceiling: it was definitely a statement room, one designed to attest the scholarly credentials of its owner.

Hetty knocked on a plain door at one side of the room. "Matron? I brought you the new girl!"

The door opened to admit Matron, and Eve startled. Matron was none other than Tiffy Ffoulkes-Ward—Number Twelve—now wearing the starched habit of a nursing order. She faced Eve with an expression of deep disapproval and a flintlock pistol, which she aimed unerringly at Eve's midriff. "You!" she snapped, lightning flaring deep within her sapphire eyes.

"Me?" Eve shrugged off her confusion. "What are *you* doing here?"

"That was *my* next question!" said Tiffy. "But it will have to wait. All new admissions are to be seen by the doctor immediately. He gets very upset if he can't make his little diagnosis, and when he's upset he gets fractious and hard to handle. He tends to overprescribe: ice baths, leeches, and galvanism, in case you were wondering, but mostly leeches. So let's not keep him waiting, shall we? You can tell me what brought you to the Institution afterward and we can try to work something out."

Tiffy stepped sideways and motioned Eve toward the doorway. "This way," she said, gesturing.

"Do you always meet your new admissions with a gun?"

"Only the deadly ones. Go on, get in there."

There being no obvious alternatives that didn't run the risk of giving the doctor a gunshot wound to run his hands over, Eve entered the examining room. Hetty trailed behind. The chamber stank of thaumaturgy and despair. It held a sideboard, an examining couch fitted with leather wrist and ankle restraints, and an individual whom she took to be Dr. Clements. He was all but salivating as he watched Tiffy usher her into the room.

"Ah yes, ah yes, new patient, new patient! Who do we have here today?" he asked, flapping and squinting at Eve.

"This is Lady de Montfort, sir," said Tiffy. "Take care, she's a violent one." A feral smile played around her lips as Dr. Clements scrutinized Eve, but by the time he glanced back, Tiffy had Matron's impassive mask firmly in place.

I'll violent *you,* Eve promised silently. This version of Tiffy—a heavily armed nineteenth-century nursing nun—was completely at odds with the flighty spy-or-sorceress Eve had met in the Village, which strongly implied something hinky was going on that involved subterfuge and impersonation. "Over here." Tiffy steered Eve toward the examining couch with her pistol. "Sit."

Eve sat. The doctor zeroed in on her, blinking luminous eyes set in deep sockets beneath luxuriant brows. His pupils fluoresced, emitting the characteristic green glow of decaying *mana.* He was either possessed by eaters or something worse. *Where is Number Seven when I could use some beefcake with a sword?* Eve wondered.

"What brings you here, my dear?" asked the doctor.

"Happenstance," she said, allowing her hand to be taken and raised alarmingly close to the doctor's lips—but he merely sniffed repeatedly, snorted loudly, then muttered something in medical Latin. "My coach was held up by highwaymen last night but I escaped, as you can see. I am in a hurry to be on my way to London, and if you would return my clothes and property I would appreciate—"

"Matron holds our visitors' personal effects," Clements said dismissively. To Hetty: "She arrived last night, yes?"

"I found her on the front step, in the storm, sir." Hetty bobbed nervously. "She was feverish and shivering."

"But she's better this morning? Jolly good. Please lie back, my dear, Lady Elena, was it? I must examine you. Matron, Hester, if you could just fasten—" The doctor picked up a large pair of calipers. "I shall take some measurements," he announced, then began muttering under his breath. "It's all in the skull you know, according to *Herr* Gall, the leading professor of cranioscopy. We practice only the most modern of the sciences here, my Lady! I specialize in galvanism and the hysterical paroxysm, while Dr. Baker is an expert in the homeopathic arts, leeching, and cupping. No archaic humors here! We will get to the bottom of what ails you, to be sure!"

Eve had enough and was about to cut loose, but Number Twelve was expecting it. "Lie *still,*" Tiffy hissed, and pressed her pistol to Eve's temple. "Stop struggling!" Eve subsided. Hetty buckled the restraints with practiced efficiency, then stepped back. Number Twelve remained, but removed the gun from Eve's head.

"I'm not ill!" Eve protested while the doctor pinched one earlobe with a glass clamp, then peered into her ear canal with a tiny lens mounted on a brass speculum, muttering angry incantations in fake medical Latin. "I don't want treatment, I just need my bag and clothes and directions to the nearest coaching inn!"

"Nonsense, my dear, every lady who comes to Saint Hilda's needs our care." Clements finished with her ear and dashed to his desk to make a note in a ledger. "Why else would they be here? Nobody in possession of their wits would bang on our door in the night if they didn't know they needed our help, so it only remains to identify the nature of your malady and determine how to treat it. And to determine how much your guardian is willing to pay for your lodging, of course."

Eve glared at Tiffy, who wrinkled her nose. "Listen to me, you idiot, *I'm not ill*! I'm here because my coach was held up by armed robbers! I'll pay you for your time but I need to be on my way *immediately*. Lives depend on it!"

"Subject is hysterical and vocal," Dr. Clements intoned. He turned to Matron. "If the patient continues to vocalize excessively, you may gag her," he instructed. Tiffy smirked at Eve, who fell silent. She could take a hint.

Despite pinching Eve with calipers and peering into her eyes, ears, nostrils, and mouth, Dr. Clements refrained from committing significantly more intimate outrages against her person. Whenever he paused to turn away and scribble notes, she tried to make eye contact with Tiffy, but Number Twelve refused to play ball. *What the hell is she doing here?* Eve fumed silently.

To distract herself from murderous fantasies Eve reminded herself that Clements hadn't done anything that quite justified murder yet—and she wanted answers from Tiffy, which she was unlikely to obtain from a corpse. Besides, boiling their eyeballs in their sockets would give her another migraine, they'd taken her ward, and she'd still be strapped to a couch in the examining room of a doctor with an unhealthy interest in leeches who had somehow acquired the kind of supernatural infection that left him with eyes that glowed in the dark. *Groveling apologies first, cornfield later,* she decided.

Clements finally sequestered himself with his notes. "No fever and no obvious signs of hysteria or uterine disorders, but there's clearly something wrong with her," he announced, scowling at a piece of paper. "She's unnaturally forward and her vocabulary is fresh—probably a bluestocking who reads too much. Look after her, Matron: she needs plenty of bed rest and fresh air. Put her in the locked ward on the unspiced diet, absolutely no books or periodicals, and I'll see her again on Monday," he told Number Twelve. "Bill it to her account and I'll write to her guardian to solicit payment when she's run up a tab."

▸◂▸◂▸◂

The doctor swept out of the examining room and slammed the door. Tiffy gave Eve a sharp-edged look. "So. Are we going to do this the easy way or the hard way?"

"I always prefer to do things the easy way," Eve told her. It wasn't entirely a lie, and it was *definitely* the reply Eve would have wanted to hear had their positions been reversed. "What is this place, and what are you doing here?" Saint Hilda's appeared to be a locked-ward asylum with more quacks than a duck farm, but Eve thought it unwise to jump to conclusions prematurely. Tiffy's presence and the doctor's infestation suggested a connection to the Invisible College people. She assessed Tiffy's nunlike habit, noticing disturbing details: dark stains that were not ink on the fingertips of her gloves, a well-polished rosary with beads like toddler finger bones.

"Fetch the bath chair," Tiffy told Hetty, who hurried away. She returned her attention to Eve. "Don't bother trying to escape, you won't get far. Fair warning, we run a tight ship at Saint Hilda's." Hetty returned with a wheeled wicker chair. They shackled Eve's wrists and ankles together, released her from the examining couch, and lifted her into the chair. Hetty was surprisingly strong despite her diminutive height. "Bring her," Tiffy commanded.

They rolled Eve along a corridor that brought them into a wing that seemed to have been built by an architect with cathedral envy: it was replete with arched windows, vaulted roofs, and devotional niches occupied by sculptures of figures lasciviously depicted in the death agonies of martyrdom. Then they arrived at a hall with locked doors on either side, patrolled by women built like nuns from an order who expressed their devotion through powerlifting. They genuflected at Tiffy as she passed; she responded each time with a terse "sister," like a general acknowledging her troops.

"What is—" Eve began, but Tiffy shushed her vehemently, making a curious gesture with her left hand. Eve lost the inclination to fuss, along with her voice. They came to a locked door that opened for Number Twelve's key ring, revealing an austere office.

Eve waited placidly while Hetty padlocked her ankle chain to a ring on the floor. *Why am I letting this happen?* she wondered. *I should be outraged.* But it all felt very distant. *My ward is missing,* she remembered, but following the train of thought was like trying to swim through congealed oatmeal. *A geas,* she finally realized. Without her magical defenses Eve was vulnerable to manipulation. Perhaps there were reinforcing wards scribed inside the manacles—

"Tell me how you escaped from the Village," said Tiffy, placing her pistol beside the writing slope on the table. She took her seat behind it. "Start from the moment you left the ballroom, if you please."

"I—" Eve's tongue began to move without her conscious volition. It was most vexing, like the loss of control that came over one when driving a car across black ice, as the wheels began to slide—a stab of déjà vu reminded her of the Prime Minister's warning, and Number Two's interrogation. *I can't let this happen again.* And maybe her resistance was strengthened by practice, or perhaps Number Twelve's geas was simply weaker, but Eve managed to bite her tongue and pause the flow, then take back control. "I don't think so."

"Oh, really!" Tiffy glared at her. "You're *not* getting out of here until you talk, you know. Even to go back to the Village."

"What do you *want*?"

"We want information!" Tiffy's glare intensified.

"Whose side are you on?"

"That would be telling. Give me *information*."

Eve dug her heels in. "You won't get it!"

"By hook or by crook, we will. Did you think you could simply barge in and take the Sisterhood from me?" Tiffy demanded.

What Sisterhood? Eve blinked rapidly. The one the PM had warned her about, or something else? Hadn't Tiffy mentioned a Sisterhood, back in the library? Her forehead throbbed and her shoulder blades itched, but the sense of being swaddled in cotton wool was receding. And now she could feel her wrists and ankles, hot ripples of magic crawling across her skin where it was in contact with the iron cuffs. "Get these things off me, stop trying to force me, and I'll consider telling you," she said. "Otherwise, you get nothing." Then she set her jaw.

Tiffy glared at her in silence for a while. "Let's try again. You escaped from the Village," Tiffy said. She looked at Eve askance. "How?" Eve looked right back at her and held her tongue. "All right, then. You'll talk eventually. You'll have to if you want to leave." Tiffy shrugged and touched her rosary. Of an instant, the sense of magical compulsion faded. Eve was still fettered to the floor, but now the fetters were just dull lumps of iron. "Number Two was *most* irate when you and the baron disappeared. Imagine my surprise when you turned up on my doorstep." She leaned forward. "Do you know where the baron and the boy François are? Did Number One send you? Do you even know what's happening?"

Eve was secretly pleased to see that Tiffy was dialing back the confrontational stance. Or perhaps she'd realized she could catch more flies with honey than with vinegar. "Saint Hilda's Home for Hopeless and Hysterical Harridans? Something like that. Near Grantham? I don't know precisely—my coach was on its way to Peterborough when we were ambushed."

"Of course it was," Theophania said flatly. "Ambushed. You expect me to believe that—like something out of a penny shocker?"

"You've got my clothing and my personal effects. How much blood was I wearing when I arrived?"

"Do I look like a laundry maid?" One eyebrow arched: razor-thin lips narrowed into near invisibility. It was disquietingly like being confronted by her own historical counterpart—a preincarnation, perhaps. "You really aren't making this easy on yourself, are you. Who are you *really* working for—Metternich? The Invisible College? Fouché? Rosicrucians or Illuminati?"

"I—" Eve's tongue stuck to the roof of her mouth: she coughed horribly. "*Can't* tell you. Number Two's doing."

Theophania *humphed* irritably. "He put you under a geas that prevents you from speaking? Deny it if you can."

Eve shrugged. It was true.

"Well, of all the—bah!" Tiffy's scowl intensified, bespeaking immense frustration. "Why did he *do* that?"

"I think he may have thought I was a French spy? Or a messenger with secret orders for one of the other inmates? I'm not sure, he didn't confide in me." Eve poked the limits of Number Two's compulsion. It was like using her tongue to explore the socket left behind by a pulled tooth. "I'm fairly certain I'm not what he—or you—imagine me to be."

Tiffy's expression suddenly sharpened into focused intensity. "Then what *can* you tell me? To pay for your rescue, if rescue is really what you want: the asylum must pay its bills, after all."

"I—" Eve stopped. "A moment please? I'm not allowed to tell you about myself." *And never mind Number Two's geas: what about the PM's warning? Could I create a temporal paradox that'd stop me returning?* (Assuming she was really in the past, rather than trapped in a mad dream of history: she wasn't sure. But it wouldn't do to take unnecessary risks. . . .) "I was traveling by coach with the baron and his ward. We met up in

Liverpool and agreed to pretend to be a family. But when we were waylaid, the robbers hauled everyone out of the coach. One of them tried to drag me into the bushes, but I escaped. I left him in no condition to follow me or raise the alarm: I don't know what happened to everyone else after that."

"I see." Number Twelve looked thoughtful. "Then how much can you tell me about the baron? Consider it a trade."

"It's not so much what I know about the baron as about his, ah, *son*." Eve had been assembling the jigsaw puzzle during the long, hard miles in the coach, and while she didn't have the full picture she had several very illuminating pieces and most of the frame. She waited a few seconds. "What's it worth to you?"

Number Twelve shrugged, then met Eve's gaze with a clear-eyed stare of her own. Eve shuddered: it *was* like seeing herself in the mirror, if the mirror looked back six months in time and showed the more ruthless, hard-edged Eve who had been stealthily compelled to follow Rupert's orders mindlessly.

"It could buy you a ticket on the first stage to London next week. And the return of your possessions, and a clean dress. But you'll need to tell me everything, and then I'll have to make enquiries to confirm your story, and it's nearly the High Sabbath so you'll have to enjoy the Sisterhood's hospitality for a few days more before I can release you safely."

"High Sabbath? Sisterhood?"

"All in good time." Number Twelve scribbled a spiky cursive note on her writing slope. "Tell me all about the boy, then I'll make up my mind."

▸◂▸◂▸◂

Eve wasn't proud. She'd seen the Muscular Marys patrolling the locked ward, she'd tested the strength of Number Twelve's ward, and while she was confident she could slip the cold iron fetters in a trice and get the drop on Tiffy, she was loath to cut loose without a plan. Nor had Eve sworn undying loyalty to the baron and his charge: theirs was purely a temporary alliance.

"François is the middle name of the Emperor Bonaparte—ex-emperor," she explained. "The boy looks to be twelve, but claims to be only six years old, which is odd, but would put his conception in 1809." Tiffy twitched at the indelicacy, but let it pass unremarked. "My suspicion is that not only is the baron not François's father, but François doesn't even have a father in the normal sense of the word: he's a graft created from the emperor's stolen tissues and incubated. . . ." She stopped.

"Please, pray continue," Tiffy said coolly. "You already alluded to the procreative act: this is no time to get missish with me."

"I'm not," Eve replied. Tiffy gave her a look that was hard to interpret. Disgust, perhaps? Or *you're not fooling anyone*. It was ambiguous.

"What makes you think the boy is a, a bud from the emperor's branch?"

"Give me a moment." Eve gathered her thoughts. How to explain cloning, a century and a half before its invention? "The emperor's marital problems are well known. And a German natural philosopher obsessed with galvanism, bringing life to dead matter, and possibly to transferring the vital essence, might well have offered the perfect solution . . . if the Empress Joséphine could not give him an heir, why not try to create an heir by other means? The perfect heir at that: an exact copy of his own person, who could be raised as a prince and who would naturally have the genius for conquest of his father. But Von Franckenstein either took fright at his prospects for survival, or took flight in the direction of a better paymaster—or perhaps he simply wished to pursue even more arcane research. The boy is very precocious, though. When did the baron arrive in the village?"

Tiffy blinked slowly. "If I were to tell you . . . ," she began, then paused.

"Yes, yes, you'd have to kill me," Eve said irritably. "Don't bother, the answer isn't important. Just saying, the baron seemed very interested in taking ship for Asunción. Perhaps he seeks to curry favor with *El Supremo,* by bringing him a young and malleable military genius to conquer South America on his behalf? Or he intends to escape some other threat closer to home? The baron mentioned babes, an army of Napoleons that would be ready to harvest in another decade. I can quite imagine the War Office taking a keen interest back when Boney was setting Portugal ablaze—can't you?" Tiffy's poker face might as well have been a porcelain mask, but she couldn't quite hide a catch in her breath. It was the sort of tell that tempted Eve to keep digging, but: manacles, guns, an elite squad of Nurse Ratcheds lurking in the corridor. *So let's maybe not,* she thought. "What's the Sisterhood you mentioned? Something about the High Sabbath?" She reached for scandal, 1816-style: "Are you by any chance *nonconformists?*"

"Nonconformists?" Tiffy's ceramic cheek finally twitched. "You *could* say that—we are sworn not to marry the first rake who comes along and gets one over on our families, so there's that! As I'm sure you've noticed, the world is unkind to women of an independent mind. So our foremothers established the Silver Sisterhood. We began by swearing an oath of loyalty to one another, not to God, and we celebrate our own calendar, to remind ourselves we sought sanctuary through piety, prayer, and good works. A little like the Beguines, but without the popery and Satanism. Only these days we have a better faith to follow."

She stood up abruptly. "Your bed is in room twenty-three, just down the corridor. I told Hetty to lay out a habit for you. We break our fast at six, luncheon is at noon, and dinner is served in the refectory at five. If your intelligence is confirmed, I will arrange for Dr. Clements to discharge you next week: if you've been lying, it will be the worse for you." She opened the door. Eve silently raised her wrists. Tiffy smirked. "I'm sure you can let yourself out whenever you're ready! Be seeing you."

Who just mugged who? Eve wondered as she fumbled at the crude padlocks with her mind's fingers. Tiffy was clearly playing at least three different deep games: she had a mind like one of those ancient screen savers that generated a mess of twisty 3D plumbing with multiple sets of pipes, none of them intersecting. Making Eve escape from her shackles was itself a form of interrogation. Eventually—but not as soon as she might have—Eve freed herself and stood. Then she opened the door and set out to explore.

▸◂▸◂▸◂

After Sally Gunderson's people pronounced the house safe and Wendy hared off to brief her boss, Imp ghosted through it like an unquiet spirit. Game Boy pronounced himself freaked out, grabbed his day pack and portable console, and bailed. Doc Depression was still busy with his parents and Del was doing some sort of training course with HiveCo Security, so Imp was on his own in a house with an open gate to the dream roads on the top floor.

"Fuck this shit," Imp complained, and propped the broken door up in front of the gaping passageway. It didn't help much—a baby squirrel could knock it out of its frame—but Imp had other ideas. So he went downstairs to a bedroom on the first floor and began searching.

Unlike his elder sister, Imp had never had much of an interest in ritual magic: his natural talent for persuasion was so much stronger than Eve's telekinesis and pyrokinesis that he neglected the basics, and he studied theater and cinematography rather than accounting or demonology.

But Imp was not completely useless at sorcery, and since his sister had reestablished contact some months ago he'd been catching up on his reading. Or at least on the filing. He'd slowly removed the contents of the storage locker containing his father's books and artifacts, brought them here, and had been sporadically engaged in an attempt to make sense of his father's not-entirely-successful magical career.

Magecraft ran in the Starkey bloodline (as did a far more sinister generational curse), and although his father had not been notably successful, that was largely attributable to the majority of his career coinciding with the sorcerous drought that persisted through much of the twentieth century.

The bedroom was, frankly, a mess. Imp had decided some months ago that he wanted to clear it, redecorate, and turn it into his own love nest: but he'd hardly made a start. He was still sleeping downstairs most of the time, and the bedroom furnishings consisted of a battered futon, an electric fan heater, and a folding chair. He'd needed to get under the floorboards to plug in—

Record scratch.

—a power brick for the Wi-Fi repeater screwed to the doorframe, so at least he had internet on this floor, but the nearest thing he had to an office desk was a gradually collapsing stack of boxes, one of which was full of spell books, and to get at it he had to partially dismantle his entire work space.

The spell books of a working part-time sorcerer and full-time accountant (as Clive Starkey had been: he had to support his family somehow) were not a cyclopedia with an alphabetized list of spells indexed by keyword and purpose. They were a series of journals documenting experiments, outcomes, and conclusions, much like laboratory notebooks: lines of research skipped between volumes with page references pointing forward and back, tables of contents frequently appeared upside down in the tiniest of handwriting on the end papers with continuation sheets taped inside, sometimes in faded Biro ink, sometimes in human blood, and very occasionally in ink enchanted so that it was unrecognizable as writing, except to those of the Starkey lineage.

"Hey, spell book, show me how to ward doors against intruders," Imp muttered irritably, cracking open the spine of the last notebook at a random page and revolving three times widdershins with his eyes tightly shut. On the last spin he rapped his right ankle on the side of the doorframe just above the skirting board, sending a bright stab of pain up his leg: he swore and toppled over, coming to a barely controlled landing on the mattress. "*Ow,* shit."

He sat up and glared at the doorframe. "You'll get yours," he warned the inanimate lump of lumber: "I'm going to redecorate in here and *then* you'll be sorry." The room needed carpet, wallpaper, curtains . . . all jobs Imp had been shirking until now. But first, he picked up the spell book.

"Show me . . . ah." A blank page, with a neatly scribed note on the very bottom line: "see book five, page twenty-two, bottom para." "Well, blow me." Imp rummaged around until he found the relevant notebook, turned to page twenty-two, and read: details in "book seven, page fifty-five, top para." He swore some more, and continued the treasure hunt through a linked list of sorcerous cookbooks until finally he fetched up at another empty page in the middle of nowhere—Dad had been a terrible one for leaving the last third of his books empty, as if he was hoarding space for footnotes—bearing just one instruction: "tidy up your bedroom and everything will become clear."

"You are shitting me," Imp growled, but then he picked up the book and slid it under his grubby pillow. There was, as it happened, a divinatory ritual he'd memorized when he was fourteen and first getting used to the family trade, and Evie (as she had then been) had been sixteen and gangly and going through a phase of pranking him. Oneiromancy, the study of dreams, ran in their blood. And Imp knew as well as any of them how to use a directed dream to get to the truth of a proposition. In this case: "I need confirmation. If I tidy up my bedroom, will it help me find Eve?" he said aloud.

It sounded silly on the face of it—she was missing in the dream roads, not hiding under the mattress. But if you followed a divination process and it gave you a seemingly nonsensical answer, as often as not the problem existed between spell book and sandals: you were more likely to be missing the point than the point was to be missing you.

So Imp unfolded the futon, lay down with his head on the pillow, gathered his wits, and began to chant a rhyme that would help him focus on the object of his attention. And presently, when he drifted off into a hypnogogic fugue, he began to dream.

THE SILVER SISTERHOOD

Four hours later Eve had succeeded in baffling and annoying herself—but was no closer to London than she had been the day before.

She'd gone to her room and dressed in the outfit provided—it was similar to a nun's habit, but lacked the religious symbols and funky headgear—then went exploring. She expected to be challenged at some point but nobody had bothered. It rapidly became clear why. Tiffy had brought her to an unlocked residential wing, but whenever she found a door or staircase that promised to take her to another part of the asylum, she blanked and came to an indeterminate time later, facing away from it with a sense of dread that deterred repeated attempts. Saint Hilda's was protected by a really powerful ward that she couldn't detect, or it existed in a closed manifold of dream roads that looped back on themselves with no obvious exit—much like the top floor of the Starkey house in Kensington. Indeed, it felt as if she'd been snatched from a bad dream of 1816 by a passing Regency gothic, an entirely different genre of claustrophobic pre-Victorian nightmare. Dream roads didn't often lead into the literal past. They could lead you into an exaggerated burlesque of history rather than the real thing, and sometimes the archetypes were both obvious and brutal—a runaway woman waylaid and incarcerated in a gothic mansion or lunatic asylum was an absolute classic. Number Twelve had her on a short leash, and escape would not be easy.

There were twenty-four beds in this wing, in single-occupancy rooms as sparsely furnished as cells save for the lack of locks on the doors. There was a refectory and a kitchen, a chapel with disturbingly familiar trappings—they reminded her of Rupert's cult churches in her own time—and a communal bathroom. There was cold water from a hand pump; the sanitary arrangements could best be described as rudimentary.

When a bell rang, one of the sisters or inmates took her elbow and practically dragged her to the refectory. Here they were served an underspiced stew with overcooked root vegetables and chunks of undifferentiated mystery meat—but only after reciting interminable prayers from the same psalter used by the Church of the Mute Poet. Eve recognized the liturgy with a sinking heart: *Rupert's been here,* she realized. After they said grace Eve tried to ask her tablemates about the cooking arrangements, but her social overtures were met with librarian-grade shushing and grim expressions. One of the sisters stalked to a lectern at the front, opened a book, and began to read aloud a sermon that slithered through her prefrontal cortex like a lobotomy pick and left her head ringing. *Make a ward,* she told herself desperately, *make a ward and hang on to it for grim death.* But she hadn't seen any writing implements at table and there was no telling what buried commands the sermon was intended to reinforce and it all felt like far too much hard work, so she gave up.

After lunch, her neighbor led her to the kitchen, where she washed and dried bowls and cooking pots for an endless hour. Time blurred, until she found herself out in the corridor with prune-wrinkled fingertips and damp sleeves, listless and depressed. So she went to the sewing room where she'd seen some sisters patching and darning. She took a stool and sat by a basket to make herself useful: it seemed like the least she could do to repay her keep. *Make a ward,* a tiny copy of her screamed through the bars of the padded cell in her head. *Steal a needle and kerchief, write it in blood!* But there were stockings to be darned and robes to be patched, and she needed to make herself useful. So she darned in silence as the afternoon hours blurred together, until it felt as if weeks had passed in minutes.

The silence—both the lack of conversation, and the stilling of the warning voice in her head—was soothing, if depressing. Eve embraced it uncritically. They weren't a silent order, Eve understood, but stilled their tongues to honor their god—

Record scratch.

Somewhere inside her head the inmate struggled in her straitjacket, nose bleeding from sheer rage. Her fingertips throbbed from the pinpricks of unaccustomed needlework. There hadn't been a thimble in Eve's sewing basket and she hadn't felt like breaking the silence to ask for one. Now her index finger was red and sore, throbbing but not yet forming a callus. Each throb felt like an echo of freedom, and eventually Eve realized why: the blood of a practitioner was a potent source of *mana,* and Eve, as a sorcerer of the Starkey lineage, was not weak. The pricking of her fingers was bound to bring her back to herself sooner or later—

She blinked and shook her head as she put one last darned sock back in the basket. Almost reflexively she stuck a pin through the belt of her habit, concealing the action with her hand so that it looked as if she was pulling the belt tighter. She shoved a scrap of patching cloth up her sleeve, then she rose and headed back to her cell. She still had work to do.

Inside the padded cell of her skull her imprisoned volition mouthed silent defiance: the straitjacket straps were fraying, the guard lulled asleep in the hall outside. Still Eve struggled against the iron and canvas restraints of the asylum's binding wards. The fetters of the Invisible College were far more obvious here than back in the Village. Clearly the two institutions served different purposes, possibly different masters, but they were of essentially similar function. (Or possibly they served different mistresses, if the asylum was indeed run by the Sisterhood. Eve's working hypothesis was that Tiffy the Tormentor was both Sister Theophania and Number Twelve, depending which institution she was embedded in at the time. How and why she moved between them—seemingly freely—was a most vexatious question.)

Eve laid her precious scrap of patching cloth across her knee and, biting her lip, stabbed the ball of her left thumb with the stolen needle. Blood beaded and she painstakingly teased it onto the scrap, drawing a design similar to the one she'd made for Flora back in the Village. *I'm not escaping,* she silently chanted. *I'm not resisting:* and it was true. The field-expedient ward would work for anyone she gave it to. *Stab,* and another arc and curve inked itself in carmine that faded to rusty brown as it dried; *stab,* and an Elder Sign took shape. By the time she finished her thumb was burning, she'd worked right through suppertime, and she was exhausted and hungry, but she had created a replacement ward and sealed it with the blood of a sorcerer. Taking pains not to think too hard, she slid the scrap around the back of her neck, so that it was hidden by her hair covering.

▸◂▸◂▸◂

Eve went to bed, deferring further plans until the morrow. There was absolutely no point trying to escape while penniless and wearing the uniform of an asylum inmate. She slept right through until morning, when Hetty banged on cell doors up and down the corridor to announce breakfast. Then she dressed and filed downstairs with the other inmates—whose names, she realized, ashamed, she hadn't even attempted to learn. (Was it the ward around the asylum?) But things seemed to be different today, with a barely suppressed sense of expectation. Residents were whispering to their neighbors when they thought themselves unseen by the sisters or Matron.

"What's happening?" Eve quietly asked the woman on the bench next to her.

"Sabbath's tonight." Her neighbor was a plumpish woman in her thirties. A row of pockmarks marred one cheek but her eyes were livelier than they had been the day before. "And it's a *High* Sabbath!"

Eve blinked. "I have questions," she murmured.

"Join me in the kitchen after grace. What may I call you?"

"Call me Evelyn. And you are?"

"Edwina—"

"*Shush.*" They had attracted the attention of one of the sisters. Eve bided her time.

Washing up went faster without mind control, and was less tedious with a neighbor who was willing to answer her questions in return for tidbits of gossip (which Eve possessed more of than she'd realized). Saint Hilda's was indeed an asylum, a country house where the upper echelons of the English aristocracy warehoused their unwanted and inconvenient women. The asylum held surplus daughters, wives who kicked up a fuss about their husbands' mistresses, and anyone who could be labeled shrewish or wicked or a bluestocking and thereby diagnosed as hysterical (a peculiarly female form of insanity that orthodox medical opinion blamed on a wandering uterus). Saint Hilda's had been founded twenty-five years ago. Today it was run by Drs. Clements and Baker, assisted by nurses drawn from a lay order called the Silver Sisterhood. In practice, the Sisterhood had infiltrated the asylum almost from the beginning, and the doctors were figureheads. The Sisterhood had their own agenda, and it involved following certain esoteric rites that were shockingly familiar to Eve. "Do they recite the Hymn to the Black Sun before or after the Suffering of the Tongueless?"

"Before! But then there's the—"

"Reading from the Book of the Flowery Penumbra?" Eve nodded, even as her heart sank. "*Sister,*" she said, and tried to reproduce the genuflection she'd seen the cultists use in London, two centuries from now, in a church established by Rupert to harvest souls and animate nightmares to serve his alien god. Edwina mirrored her gesture, and with a dawning sense of horror Eve realized why Tiffy seemed so familiar: Rupert *definitely* had a thing for skinny blond ice queens. Tiffy was, at least superficially, of a kind with the priestess in Chickentown, or (a rueful cringe of recognition) herself.

"I knew you were one of us!" Edwina enthused. "Sister, you were *destined* to come here."

"The Silver Sisterhood serves the Prince of Poetry and Song?" Eve sought confirmation.

"He who is Ppilimtec, the Mute Poet. Or Saint David, as we name him in the presence of infidels. I mean, Christians." Edwina stacked another bowl on the wooden drying rack. "You can never be too careful," she confided. "There have been no witchfinders in Lincolnshire for over a century, but Sister Garcia has the most horrifying stories from Andalusia! Tales of the Inquisition to curdle your blood."

Eve nodded along agreeably as Edwina regurgitated ghastly accounts of martyrdoms carried out by the *Inquisición Española,* although she gathered they predated the Bonapartist ascendancy. The Inquisition had maintained a secretive arm dedicated solely to the suppression of mystery cults like the Church of the Mute Poet. Which just happened to be the cult of which Rupert had been a bishop—possibly the supreme bishop—in the British Isles during the twenty-first century.

While she sat in the sewing room inexpertly fixing a threadbare hem, Eve considered the big picture. The activities of the sisterhood echoed those of the cultists she'd uncovered inside FlavrsMart, a supermarket chain in her own time. One of Rupert's more alarming priestesses had been tormenting the workforce in order to harvest the *mana* released by souls in a state of existential despair. The unhappiness of women unjustly imprisoned in an inescapable asylum was a similar power source for Rupert's magic. As had happened in her own time, he'd enlisted the true believers into his cult, turning them into prison guards in a bizarre version of the Stanford prison experiment. He'd done the same on Skaro, only using a different group as his minions. It was a consistent methodology, as consistent as his taste in handmaidens.

But still: *twenty-five years?* "How long has the Sisterhood been headquartered in this—" She paused, unwilling to risk any words that hinted of the wrong religion. "—establishment?"

"I can't really say, to be sure, but Sister Theophania is the fifth name inscribed on the roll of honor of Eldest Sisters, on the chapel wall? She came here before I did—" And Edwina was off on another anecdote, something about Number Twelve's coming and going at all hours and seasons. Eve screened her out, thinking furiously.

If Rupert had indeed started the congregation here a quarter of a century ago, then he must have arrived in the early 1790s. Which would explain . . . quite a lot, actually: why the Village—a blatant rip-off of Portmeirion, which had been built in the 1920s—was so well established, why the version of Rupert who had ambushed her with his unwelcome return to the twenty-first century was so decayed, and more. How he had survived this long if the dream fistula was kept going by dissolving his soul.

Obviously his search for the missing manuscript of the *Necronomicon* had gone badly during the years of Tricolour and guillotine, as Napoleonic Sturm und Drang reverberated from the warm waters of the Mediterranean to the icy roads from Moscow. As an Englishman he lacked the freedom to move at will on the Continent without being arrested as a spy. But Rupert was never one to place all his money on a single bet. He had manifestly succeeded at other projects—including the construction of a magical power base in England, with links to the government bureaucracy for suppressing and controlling sorcery on behalf of the Crown—what had the PM called it?

The Invisible College. Yes: a Rupert with tentacles spreading through the mahogany-paneled corridors of Whitehall was not someone to trifle with lightly.

So. Ten or twenty years passed before he left and returned to 2017. *He came back for revenge,* she realized, or *to collect something he needed.* The date might not be an accident: perhaps he saw himself as an Edmond Dantès, unjustly imprisoned in an oneiromantic Château d'If. It'd certainly fulfill the mythic requirements of the dream roads. After his escape he returned for revenge, but then dived down-time, not all the way back to 1790, or even to the end of his last stay. *Maybe it was something in his office. In the safe. But what?* Abbé Faria's fortune in treasure? However she racked her brain she couldn't recall him taking anything magical: just money, gemstones—another form of money—and a pistol. Whatever business he'd had in 2017, he hadn't conducted it in front of her.

"When does the Sabbath service begin?" Eve asked as the well of Edwina's gossip finally began to run dry. "I assume it's tonight? All day tomorrow? What will I be expected to do?"

"Oh!" Edwina shook herself, then laid her darning aside. "Is it that late already? Eldest Sister—Matron—will want to prepare you. It's a great honor to be inducted into the order on a High Sabbath," she blurted admiringly. "You should be so excited about the midnight feast of the body and the blood of the lamb undying, where you will swear your vows as a Bride of Saint Ppilimtec!"

Eve tried to turn her shudder into a fervently prayerful wobble. She'd seen the rites of the Mute Poet, and wanted nothing to do with it: she loathed such cults with a fiery passion. "I haven't been here long enough, surely, to be taking vows?"

"Don't worry about that, the Mute Poet won't keep you waiting like the Catholic orders! He is eager to increase our numbers, to carry out his will and spread his word. We are a cloistered order for the most part—it is well suited to the outward guise of an asylum—but Eldest Sister and the other externs go into the world to wreak his magic upon it. If you are as gifted as rumor says, I'm sure you'll be elevated very quickly!"

Edwina expounded at length about the duties of a Bride of Saint Ppilimtec. They seemed to be a knockoff of one of the Benedictine traditions: a dismal trifecta of poverty, obedience, and chastity (with occasional human sacrifice and demon-summoning thrown in for variety). However her description of the ritual was so flowery and full of euphemisms that Eve might have completely misunderstood what Edwina was talking about had she not already encountered Rupert's coreligionists. None of Edwina's anecdotes gave Eve the warm fuzzies. Her jury-rigged ward was all very well, but the rites of the Mute Poet were blood-fueled and powerful, designed to corrupt the minds of the new members. Few things were more upsetting to Eve than loss of control, and she resolved to make her escape before the midnight Sabbath.

"So it's tonight, is it?" Eve asked, trying to sound convincingly intrigued, if not enthusiastic. "I should like to speak to Eldest Sister first—do you think she'll be in the Matron's office?"

"I should think so!" Edwina nodded cheerfully. "If you need to visit her in the doctor's wing just think of Matron and put your best foot forward."

Eve tried not to gape. When she'd tried to leave the locked ward, all paths had led her back to her starting point: but she'd been thinking about escape, hadn't she? If the dream roads responded to intent, perhaps that had been her mistake all along—setting her mind on a forbidden goal rather than a permitted one. "I shall try to do that," Eve managed, then stood and stretched.

"Be seeing you!" Edwina winked as Eve left the sewing room and went in resolute search of Number Twelve.

▸◂▸◂▸◂

Number Seven rode through the rain-soaked woods for hours before he finally spotted a pair of gateposts. The silvery tingle of a ley line underfoot set his horse to shying, and it took him a while to settle the beast. He was certain Lady de Montfort had come this way—his tracking spell was certain—but how long ago was debatable. Hours, certainly: the moon had set and it was nearly full dark.

"Well, well, well," he muttered, stifling a yawn. It came as no surprise that the prickling of his fingers led to the front door of Saint Hilda's, although it complicated matters somewhat. The Silver Sisterhood took a dim view of untamed males encroaching on their retreat. Number One's handmaidens had brutally enslaved their former tormentors when they took over, and while he held no brief for Drs. Baker and Clements (or Corrupt and Crankish, as he thought of them), he made it a personal rule to never spend a night under their roof. Too much risk of not waking up in his right mind the next morning. Likely Tiffy the Treacherous had her own plans for Number Six, plans that would not redound to the benefit of George, sixth Earl of Marsden and agent at large of the Invisible College. Really, it would be prudent to wait until morning then present himself at first light, to execute the warrant he carried as a matter of course. But George wasn't known for his timorous nature.

"Faint heart never won fair maiden," he told himself, then hammered on the front door. He meant it semi-ironically—Number Six's temperament tilted more toward Medusa than maiden—but she was certainly fair. And, he thought, almost certainly in need of rescue if she'd arrived here on the eve of the High Sabbath. A minute passed before George pounded on the door again. "Open up!" he called, "by order of the Crown!"

Shuffling and heavy breathing approached, then the latch rattled and the door creaked open. "Who comes hither?" croaked the elderly butler, blinking shortsightedly up at him.

"You know perfectly well who I am, John. Have my horse

stabled then bid Miss Ffoulkes-Ward meet me in the pantry in ten minutes." He glowered at the butler as he drew himself up. "Do *not* force me to share my disappointment with the doctors, you know it won't end well."

John whimpered then winced as his old bones rewarded him for his brisk cringing. "At once, sir! If you shall just make yourself at home I'll have the maids see to things." He lurched off into the gloomy depths of the hallway. George tossed his reins to a footman who materialized out of the twilight, then squelched his way to the room adjacent to the kitchen. It backed onto the hearth, and was always warm. He collapsed heavily into an armchair and slid his boots off, but then his eyelids ambushed him by sliding closed without warning.

George awakened in a bed with daylight streaming in through an unshuttered window. Outside the sash, a gaggle of geese were squabbling angrily about something—food, or encroaching hens, or maybe a dog—and someone was chopping firewood, just erratically enough to set his teeth on edge. The sun was descending—he'd slept past noon.

Damn it, he thought, *should have checked the rug for wards.* Or maybe not: he'd been just about tired enough. . . .

He threw back the bedding and stretched, then rolled to his feet. Whoever had brought him here had left him in his smalls, but his breeches, neckcloth, and waistcoat were neatly folded on the dresser. It was the third guest room in the main wing, he realized. The doctors were clearly maintaining it for visitors, perhaps relatives of the inmates. The doctors who ran the institution lived in this part of the house, rather than in the cloister with the sisters. *Damnable interlopers.* He eased his feet into his boots, then slipped downstairs in search of food and answers.

Unfortunately he didn't get them. Dr. Clements had ridden off to the nearest village on some errand to the curate—this was not unusual, although the doctor's horse frequently brought him back blind drunk, often in custody of a dead pheasant or two—and Dr. Baker was off to London on business. George demanded that the butler carry a message to Lady Ffoulkes-Ward, and the man groveled and apologized that there was a witches' sabbath tomorrow night, the Matron was undergoing some sort of purification rite, and seeing a male visitor was simply not going to happen today. Or, probably, tomorrow.

George ground his teeth and growled, but managed to bully the fellow into letting slip that an unaccompanied young lady *had* presented herself on the doorstep in some distress, and had been admitted. *Number Six,* George inferred, and if she'd been admitted as a patient she certainly wasn't going to get out on her own.

It was a bit late in the day for an escapade, so George decided to spend the day laying the groundwork for a proper extraction on the morrow. First he scoured the grounds around the hall. His tracking ward confirmed that Number Six hadn't departed, which was well and good. Next he checked with the stable that his horse was well looked after, then he retreated to the library before dinner. He ate alone, for Drs. Clements and Baker still hadn't returned. Finally, he retired early. He was still tired from his lengthy journey, and he needed to be fresh and sharp if he was going up against Number Twelve.

The next morning George rose in a timely manner and went downstairs to break his fast in the kitchen. "Are the doctors home?" he asked the butler the instant he found him.

"I'm sure I don't know, sir," the fellow quavered.

"Well, then." George smiled without humor. "You said Matron was not taking visitors *yesterday*. But today is a new morning, and I am here on business. Perhaps you can tell her I will see her in the drawing room in half an hour? No more delays, otherwise Number Two will be *most* displeased."

"Numb"—*squeak*—"Two, sir?" John seemed close to fainting.

"Delays have consequences, and while a day of rest was not unwelcome"—after riding most of three hundred miles in eight days, Number Seven spoke with considerable sincerity—"I am engaged on a mission." He clapped his hands. "Make haste!"

The butler vanished at a rapid (if creaky) shuffle, and George got down to business.

Perhaps it was uncharitable to anticipate treachery from Tiffy—even though it was her middle name—but his first act was to go to the drawing room, raise the Persian rug, and scribe a binding circle on the floor under it. That should hold Number Twelve for a while when she came to meet him. Next he felt along the windowless, doorless wall that separated the blue room from the morning room next door until he found a discreetly hinged panel, which he opened. The panel let him inside a servants' corridor that a more uncharitable soul might have described as a secret passage. George was familiar with the hidden shortcuts in the asylum from his infancy: it had been his family's country seat and part of his entailed estate, before a series of unfortunate financial decisions had compelled his father to rent it to Number One during the Jacobin Reign of Terror. Number One had in turn sublet it to the doctors, at which point it became the Invisible College's problem. And thereby altogether infuriatingly complicated.

In addition to the mission Number Two had given him, George had questions he sought answers to. Firstly: *If I was Tiffy, how would I put Number Six to use?* And secondly: *What has Number Twelve learned about Number Six that Number Two failed to discover in the Village?* Six was clearly a powerful sorcerer, albeit isolated and bereft of allies; Twelve, being ambitious, would seek leverage. But the Invisible College had powerful sorcerers by the dozen, and so did the Village. Eve was nothing special. Or was she? The answers—George came to a narrow staircase, and added a third question: *Why is it always servants' staircases with Number Six?*—would probably be found in the Sisterhood's files. And those were stored under lock and key in the doctors' suite, where inmates and visitors could not venture without an escort.

The great house was laid out in three wings. The main wing had once held the function spaces and family rooms (with servants' quarters and a nursery upstairs). These were now the doctors' abode, the examination and treatment rooms, and the guest quarters. The east wing had been turned into cells and facilities for the inmates, its entrances and exits magically turned back on themselves by Number One, in an alarming demonstration of power. The west wing was, if anything, even worse: not that George knew exactly what was going on behind those shuttered windows where the Sisterhood lived, but just walking past them made his skin crawl. He might be the manorial lord of this estate according to the title deeds, but his father had sacrificed his rights in settlement of his gambling debts. George had other properties, but the loss of his childhood home bit deep.

George pulled his cloak tight about his shoulders as he swept up the stairs, then twitched irritably. A minor exercise of willpower fed *mana* into a design embroidered in the lining of the garment, shedding residual road grime and mud in a thin spray that landed everywhere except back on his person. *Better.* Now clean, the garment was a better conductor for magical energy. Another formula invoked a willful misdirection, not rendering him invisible but redirecting the gaze of anyone who pointed their eyes in his direction. Just in time, for he was now at the top of the staircase.

He stepped out into the empty hallway connecting the doctors' offices and treatment rooms on the first floor. By now Number Twelve would surely have been called away to the blue room, where George's trap would hold her while he retrieved Number Six, which meant—

"*Oof!*"

I need to find Matron, Eve silently repeated as she marched to the end of the corridor, gripped the door handle, and pulled. *I am not trying to escape.* It was entirely true, but she still shuddered as the wards that guarded the wing dragged ghostly filaments of scrutiny through the upper layers of her mind, seeking mendacity.

It was trivially obvious that merely wanting out must be permissible, otherwise there'd be no way to drag any of the inmates in front of the doctors in their examining rooms: the knotted space behind the door would turn them back. The invisible gatekeeper, the jailer in the very short ghost road linking the locked wing to the real world—if you could call it that—must be able to discriminate between intention and desire, turning back those who were actually trying to leave, as opposed to simply wanting to be elsewhere. So Eve, who as a sorcerer was well accustomed to controlling her state of mind, made sure that she was *absolutely certain* that she was going in search of Eldest Sister to give her a piece of her mind. Not running away: never running away. Control over one's own inner state was one of the first skills a trainee sorcerer must learn, else they would not be a sorcerer for very long. *I need to find Matron and then I will give her a piece of my mind,* she repeated. That it was the particular piece of mind involved in setting Tiffy's hair on fire and boiling her brain until steam blew from her eyeballs should make no difference to the gatekeeper ward. (It would also be *most* satisfying, even if it drastically increased Eve's risk of Metahuman Associated Dementia. But brain-boiling would have to wait: she had questions that needed answers first—and some personal effects to retrieve.)

The process of opening the door lasted a mere second but it felt like a century. Perhaps the ward was confused by her lack of an escort, or sensed her hostility? It'd be just her luck if rather than *intent* the ward sensed *submission,* for while they weren't nuns the Silver Sisterhood had something of the stench of a lay order to them; there was the inevitability that Rupert would demand submission from his female followers, and when not compelled by a geas Eve was absolutely *not* a submissive—

Record scratch.

She stood in the corridor, blinking to clear her watery eyes, and almost gasped with relief as she saw that the doors had changed. She'd made it into another wing of the house! It wasn't familiar, but then, she'd only seen the main wing while manacled to a bath chair.

Now where? Eve crooked three fingers, the mnemonic to summon up her macro for locating that which was misplaced. She visualized her fake-pearl choker, held it in her mind's eye, remembered the flow of weight as she tipped it from the palm of one hand to the other. *There.* Her nose itched with a near-uncontrollable urge to sneeze: it came and went as she turned her head. *How inconvenient!* She cast about until she caught the scent of the chain—seawater and slightly past-it oysters: dust. Then she followed her nose blindly. The scent dead-ended in a locked door, but the lock had recently been oiled and she sprang it without too much effort. Behind it she found a narrow staircase ascending toward the attic.

Upstairs she found a room full of dust-sheeted furniture on bare boards beneath the inner slope of the roof. The trail led straight to one end wall, where a wooden cabinet with padlocked doors filled almost the entire width of the attic. She sneezed convulsively, then bent to inspect the lock.

Someone had inexpertly warded it to sound an alarm if picked. Whoever they were, they were far less proficient than the unseen hand that had enchanted the doors and window casements of the locked wing. It was like a child's crude crayon scrawl beside a carefully composed portrait. *Tiffy, or one of her subordinates?* Eve sniffed disdainfully as she lulled the ward to sleep. Then she unlatched the lock and opened the cabinet.

The doors concealed a row of cubbyholes containing tightly rolled bundles of cloth, and canvas sacks full of indeterminate items. All bore name tags, the ink fading into illegibility. The dust tickled her nose mercilessly. One of the cubbies seemed less dusty than its neighbors, and as she reached for it she recognized her traveling gown, dirty and bloodstained about the hem. She drew it from the niche and discovered her underpinnings inside, along with her bonnet and the detachable pocket she'd bought in York: it was all there! The enchantment on the pocket had burned out, but not before it had done its job and concealed the contents. Her boots were stuffed to the back of the cubbyhole. They'd been put away damp and muddy and now they were rock-hard and smelled bad.

Needs must, Eve decided, and shoved her feet into the crunchy leather. It cracked as she shifted her weight, and she winced, but they were more durable than the thin slippers the Sisters had given her. She swapped her habit and headpiece for her own clothes, pulled on her filthy pelisse, bonnet, and gloves as if stepping out for a walk, then shoved the prison outfit into the cabinet, closed it up, and locked it. At least now she looked less like an asylum inmate and more like a woman who had merely met with an unfortunate accident while traveling.

Ready to leave? she asked. Not without trepidation: she still wanted answers, dammit—the Silver Sisterhood *reeked* of Rupert, and she was aware that an unseen clock was ticking—but she didn't dare go back. If they laid hands on her they wouldn't allow her to escape again. Treacherous Tiffy was Number Twelve, so presumably somewhat weaker than her, but this was Tiffy's home turf and Eve was deeply unenthusiastic about tackling a cult priestess in her place of power. *Let's find the nearest exit,* she decided, then swirled her little pinkie to deflect unwanted attention. She turned and headed back downstairs, assembling a mental to-do list: avoid detection, walk to the nearest road, flag down a ride without being murdered, find an inn and hire a paid companion, then—

"*Oof!*"

▸◂▸◂▸◂

George staggered as a female person barged into him chest-first. A *very* female person, judging by the impact, and very substantial, but he couldn't see her, so he folded his arms around her before she could run—

"Let go of me, you great oaf!"

The termagant tone was instantly familiar. "Lady de Montfort?" he greeted her, amused despite himself. Once he assured himself that she wasn't about to fall over, he released her. He wasn't a ruffian, and besides, Lady Evelyn was doubtless making her escape under cover of her own obfuscatory magic. "Please show yourself."

He would swear he heard her mutter, "pearls before swine," but a moment later his eyeballs unkinked and he saw her squinting at him, less than a foot from his nose. She was uncommonly tall: her eyes were nearly on a level with his own, and he was not a short fellow. Her traveling gown was filthy, but when he looked at her with his inner gaze she burned with angry magnificence, no longer bothering to mask her power. He released his veil of misdirection and her squint moderated into a baffled glare. "What are *you* doing here?" she demanded.

"I thought it was obvious, I'm here to rescue you." He raised an eyebrow. "I got here just in time, I think." He offered her his arm. "Would you care for—"

She snorted like an angry bull. Clearly her patience had reached its limits. "I can make my own way, *sir.*"

Normally George would find this amusing, but: "It's the eve of the *High Sabbath,* m'Lady. The Sisterhood are at their most dangerous tonight because they can draw directly on the power of their Mute God." She paled visibly at this: *good, no need to explain.* "I've tried to ensure Number Twelve will be detained elsewhere, but it won't hold her for long and I have no more desire than you to be a guest at their unholy communion tonight. I grew up in this house—before it was an asylum—and I know where the secret passages are. So, my Lady, I repeat myself: would you care for a local guide? If so, we should leave immediately." Again he offered her his arm, and again she sent him a look hot enough to boil ice, but this time she took his elbow. At her touch a spark ran through him from scalp to floor. *Astonishing,* he thought dizzily.

"If this is a subterfuge I swear I will gut you like a haddock," she said, tightening her grip. "I am *completely* fed up with this place."

"No traps," he promised. "Let's get out of here, then we can talk." *And you can tell me how you entered my thoroughly warded town house, how you escaped from an escape-proof internment camp for sorcerers, and how in the name of all that's unholy you then escaped from the locked ward of the Sisterhood's cloister.* But he said none of that now: they had at most ten minutes before their escape was discovered, and there was no time to waste. Besides, she was strung so tight, if he provoked her she might snap. There'd be no sweet-talking her until she knew she was safe.

George led Number Six—who clomped along in a most unladylike manner; he'd have to find her some more appropriate footwear—toward the back of the house. There were more servants' passages. He led her to the corridor behind the butler's pantry, then through the mudroom and straight to the back door adjacent to the vegetable garden. "You need to veil yourself again," he said quietly, then waited for her to nod and for his eyeballs to develop an involuntary squint. She could follow orders when it suited her, he noted; she just didn't suffer fools gladly. Or at all. He'd met more biddable mules.

George wrapped himself in his own aversive magic, eased the door open, and led her down the steps into the yard.

The sky was overcast and a thin drizzle falling, but night was a way off. George hustled Number Six along the back wall of the coach house toward the stable. The groom and boys were busy at one end, the boys mucking out stalls and their master checking over the tack on George's mount, which—he was displeased to see—had not yet been saddled.

George gently prodded Lady de Montfort toward a nearby empty stall, then dropped his guise. "Ho, stableman! I've changed my mind: I'll be taking him off your hands," he called. "Not staying overnight on Sabbath's Eve."

The groom turned and gave him a slack-jawed look. "Aye, sir? Are you sure? He's still tired and I won't speak to how far he'll carry you in this state."

"I'm sure." George approached. His mount snorted softly and shifted, sensing his urgency. "I'll rest him properly in an hour or two, but I must be on my way right now. Duty calls!"

The groom set about saddling the horse. George took the reins and led him to the yard. Once outside, he wasted no time in setting boot to stirrup and climbing into the saddle. The skin in the small of his back was crawling. Surely Number Twelve would be on her way by now? He glanced left, back at the stable, and saw that the head groom was watching him. "Dammit," he muttered, "show yourself so I can help you up."

Something warped the air to the right of his mount, and he leaned sideways to see Number Six looking up at him with an expression of deep suspicion on her face. "Take my—" He paused. "What?"

"I can't ride," she blurted. "I mean, I've never—"

"What? Never?" He blinked in disbelief. "No time for that now, woman, take my hand and . . ." He leaned down and grabbed her wrist. "It's perfectly simple," he said as he tensed and lifted. In truth it was less simple than he'd imagined—she was not only tall but as muscular as any soldier he'd led—but pride forbade him from complaining. "Now wrap your arms around me and whatever you do, *don't fall off.*"

A shout went out from the direction of the house as he nudged the bay gelding's flanks, startling it into a side step as Lady de Montfort landed in front of him like a sack of potatoes. For a moment he feared she was going to slide right off again: she seemed to have no idea of the correct posture for riding sidesaddle, let alone how to do so without stirrup or pommel horns. Somehow she managed not to topple over. Then there were more shouts and they were moving at a brisk walk, although he couldn't discern in which direction because he had a faceful of bonnet and a double armful of trouble clinging tightly to his waist.

"This is most undignified, and the only reason I'm not going to kill you just yet is because here comes Tiffy and she looks *mad. . . .*"

There was a flat, percussive bang. A pistol ball buzzed past George's head. He nudged his horse harder, then harder still as Number Six shifted, seeking stability, and then they were going at a trot, although how long the animal would be able to keep it up with two riders was an open question.

"This is bad," Number Six told him breathlessly. At least she wasn't screaming or swooning. He supposed it was easier to rescue a fiery-spirited sorceress than a fainting wallflower. But then she began patting him down in an alarmingly intimate manner.

"What are you—" he began to ask as a slim hand invaded his coat pocket. "Stop, no, don't touch that! It's—"

"A pistol!" *Bang.* "Dammit, missed. Do you have any more ammunition?"

"Yes, but I can't reload right now." At least she'd gotten her head out of his line of sight, although her chin was drilling a hole in his collarbone.

"Huh. Well, at least she'll think twice about following us," said Number Six. She sounded frankly bloodthirsty. "They went back inside."

George swallowed a curse unfit for a lady's ears. "That's not good." The gateposts were coming up. "In fact, it's really bad."

"Why is that?"

"You shouldn't have shot at her. Number Twelve can't afford to let you go now: she'll lose face. It's the eve of the High Sabbath. She'll rally her followers and summon the hounds to take up our trail."

Number Six gave a most unladylike chuckle. Then she abruptly stopped. "I take it we're not talking about foxhounds," she said tensely.

Centipedes writhed over every inch of his exposed skin as their mount ploughed across the ley line that marked the edge of the estate. *Foxhounds*. How was such a powerful practitioner so ignorant of the basics? "The hounds that live in the angles of time," he said. "Summoned from an alien hell to serve blasphemous beings that claim to be gods. She will summon them, and if you left any articles of clothing behind she'll give them your scent. They can appear wherever man-made right angles exist, so taking shelter indoors is futile."

"*Oh*," she said, then added some words that well-bred ladies weren't supposed to know. "Then we'll just have to not do that, won't we? How long do you think we—" A hunting horn sounded behind them. "You know what? Forget I asked."

An eerie wavering howl split the twilight behind them. The horn sounded again, slightly off-key. "We have company." Their mount surged forward. He was clearly tired, but the belling of the alien hounds had him spooked, so he ploughed ahead, desperate to outpace the thing trailing them. George had to rein him in to a more sedate pace: he was on the edge of bolting. "He'll be blown if we keep this pace up." The bay might have a couple of miles in him if George was any judge, but then they'd have to dismount and walk the rest of the way. The horse already needed a couple of days' rest: push him much farther and the poor thing would break.

The horn sounded again. It wasn't falling behind, so presumably their pursuers were also mounted. Knowing his luck their steeds would be fresh.

"I have an idea," said Number Six, "but you're not going to like it."

"Tell me," he grunted. Was it his imagination or was there a fine carpet of mist forming above the road?

"We need to ambush them before they catch up," she said calmly. "Let me dismount, then buy me a couple of minutes while I set up a circle in the road."

The horn sounded again. From back down the driveway he heard Lady Ffoulkes-Ward shout, "This is your last chance! Surrender right now and I'll call the hounds off!" Another horn blew, and the hound voiced a discordant whining plaint. George listened to his horse's breathing. It didn't sound good.

"We'll—" he began.

"Stop and let me down!" Number Six hissed in his ear. She raised her voice to shout, "We're stopping!" Then she let go of George's waist and slid from the saddle. The madwoman obviously thought she could take on the Silver Sisterhood on their night of power, riding with the hounds of Tindalos. He was torn between frustration and admiration. He'd met soldiers with less spirit, but she was going to get herself killed. He couldn't leave her to die: he'd never get his hands on her . . . her so-called husband, he hastily amended. So in addition to getting herself killed, she was going to get *him* killed. Number Two would be very displeased.

He brought the horse around sharply and followed her down to the deadly ground, swearing up a blue streak as he reached for his powder horn and began to reload. This was *not* how he'd planned to entertain her this evening.

Eve was unsure if George—Lantern-Jawed Trouble in Skintight Breeches, as she thought of him—was going to prove a liability in the long term. He'd been extremely obliging in showing her the back door to the asylum. He had *amazing* abs and knew how to operate a nineteenth-century grass-fueled motorcycle (although the one they were riding right now appeared to have a cracked cylinder head and four flat tires). Moreover he'd actually *asked* her to come with him, rather than simply grunting and flinging her over his shoulder, which would have obliged her to stab him in the kidneys. These were all positive qualities in this dark and unenlightened century, and he was ticking all the boxes on her dating checklist, and the archetypes whose logic the dream roads obeyed seemed to require ladies in peril to be rescued by hunky males rather than liberating themselves: so she decided to keep him around. (Purely for tactical reasons. It was absolutely nothing to do with the way he filled those breeches, she told herself.)

"Can you hold the horse while I . . ." She screened him out. Instead, she focused and, through an exercise of raw power, dredged a circle in the crushed stone of the driveway. It wasn't as efficacious as a spray can full of conductive paint or a pump bottle of blood from a still-screaming sacrifice, but it served to cut them off from their uncanny surroundings.

"Do *not* let the horse cross the line," she warned.

"What are you doing?" George was fiddling with the pistol she'd discharged.

"Avoiding right angles." She shut him down because the horns were sounding again, and where the horns went the hounds followed, and she hadn't finished dialing in the parameters of the containment diagram. She drew a second outer circle and filled the space between them with symbols in Old Enochian script, the formal language of sorcery. She tried not to hurry, for even trivial mistakes could be rapidly and gruesomely fatal. By the time she completed the last ideogram the hunting horns and the eerie wails of the hounds were just around the bend in the road. "Done," she announced, gritting her teeth, for she expected him to belittle her work.

George squinted at her circle of protection, then merely nodded. "I'll build on that as an anchor for a deflection ward," he said, and began to chant an invocation that Eve recognized as a more powerful version of the aversive spell she'd used to hide her presence—powerful enough to bamboozle and confuse even an attentive audience. The world beyond the circle blurred as he finished his recitation. "Stand behind me," he added, stepping toward the approaching hooves and raising his pistol to cover the road.

"Ahem." She elbowed him in the side. "You're blocking my aim."

"What are you shooting—" She saw his eyes widen as he took in the handful of nacre-coated buckshot hovering above her upturned right hand. "—jewelry?"

"Ball shot disguised as false pearls." He nodded then turned his attention back to the road without comment, still seemingly intent on shielding her with his body. Eve swallowed a sharp rebuke. She could work with misplaced chivalry, but she wasn't sure she approved of the implications. "Where are they—ah." The wavering world outside was definitely misting over. Or was it smoke? An eldritch caterwauling like Aztec death whistles raised the gooseflesh on the nape of her neck. Half-glimpsed shapes cast about beneath the branches of the trees to either side of the lane, sniffing and ululating. There were at least two of the things, sleek black beasts that bore no resemblance to any earthly animal she'd seen. Calling them *hounds* was like describing a tiger as a large cat. George whispered a charm in his mount's ear to keep it from bolting: the horse shivered in terror and its eyes rolled in their sockets, but its feet stayed rooted to the ground.

The hunting horn sounded again as the riders flowed around the curve of the road. There were half a dozen of them, robed in white fabric edged in silver, their faces concealed behind veils like funeral cerements. They looked for all the world like a cluster of fashionable ladies taking the air on Rotten Row, save that they bore staves crawling with aurorae that hurt the watcher's eye, and their steeds were beasts out of nightmare. The mounts had front-mounted blue-glowing eyes, raptorial claws to either side of their hooves, and scars in their equoid foreheads where their horns had been crudely amputated. These were not horses but neutered unicorns, their slavering jaws barely constrained within gibbet-cage muzzles. And the riders were clearly fearless, fanatical, reckless, or all three at once, for they rode their horrific steeds without a steel safety cage.

The hunting beasts circled the perimeter of Eve's ward, and the Sisters drew up before it. They couldn't see inside or cross the circle, but they certainly knew it was there. Their leader edged closer. "Really, Number Seven! I expected better of you than this." The Matron of the Silver Sisterhood threw back her veil with theatrical elan. "As for you, Lady de Montfort, when you are back in your cell there will be *extra punishments*—"

Eve whacked a pearl into Tiffy's shoulder with her mind. Number Twelve screeched and dropped her eldritch glowing wand. It was a lucky miss: Eve had actually been aiming for one of the alien hounds that circled in front of the sisters on limbs that stretched and contracted like molten tar. But the thaum field around the stave had grabbed her pearl like a superconducting electromagnet, warping its path straight into its bearer's arm. The amped-up wand, pumped full of who-knew-what malignant *mana* by the followers of the Mute Poet, fell to the ground and went off like a bomb.

When Eve could see again—let alone hear, for her ears were curiously numb apart from a high-pitched chittering like hell's own tinnitus—it was dark, and there was nobody outside the circle of protection. Splintered trees showed their pale bones, nude in the moonlight. A thin rain was falling, and when she wiped her face she saw it was the pink of dilute blood. "Gaah." She shook her head, just as George stepped in front of her and folded her in his arms. After a moment she realized he was talking, or rather shouting, in her ears.

"What?" she shouted back.

"—said, it's full dark. At least an hour ago, by the angle of the moon."

Eve pushed him away then took a step back. "But we're—" She thought hard, then *looked,* opening her inner eye. Within her circle the ground was dark, but outside it was stained the luminous green of a magical fallout zone. Blast shadows etched the negative images of mounts and riders across the road, stretched nightmarishly outward.

"It struck the hound," Number Seven said, pointing at a weirdly distorted shadow that seemed to flicker and twinkle and bend away from her sight. "And the hound took everything else back with it from whence it came. In time, I mean. Or it hurled us into the future." *He actually said "whence,"* Eve thought dizzily. So that was how you pronounced it. *I think I'm in love. Or maybe concussed.*

"Horse," she croaked, all the shouting catching up with her. She felt dizzy from her magical exertions, and more than a little nauseous.

George's horse was gone, presumably having had enough of their scary magical shit. It had most likely bolted for safety in all directions at once, driven to escape the equoids and the hunting hounds.

"I'm afraid we have only shank's mare for the time being." He had the decency to look apologetic as he raised his left hand. A silvery glow spread between his caged fingers. "It's two or three miles to the nearest inn. Can you walk that far?"

Eve sniffed and took his offered arm. At last all those hours pounding the treadmill in the gym would prove useful.

▸◂▸◂▸◂

As they walked, Eve contemplated her prospects. The chance of making a successful break for it on her own were somewhere between slim and vanishing. She was lost in the middle of Ruralshire without a map or a compass, and although she hadn't confirmed this, her traveling companion had most likely been sent by Number Two to bring her back to the Village. But George had proven unexpectedly considerate: she had many questions, and as long as she didn't seek them too eagerly he could probably be induced to provide answers. So she refrained from escape attempts for now, and focused on obediently putting one foot in front of the other.

George was clearly a master of the long silence. By the time he started talking she was cold, faint from hunger, and beginning to truly hate the blister forming on her right heel. "My Lady, I know you're unable or unwilling to answer certain questions about yourself. But would you be so good as to confirm or deny some of my suppositions?"

Eve pretended to ignore him, but he continued regardless. "It's quite obvious that you don't want to return to the Village. Equally obviously, you wouldn't be running away from the asylum if . . . well, your actions speak louder than your words. Number Two bound you to silence, which I find rather annoying, but it's plain to see that you speak English like a native, you have good manners—when you choose to use them; you have a tendency to stab trouble in the eye in lieu of gracious words—and you are a powerful sorceress."

At this transparent flattery Eve skewered him with a glare that promised future retribution. But she managed to bite her tongue rather than show him its vicious edge (her temper had not been improved by sore feet and cold drizzle). So, not being fatally discouraged, George continued to speak at her. "Number Two and his superiors think the obvious explanation is that you are a foreign agent of polite breeding, but I happen to disagree. I think Lady Ffoulkes-Ward snared you in passing because she knows or suspects something about you. The same thing *I* do, I mean. Tell me, Evelyn, you got into my town house—did you wander in from the dream roads on the top floor?"

"That's—" She stopped dead in her tracks, her resolve to hold her tongue shaken. "—that's *your* house?"

George looked at her. She met his eyes. He nodded, she resumed walking. Every step hurt, so she barely noticed when he added, "You're not the first visitor we've had over the years. Another fellow arrived before my time—it would have been in 1790, 1791? I think—and made himself useful to the Invisible College until he disappeared again, back in '12. To be honest he'd become a liability. Chap was a bad penny, powerful bad, although all the ladies seemed unaccountably weak for the scoundrel." He paused, evidently reconsidering his words. "Except yourself, of course."

"*Rupert,*" she whispered.

"Yes, that was his name." Eve turned and glared at him. Either George was using a charm on her or—*no,* her home-brew ward wasn't that weak. She was simply tired, her defenses were weak, and George was that most subtle of menaces, an attractive man who actually listened to women and understood what they told him.

"Tell me, Lady de Montfort—if you can, that is—would you consider Rupert to be friend or foe?"

She realized her fingers were clenched in his sleeve. She forced herself to relax her death grip before they turned white. "Rupert is the enemy of all humanity," she said vehemently, as soon as she could trust herself to speak again. "He mortgaged his soul to an abomination that seeks to murder or enslave everyone on Earth." Neither Number Two's geas nor any residual compulsion Rupert had left her with prevented her from confessing. "He came here—through the dream roads—in search of power."

"You followed him."

"I had no alternative." *Besides, the Prime Minister commanded me to bring him Rupert's skull.* "I meant no harm by doing this, at least not to the Invisible College, but Rupert *must* be stopped." She took a deep breath, nostrils flaring at the scent of petrichor in the damp air. "Sounds like I'm too late."

"Perhaps not." Something in George's posture changed, bringing Eve's attention back to the road ahead. A dim light flickered ahead. "Look, we're nearly at the inn."

"Wonderful." She wished she could sound excited, but right now the only thing she could muster any enthusiasm for was a bed.

"We shall talk more tomorrow. For now"—*here it comes,* she thought tiredly, nerving herself—"I intend to return to London tomorrow—I have some business to attend to there. I believe our goals are aligned, and you are welcome to accompany me as my guest. Does that suit?"

"Does that—" She shook herself dizzily. It felt as if she'd been pushing on a locked door, and George had just yanked it open from the other side. *Have I been rolled? Or did he just—* "Tomorrow?" she asked, finding it difficult to focus her awareness on anything but the last steps to the doorway beneath the lamp. It was more than just physical exhaustion, or the mental backlash from a series of workings: from pushing through the knot of dream paths around the locked wing, then sneaking out of the asylum and fighting off the Sisterhood. What finally weakened her knees was the sheer relief of finding someone who might be an ally.

"Tomorrow," she heard George say. "We can talk after breakfast—" Then the door opened and she shuffled inside, almost asleep on her bleeding feet.

▸◂▸◂▸◂

Eve awakened the next morning in an unfamiliar bed. The innkeeper's wife had found her a clean nightgown and the bedding was recently laundered and flea-free. The window was open to admit daylight and a fresh morning breeze, and from downstairs she heard the sounds of a household going about its morning business. She took stock of her limbs, half-surprised to find no fetters. *Not a prisoner,* she thought fuzzily, *how strange!* She'd been a prisoner almost continuously since Rupert had reappeared in her life. Even her brief escape from the Village and the run up the coast and down the Great North Road felt as if she'd been playing cat and mouse with her jailers. In a sense, she'd been a prisoner—except for the months following Rupert's disappearance—for years before that. George couldn't be any worse than Rupert or Number Two, could he? *Time to see,* she decided. She threw back the blankets and sat up.

An hour later she was sitting pretty in George's liveried coach, which had driven up from London to collect him—how he had sent for it she had no idea, but right now she couldn't care less. It was a vast improvement over the crowded, bumpy stagecoaches. Nevertheless she was regretting her spasm of early-morning enthusiasm. There had been no time for a bath or clean clothes: consequently she felt frowsy and her right foot hurt whenever she put weight on it. Also, although the springs and the interior padding were vastly better than the commercial carriages, the coachman was racing between villages. The results were all too predictable. "Are you feeling all right, my Lady?" asked George. "You seem to be a trifle pale?"

Eve forced a smile. "It's nothing." He actually looked genuinely concerned for her well-being, and she felt a treacherous flash of gratitude. She resolutely suppressed it. This was not the time to go all softheaded because of the first human kindness she'd encountered in ages, even if it *did* come in a package with rock-hard abs, a luxury coach, and a killer smile. "How far do we have to go?"

"A little over a hundred miles." George paused a moment. "But I sent word to have fresh teams waiting along the way—we could be home before midnight, my Lady. A little faster than the commercial stage, and much more comfortable."

Eve didn't know whether to laugh or cry. The long day of tooth-rattling tedium ahead was simultaneously a display of enormous wealth and a dismal reminder of the limitations of power. Everything screamed *privilege,* from the armed footmen on the roof to the dozens of horses George thought nothing of mobilizing for his own convenience. And yet, they were less than forty minutes away as the helicopter flew.

"You came through the ghost roads," George said after a moment. "Pursuing Rupert Bigge, yes? That's what you said last night."

Eve winced. So, the interrogation was to continue, was it? "Obviously I said too much. I was not myself." *I haven't been myself for weeks,* she thought despondently.

"Well, let me say what I surmise you cannot and you can deny it if I get it wrong? Ghost roads connect different times and different possibilities, not just different places. Rupert knew secrets he could not possibly have obtained through espionage—indeed, he was in possession of secrets about the *future* when he arrived for the first time in 1790. He predicted Louis's execution to the very day, in a sealed envelope he placed in our custody. You can understand how that caught the undivided attention of Their Lordships on Mahogany Row? He brought the architectural drawings for the Village and proposed a prison for enemy sorcerers captured during a war that hadn't even started yet. Made himself as useful as only a man from the future might." Eve's skin crawled. A panicky sense of inevitability gripped her: *here it comes.* "Then he vanished in August of 1812, shortly after Wellington entered Madrid. When he returned after three years of absence he was . . . changed. Murderously so. He disappeared, but not through the ghost roads—he cut a bloody trail through London before he vanished. Then you arrived a few months later, via the same route." George raised an eyebrow. "What *is* your future like, my Lady?"

"I—" Eve shuddered, tight in the grip of an uncontrollable horripilation. "If I told you about the future it might not happen, and then I wouldn't exist!" she burst out. *Or worse, it might not happen and I'd still be here, trapped for the rest of my life,* she thought grimly. Cupping and leeching, no divorce, lunatic asylums for women who challenged their masters—the past was a nightmare. "I just want to stop Rupert and go home," she confessed.

"On that we can agree. But is life here really so bad? A sorceress of your power is not without options. You could marry well, lead a life of luxury, be the envy of society. If you were a countess, for example . . ."

Is he propositioning me? she wondered, startled into momentary speechlessness. George was either an earl or the heir to an earldom, wasn't he? He watched her from the opposite side of the carriage—she had taken the rear-facing seat—his expression open and earnest.

"Please don't joke about such matters," she said tightly. "I have responsibilities back home." She needed to remind herself that the Black Pharaoh himself had tasked her with the return of Rupert's head. (*The right one,* whatever that meant.) Who knew what might happen if she deserted her duty? His Eldritch Majesty had a long reach, and surely the ghost roads would be no obstacle to Him. "The Lords of Mahogany Row—you speak of the House of Lords, do you not? I serve a, a very similar institution in my time."

"Curious that they would employ a female agent." If Number Seven had a beard he'd be stroking it.

His unconscious chauvinism put iron in her spine, and she sent him a thin-lipped smile. "Not really. The past is a foreign country: they do things differently there."

George sat up and stared at her admiringly. "That's a wonderful aphorism! Is it yours?"

"No, and—" Eve swallowed, her mouth suddenly dry. "—please don't write it down anywhere. It might—small changes can snowball."

"Ah! For the want of a nail the shoe was lost, et cetera?"

"Exactly so." Eve forced herself to breathe again.

"Something commonplace out of your time, then." George nodded to himself. "Well, I hope you can be my guide to Rupert's intentions, because if you come from the same time—a foreign country where they *do things differently*—you may anticipate his movements when I fail to do so. On the other hand, you need a partner, someone who gets things fixed. I've got the brawn, you've got the brain: how about it?"

Eve opened and closed her mouth, stuck on a hook of acute déjà vu. Most of the time she could forget that this was merely a fever dream of 1816, a re-creation by the dream roads rather than the thing itself: then it punched you in the face with Pet Shop Boys lyrics. Truly, the collective subconscious was *weird*. Eventually she nodded. "I can work with that."

"Good enough for now." He nodded and pulled out a pack of cards. "Would you care for a game?"

▸◂▸◂▸◂

Eleven interminable hours and about two hundred hands of piquet later, they finally pulled up in the mews behind Kensington Palace Gardens. Eve had dozed for the last couple of hours but awakened in time to be handed down by the coachmen and ushered into the drawing room. It was the same room she'd fallen so oddly asleep in when she first arrived, but the dust sheets had been removed and the candles burned without any cloying scent and strange smoke. Number Seven poured her a brandy from the decanter on the sideboard. "I'll have Mrs. Dorling make up a guest room for you. We can start searching tomorrow."

"Thank you." Eve sipped her glass as she reclined on the chaise, grateful for a seat that wasn't constantly moving. Her thought processes were blurry. (Wasn't there a bloated carnivorous lounger here in her own time? *Jabba the Sofa,* Imp called it.) "Rupert is looking for a book." She yawned. "And I, I need a maid, I think? And a chaperone? To be respectable."

"Of course, and I'll see to it tomorrow. Of course, if, er, if I were to introduce you as my wife no questions would be asked—"

It was hard to tell by candlelight but Eve was certain his cheeks were glowing. Hers certainly felt as if they were: best to nip this in the bud. "My Lord. Anyone might think you were *trying to propose.*" Because that was inevitably what a twenty-first-century hallucination of the Regency era would demand of its protagonists once they were ensnared in its coils, wasn't it? The narrative unfolded with gentle but inexorable pressure: *heiress in jeopardy, unjustly incarcerated in a most peculiar prison, from which she escapes to seek exoneration; chased by a hunky spy, captured, and locked up again in an asylum, she is rescued by her beau, a marriage of convenience ensues to avoid social ruination—or maybe a fictitious one?* The echoes of a hundred TV costume dramas and a thousand romance novels demanded it. Indeed, it practically wrote itself.

"Er, yes? I mean, am I?" asked Number Seven, sounding as punch-drunk as Eve felt. "I mean, it would be the honorable thing to do, I'm sure I could petition for a special license—in view of your lack of a parish in which to post the banns—"

Just say no, Eve told herself. She opened her mouth and heard herself say, "Yes."

"My dear—" He went down on one knee and drew breath, even as her eyes widened in horror.

"I meant, no! Wait, *yes,* no—what I meant to say was—" The ward strung around her neck stung her: it had become so hot that a trickle of smoke began to leak from it. "—I can't marry you because I think I may already be married but I'm not sure," she gasped out hurriedly before her ward made a muffled popping noise and crumbled to ashes. *Deep breaths,* she thought, *take deep breaths.* She clenched her thighs together, trying to ignore the shivery ache in her core.

George winced but didn't interrupt. "I'm terribly, terribly sorry—please accept my apologies. I must be overwrought to have asked you so thoughtlessly, it has been a very strange day." He sounded slightly stunned. He rose and walked toward the door without any further ado—or questions, which Eve found worrying. "Mrs. Dorling will show you to your room: I think it best if we leave further discussion until the morrow. Good night."

The instant George left, a pressure lifted from her mind. Eve drew breath and only narrowly restrained herself from busting out a stream of invective that would have turned the air blue: it might even have impressed her brother. *What the ever-loving fuck was* that *about?* she asked herself.

She tipped her head back and stared at the ceiling. When she and Imp had tackled the dream roads before, to visit a ghastly version of 1880s Whitechapel, all pea-souper coal smog and Jack the Ripper vibes, it had felt claustrophobic and brutal: but she hadn't been sucked into the narrative slipstream like *that.* On the other hand, Imp had a very bad time coming back, and she'd been in 1816 for much longer than he had spent in 1888. Maybe that explained Rupert's decayed state when he'd returned from his first trip. Twenty years in the dream roads, two decades living in a magical hallucination leeching off his life force, had strip-mined his soul.

She'd only been here a handful of weeks and she was already noticing it, dragged down by the powerful undertow of the shared universe of Regency fiction. Rupert's version of the Napoleonic era was likely misaligned with the one that had snared her: else she'd already be trussed up and delivered to the altar, starry-eyed and leg-cuffed to an adoring but overbearing husband while her *mana* was drained to power a romance-fueled pocket universe.

Not that marrying George was the worst thing that could happen to her, a confused part of her mind insisted. He might be imaginary but he was a very *attractive* kind of imaginary: a total hunk, wealthy and titled, anomalously kind and considerate for a man of his time, and with a glamorous side serving of derring-do: *he does secret work for the government.*

On the other hand, she reminded herself, she couldn't stay here. She could die of a tooth abscess or childbirth, the dream would steadily consume her soul for fuel, she'd be a second-class citizen, and in any case, *why am I even thinking about a man?* Eve shook her head. Her sexuality was a sore point, so she mostly tried to avoid thinking about it.

Before she'd gone to work for Rupert, back when she'd been studying at university, she'd figured out that some men (and some but fewer women) interested her: but what got her particularly excited were fantasies involving partners in latex and leather wielding whips and restraints. She'd gone to fetish clubs a few times and enjoyed herself immensely. But then her mother had died and she'd conceived her plan for revenge on the cult responsible, and she'd taken the devil's shilling. Rupert repelled her so much that after meeting him she pretty much lost interest in sex, vanilla *or* kinky. In hindsight that might have been his geas's work—because *of course* Rupert wasn't a submissive, and if she wouldn't willingly touch him it wouldn't let her be with anyone else, would it? But now this place was trying to squeeze her into conformity with a frankly tedious heteronormative narrative, and—

Record scratch.

She was sitting at the breakfast table, holding a half-full cup of tea over a plate that she'd apparently cleaned of food. Her pulse pounded in her ears as she took stock of herself. She was alone in the breakfast room, wearing an unfamiliar (but clean, and expensively embroidered) frock. The morning sun was shining in through the window and she felt as rested as if she'd had a full night's sleep. But she had no memory of going upstairs to bed, or of having slept and dreamed before rising again. Her last memory was of George leaving her in the drawing room, and thinking herself in a pretty mess with the world pressing in around her. Then she'd had another of those funny spells.

The first fugue happened when she met the Black Pharaoh. Another, when the Sisterhood trapped her. The third, as she fled through the knotted dream door separating the locked ward from the main wing of the asylum. The latest . . . *I was questioning this reality, wasn't I?* she realized. *Is it that unstable?* If it had been sustained by Rupert for all these years, sucking him dry until he was barely more than an animated corpse searching for the lost *Necronomicon,* maybe it *was* that unstable. Maybe it was looking for a new host to leech off. Or perhaps it depended on her sustained belief in it to persist. If she stopped believing it was real rather than a dream, would everything around her stop existing, leaving her stranded in the middle of nothing?

She raised her teacup and drained it. Her hand was shaking so badly that it clattered when she replaced it on the saucer. The door opened. "More tea, m'Lady?" She glanced round. George looked as if he'd barely slept, with dark bags under his eyes and a pronounced five o'clock shadow.

"I don't—yes," Eve amended as he entered. "Listen, about last night—"

"Please." He picked up the silver teapot as he approached. "I must apologize. I was overwrought and tired—"

"—There is a geas," Eve said simultaneously. "What?"

"You first. Please."

"I don't know how much I can say," she said while he refilled her cup. "You first."

"I sent Number Two a message this morning, to which he replied an hour ago: you are released from his geas," he said, and uttered a furious, silent phrase that hung colorlessly in the air for a moment and made her ears hurt. "If you are under no compulsion, *now* will you tell me what's going on?"

"You deduced most of it." She shivered. "Number Two isn't the only one to play fast and loose with bindings. Rupert placed a geas on me when I was in his employ, then tricked me into a marriage by proxy from which he obtained the power to compel me to absolute obedience. It relies on sympathetic magic: the *feme covert* is bound as tightly to his will as his own flesh. But we are not married *in this time*: all this happened or *will* happen in the future; the date on the wedding registry has not yet come to pass. So his geas slackens when I'm not in his presence, and as far as I know it doesn't control me here. But if he returns to the future and I follow him, I will be under his power for the rest of my life. And a lot of people will die if he gets his way—either the artifact he seeks, or whatever his new plan is."

"If you obtain this book can you return to your future safely? Will all be well?"

Eve bit her lip. "I am under orders from the government. The successor to your own employers, as I understand it." Best not say their name. "But the book is secondary. I am to bring the—the Prime Minister—Rupert's skull as evidence of his demise."

"Well!" George leaned back in his chair. "The Invisible College is commanded directly from Downing Street in your day? And they trusted such a mission to the fairer sex?"

"Yes. And I don't have to kill him myself, just return his head as proof of execution." Eve's cheek twitched. "The skull previously believed to be that of Rupert de Montfort Bigge was unsatisfactory for some reason. Time travel and the dream roads mess everything up." She paused. "Also, things here turn out to be more complicated than I imagined."

"The Sisterhood," George proposed, raising his teacup ironically. "They're his doing. As is the Village, as I suppose you realized. You are surrounded by his works, but no sign of the man himself."

"Correct. He first came back here to go after the book, which is probably why there's no sign of him—he's given up on trying to work the system from within. Instead he said something about a great wreaking to be carried out in this time which would affect my own present—your future."

"What is this book that's so important for this master spell?"

"It goes by a variety of names." Eve put her teacup down. "Tell me if you've heard of any of them? *Al Azif. The Book of Dead Names. The Necronomicon*—"

"*Stop!*" George looked horrified. "Utter not that name! You may have said too much already—"

The hairs on the back of Eve's neck stood on end. A moment later columns of blue-white mist began rising from the floor, as if the joists beneath the parquet were on fire. She pushed her chair back as George grabbed her hand and pulled her toward the doorway. There he paused, for the strange smoke was leaking in from the corners of the front door and along the skirting board in the hall.

"What's happening? Are we on fire?"

"I wish that was all it was." George drew his pistol. "I fear the hounds have run us to ground."

▸◂▸◂▸◂

Directed dreaming was the Starkey family talent: always had been, going back most of two centuries. Which was, of course, why Imp generally avoided sleeping unless he was stoned, drunk, or exhausted close to the point of hallucinating. Yes, you could indulge in fascinating lucid dreams and enjoy the most outrageous orgiastic fantasies; but you ran the risk of visitors popping in from the dream roads to say "*pthagn*" and wave their feeding rhizomes from your imaginary lover's eye sockets. (Then you awakened in a state of fright with a damp crotch if you were lucky, and needing a shower and a change of sheets if you weren't.)

You could also find things that were lost, or seek hidden knowledge. But to find anything useful always required a sacrifice, and the price was usually more than many would be willing to pay: it was very much a monkey's-paw talent, and Dad had died before he could really make a start on teaching Imp and Eve how to make use of it.

However . . . truth or falsehood was a much easier ask for the oracle of dreams: especially when that which was sought was only misplaced, and even more so when the person who was lost actually wanted to be found.

Imp awakened inside his dream, lying on a stained futon in a darkened bedroom—though it was only midafternoon—with corners that faded into mist and walls of disturbingly textured paper. *So you may find yourself,* he found himself humming, *in a beautiful house, with a beautiful life, and you may wonder*—it was very strange. *And I don't even* like *Talking Heads!* But for some reason he'd been thoroughly earwormed, as if the song was woven into the very fabric of this dream, stitched firmly in place by an overlocker.

He sat up, weightless but somehow fastened to his surroundings. It was oddly quiet in the house, as if he was alone. But he had a premonition that he was anything but alone, that someone or something was paying attention to him, and that he shouldn't linger long. "Where is she?" he asked, but there was no reply.

The LED light on the Wi-Fi extender above the door glowed a cheerful steady green as he looked around. It seemed to be pushing back at the darkness and he found himself glad of its company. He remembered levering up a floorboard to wire its power brick directly into the wire feeding the antiquated single-plug socket in the skirting board—

Oh.

If it hadn't been a dream Imp would have smacked his forehead. "How could I forget?" he asked, rhetorically: for now he was asleep, the—*record scratch*—no longer fogged his memory. The recess under the boards had been dusty, soiled with ancient mouse droppings, and there'd been an envelope: more of a folded sheet of paper, actually, the seam where it had been fastened sealed with an archaic wax blob. And on the outside, in a vaguely familiar spiky copperplate handwriting (the ink faded by the passage of decades), a message.

It was addressed to him, with a "do not open until" date and a stern injunction: "Do not open this envelope under any circumstances or *you may cease to exist.* Put it back where you found it and forget you saw it."

Imp dreamed that he blinked, and suddenly he was holding the letter.

It bore today's date.

Imp cracked the seal, unfolded the sheet of foolscap, and began to read the instructions that had been letter-locked within.

THE HOUNDS OF MEMORY

The hounds coagulated from the smoke curling out of the angles where the walls intersected. They weren't dogs, although they were—probably—quadrupedal, with a blunt, questing end opposite a skinny whiplike end that seemed to fade from view, as if dwindling to an infinitely remote vanishing point. But it was impossible to count their limbs, or even the number of joints in each limb, or even to be certain how many hounds there were: for they warped in and out of sight as they moved, merging and separating.

"Hurry!" George urged Eve toward the curve of the hall staircase. "Before they manifest fully."

Eve hurried after him. "How do they sense us?"

"Not by eyes, ears, or nose. They follow arcane spoor—our *mana* traces, according to Hermes Trismegistus, although the Ramban thought they consumed emanations of the holy—"

Eve ignored his nattering. At any other time she'd have been fascinated but right now she had other priorities—starting with not being eaten. She paused on the landing halfway up to the first floor. The ground-floor hallway had filled up with smoky mist to knee height, and where the mist swirled thickest the shadows of the hounds began to flicker in and out of view.

Eve knelt.

"What are you doing?" hissed George. "We don't have time! If we make haste into the dream roads we might be able to—"

"Nope, not going there," Eve said as she hastily sifted through her pocket contents. She had no ritual chalk or charcoal, but—*oh, that might work*—she tugged the false pearls from her necklace. Six were a start: twelve would be better. She shoved them into position with a thought, setting up a circle on the landing. "Get in here," she told George as she concentrated on heat, willing the arcs and lines she was visualizing between the bullets to warm up and up and *up,* hot, hotter, charring the carpet runner. Smoke began to tickle her nostrils as a dull throbbing headache clamped vise-jaws around her temples.

"What are you"—George stepped across the last line as it began to glow eerie blue, decaying *mana* radiating light as Eve pushed power into the circle—"*doing?*"

"Get behind me and push," she wheezed, trying not to inhale through her itching nostrils. The scent of burning wool gave her an almost unbearable urge to sneeze, which would be disastrous at this point. "Because your life depends—"

George needed no further urging: he was proficient enough to sense the herculean effort Eve was putting into the circle and to work out what she was doing. He began to chant in Enochian, his tone dark and forbidding, every phrase gravid with crackling power. The improvised protective ward lit up blindingly bright, the glowing circle throwing stark shadows that underlit his face and made dark holes of his eye sockets. Eve felt lightheaded, but kept pushing her own power out. It felt as if a heavy weight hung from her shoulders. Dizzy, she was unsure which way was up: a swoon threatened, but the mist was still rising. The many-legged phantoms cast about agitatedly in the turbid darkness. She began to flex her fingers in sequence, discharging all the *mana* she'd bound up in her spell macros, for there was no point in holding anything back at this point.

The thickening mist billowed up the stairs as if blown by an intangible breeze. Shadows writhed and tumbled inside it, and Eve sensed rather than heard the eerie keening of a hunting pack that had scented their prey at last. But the vapor paused when it reached the landing, bulking up and flowing around her ward as if it was the solid dome of a glass bell jar sized for two. She breathed deeply and chanted her aversion spell aloud, merging it with the shield. A moment later George joined in, reciting in close harmony with her. It was draining, and a deep ache settled into Eve's every muscle and joint. But the baying of the hounds became uncertain, and the mist began to ebb away.

In her near swoon Eve thought she heard human speech, the voices of the sisters directing the beasts from beyond the smog. "*Where is she? I swear she was here a minute ago—in this room—the candles still burning—why aren't—*" The complaint gave way to a smothered unearthly shriek. The hounds belled eerily once, then the mist receded: and just in time, for Eve's knees gave way and she slid to the floor, breaking the circle. A moment later George crumpled on the landing beside her, out cold. She could barely muster the energy to raise her left hand, dismissing the power they'd pumped into the circle of protection, and when she let it drop something hard burned her wrist. She twitched away involuntarily, shocked back into awareness. It was one of the nacre-coated bullets, now a shapeless melted mass that had begun to cool.

Time passed. George groaned quietly and struggled to sit up. "Are you injured, my Lady?"

Eve shook herself. "Only my dignity. That was a close call. If they'd come in the night, or even a couple of hours ago—"

"Indeed." He sounded shaky. "This is intolerable! Number Twelve has overstepped. Seeking to recapture runaways from the institution is expected, but the hounds consume the souls of those they run to ground if not restrained by their handlers. I take it your—Rupert—would not have told her to unleash them?"

Eve noticed the pause as George caught himself short of the word *husband*. "I very much doubt it. If he knows I'm here, that is. He ordered me to stay at my post back in my own time, so he has no reason to expect to find me here unless someone told him. And you say he's in the wind."

"Your post?" George looked puzzled.

"Some of us work for a living," she said, allowing a little acid to dribble into her voice. "And I don't mean on our backs."

George rose to his feet. "I assure you I did not think that of you. But in the meantime we have a problem. Excuse me . . . ?" Before she could object he bent down and picked her up in a bridal carry. *Memo to self: if fleeing this one, remember to stab him first*, then *run*, she noted. Otherwise she'd never get away. Not that she was planning on fleeing anyway—George seemed excessively devoted to preserving her well-being—but he was built like a tank. A tank that had ideas of its own and was now carrying her upstairs whether she liked it or not (and to her surprise she realized that she did, in fact, like it a *lot*).

"Where are you taking me? Put me down!" Her protest was pro forma.

"I have inquiries to make about town, and I shall feel much better knowing you are in a circle of safety while I pursue them. If you please?"

George opened the door effortlessly despite holding a double armful of Starkey sorceress. She thumped his shoulder lightly: a warning, rather than a serious protest (for now). He was mindful enough to turn sideways to spare her head an encounter with the doorpost. It was all rather confusing but very hot, she thought fuzzily, before she realized where he'd brought her.

In two centuries' time this would be her brother Imp's bedroom. Eve recognized it from the door and window layout, which hadn't changed at all. Right now it was . . . not very different at all: Imp tended to be a hoarder, not to say a trash magnet, and it seemed George too needed some sort of bizarre man cave to sit and brood in. A stuffed crocodile hung from the ceiling; a ship's wheel graced one wall: there were bookcases and a cabinet of glassware, alembics, retorts and the like: and in the center of the room a cast-iron containment grid sat atop the scraped wooden boards.

"Here we are!" he said as he lowered Eve's feet to the floor as delicately as if she was made of the finest Venetian glass. "Welcome to my laboratory, Number Six. What else was I looking for . . . ?" A desk and chair were shoved against one wall, the desk elbow-deep in papers. George picked up the chair and planted it in the middle of the grid. "Sit here, please." He gestured, clearly expecting Eve to submit meekly after her encounter with the hounds.

Eve shook her skirts out then crossed her arms and introduced him to a glare she'd spent years honing on underperforming minions. "*Not* until you tell me why!"

George looked unimpressed.

"We discussed a partnership," she pointed out, trying to keep her tone icy, because melting all over him wasn't going to help. "This is *not* how partnerships work. I expect to accompany you as you make your enquiries—"

"My dear lady."

Eve steeled herself, marshaling her objections before he finished his sentence: *here it comes, the standard early-nineteenth-century don't-worry-your-pretty-head-my-dear.* She almost regretted having expended her necklace of bullets.

"I agree with you completely—"

"*What?*" She was taken aback.

"But the clubs I need to visit do not admit the fairer sex."

"Oh for—" She managed to bite her tongue just in time: Ladies weren't supposed to know those words. *Sailors* probably weren't supposed to know them. "Listen. If you have a footman of about my height whose uniform I could borrow—"

"No, my Lady: you're a practitioner of the highest art, do you believe for an instant that you could cross the threshold of the Invisible College unnoticed? It'd be one thing to maintain your disguise in a molly house or a brothel where they cater to the English vice." His cheeks pinked slightly as he realized what he'd just implied. "Ahem. But I need to consult certain most-secret archives in Whitehall, and you are not a member of the House of Lords, and there are *things* bound to the doorposts—for want of a better word, demons—"

"Oh." Eve subsided. It wasn't just her testicular deficiency excluding her for social reasons: it was actual no-shit national-security policy. "So this"—her gesture took in the room—"is for my own protection? Not simply another jail?"

"I shall not lock the door on you, but can I presume upon your common sense to keep you safe? If the hounds return you may retreat within the circle here." Which was not unreasonable, she conceded: a closed cold iron circle was far easier to energize than her improvised carpet-scorchings. "I shall only be two to three hours, and I'll leave word with Mrs. Dorling to bring you lunch, and to see to the carpet on the landing." (Was that an attempt to guilt-trip her?) "Once I have some answers we can discuss what to do next. There are some other avenues of enquiry I need to pursue, where your presence is not only permitted but will probably be helpful: just not this one."

He made it all sound so *reasonable,* that was the worst part. "Before you go—what did Rupert do when he returned from the dream roads? I mean, what did he do here, to get you so upset?"

"Upset?" George looked appalled. "Apart from murdering my parents in their beds? Nothing of any greater consequence!" Then he closed the door behind him, leaving Eve utterly at a loss for words.

▸◂▸◂▸◂

George had made good on his promise not to lock the door. When Eve stopped fuming about his high-handedness, she realized that he'd given her an unexpected gift. She knew this house better than he suspected. And given that this was indeed Imp's bedroom in her own time, Number Seven had granted her a unique opportunity.

"The only question," Eve mused aloud, "is whether time travel via the dream roads is call by value or call by reference."

The coding metaphor sprang to mind unasked. Almost before she was out of nappies, her mother had begun teaching her to program on a dusty BBC Model B. Mum had been a mainframe programmer before marriage, children, and a series of increasingly manipulative cults had done a number on her mind. Eve hadn't had much cause to use the skill in recent years—not unless you counted spreadsheet macros, for she'd specialized in finance and management at university—but the mode of thinking was useful for structured magic.

You could generally call a subroutine embedded in a larger program through two mechanisms. In call by value, you invoked a subroutine, giving it a bunch of variables, and it would do something, then return without changing them. All it could do was look at their values at the moment where you triggered it: there were no side effects elsewhere in the program. But in call by reference, you handed the subroutine the location in memory where the data was stored, and implicitly gave it permission to meddle.

Time travel via the dream roads didn't mean actual travel into the past: instead, it sent you into a pocket re-creation. But the re-creation might have external side effects when you returned to the waking realm. It might even set up resonance effects with the real historical record. It was how the Invisible College had suppressed magic, once upon a time, when it threatened to become too strong. (It was a technique that had failed spectacularly when they suppressed it so thoroughly that everybody forgot it was a thing—until it came roaring back again, stronger than ever and out of control, once they'd almost completely disbanded.)

Not all dreams remained in memory when the dreamer

awakened. It was possible that nothing she changed here would have any effect when she got back to her own time: that was how call by value worked. But if this was hooked into the real thing, if she'd been handed a stack pointer into history itself . . . she'd have to be very, *very* careful.

It seemed most likely that Rupert had returned because he believed he could edit the modern era's history, using the dream roads' tendency to converge on archetypes to lure his enemies here—where they were weakest—and crush them.

Well, Eve could come up with a strategic plan, too. And she knew the rules of the game.

Desk. Paper, pens, penknife, inkwell, *tools*. Eve smiled a feral smile, cracked her knuckles, and went to work.

First, the letter. Keeping a weather eye on the iron grid—she was ready to jump for the chair at the first sign of mist—Eve picked up a spare sheet of foolscap and wrote on one side:

"To Imp (Jeremy Starkey). If you are not Imp and it is not yet" (she wrote in her date of departure) "do not open this envelope under any circumstances or YOU MAY CEASE TO EXIST." (A reasonable supposition, where temporal paradoxes were in play.) "Put it back where you found it and forget you saw it."

She turned the page over and jotted down information and instructions for her brother in the future, hoping like hell he wouldn't be stoned when he found it this time. Assuming he *did* find it: also assuming her theory of time travel in the dream roads was correct. George had left a candle and a stub of sealing wax behind. Using the penknife she cut a short lock of her own hair and used a drop of wax to attach it after her signature. Then she folded the letter repeatedly, making tabs and slots from the edges to lock the text (and the lock of hair) inside so that it could not be read without tearing the tabs, as was common practice with letters in this era.

She melted another blob of wax over the edge of the paper, then in lieu of an actual seal she pressed the ball of her right thumb on it. *Ouch.* Sealing wax, it turned out, stayed hot even after it solidified.

She sucked her stinging thumb, then stood up and began to search the skirting boards, trying to remember where Imp had positioned his mattress and where the electricity sockets had been. She briefly considered Number Seven's palette knife and the wallpaper, but decided there was no way the walls had survived without being stripped and replastered several times over. It had been two centuries, after all. Avoid the window casement where radiators would later be installed, and the boards that covered the future hot-water pipes. Avoid . . . yes, *here* and *there,* she was sure there had been mains sockets. What else . . . ?

Wi-Fi. Wi-Fi was a twenty-first-century innovation. Imp had installed a mesh network to flood fill the house, and of course he'd nailed a repeater to the doorframe with a trailing power cord. The penny dropped, and now she knew where to dig. A floorboard beneath the future hot spot was easy enough to lever up with the tools available. Eve took another sheet of paper, hastily scribed a ward and an intent upon it—a spell to attract his attention only at the right time—placed it on the exposed lath and plaster between the joists, and laid her letter on top of it. Then she replaced the board. Her letter to the future should remain undisturbed until Imp installed the internet extender—and if he had the sense of a boiled frog he'd wait to open it until the date on the front, the day after her hasty disappearance. And then . . .

Eve explored the second floor of the house after she planted her time capsule. There were changes: what in her time was a bathroom was in this time another guest room. There was a nursery, the furniture shrouded in dust sheets. And then she found George's private chambers. He had a padlocked armoire by his bed, and when it yielded to her mental fingers it revealed a collection of very interesting toys: it seemed her bedroom interests were unusually closely aligned with her host's.

But then the morning's excitement caught up with her. Eve's expenditure of energy diverting the hounds then creating a message in a bottle left her feeling quite drained. So she took a book from George's shelves, requested a pot of tea (which came on a collapsible table with a plate of slightly stale cupcakes), and made herself at home in George's laboratory.

The book was a dry thesis on certain irregularities in Enochian metagrammar, but written with a degree of theoretical knowledge she was surprised to find in such an early text. She was completely engrossed—aside from brief checks of her surroundings—when George returned. He cleared his throat. "Oh, it's you," she said, affecting disinterest while watching him out of the corner of her eye (she had decided against letting him know he was forgiven just yet). "Did you discover anything?"

"Oddly, yes." George sounded tired and frustrated. He helped himself to the dregs of the tea, then leaned his hip against the desk. "The right hand washes the left, but not vice versa. There are many mansions in His Majesty's house, but I only found out what I needed to know by accident when I stopped for a pie and a pint between offices."

Surprised, Eve glanced at the window. The sky was overcast but the direction of the shadows had shifted. He'd clearly been gone a lot longer than three hours. "You have news, then?"

"I see you've been reading: a novel, or—"

Eve hid the book inside her sleeve before he could scan the embossed title. "You first." She waited.

"Oh, I see." He chewed his lip. "You are quite right to be upset, I did not expect to be so long. Unconscionable of me, I know."

"That's not what I meant. What news of Rupert?" Eve demanded. She caught the direction of his gaze. "I have no complaints about Mrs. Dorling's catering."

"I confess to some relief. To business: the Invisible College is clearly unaware of Rupert's location. If they could tell me where he was, I wouldn't have needed to spend the past week tracking you down, or an entire morning wasting my time traipsing around Whitehall. Headless chickens running around the farmyard, all of them." He sounded frustrated. "But the Admiralty, of all people, had word of Rupert. Or should I say they had news *about* Rupert de Montfort Bigge—"

Eve was on her feet instantly, tea and text on theory of thaumaturgy forgotten. "Yes?" She demanded, "Where *is* he?"

"Involved in smuggling!" George shook his head. "It seems he came storming back to London six months ago, only to run away to sea! There's plenty of money to be made in smuggling; he found a brig engaged in the cross-Channel trade to Normandy—although where it lands in England is a question the Excise are *most* interested in answering—and bought a controlling interest from the former owners, then replaced its captain. It sometimes puts in to port in Bristol, and is seen on the Mersey for repairs, but whenever the customs men board him they find only empty holds and an insufficiency of cargo to explain his well-lined wallet. Merely being inexplicably rich is not a crime in England—were it so, half of Parliament would be in jail—so they had no grounds to hold him."

"A ship." Bones in a gibbet cage rattled Eve's memories. What had Wendy said . . . ? "Was the vessel by any chance called *Prince of Poets*?"

"*Prince of*—?" George shook his head. "Yes," he said slowly. Crow's feet deepened adorably around his eyes. "How did you know?"

"There *was* an abandoned hulk—a two-masted brig—found in a smuggler's cave on Skaro, in my time. It had been there for well over a century, possibly long enough that it dates to the here and now. Rupert is an initiate of the rites of a ghastly entity that is called the Prince of Poetry and Song by its worshippers, and that was the hulk's name, so I thought . . ." She trailed off.

It must *be the same vessel*, she thought. *Surely?* How much could she safely tell him, without putting the future at risk?

"What are you not telling me?" George prompted her. Despite his obvious unease, she saw that his suspicion was not hostile.

Eve took a deep breath.

"I have a confession to make: my family lived in this house for over a century. This was my brother's bedroom." George's eyes widened, but before he could interrupt she pressed on. "That's two hundred years from now. Rupert tricked me into marriage for reasons I am not certain of, but most likely because he wanted the title to the house and the door to the dream roads—which I thought my ancestors had created, although that hasn't happened yet, maybe? Apparently it predates them. The ancestor who came into custody of the book Rupert wanted—the great-great-great-grandfather who bought the house—hid it in a dream library to keep it out of the wrong hands. I thought at the time Rupert wanted me because I could handle it—it was under a curse tied to my bloodline—but there was more to it than that. Or so he said when he returned from the past."

George shook his head. "The more I learn, the more confused I become. The Sisterhood are hunting you, and they were founded by Rupert. He knows you are here by now—"

"How can you be sure?"

"Because you were detained in the Village. To say nothing of Saint Hilda's." At her blank look, George explained. "Rupert built the Village for the Invisible College as an internment camp for captured enemy sorcerers. It was his idea. He appeared out of nowhere twenty-five years ago, acquired a fortune—whether through gaming or playing the stocks is unclear—then made himself known to Their Lordships. He claimed to be just another patriotic Englishman, stranded outside his own time, with some creative ideas for aiding the war effort. Who did you think Number One was?" He shook his head in disgust. "He has a bloated opinion of his own self-worth; they should never have trusted him."

Eve stared at him slack-jawed. It seemed their exchange of secrets was escalating.

"Hello?" George looked concerned. "My Lady? Are you all right?" He knelt before her, a sudden urgency in his manner. "Can you speak? Can you raise your hands? I fear—"

Eve swallowed. "I've been a fool," she confessed.

George looked relieved, then slightly resentful, as if he thought she'd tricked him into believing she'd suffered an apoplexy. "Please don't do that again."

"What, confess to my own stupidity?" She sounded too sharp even to her own ears. "I'm sorry. I'm angry at myself, not you."

"Well, regardless of who you're angry at, please don't leave me wondering if you're about to die of apoplexy? It was most unpleasant." He stood up again, then offered her his hand. Eve took it and stepped close.

"What?" she asked, looking him in the eye.

"If the Sisters are searching for you, Rupert is obviously behind them." George spoke just slowly enough to make it clear he was giving her time to catch up without intending any insult. "They won't give up, and they'll try here again if he has informed them of your family connection, and there are too many right angles in this house. And the book *isn't* here, or Rupert would already have found it. I'd wager good money on it. And that's before we come to the baron and his boy. We need to leave."

"The baron." Eve was thinking aloud. "He's a mad natural philosopher, correct? One who works with life energy and bodies. Bits of bodies."

"Yes: he created the boy by means most foul and necromantic."

"Let me see: he used blood or skin or saliva stolen from the emperor, and"—Eve shuddered as she realized what this meant—"implanted the boy in some poor soul's womb?"

"Yes." George paused, then remembered who he was conversing with and continued, "If you must know—it is not a matter for delicate ears—" He proceeded when Eve nodded encouragingly. "He grew his first boy in the unnaturally animated corpse of an executed aristocrat—"

Eve shuddered again and forced herself to ignore the horrifyingly intimate implications. "So the boy is a valuable government asset that has gone walkabout for some reason, right after I arrived on the scene?"

"Yes. My second objective was to retrieve him. I left them both in the capable hands of Sergeant Benson, who was to return them to the Village. But he should have sent me a letter by now."

"When?"

"The day before I rescu—excuse me, the day before you rescued *yourself* from Saint Hilda's? So, three days ago—"

"You should have heard from him by now," Eve determined. "If nothing else, he has had time to get as far as York and write you a letter, which should have—" She froze. "Why do you imagine Rupert might have an interest in the baron, too?"

A memory of Rupert's state of decay returned to haunt her. A sorcerer-lich sustained by malice and bloody-mindedness might indeed want Europe's greatest reanimator on his staff. Worse: the doctor in question had been experimenting with cloning and memory transfer, achieving a degree of success that eluded twenty-first-century scientists constrained by pettifogging concerns about medical ethics. (*Not so good for any hapless woman Rupert decided to use as an incubator,* she thought with a very personal sense of horror.)

George slid an arm around her shoulders and stated, as if it were a settled matter and not open to debate, "I shall not allow him to take you as long as I draw breath. It will only happen over my dead body."

Eve shivered. "Don't say that," she murmured, "you never know what will happen."

George pressed his lips to her forehead briefly, and she shivered for an entirely different reason; then he released her, seemingly unaware of her confusion.

Quick, change the subject, she thought. "Can you send a message to the Village?" she asked. "One that Rupert can't intercept?"

"Yes, but secrecy is time-consuming: we might not get a reply until next week—why?"

"Thinking. Would Rupert's brig have been smuggling port or madeira wines, by any chance? From Spain?"

"Why? Oh, you think he was looking for the copy of the manuscript in Madrid? It's possible."

"It's one option," she said aloud. "Although I think it more likely he's looking for the baron these days, not the book." The book was a necromantic reference tome, among other things. But if the baron had worked out how to clone men and copy their memories, Rupert's plan might not require the book anymore. (*Just the baron and an obedient host womb for his scheme,* she thought dismally, assuming she had correctly deduced his scheme. Being trapped in an undead, decaying body need not be a significant obstacle if one could clone oneself and transfer into a new body . . . immortality of a sort would open all sorts of new opportunities to someone like Rupert. She set the insight aside for later contemplation.) "A ship would be useful if he was considering a retrieval from the Village. And the baron will be with the boy, or looking for the boy. I don't think Number Two really expected him to get away by balloon, did he?"

George looked affronted. "Would *you*? The whole idea of flying is unnatural!"

"Oh, you have *no* idea." Eve snorted out of sheer frustration. *If only I had the helicopter, or cellphone coverage*—but then so would Rupert. The loss of communications and high-speed travel made the world feel so much larger and more intractable. But on the other hand, it afforded her more space to hide in. "We need to know if the baron and the boy are still in custody."

"We—" He paused. "Yes, we do," he said hesitantly, with a faint hitch in his voice. "I shall write to Number Two immediately. We can probably survive another night here, with precautions—I shall have the servants make up a bed for you in the circle—then I'd like you to help me with some enquiries tomorrow."

Eve stood up. "At last!"

"Yes. And I have an idea." He had a number of smiles, she was discovering, all of them unique. The one that he wore now was new to Eve. It was feral and a little bit mischievous and she loved how it made his face light up darkly: it was the smile of a dangerous man, one who was about to invite her along on an adventure. "Would you like to help me set a trap for Rupert?"

▸◂▸◂▸◂

Eve spent an uneventful night on a folding cot inside the protective grid on George's laboratory floor. She didn't ask after her host's own arrangements, but assumed he'd set up a similar protective system in his bedroom. (Unmarried ladies very emphatically did *not* ask men about their sleeping arrangements in 1816, or so she had been led to understand.) The Sisterhood refrained from sending their hounds after George and Eve overnight for whatever reason, and after breakfast the next morning George suggested a walk. "The weather is good, and there are people I should like to make enquiries of at the Inns of Court—it is a long walk but it takes us past the park, and thereafter we could take a hackney the rest of the way? There's a rank near St. George's Fields."

"A walk would be good," Eve agreed, surprising herself. "What do you hope to discover?"

"Well." George sipped his cup of tea. "The Admiralty are all very well, but if one is seeking word of events at sea, one really should consider making enquiries with Lloyd's Agency. And while that might normally require a visit to Pope's Head Alley, I happen to know of a Name who is in chambers close by Lincoln's Inn Fields, which is considerably closer and doesn't take us past as many rookeries."

Eve blinked. "Rookeries?"

George gave her an odd look. "Come, my Lady." He put down his cup. "Surely you—"

"There are rookeries near *the Bank of England*?" In her own time it was all glass-and-steel skyscrapers, picturesque listed buildings (part of a designated World Heritage Site), tourists, and armored police with machine guns.

"Where was it you come from again." His tone was flat, disbelieving. "Fairyland?"

"No, London—" She paused. "Just, the early twenty-first century is very different." She put her own teacup down. "They cleared the rookeries, for one thing." She'd blundered into one in her nightmare visit to 1888, and managed to blunder out again without getting her throat cut, although her bodyguard had been less lucky.

He shook his head. "Stay close to me and I shall keep you safe."

Kensington Gardens and Hyde Park were relatively salubrious—this was, after all, where the Horse Guards and the upper classes went riding along Rotten Row and South Carriage Drive, even if George was not escorting her that far south. As they neared the tollgate close by the site of the former gallows, George hailed a passing cab and handed Eve up into it. "To the Bar Gate," he told the jarvie through the hatch behind his head.

Hours of traipsing between stiflingly cramped chambers near Temple Bar did not improve Eve's mood, especially as most of the barristers George wanted to visit insisted on parking *the lady* in a waiting room outside, lest she be exposed to the lurid and corrupting influence of the law (which, it was made clear, was for men only). The presence of the fair sex in public appeared to be viewed as an alien intrusion. Indeed, at one point an unwary clerk entered the waiting room by mistake, panicked, and spilled the inkwell he was carrying when she *smiled* at him. That was the highlight of her morning, and Eve was mightily vexed when George emerged, blinking, to escort her back toward Chancery Lane and the next set.

As they reached the front door, she turned to him. "This seems to be a safe neighborhood, so I shall go for a stroll while you're busy—there are shops to see." She smiled pointedly, this time closing a door on conversation rather than opening it. "I'll meet you back here in exactly an hour." She wiggled her fingers, triggering a macro for keeping track of valuables, and touched her index finger to his lapel. "Be seeing you."

George looked about to protest, but then looked at her again and did a double take. He nodded gravely. "No rookeries, mind you," he warned her.

"No rookeries," she echoed. Then she turned and stepped out on her own.

The area around High Holborn was not uncivilized or particularly dangerous in this time, which is to say it had no more than its share of dung-strewn cobblestones, barking costermongers, dead drunks in gutters (or perhaps they were just plain dead), stench, flies, and rotting food waste. The back streets were narrow and stank of piss and shit, and the shop fronts at ground level were overhung by quaint upper-floor dwellings, but they were recognizably shops, and in a good enough state of repair that she did not fear their imminent collapse. Some of them even smelled inviting—here a baker, there a coffeehouse. Eve stayed out of these, preferring to remain a moving target, but she noted their location for when she retrieved her escort. Some of the shops were perplexing (from the window display this one appeared to sell nothing but wooden brooms; that one specialized in balls of string), but others were more familiar. She was about to pass a shop with a narrow window frontage crammed with crude toy soldiers and wooden horses—NOAH'S ARK shouted a sign above the door—when a familiar figure loitering on the pavement outside caught her eye.

"Hello there," she said, gripping François's shoulder before he could bolt. "Remember me?"

"Ma'mselle!" Wide eyes peered up at her. "Please, you must help me!" Other details came into focus: his tousled hair, hollow cheeks, the rip on his sleeve. One of his shoes was missing, his foot bare and filthy. This was not the well-put-together lad she had parted company with on a rainy highway near Grantham, the charge of a German baron.

"What happened to you?"

"The soldiers took me and Monsieur *le* Baron, but before they could put us aboard a coach the monsters, they attack—"

"Monsters?" Eve peered at him. *Is he hallucinating?* she wondered, then remembered: *Wait, near Grantham—*

"Monsters like dogs, they hunt the soldiers but I run away from them and—" He glanced around furtively, continuing very quietly. "—took a horse. It was not theft for the soldier was beyond needing him. But he is lame, and I walk the rest of the way to *Londres* and now I am starving and penniless."

"We'll fix that," Eve assured him, and felt his shoulder slump with relief. "When did you last eat? Or sleep?"

François looked baffled. "Days," he said uncertainly.

"Well, then." George would be finishing soon, and he'd surely be pleased to find François in her company. "We should get going. If you're coming with me, there will be food and a bed for you."

"But—" As if by magic, the lad's eyes swiveled toward the shop window and glazed over. "I need the, the tiny men of tin? For the kriegspiel spell—"

Eve followed his gaze. Below the shop sign (NOAH'S ARK, PROP. WM. HAMLEY SINCE 1760), rank after rank of toys menaced the unwary passerby from the window. One entire shelf was full of porcelain dolls; another was covered with an array of miniature soldiers drawn up in a thin red line, opposite the white-and-blue figurines of French imperial grenadiers. *Kriegspiel spell,* she thought, then, *Hot damn!* "I don't have the money to buy them," she began, "but we can return with—"

Too late: François had already opened the door and walked inside. Despite his evident exhaustion (and blistered feet) his back was ramrod straight and his head tilted back in the self-assured posture of a general about to inspect his troops. *Fucknuggets,* Eve thought, *that's a geas at work for sure.* She swept through the door in hot pursuit.

The shop was rammed full of toys from floor to ceiling. Various puppets dangled from the rafters, necks drooping and limbs limp as if participating in a mass execution. More dolls and stuffed animals took up one wall, while rows of toy soldiers filled up a glass-topped display case in the middle of the room. Hobbyhorses and hoops and balls filled every available corner. As shops went it wasn't very large, but then nothing in this era was built to any scale except the mansions and palaces of the hyperrich. An elderly shopkeeper leaned over François. "Nay, lad, you can't be in—" Eve drew herself up behind him. "Oh, my apologies, ma'am, is this urchin bothering you?"

Eve glared at him. "My nephew is no bother to anyone!" she insisted indignantly, twitching her fingertips frantically. "He was robbed not five minutes ago by a gang of thieves working the street. We barely got away with one of his shoes—"

Behind the shopkeeper a drawer slid open and fell to the ground as Eve tugged on it with her mind. While she distracted him François flexed an arcane power that made the skin on the back of her neck crawl.

"What's that?" the shopkeeper asked querulously. "How did that come open—hey, you! Stop that! Wait, what's—how are they—*eep*! Witchcraft and devilry!"

A company of blue-and-white-clad Immortals—the Old Guard of the French emperor—came boiling up and over the sides of the fallen drawer like living troops storming a rampart. They formed up around their raised standard with fixed bayonets and marched out from behind the counter like a column of army ants. Half a dozen horse-drawn artillery carriages rode behind them. The smell of burning gunpowder seemed to hang in the shop's stuffy air, and screams and distant bugles echoed in Eve's ears. It was all François's doing, she realized. The shopkeeper cringed in horror, as if the floor was on fire—as well it might be to him, for now she looked close she realized his coat had once been red and one side of his face bore the scars of a powder burn.

"Come on, Jack, we're leaving now," Eve said firmly, clapping her hand on the lad's shoulder and triggering her other macro, the eyeballs-can't-track-me spell. She backed toward the door, pushed it open, and dragged François out of the shop. He stuck in the doorway and refused to budge for several seconds and Eve was about to tug him harder when she glanced down and realized she couldn't see the paving stones. "Nothing for us here, boy," she said, and nudged him hastily toward the next door along. "Tell them to meet us in the alleyway round the corner," she hissed, then gave him another poke.

Ten minutes later Eve strolled up behind George as he paced the street outside the barristers' chambers, cursing volubly and casting about for her. "Boo," she said, just to watch him jump. "You'll never guess where I've been!"

"You were supposed to be here a quarter of an hour ago!" George grumbled like an approaching storm of disapproval. "I thought you'd been abducted!"

"Nothing so convenient for you," she said, artlessly tucking her hand inside his elbow. "I made a discovery."

"I don't care! You could have been kidnapped! Sold to Barbary pirates! Throat slit and left for—"

"Don't be ridiculous. I was simply shopping for cleaning materials and lost track of time." Eve flipped open her tessen and fanned herself, even though it was a cold afternoon. "My fan is silk, and I don't seem to be able to get the dried blood out of it."

"Blood—" George tried to grab her fan and she hastily furled it. "Whose?"

"Nobody you care about." She tilted her nose up at him and sniffed delicately. "A highwayman, if you must know. Days ago, before I arrived at Saint Hilda's. He bled copiously."

"A—a—" George visibly struggled to control himself for a few seconds. "A-choo," he finally said weakly. "All right." A pause. "So what havoc have you wrought behind my back this time?"

"I learned something useful. I take it there were no reports from your friend?"

"No. Tell me what you found?"

"I have good news and some bad news. First, the bad: your soldiers ran into the hounds and lost track of the boy. I don't know about the baron." She waited politely until George stopped swearing. "But the good news is, I found François again." She looked round and beckoned discreetly. "He's starving, so I promised you'd take us to a carvery and buy us all lunch. Then he can tell you what happened. How about it?"

▸◂▸◂▸◂

Eve was learning to hate travel by carriage, even though the earl's landau (replete with luxuries like a spring suspension, glazed windows, and only two other passengers) was nothing like a stagecoach. It wasn't the carriage itself she objected to on this trip, or the hunky company—seated opposite, she was constantly tempted to ogle him—but the interminable journey. London stank of coal smoke and sewage, which barely covered the even more noisome stench of decaying food waste. It also rang with shouts, screams, the bellowing sales pitches of barkers, the complaints of sheep and cattle being driven to the slaughterhouses, and the conversations of a million people. It was so loud it made her long for the London of diesel engines and police sirens. What made everything so much worse was that it was *slow*. Ploughing through central London at about four miles per hour wasn't new to Eve, but when the buildings thinned out and they were rolling along macadamized roads between trees, farms, and villages, they were *still* making no more than eight miles per hour.

Eventually they stopped at a coaching inn. "Ah, excellent," said George. "Hatton Cross already!"

"Are we there yet?" demanded François, giving Number Seven the royal stink eye. Once fed, bathed, dressed in the earl's childhood castoffs, and allowed to play general with his tin soldiers for half an hour, the boy had calmed down considerably. But today he was a trifle fractious. George had decided they needed to hit the road as early as possible, but clearly hadn't reckoned with the needs of a twelve-year-old. Or rather, a six-year-old clone who had been force-grown to physically resemble a twelve-year-old, imbued with a personality and memories copied from the emperor when he had been thirty-nine; but who, whichever way you cut it, had the energy and impatience of any other twelve-year-old, and no greater tolerance for long-distance coach travel.

"We may be halfway there by nightfall."

"Halfway *where*?" Eve asked as he climbed down, then extended an arm to help her. "You said this was the fastest route!"

"Halfway to Bristol, of course. Come, let us sample the ale

while John Coachman sees to our horses and hitches up a new pair. You too, lad, you need to stretch your legs."

François muttered something extremely rude in French, which George pretended not to understand.

"Bristol—" Eve paused. "Why are we going to Bristol?" Bristol wasn't quite in the opposite direction from the Village, but it wasn't far off.

"To take ship, of course." George led her around to the front of the inn. (François trailed behind them, muttering dark imprecations about the fate George could expect once he regained his throne.) Number Seven's expression was bland. "It's barely slower than the Great North Road, and there are far fewer right angles on board a ship than in a landau. Best not to tempt the Sisterhood, don't you think?" He cast the boy a significant look. François sighed noisily and shrugged: he seemed to be no keener to meet the hounds again than Eve was.

"But the Sisterhood . . ." The asylum at Grantham was on the road back north. And even taking into account her involuntary detention it had taken her a week of solid travel to get from Liverpool to London. "Right angles attract the hounds, don't they?"

"Creatures of fatal geometry and precision, they come from beyond the boundaries drawn by Euclid. But they dislike curves, and the sea is nothing if not full of shapely waves."

Eve suppressed a snort of amusement at his arch look and florid misuse of allusion. "Tell me you're not an aspiring poet."

George gave an exaggerated shudder as he held the door open for them. "No, the dubious honor belongs to that jackass Byron's personal physician. He's my idiot shadow or something. Luckily he's embarked on the grand tour with his master and won't be back this year. Would you believe he accused me of being some sort of demonic hell-fiend? Mad fellow poured holy water in my whisky last time I saw him. At least he *said* it was holy water."

"Why would he do something like that?" Eve asked after he

led her to a side room and returned from giving instruction to the publican.

"I suspect he might have seen rather too much for his own good when I was consulting with the Royal College of Surgeons in Edinburgh last year. Enough of that: my point is, the hounds do not visit ships at sea, for whatever reason, any more than they trespass in circles of safety. There is security in geometry, so to speak. Unfortunately where the hounds go the sisters who summoned them may follow, and as natives of our own realm they are not so limited."

"What did Byron's doctor see?" Eve couldn't let it pass.

"I was only there to take the baron and his ward"—he nodded at the boy—"into protective custody." Number Seven shrugged and pretended not to notice François glowering at him. "Von Franckenstein came quietly, but before I arrived he had given a most disturbing demonstration of reanimation. It was of considerable interest to Their Lordships at the War Ministry, for obvious reasons: there are lots of spare body parts lying around on every battlefield, wouldn't it be good if the surgeons could assemble new soldiers from giblets and limbs? But the baron's method suffered from worse than the usual shortcomings, and besides, the war is now over."

"Body parts," echoed François, with a defensive hunch of the shoulders.

George paused as the servants arrived with cutlery, ale, and food. Eve nodded thoughtfully to herself. "Was the baron by any chance one of Rupert's initiates?" she asked when the maid and manservant departed. "Or had he spent time with Number Twelve?"

"Number Twelve, she is horrible," François volunteered, unasked. "She threatens Monsieur *le* Baron."

"Did she now." George looked thoughtful. He contemplated Francois. "Did he say anything about Rup—about Number One?"

François shrugged truculently. Having demolished his bowl of stew and chunk of bread he seemed restless—uninterested in sitting still. "Run along now," Eve told him, "I'm sure your soldiers are in need of a surprise inspection." François wasted no time in making for the door, where he paused and saluted her before leaving. "He won't talk to you yet," Eve told Number Seven. "Even *I* know you have to gain a child's trust, and you haven't even tried."

"For good reason: he's a headache, that lad," George observed sotto voce. "Just another twelve-year-old, but he's already a threat to the nation."

Eve let it slide. Obviously any version of Napoleon was regarded with considerable suspicion after the war, even a tousle-headed preteen one who'd been cloned by a War Office research program. "What about the baron and Rupert?"

"The baron? And Number One?" George shook himself. "Why do you ask?"

"It's a long story and parts of it will sound very odd to you. . . ." Eve explained her speculation about Rupert's motives as best she could. "In my time the process is called cloning, and the baron appears to have made unprecedented progress at it. I think Rupert intends to make himself effectively immortal by means of the process that gave you the boys—who you *really* want to keep away from South America, that won't end well."

"Oh dear." George continued to look thoughtful, but it was a worried kind of thoughtful: as if he was a general and she an enthusiastic junior officer, who had just bought word that the enemy was sneaking round the next hill over to outflank his front line. "Steps have already been taken to keep the boys from Brazil . . . meanwhile I find your speculation about Rupert's goal worryingly plausible." He cut into the slice of grayish roast beef in the middle of his plate. "If Rupert has captured the baron—and if he was taken by the Sisterhood that seems likely—that is a problem for both of us. But at least where we find one we will most likely find the other."

"And François?"

"As long as we have him he can't do much damage. . . . It is more the potential for damage that he represents that is of concern, rather than the boy himself."

Eve sniffed quietly. She hadn't told George about the toy-shop robbery yet. He was an upstanding citizen who might not appreciate the necessity of obtaining François's willing support. The boy's ability to animate his toys—not rare among magically gifted children; the offspring of Captain Colossal and the Blue Queen had such a talent—was not particularly notable. But George's high-handed dismissal irritated her; it rankled for some reason she couldn't quite articulate, so she withheld her counsel.

"Please eat your lunch before it gets cold, we still have miles to ride before nightfall."

Eve forced herself to finish the meal: overcooked roast beef, potatoes, and vegetables boiled to mush, all of it swimming in greasy gravy. It gave her time to pull her thoughts together. Von Franckenstein, like Tiffy, was obviously a member of Rupert's cult. Indeed, Rupert must have initiated him years ago—long enough for his work on force-grown clones to give rise to the lad, long enough to account for the Crown's *extreme* interest in his research. Research that led down some insalubrious alleyways and would later contribute to the passing of the Anatomy Acts. And *of course* the Shelleys would learn of Von Franckenstein from George's stalker, Lord Byron's physician—and come to think of it, hadn't he published a gothic yarn of his own after the house party by Lake Geneva? Byron, the Shelleys, Polidori, and their other hangers-on would be there right now. Nothing to do with Rupert; it was just another horrible narrative archetype of the sort the dream roads seemed to throw up like poisonous toadstools on the rotten log of history.

Rupert seemed to have an obsession with animating corpses in wholesale quantities, as well as setting up underground networks of fanatical worshippers to feed him *mana* and keep him supplied with tightly wound blond sorceresses. He'd had his followers working on it under cover at FlavrsMart in their own time, and the Sisterhood appeared to be the same sort of project by other means. It was absolutely infuriating: before she had awakened in the Village Eve would have sworn she was incapable of learning to hate Rupert any more—her rage trait was maxed out—but at every opportunity he presented her with a bottomless buffet of resentment and spite. She couldn't even bring herself to despise Tiffy: she'd been there herself, she knew what it was like to have her individuality drained and her goals warped into conformity with Rupert's diseased desires. He'd used the geas he'd bound her with to nudge her toward a course of plastic surgery that, if completed, would transform her into his perfect plastic playmate. He'd laid the same whammy on that HR manager and priestess—Jenny? Jennifer?—at FlavrsMart, and doubtless if plastic surgery had existed in 1816 he'd have done it to Tiffy. And the worst thing about it was, he'd made her think it was all her own idea. Jenny and Tiffy were horrible, terrible people, but no less his victims than Eve herself.

His treatment of women was degrading, and the more she thought about it the more steamed Eve became. It was as if her perceptions had been obscured by a fogbank, but there was no fog to blur her mind in this version of 1816—whether it was the real past or an oneiromantic pocket re-creation—and now her thoughts were sharp enough to draw blood.

It didn't matter a jot why he was doing it. He claimed to be doing it to fix some vast, overarching magical crisis caused by overpopulation and too many brains and computers. But the ends did *not* justify the means, and even if they did, Rupert's means were so conspicuously cruel that if they were the only way to save humanity, then humanity wasn't worth saving. Not that she believed Rupert's was the only viable plan: it was just the plan he had chosen to follow because it appealed to his depraved appetites.

I will kill him, she thought as she stabbed an innocent root vegetable to death. She needed a plan: a plan to run him to ground, a plan for the endgame, a plan that leveraged the dream roads' demented desire to rack her upon a procrustean bed of archetypes. She needed a *story,* one that she could control and turn to her own ends.

Finally they had both cleaned their plates. "Let us collect our ward and take coach once more," said George, taking her chair as she rose. "Onward ho!"

"Onward," she echoed grimly.

A SEA VOYAGE

Another night in an inn: then another day of tooth-rattling coach travel. They changed horses regularly at profligate expense, for George was spending money like water to maintain their rate of onward travel. François spent much of his time riding on top with the coachmen, but grumped incessantly about the tedium. They didn't stop to sleep at coaching inns, but instead George bought blankets and pillows into the coach for Eve, then rode up top for a few hours himself to lend her the illusion of privacy. (The coach was all curves: it gave no traction to the blue smoke and scrabbling claws of the hounds.)

Eve, being naturally suspicious, was curious about the lad's reasons for going along with them. After all, he'd previously embarked on a perilous escape attempt with the baron, then run away when things got tough. This abrupt tactical about-turn in his inexorable march on the Continent smelled somewhat fishy to her. Then again, he was a six-year-old in a twelve-year-old body. Wouldn't he want to stick close to an adult provider of meals, clothes, shelter, and toy soldiers? He had to know that nobody would take him seriously as a pretender to his progenitor's throne for at least a few years. She couldn't make her mind up on the basis of his behavior, but she didn't want to ask him directly, for he was not a terribly forthcoming child and she didn't want to spook him; the last thing she needed to deal with was a panicking magically endowed Napoleon clone. For the time being he seemed content to return to the Village, so there was nothing to be done but stand watch and fret.

After a couple of hours of uneasy sleep, Eve awakened with a sore neck and a bad taste in her mouth. She wished she'd filched a book or two from George's library, however dry the subject matter might be. The miles passed slowly, and with only her worries for company Eve's thoughts drifted down some very dark paths.

Why am I even here? she wondered, not for the first time. *Because Rupert* was a good first approximation. But it was a superficial one: she was here because she had to stop Rupert, both for her own safety and to propitiate His Dread Majesty beyond the dream roads. But what was Rupert doing here that required two trips into the past, decades apart, and no longer required the retrieval of the one true *Necronomicon*—as if he'd started on that project then discovered a new and far more promising objective to pursue? Obviously the self-cloning stratagem was a reasonable supposition, but if that was the path he had embarked on, why did he bother returning to the future at all? And what had turned Rupert from a willing collaborator with the Invisible College into a burn-your-bridges enemy on his second visit?

Did he, a nasty, paranoid corner of Eve's mind asked, *return to 2017 and tell me all about his plans—no*, not *about his plans, about the* shape *of his plans—simply because he could never resist an opportunity to gloat, or because he wanted to trick me into coming here of my own volition—*

Record scratch.

They were bouncing across cobbled streets between houses and shops by late afternoon. Not long after, they pulled up in a final courtyard. The air outside stank of road apples and fish guts overlaid by the brackish smell of rotting seaweed. Gulls circled overhead, screeching mournfully.

"Bristol," George announced with some satisfaction, "and still two hours to go until sunset!" He escorted Eve and François into the inn—more of a hotel than a pub—and demanded two rooms in the attic (where the eaves dipped low and the angles were obtuse). "I must go to the harbor forthwith, if we're to take ship in the morning," he told her. "I trust you not to make trouble while I'm gone. Come with me, lad, for we have ships to view."

"Yes, well, I'll just wait in here like a good little wifey," Eve said with ill humor, but her sarcasm went unnoticed: her traveling companions disappeared, leaving her to her own devices. "Fiddlesticks," she grumbled, then snapped her fingers for the maid. The inn was old enough that the joists sagged and none of the interior angles were true. "I require a bath," she said imperiously. She'd been on the road for days without benefit of luxuries like flush toilets or showers; to sweeten the pill she passed the girl a sixpence. "Bring it promptly and there'll be more where this came from. Also, where is the washerwoman? I have work for her. . . ."

By the time George returned from his errands the sun had set and the tin bath had been and gone. The maid had laced Eve into her spare gown, her traveling habit was with the laundry, and now she sat by the bedroom window with a pot of tea and a lit candle. She'd paid the landlord's wife to send out for some necessities: ribbon, paper, a small linen bag, and herbs. It made a plausible pomander, and with the right contents it would make a much more effective ward than the bloodstained rag she'd improvised in the asylum.

She'd given up on George's discarded newssheet when the sun went down. Now she was working through her fingertip macros, reminding herself of her spells as a way of distracting herself.

George watched her from the doorway with an unreadable expression. She supposed she must look a little strange, mumbling under her breath and contorting her hands through weird shadow-play shapes, but then she saw his face. "What is it?"

"I've found us a ship, and high tide is tomorrow around noon, that's the good part. My Lady, are you quite well . . . ?"

"I'm fine." Eve flushed, and shook her hands out. "Just practicing."

"Ah." Her stomach rumbled embarrassingly. "Then perhaps we should go in search of something to eat?" She stood up without prompting. "I'm sorry to have kept you waiting," he hastened to add.

"Supper would be good," she conceded. "And tell me about this ship."

The next morning, they went to the harbor—a forest of masts and yardarms at the bottom of a canyon of stone—where they boarded a small schooner. It was about the size of the Village's supply ship: Eve had been aboard larger yachts in her own time.

"This is Captain McNally, my Lady," George introduced as she came aboard. McNally was a forty-something fellow who looked as if he'd been left out in the rain every night, but he seemed sharp enough as he barked orders at the mate and bosun. He kept a wary eye on Eve and only addressed her through George, which she ascribed to yet another charmingly antique misogynist tradition and resolved to ignore.

"If you and your wife would do me the honor of attending my table for dinner tonight, I'd 'preciate it," McNally told George. "I'm sure your son will be at home with my midshipmen. My wife would normally sail with us but she's ashore for the next month. We're increasing." He gurned at Number Seven with proprietorial smugness. *Pregnant,* Eve translated, and couldn't make up her mind whether she wanted to congratulate the captain or punch him.

At least on this voyage she wouldn't be sleeping in a chest in the hold. The owner's quarters in the stern were next door to the captain's cabin, up against the port side of the ship's hull. Although the rooms were compact the carpentry was luxurious, and every available side panel seemed to conceal a drawer, cupboard, folding table, or stowaway bed. It made Eve feel like a piece of delicate silverware, wrapped in cloth and locked away in a meticulously crafted oak and mahogany sideboard, only to be taken out at mealtimes. Luckily for her state of mind there was no lock on the door (just a bolt on the inside, for privacy), and she had a small hinged porthole to puke out of if the sea became rough.

Still tired from the madcap carriage dash across the breadth of southern England, Eve retired to take a nap. When she awakened a couple of hours later the ship was rolling gently, with the banks of the Bristol Channel drifting past outside her porthole. If her cabin had been to starboard she'd have a view of Cardiff, she supposed. Now there was nothing for it but to wait while the ship sailed out onto the Irish Sea and turned north to skirt around the coast of Wales, which would take at least a couple of days. *But hey, the hounds can't catch us here*—and there'd be none of Rupert's minions sneaking aboard to slit her throat, either.

Eve left her cabin in search of George, and when she found him she chivvied him into giving her a guided tour of the vessel—or at least asking the questions the sailors didn't want to hear from a strange woman while they went about their not-terribly-mysterious duties.

The *Linda Lee* out of Bangor was a packet boat, a two-masted schooner that hired out to transport passengers and goods across the Irish Sea and up and down the coasts of Great Britain and Ireland. George had found Captain McNally just as he put in to Bristol in search of cargo, and promptly chartered the ship to Portmeirion. Equipped with a letter of introduction from the War Office, he refused to take no for an answer—but to be sure, he was careful to write a note committing the government to pay half again above the going rate, which sweetened the pill considerably. McNally was mildly grumpy, more about the principle of the thing than the money on the table: hiring a ship and all thirty of its crew just to ferry a man and his wife about the Welsh coast was an extravagance that didn't sit well with his Presbyterian principles. But it was hard to say no to a peer of the realm, and even harder to say no to the government, so after loading enough ballast to keep them on an even keel they hoisted sail with the ebb tide.

That evening, McNally entertained his adult passengers in the wardroom with those officers who were not on duty. His cook was better than those at most of the inns Eve had been subjected to, and the ingredients were still fresh. "Monsieur was chef aboard a French ship of the line," McNally confided after the monsieur in question dished up a passable clam chowder and retreated to finish the next course. A midshipman (one of McNally's sons) took turns around the table with a bottle, keeping their wineglasses topped up. "Shipwrecked at Trafalgar, impressed by Collingwood, then discharged three years ago—lucky to get 'im, I was. 'E'd already learned to cook decent English grub instead of fancy French mush, but 'e's good at it and no mistake."

Eve left the questions to George and kept her eyes down, making inroads on her meal. It was as good as promised, if somewhat underspiced (which seemed to be the norm for English cuisine in this period). When the main course arrived it proved to be a spit-roast chicken with chestnut stuffing and Jerusalem artichokes, green beans, and grilled courgette on the side: her taste buds thought she'd died and gone to heaven. *I've been here too long,* she thought, trying not to moan with delight. *I've gotten used to the terrible food.* (Clearly there was some truth behind the legend that the English had set out to conquer the world in order to escape their homegrown gastronomic atrocities.)

Eve listened quietly as she ate. George was a good interrogator, discreetly alternating between probing Captain McNally for news of smugglers and privateers in the western approaches and flattering him for his good taste, excellent choice of ship's cook, marvelously clement weather, and anything else he could think of. McNally was gruffly self-deprecating, but became increasingly smug and opened up as the meal progressed and the flattery escalated. The wine, he freely admitted, came from a fellow whom he thought *might* be a smuggler, but as it was for his personal supply and never touched land—it was transferred at sea and drunk there—the Excise couldn't possibly have a problem with it, could they? It was a passable Bordeaux, even though France had been under navy blockade until relatively recently.

"And pirates?" George nudged. "I heard a rumor that a couple of former privateers who surrendered their letters of marque after the colonial war have been sighted plying their trade in home waters. Is that likely to prove a problem?"

"Och, not to worry! If they've the good sense God gave a wood louse they won't be seen dead within a thousand miles of Greenwich, not now the French threat is ended and the blockade has been lifted. Lots of navy captains will be in search of a line o' work to replace their missing prize money." McNally shoveled a slice of chicken into his mouth, then poked a beautifully carved piece of courgette through the gravy with an expression of great dubiety on his face. "Hunh, Monsieur's tryin' to impress youse with 'is foreign greens," he grumbled. "No, there'll be no chance of ambush on this trip, you'll see. Not unless the colonials start up their rebelling again."

Eve had been wary of the sleeping arrangements since George introduced her as his wife and François as his son. It was ostensibly to protect her reputation as a virtuous woman—an infuriating necessity in this era—but Eve had concerns that went beyond Number Seven's intentions. The collective subconscious's vision of the Regency era had already thrown a whole bunch of shitty AU fanfic tropes at her, before settling on "fake marriage": she didn't have to be a romance reader to see "only one bed," "enemies to lovers," and "marriage of convenience" lurking in the wings.

This particularly deranged dream of 1816 seemed determined to marry her off to someone. Perhaps it was simply that her proxy marriage to Rupert was invalid here, and narrative abhorred a plot vacuum. Whatever the reason: it had thrown a fortune hunter at her, locked her in an asylum for wayward women, and having failed to get her into George's arms by means of natural attraction, it was about to play dirty. It was a crying shame: George was considerate, ripped, and loaded, and if Eve had met him during the white-tie reception at Lancaster House (or at a play party in the right kind of fetish club), he might well have scratched her post-Rupert itch. But this was the nineteenth century, and even if he shared her taste for kink—the trope engine would see to that if it came to it—they would never suit. The cottagecore lifestyle lost its charm when toilet paper wouldn't be invented for another forty years, and the dream realm would suck her soul dry if she tried to stay, doing to her what it had already done to Rupert. UwU: nope!

She retreated to her cabin after dinner while the officers and her faux husband passed a suspiciously crusty bottle of port and the captain broke out a deck of cards. As she'd expected, the cabin boy had unfolded the bed. It was a wooden box suspended from the ceiling by ropes, and it was indeed singular and big enough for two adults only if they were extremely friendly. "Bah," Eve grumped to herself. "Fucking collective unconscious." There ought to be a way to get a judo grip on the archetype and throw it over her shoulder, but she wasn't quite seeing it. So she rummaged through the nooks and cubbyholes until she found a couple of blankets and a spare cushion, built herself a nest against the bulkhead, and bedded down. A variation on her aversion macro sprang to mind easily enough, replacing "don't see me" with "don't touch me": having applied it to herself, she fell asleep wistfully imagining what it would be like to run her hands over George's well-oiled abs (preferably while he was blindfolded, hog-tied, and unable to resist).

Sometime later Eve was awakened by a startled curse and a thud. She opened her eyes to find George sprawled against the opposite wall of the cabin, shaking his hands and swearing. "Did you try to touch me?" she asked, fully awake and on her guard. *Man behaving badly!* her reflexes screamed. He'd made no attempt to molest her on their journey, but—

"Your damnable ward bit me!" He scowled in the dim lantern light.

Eve shoved herself upright. "*Why* did you try to touch me?"

"You can't stay there! It's not right. I only meant to lift you into the bed—"

"I'm not sleeping with you." Now they were *both* scowling.

"*I* know *that*, I'm going to sleep on the floor—where *you* are." *A likely story,* she thought—but on second thought, oddly plausible coming from George. Nevertheless, she kept her guard up.

"It's *my* floor and I'll sleep on it if I want to. You can't have it!"

"Are you always this willful, or do you reserve it just for me?" He'd taken his shoes off and removed his neckcloth and waistcoat, presumably in readiness for bed. She refused to admit how attractive she found this disheveled version of George. *Absolutely not!*

"*I'm* not willful, *you're* encroaching." She crossed her arms. After a pause she added, "So there."

"I'm attempting to ensure *one of us* gets a good night's sleep, and it's going to be you." Now they were leaning against opposite walls, knees raised before them and arms crossed, wearing identical scowls.

"You're not the boss of me," she warned, suddenly acutely aware of how ridiculous the situation was. She stifled a snigger as she realized that he was about to say—

"I'm a gentleman, you're a lady, it is my duty to protect you!" He seemed unable to comprehend that she might think otherwise, as if he believed his ridiculous statement was as physically real as the law of gravity.

"Protect me from what?" The snigger tried to escape as a giggle but she managed to strangle it in time: Eve did not *giggle*. Giggling was frivolous, and frivolity was the antithesis of dignity. Eve relied on dignified disapproval—not to say frigid hauteur, or even supercilious envenomation—to insulate her from inappropriate behavior. Working for Rupert had reinforced the no-giggling rule until it was a reflex, for any other strategy was an invitation for trouble. "Is the floor going to attack me in my sleep, by any chance? Do you think me so fragile that I'll bruise if the bed's too hard? Is an injury to my dignity likely to prove fatal?" She pointed at the suspended bed swaying slowly between them. "Take the bloody thing, man!" He recoiled as if she'd slapped him. *Oops, language.* "I'm not made of porcelain."

"It would be wrong for me to take the bed and let a lady sleep on the floor," he insisted, "so I suppose we will both be bruised in the morning. Good n—"

Eve forced herself to her feet, leaned forward, and grabbed his hand. "Go to bed, man," she snarled.

"After you, my Lady," he snapped.

They faced each other across the swinging bed, breathing hard, for a good minute. Then Eve lost it. The snigger returned, rising up from the depths of near exhaustion, and as it leaked out it lightened and gasified and bubbled into an all-out attack of the giggles as ghastly as any that she'd given vent to since her teens. It was mortifyingly embarrassing—until she realized that George was shaking with mirth, too.

"This is ridiculous," he finally gasped, taking hold of her other wrist with exaggerated care.

"I agree." She gritted her jaw, caught the laugh between her incisors, and bit down on it. (*So undignified.*) "You won't sleep on the bed if I'm on the floor, I won't sleep in the bed if you're on the floor, and neither of us really wants to sleep on the floor." She took a deep breath. "That leaves us sharing the bed. But listen—" She released his wrist only so that she could wave a pointed finger in his face. "—no funny business. Or I *will* cut you."

"No funny business," he agreed. He bent down, picked up the lantern, and hung it from a bracket clearly intended for that purpose. When he turned to face her again his expression was sober. "On my honor."

"All *right* then," she breathed, then George picked her up bodily and tossed her onto the mattress. It swayed alarmingly and tipped sideways, then almost spilled her out a second time when he climbed in alongside her. They were both still dressed. "No hanky-panky," she warned again.

"No what?" He looked confused. "Never mind." He reached over the edge of the bed and turned the wick down. "Good *night,* m'Lady." Then he rolled over and turned his face to the wall, and she was confronted simultaneously by his ridiculously broad back and the problem of how to get comfortable in the third of the bed he'd left her. The night was cold and most of the blankets were languishing on the floor. *Men, feh.* Did they have to take up the *entire* mattress?

▸◂▸◂▸◂

Eve awakened to the light of dawn dribbling in through the porthole, and discovered that George had rolled onto his back. He sprawled across almost the entire bed and she was curled against his flank for warmth, like a cat on a warm patch of floor. Worse, she'd thrown an arm across his chest and curled her knee over his hip, and he'd tucked a protective arm around her shoulders and was *cuddling her* as he snored. *Disengage! Disengage!* her brain shrieked, but there seemed to be no way to extricate herself without waking him, which would be even more horrific than the previous night's fit of the giggles. Despairing, she considered suicide. Or perhaps embarrassment was a fatal condition? She tried to remember if she'd ever heard of anyone dying of it. Maybe a romantic poet? But Eve was not a romantic poet: Eve did not have a poetic bone in her body (or if she'd started out with one she'd deliberately buried it in the catacombs under Rupert's manse).

On the other hand, embarrassing or not, being cuddled in his sleep by Lord Hunky of Perfection was *really nice*. Surely it would be all right to just lie here enjoying it for a bit longer, if he didn't wake up?

"Mm-hmm." The arm around her shoulder tightened as he moaned and rocked against her in his sleep, inadvertently setting fire to her core. She tensed and tried to resist the urge to rub herself against—*oh my,* she thought, as she discovered the hard way just how tight his breeches were. But just as her crotch was approaching atmospheric reentry temperatures, he woke up. "Mmm-*oh no*!" He made an inarticulate gurgle and recoiled, wide-eyed. "I'm so sorry, my Lady! I didn't mean to—"

This was what was known in the literature as a compromising position. But Eve had been going through a dry spell of biblical proportions, ever since she started working for Rupert. She certainly knew better *in theory,* but in practice her lady parts had awakened and her analytical mind was just along for the ride. Also, there were no witnesses. So it was with no surprise whatsoever that she observed her arm tighten around his shoulders as she dragged herself up and onto his chest, leaned in, and kissed him.

Dry spell aside, Eve was no stranger to kisses. She'd kissed men before—and a fair few women. But, kissing George *was* different. Sweet, passionate, engaging: she found herself running out of adjectives to describe the experience as she felt his tongue sweeping between her lips. She might have worried about morning breath if she'd paused to think, but the dream roads weren't about to let mundane realities like volatile sulfur compounds and diamines produced overnight by bacteria get in the way of true love. Nor was George one to protest her need to be on top, so she found herself kissing and fondling, and being kissed and fondled from beneath, with extreme enthusiasm: so much so that her knees went weak and her nipples tightened into hard knots as her heart hammered against her rib cage. She pulled back for breath after a timeless interval, her head spinning. "*Fuck,*" she breathed, feeling him tense beneath her and not caring what he thought about her language. And she was absolutely determined to kiss him again—then get down to the vitally important business of stripping him out of his clearly too-tight-for-morning breeches—when someone hammered on the door.

"*Fuck,*" breathed George, with an apologetic look. "Just one minute, my Lady." He spilled her across the mattress as he rolled out of bed and strode barefoot across the room. "What is it?" he shouted with barely concealed ill-temper.

The answer was muffled into inaudibility, but sounded distinctly unhappy. George threw the bolt and opened the door a crack. Eve sat up and watched over the side of the bed, holding her chemise up to cover her breasts. "Would you repeat that?"

"Captain's compliments, sir"—it was the cabin boy, red-faced and clearly even more embarrassed than Eve—"and you're wanted on the quarterdeck?"

"I see." George was clearly no happier to be interrupted than Eve, but as the haze of insta-lust cleared from her brain she began to wonder what was up. "What's going on?" George demanded.

"We're bein' hailed," said the cabin boy. "Got to run!" He dashed away, and now the door was ajar, Eve could hear the rapid thud of feet beating across the deck overhead.

"Something's up—" she said, as George turned to her and simultaneously said, "I should go and see—"

"Go." She made shooing motions. "Find out and tell me." She clenched her thighs together and wished that lying back down and thinking of England would help.

"Yes, m'Lady." George retreated into defensive formality as he pulled on shoes and jacket, then hastily knotted his neckcloth. "I'll be back presently." He took a deep breath. "You might as well get some more sleep."

"*Go*." She practically shoved him out the door, then began hunting for her abandoned stockings and shoes. She had a very bad feeling about this. Surely the narrative archetype wouldn't interrupt "only one bed" for anything short of a pirate attack?

▸◂▸◂▸◂

Ten minutes after George headed up to the quarterdeck—the platform at the stern where the captain and watch officers stood alongside the ship's wheel—Eve ascended to the main deck. She'd taken the time to dress in bonnet, pelisse, and gloves: it had been cold ashore, and she expected it would be even chillier on deck.

George appeared at her side. "You shouldn't be up here unaccompanied," he admonished her.

She ignored his rebuke. "Have you seen François today?"

"He's with the midshipmen," George said dismissively. "You should go back down—"

"What's going on?"

He harrumphed, then pointed to the port side, where the full sails of another ship were visible. She glanced in the other direction, saw the barest sliver of land on the horizon—the Welsh coastline. "Over there."

"What is it?"

"It's a navy ship, and she's signaling to us to heave to."

"Is that—" Eve thought for a moment. "—is that a particularly bad thing?"

George's gaze took in the officers on the quarterdeck. "I don't *think* so," he said, but there was a note of doubt in his voice. The captain's shoulders were stiff, his posture affronted.

"As long as Captain McNally isn't smuggling, we have nothing to fear. Right?" She slipped her hand through his arm.

"Mm-hmm." He nodded, but she could tell he wasn't in complete agreement. "They'll be on us in an hour or two at this rate. I think we should go below and see if there's any breakfast. Then back inside the cabin." George had already made it clear that he intended to protect her whether she wanted it or not. Eve didn't fancy picking a fight on an empty stomach if the dream roads were about to drop a naval battle in her lap, so she ducked her head and went back inside for now.

Eve made her way to the galley, where a young sailor fetched her a bowl of gruel and a couple of smoked kippers. She sat fuming after she'd eaten, for her cabin's porthole didn't offer a good view of the approaching brig. Everything seemed to take forever. The schooner rolled more than usual, for the captain had ordered one of the sails taken down while the navy ship approached. Eventually Eve ran out of fucks to give and stopped waiting. She went up on deck again in time to see the brig standing off about two hundred meters away. A man on the quarterdeck was frantically waving semaphore flags at Captain McNally, who had a flag-waggler of his own standing by. The warship's gunports—she could see eight of them—were shuttered. *That has to be good?* she thought.

George sidled up to her. "I thought I told you to stay below," he muttered.

"You"—she poked him in the side—"are not the boss of me, as I keep having to remind you *for some reason*."

"Firstly," he spoke quietly through gritted teeth, "it was not a certainty until just now that this *was* a navy ship—"

"Why? Who else might it be?"

"A pirate running under false colors. And *secondly*, if you can see them they can see *you,* so if he *was* a pirate, for example the self-proclaimed Baron of Skaro, Number One gone bad, then now he knows you are here, and you mentioned a geas he has applied to you."

Oh shit. "Should I go—"

"Too late for that, I fear." George shook his head. "But sometimes a gun brig is just a gun brig, and we appear to be in luck this time. However, my Lady might perhaps pause in future, just for a *moment,* to ask herself if I might have a valid reason for—"

"My Lord?" Captain McNally interrupted George's quiet but vehement scolding. "Would you be so good as to join me up here?"

George shook his head minutely at Eve, then ascended the steps to the quarterdeck. The message was clear: *no gurlz allowed, tree house for sailor boyz only.* Eve sniffed in disgust. Snooping at doors wasn't her regular habit, but needs must. She touched her right middle finger's second knuckle to her left ear, then turned so that she was oriented to face the approaching brig and, coincidentally, point her ear at Captain McNally.

". . . know anything of pirates in the western approaches, sir?" said McNally. (His "sir" did not sound entirely respectful to Eve.)

"Perhaps," George replied abruptly.

"Well, for heaven's sake, man . . ." McNally's next sentence was an expletive-laden tirade. ". . . didn't you *tell* me?"

"It's far from a certainty, Captain. And if there is a pirate, and he's who I think he is, he won't attack you at sea. He's after—" George looked toward Eve and she turned her head away hastily. *Busted.* After a second she turned back to listen again. ". . . likely he will wait until you have set us down and departed, then send a shore party. After all, he doesn't know you're not carrying a platoon of marines below decks. Which is why I need you to signal Lieutenant O'Brien and tell him—"

Eve missed the rest because the bosun began shouting up at the sailors on the yardarm of the big mast at the rear, something about reefing (was the ship about to run aground?), and by the time she stopped wincing her macro had fritzed out like a dodgy hearing aid. But she'd heard enough, she figured. *He'll send a shore party.* Repetition did not make the sinking feeling in her chest go away: quite the opposite. Rupert knew the Village inside out—he'd designed it, along with its defenses—and, of course, he was after *her,* not to mention Von Franckenstein and the boy, not trying to loot a small merchant vessel at sea. Piracy in this day and age was rare (Barbary corsairs aside), and the newssheets had been full of reports on the parties to the Congress of Vienna agreeing to act decisively. Only a maniac, the truly desperate, or someone with a thaumaturgic edge would dare carry on in such a way this close to England's shores.

"My Lady?" It was George. "Are you well?" He looked concerned, but his tone of voice suggested his concern was not so much with her health as for her state of mind.

"Very well, thanks." She bared her teeth at him. To his credit, he pretended it was a smile and simply nodded.

"There's no immediate danger, but we should go below. The captain says the weather glass is falling and there are clouds to the west."

"Below. Go. Yes." Eve's thoughts were still clouded by her dawning dismay as she estimated the extremity of her predicament. She had to confront Rupert here, on his own turf—there could be only one survivor—but she felt increasingly hemmed in, not least by the realization that if she confronted Rupert directly she might no longer be ruthless enough to prevail.

A year ago she'd been under the penumbra of Rupert's mind-warping geas, but without the reinforcing power of the wedding contract making itself known. It had imposed a subtle and pernicious darkening on her vision, so that she wouldn't have blinked twice at killing in the service of her master. But Eve was no longer Rupert's toy and now felt a sick sense of revulsion when she remembered killing the highwayman—*I'm not the ruthless bitch he turned me into,* she realized with a sinking feeling as she descended the companionway. *I'm just me again. And I'm not up to doing this the usual way.* She'd have to come up with a plan that didn't rely on stabbing obstacles until they bled out, a plan that leveraged the dream roads to lend her additional power. Only one gambit remained—and it was the parson's mousetrap that had gotten her into this mess in the first place.

▸◂▸◂▸◂

Travel aboard ship with a berth in the owner's quarters and an earl for a fake husband was generally preferable to sharing a coach with the same earl—she could walk around for one thing, and inhale the healthy sea breeze instead of road dust and the rich aroma of passing pigsties—but it shared the same principal drawback (boredom) and some new ones (what she had come to think of as the Bed Question).

The morning's unwelcome interruption had chilled Number Seven's ardor for the time being. It had also given Eve a much-needed pause for reflection, which was mostly a jumbled blur of *what on Earth was I thinking?* alternating with *where do I get condoms in this day and age?* (Although there *were* spells for that, should she eventually need them. . . .) There was also a cautionary note of *if we go there, will he try to top me?* (*That* would be intolerable.) On the downside: he'd already asked her to marry him once; obstetric anesthesia was a third of a century in the future; and finally, *this is such a bad idea!* But on the other hand: *so sexy!*

She briefly considered dragging him back to the modern world via the dream roads. Equally briefly, she wondered how she'd feel when she got home if she discovered she'd pulled a gender-switched Orpheus, and George—her ripped, muscular, male Eurydice—crumbled into bones and nightmares when he stepped into the present.

Eve dealt with the problem the traditional way—by pretending it didn't exist. And George made it easy for her by doing the same. That night she made sure to go to their cabin early, after encouraging George to stay drinking with the officers. She curled up facing the side of the bed and feigned sleep as George clambered into the bed beside her. She dozed off to the tune of his drunken snores, and was out of the bed the next morning before he awakened. It might have been her imagination, but George seemed unusually distant over breakfast; or perhaps he was just hungover.

They made it through two whole days in this manner, ignoring the elephant (or perhaps it was a sperm whale) in the room. Then on the morning of their fourth day at sea, the cabin boy came round. "Captain's compliments, sir, but we're within sight of yon cove? I'm to help pack your chests."

George piled straight out through the door and was up on deck in a trice. Eve cursed silently, quickly told the lad what went where, then followed him. Up top, a fresh breeze was blowing and the sea was becoming choppy, spray and the first harbingers of rain splattering around her. She joined George and François, who had spent most of the voyage scrambling up and down the ratlines with the midshipmen. "Land!" piped the boy, pointing off to the right, and indeed she could see a low headland rising in the distance beyond the starboard bow. A dusting of white dandruff around the balding green dome of a hill might have been buildings.

"Is that it?"

"I think so." George screwed his eyes shut and muttered something in Enochian. "Yes, the shore wards are up but they recognize the watchword. Rover won't attack us." He turned to face the officers on the quarterdeck. "Sir, a very good morning to you and how long do you think we'll take to make landfall?"

McNally breathed deeply, squinted into the wind, then descended the steps to the main deck until he was facing George. "Two days," he announced. "Or I can put you in the longboat and you'll be home in time for lunch."

"Two *days*?" Eve asked.

"Bad weather's coming in, and I'll not risk my ship on that lee shore," McNally told George, as if Eve was a ventriloquist's dummy. "We can beat farther out to sea, then wait out the storm—maybe a day or two, might be three—but we're already closer to land than I'm happy about. The boat, though—I can have my men row you ashore and if the weather turns bad they can wait it out on dry land before I pick them up."

Half an hour later Eve found herself perched precariously in a bosun's chair, descending toward a rowing boat approximately the size of a postage stamp that was already full of sweary sailors (also one boy and a lord). Two hours after that, as the sky overhead turned the color of titanium and raindrops the size of her thumb began to spall off the planks, the oarsmen dragged the boat up the pebbled beach alongside the jetty, and George helped her ashore.

"Remember the story," George quietly reminded her as he led her up the beach toward the edge of the ward. "Can you do that?"

"Prisoners, recaptured outside Grantham, check." The simplest story was always the one that kept closest to the truth. "You took François and myself back to London where you made further enquiries after the baron, and now you're returning us both to the Village and I hate you and want you to choke on a pretzel."

"What," asked George, "is a pretzel?" He shook his head. "I probably don't want to know, do I?"

"Just look pained and mildly disdainful and I'll look pained and extremely resentful and everything will be fine. People always believe you when you tell them what they want to hear, and it's the news Number Two expects." She allowed him to take her arm, trying to look reluctant. "What happens next?"

"Number Two's office, where we beard the lion in his den. I'll take the lead. It'll be fine."

Eve nodded. The uneasy feeling that this was a fake-out and she really *was* the prisoner she appeared to be, rather than a willing collaborator pretending to be a prisoner, made the skin in the small of her back crawl; but it was a little too late for second thoughts at this juncture.

The plan she'd come up with *en voyage* was straightforward enough. Number One knew his way in and out of the Village, having designed it. Number One's minions, notably Number Twelve, would learn of Eve's capture and send word, at which point someone—most likely the Silver Sisterhood, or one of Number One's other followers—would try to abduct her. If he succeeded, Number Seven would give chase (he would supply her with an enchanted amulet that would allow him to track her easily and provide certain defenses: he just had to retrieve the necessary materials from his own chambers in the Village). The plan even included a gambit to neutralize Rupert's geas. "It's the only way to ensure he can't enslave you again," George reminded her.

("But what about you?" Eve had objected, the second time he broached the topic. "Won't you be trapped? Surely the entanglement side effects . . ." George had shaken his head. "It won't matter if you return to your own time. I can annul the binding once you're gone." And though she'd spent the rest of their trip trying to pick holes in the logic, it stood up to scrutiny. It even had the benefit of working with the dream archetypes, rather than against them.)

The rain was falling heavily as George led a bedraggled Eve to the front door of the town hall and tugged the iron bellpull.

The door swung open to reveal Number Forty-Nine's supercilious mug. The butler stared down his nose at her. "Number Two is expecting you," he told her. He bowed to George. "And you, my Lord."

"This won't take long," George said briskly, then led Eve toward the mayor's office. He flung the doors open and pushed her through them. "Behold, our runaway prodigal returns!"

Eve glared resentfully at Number Seven. "Get your hands off me," she snapped, very carefully not thinking about where she really wanted his hands.

"Ah, ah! Remember your manners, my dear." George hammed it up atrociously. To Number Two he added, "The baron is still missing but I was able to retrieve the boy. I left him with the sailors for now. They'll put him in the guardhouse until you can decide what to do with him."

Eve had the distinct impression that Number Two was watching her mistrustfully, even though she still couldn't see his face. "I see the shrew is no tamer than she was the last time she deigned to visit," he said. To the butler: "Two brandies, please." Number Forty-Nine vanished. To Eve, in a tone of mild disapproval, he added, "Next time you decide to waste everybody's time, please be good enough to send me a note first. That way I can schedule it as a training exercise and you can be home and snug in bed by nightfall without being outraged or murdered by highwaymen, what?"

George held her arms behind her, tightly gripping both elbows—and thereby ensuring that her feet did not cross the boundary of Number Two's under-carpet circle. Time to amp it up. "I'd have gotten away with it, too, if it wasn't for that meddling kid!" she announced, then embarked on an impassioned (and only somewhat misleading) rant in which she laid the blame for her capture on François, who had discovered her in the ship and insisted she accompany him and the baron on their own escapade.

Number Two put up with this for approximately sixty seconds, then raised one hand. "*Silence,*" he intoned, in a language not created for human throats. The word reverberated back and forth painfully and Eve found herself unable to move her jaw, her larynx numbed. "Enough of this disgraceful rubbish!" he upbraided her. "Number Seven, put her back where she belongs. I hold you *personally* responsible for ensuring she doesn't escape overnight. I'll see her in the morning once I have decided what to do with her."

George nodded. "And the boy . . . ?"

"He and the baron—when we recapture him—will be most thoroughly taken care of," Number Two said with grim satisfaction. "They won't escape again."

"You don't mean—" George blanched.

"I do indeed." Although his face was an unrecognizable blur—a version of her shrouding macro, but more powerful for being tightly focused on one particular part of his anatomy, she decided—he exuded smug satisfaction. "As long as they remain within the perimeter ward they won't die. A most effective solution, the explosive collars. I shall write to London and requisition three more tomorrow. I am relying on you to keep her under lock and key until they are ready." He clapped. "Take her away, there are wreakings that require my attention! And good work, Number Seven."

George turned and propelled Eve through the lobby.

Her unwilling tongue came back to life as soon as they were out in the rain again. "Explosive collars? What the *hell,* George?"

"A really bad idea and I'm sure it won't come to that," he whispered in her ear, "but you mustn't talk about it in front of the servants—they get upset. Just play along tonight and I'll be back soon with the necessary extras."

"But what—"

"Things will be different tomorrow. In the meantime, just pretend I'm your jailer."

He escorted the now-shivering Eve back to her rooms. Only when he left her—after locking her in using a mechanism that hadn't been there the last time she'd passed through her apartment door—did she realize that she couldn't tell the difference between his pretense and the real thing. Had she been a fool to trust him? she wondered. After all, what better way was there to keep a prisoner passive than to persuade them to connive at their own detention. . . .

▸◂▸◂▸◂

"I can't help thinking this is a *really bad* idea," said Game Boy, pausing in the doorway of the room with the stagnant swimming pool.

"Of course it is," said Doc Depression. "*All* Imp's ideas are really bad."

"What part of 'Eve needs help' didn't you get?" Imp retorted with some asperity. "It's not *my* idea! I'm just following *her* orders!" He shivered.

"Hey now, break it up." Wendy looked to Del for support but Del crossed her arms and shrugged. *This is your call,* she mimed.

Imp had been in a state of some anxiety ever since he found the letter. At first he'd tried to keep it secret, but the instructions had been very clear and ever since he'd read them events had been out of his control. "Eve's trapped in a copy of 1816 with Rupert," he'd eventually explained. "Rupert's cooked up another crazy-ass scheme to take over the world by warping history and if we don't stop him and get Eve back we'll cease to exist. But she left instructions."

Wendy had been paying him a visit in hope of finding out if there was any new news. To Wendy's embarrassment, Eve had authorized the HiveCo Security contract personally, and in her absence nobody was going to release payment of Wendy's invoices. Lots of stuff had simply ground to a halt when Eve disappeared, leaving the Bigge Organization in much the same state as an anthill from which the queen had been abducted. Worse: people from the government had turned up with scary warrants and taken control for the duration. So Wendy had sat Imp down and managed to get the story out of him by rolling him a fat joint and holding it just out of reach until he cracked.

"She needs us," he said, brokenly, like a—*record scratch*—"Rupert's in 1816! What's he doing in 1816?" he added plaintively.

"Fuck knows." Wendy shrugged. "But if she doesn't come back I'm not going to get paid." *Billable hours,* she reminded herself. Mr. Gibson would be upset. "Let me read that."

Imp had passed her the photocopy of the original letter and she'd puzzled it out (old-style copperplate handwriting was not her cup of tea; where had Eve picked that up? her detective brain asked) and then she started swearing. "This is bad," she said.

"Yeah, I know."

"No, I mean, this is *really* bad!"

"It's only happening in a bubble universe opening off the dream roads," Imp reminded her. "It's not real. Yet."

"The New Management is taking an interest so you bet your ass it's real."

Wendy had been doing some reading—like everyone else: the rules of magic were the stuff of newspaper Sunday supplement articles these days—and this situation meant that the stuff that had stuck with her, mostly about the laws of sympathy and contagion, were giving her bad feels. *Very* bad feels. It wasn't true time travel, classic *Doctor Who* time travel, grandfather-paradox time travel, *but* if you could warp history inside a pocket reality plausibly enough, and *if* it was connected to the real world because some dipshit demiurge-powered lich-priest had sacrificed a bunch of cultists to set up the link, *then* you might tell yourself this is not my beautiful history, this is not the world I remember, but like the water dissolving, and the water removing, you might find the ground under your feet morphed into something quite different. "If we don't stop it, what happens to us?"

"*She* told me that *He* expects me to fix this. If I don't it's going to be skulls-on-poles time." Imp collapsed on Jabba the Sofa and stared up at the ceiling despairingly. Wendy finally passed him the joint: he seemed to need it. "Can we send Sergeant Gunderson? Eve is her boss."

"So is Rupert, if he's really trapped in there," Wendy pointed out. "Anyway, Eve addressed it to you. And"—she shuddered—"*she* told you to follow the instructions like it says, to use whatever was in here to follow Eve with a tracking spell. Right?"

"Send lawyers, guns, and money. And on second thoughts, forget the money and the lawyers."

"Listen, call a house meeting. I think if you can get the others on board we may stand a chance. More of a chance than a bunch of unmagical mooks with M16s going up against an ancient undead evil, anyway."

"Yeah." Imp had trailed off. "We should do that," he agreed reluctantly. "We ought to do that."

Back in the here and now—more than a week later: it had taken time to get the band back together, arms twisted and duly briefed for another dream-roads excursion, and then to obtain permission from the Powers That Be—the inevitable crisis of compliance had materialized. Now Imp was throwing Wendy under the bus. Not that Wendy could blame him. The Lost Boys all knew about his singular talent and had metahuman skills of their own: if he tried to bamboozle them they were quite capable of telling him to fuck right off.

"I've read the letter," she told Game Boy. "I know this sucks but she convinced *me*. And you know what I think about this crap." She cast about, and ended up staring into the turbid depths of the pool. It was a really nice example of classic Victorian swimming-pool design, ornamental tile surrounds and all, except nobody seemed to have cleaned it for decades. (Any year now the residents were going to evolve lungs and colonize the decking.) "I'm here because the New Management said to go along, or else. Also, if Eve doesn't make it home, I don't get paid. Also, we maybe cease to exist, or find ourselves in a grim meat-hook future ruled over by the priesthood of a mad god even worse than the Denizen of Number Ten—a priesthood led by Rupert." She turned to Imp. "You know where we're going, right? Right?"

"The Village." Imp twitched. "It shouldn't exist, but it does," he added, hollow-voiced.

"Any particular village?" Game Boy demanded.

"*The* Village." Imp shook his head. "Portmeirion, in Wales, although why the hell Rupert built a copy of it more than a century ahead of its time—"

Del turned on Wendy. "Has 'e been smoking again?" she demanded.

"Not today, I don't think." Imp had explained about the sixties TV show his dad had been a massive fan of, subjecting him and Eve to interminable DVD reruns. "It's an elaborate spy trap with occult significance, the perfect place to imprison captured mages while you can interrogate them . . . or something. Rupert built it for the Invisible College, the Crown's sorcerers, during the Napoleonic wars. But Eve says he had some plan in mind, not just retrieving the manuscript he sent us for last time, something *worse*."

Imp produced the letter with a flourish, and read: "George Orwell wrote, 'He who controls the past controls the present.'" He stared wildly. "Don't you get it? What Rupert did to Eve with that bloody geas, he wants to do to everybody! He's set himself up as Number One in the Village! He controls *everyone* in his panopticon! And he's got a whole heap of sorcerers to sacrifice for their *mana* to back-propagate it through the dream roads to—"

Doc gently took him by the elbow. "Chill," he advised. "We're with you."

Wendy straightened. "Walk the dream roads, find Eve, bring her back. This time we're not trying to collect a cursed necromantic text, we're just aiming to rescue someone from a mad god's high priest who's trapped her inside an escape-proof prison for sorcerers. Piece of cake."

"You make it sound so easy." Del popped a piece of chewing gum in her mouth. "Something's gonna go sideways."

"Doesn't it always?" Doc Depression was characteristically downbeat. "GeeBee, you don't have to come if you don't want to."

"I don't want to!" Game Boy squeaked for a moment, then dropped his voice an octave. "Doesn't matter," he said sullenly. "Fucking Rupert. Fucking Prime—"

Doc slapped a hand across Game Boy's mouth before he could finish the sentence.

After a few seconds Wendy nudged Imp. "Go," she told him. "You're the one with the magic hair." The twist of Eve's hair that she'd placed in her letter was, in combination with Imp's blood affinity and a spell from their father's book (which she'd helpfully provided a reference for), more than sufficient to guide him to her. "Lead the way."

"Okay." Imp looked around, then headed around the pool toward the far exit. "Past this point I don't know where we're going. It's a lot farther back than Whitechapel was." A pause. "I hope we can get back afterward."

"That's my job," Del pointed out. As the team's courier she could always find the shortest route to where she needed to be: the ghost roads played hell with her talent when she was searching, but less so when returning to a previous place. "Trust me, that part I got covered."

"Go, *go,*" Wendy reminded Imp. "Who knows how long she's been trapped in there, or what's been happening?"

SEASON OF SKULLS

Eve had never been great at waiting patiently, and anyone who thought to call her biddable had clearly never bid against her at a high-stakes auction. Now she was locked in her apartment in the Village with a storm howling in off the sea, and her mood deteriorated from dark to deadly. She lit the prelaid fire with an angry snap of her fingers, sparked the oil lamp into fishy-smelling light with another gesture, hung her outer garments before the flames, and began to pace back and forth, muttering darkly to herself.

"Once you have retrieved the *correct* skull We will be able to proceed, He said. No pressure, it's entirely on your head now, He said. We shall not punish you, he said. *Fuck—*" She caught herself just in time. "*—this.*" She kicked the fireplace surround, not hard enough to damage her toes but sufficiently hard to register her resentment. "Dammit, *why*?"

Her heart ached. The facts were plain as day: His Dread Majesty had known (or suspected) that tomorrow was coming. *He* had sent her after Rupert, He had a well-earned and fearsome reputation for playing lethal games with human chess pieces; and tomorrow belonged to Number Two, who was *not* His Dread Majesty. Or at least, not *yet*.

Trying to second-guess the nature of the Black Pharaoh's game was a fool's errand, but to Eve, at least, he was a more sympathetic devil than Rupert.

Rupert was out there with his network of cultists, the Silver

Sisterhood (and whoever else he had made allies of in the twenty years since he presented himself to the Invisible College), and his knowledge of the Village. Which he had created as a trap for captured continental sorcerers, including Baron Von Francken-stein and his ward. After the detention of whom he had returned to Eve's present day, to 2016, to check that everything was in place for . . . something? Some scheme that required a woman of childbearing years to undergo forced insemination with a cloned embryo of Rupert.

It had not escaped Eve's notice that the boy François had an aptitude for the magical arts and sciences, if only from the way he marshaled his battalion of lead figurines. At a guess it was magical contagion from the guillotined owner of the womb he'd been grown in. (Probably a sorceress's womb was a necessary environment when cloning a sorcerer—some kind of epigenetic modification at work, possibly a cross infection of human endogenous retroviruses expressed in utero—she could ask a professor of gynecological thaumaturgy when she got home.)

Eve was very much afraid that she was the most powerful female practitioner currently in the Village. And she was only here, rather than trapped in Rupert's mansion in London, thanks to the Black Pharaoh's orders and Rupert's misunderstanding of how the contract-reinforced geas he'd bound her with would respond to a mangled date order. (After all the marriage contract said, "From this day onward . . .")

Think it through, she told herself. *First, he installed the geas. Then the proxy marriage that reinforced it. But the reinforcement went away the* instant *he stepped on the dream road. So its failure is definitely a side effect of time travel.* Magical contracts were notoriously literal-minded, a fact she'd exploited to her advantage when Rupert sent her after the cursed concordance that had been hidden in a dream of 1888. What were the precise terms of the proxy marriage? She tried to remember how marriage vows worked: "for worse, for richer, for poorer, in sickness and in health, until death do us part from this day hence," something like that. The date on the marriage certificate was two centuries in the future, and spells—such as Rupert's geas—were notoriously picky about temporal and spatial boundaries.

Until, she thought, *until death do us part.* "Until" implied a direction of causality. Assume the word appeared in whatever abominable contract Rupert's lawyer had signed on her behalf under Skaro's fossilized legal system. And postulate that the Cult of the Mute Poet—which had lurked like a tapeworm cyst in the brain of the Catholic Church since the sixteenth century—had borrowed its wedding vows from the Church. The arrow of time was important: There was a date in the registry, a date on the marriage certificate, and wedding vows couldn't bind you before you were married. So . . .

Eve paused for a moment to reflect that this was typical Rupert. Rupert was all about intricate schemes rammed through by brute force; sloppy and lacking attention to detail, because details were for little people to take care of on his behalf while he dreamed up new and ever more grandiloquent apocalypses.

She dragged her focus back to the big picture. All the clues pointed toward a dismal hypothesis. Rupert's immediate goal had changed. Bringing the *Necronomicon* back to 2016 was all very well, but he'd had about twenty years of subjective time in the dream roads to revise his plans. It seemed obvious in retrospect that Rupert had already gotten hold of the book, or at least the details of the ghastly rite he needed. He'd fed it to the baron, using the cover of Napoleon clones for the War Office to develop the technique and identify its weaknesses and requirements. His orders to Eve regarding pregnancy made his intentions ominously clear. Connect the dots: he meant to use her as a host for a sorcerously enhanced clone of himself—a replacement for the body he'd wrecked wandering the dream roads.

Plainly, once his youthful vigor was restored and his memories were installed in an inherently more sorcerously powerful brain, he meant to go after the Black Pharaoh.

But plans change to adapt to new realities, and Eve had disrupted Rupert's plan by following him back to 1816. And he must be thinking: if he could summon the Mute Poet in *this* here and now, why would he even need to return to 2017 again? He had the key ingredients for his plan already in place, after all—everything except a biddable wife. He might have decided that taking over the world of Lord Byron suited him better than returning to the world of tomorrow and duking it out with the PM. Then again, in the dream roads, dreams had a nasty habit of taking on a reality of their own, echoing the real world—and vice versa. Perhaps if he invoked the Mute Poet here it would have side effects that would spill over into the real world and ensure that the Black Pharaoh never returned, never *had* returned, and the New Management was ruled instead by Ppilimtec the Tongueless, Prince of Poetry and Song? (*Call by reference, not call by value,* she thought.)

With Rupert as his human avatar, just as Number Two would in time become the—

Record scratch.

Rupert did not appreciate defiance. Rupert did not permit his victims to escape, and he'd made his contempt and disdain for her crystal clear. She'd disobeyed him, and he always punished disobedience. Worse, she'd managed to do so despite his geas. He'd be absolutely furious when he caught up with her, and what he intended to do when he came for her in the Village was both obvious and horrific.

George had said, "I shall not allow him to take you as long as I draw breath." The memory was a consolation in the darkness and she clutched it tight. But then he'd added, "It will only happen over my dead body." If only he knew!

Clearly they had no future together. If she stayed in this bad dream of history she'd slowly rot away as it leeched her soul of *mana* to power the pocket universe. But in the future George would be dead and gone, just another skull to mount beside Rupert's on the Marble Arch Tzompantli. And she couldn't invite him to walk the dream road beside her—there were good reasons why that could not be allowed to happen, starting with what they planned to do after midnight.

It didn't mean she couldn't want him. It didn't mean she couldn't fantasize about having her earl and eating him. He was a decent man, physically attractive, intelligent, a powerful sorcerer in his own right, and respectful of her person. Also wealthy but not a wastrel, dedicated to a life of duty and public service, and clearly interested in her as a partner, if not as a wife.

(He'd made it clear that a family was not in his future. "I survived the mumps six years ago, but the swelling means I fear my title will escheat to my second cousin. I could not give you the children you deserve, my Lady.")

They clearly had *no* chance of a future together, and for the first time Eve—who had carefully constructed her own identity behind high and icy ramparts after her father's death—found herself wishing things could be otherwise. Her head hurt almost as much as her heart: *How did I get into this mess?* she asked. *Oh,* that's *how.* Dream archetypes could really fuck you up: and so could the PM.

"*Fuck* that—shit," she swerved, leery of taking the Prime Minister's name in vain even though she was trapped in a pocket universe outside his demesne.

From whichever direction she considered the problem, every road led back to tonight's ritual. The one that would protect her against Rupert's geas, maybe immunize her completely (albeit at a cost she suspected she'd regret later). Assuming it wasn't all a horrible gaslighting, of course, but if it was, Number Seven must have been telling her lies since they'd first met. And while he was good, she didn't think he was *that* good. He'd had plenty of opportunities to betray her already, if that's what he'd intended. And his attraction was impossible to feign. She squeezed her thighs together, remembering his kisses and the hot immensity of his body next to her in the ship's bed, like the missing jigsaw piece from the picture of her life.

Lust really *did* make you stupid, she realized. Almost as stupid as this plan. Which was *very* stupid. But it just *might* work, in which case . . .

▸◂▸◂▸◂

A couple of hours passed. The lock rattled and the door opened for Mary, who entered with a tray bearing a lidded bowl of Irish stew and a bottle of wine. A pair of footmen in white-piped black uniforms waited outside the door, and Eve's skin itched as she sensed their protective wards. She retreated into her living space and watched as Mary set out her dinner on the side table. She could take the guards in a fight, she decided, but not without injuring or killing them, and she'd sworn off killing people except in self-defense. (Anyway, she was outnumbered and she had no escape plan in place. All it would buy her was a chase around the Village green and an appointment with one of Number Two's collar bombs—or worse, Rover.)

Eventually Mary dipped her a perfunctory curtsey and left. The guards locked her in again and she was alone once more.

It felt a bit like the prisoner's last night in the condemned cell. Eve gloomily spooned up her lukewarm stew. All it needed to complete the picture was a couple of turnkeys sitting suicide watch and a sanctimonious priest reading the Bible at her.

After dinner Eve fell into a fitful doze. She was awakened sometime later by the rattle of a key in the lock. She pushed herself up from the wingback chair by the fireplace as the door opened. The fire was down to dimly glowing embers and the air held a distinct chill, but the oil lamp was still burning, and as she turned to face the door George entered the room, followed by Parson Richards, carrying a Bible. The effect was as sobering as a bucket of ice water. Instantly awake, her first instinct was to snap, "You're early. What time do you call this?"

"Ten past midnight, darling," said George. "It's tomorrow already. Are you sure you want to go through with this?"

It *was* a lot like an execution, Eve realized, this ritual that would snap the neck of her independence. She didn't know whether to laugh or cry. "Let's get on with it."

"Very well." George turned to the parson. "Are you ready?"

"Do you have the special license, my Lord?" The parson fiddled with his spectacles.

"Here." George reached inside his frock coat and withdrew a packet, which Richards unfolded and squinted at by the light of the oil lamp. "I think you'll find it's all in order."

"I still have to read it first," Richards fussed. Scrutinizing the seal and signature at the bottom, he nodded his conditional assent. "I recognize that hand." He sounded almost awestruck. "How did you convince His Grace the Archbishop . . . ?"

George smiled humorlessly. "I hold a written warrant that says, 'It is by my order and for the good of the state that the bearer has done what has been done.' You may guess whose hand signed it. His Grace knows better than to argue with him when I choose to wield it."

Perhaps it was her imagination—the lamplight was dim—but Parson Richards seemed to pale before he swallowed and returned his attention to the packet of paper. Finally he spoke. "This all seems to be correct and in order, my Lord, although the variant oath—"

"Remember my written warrant." George was implacably polite. For the first time Eve allowed herself the luxury of hope. It wasn't a setup: he really *was* going to do what they'd agreed.

"Yes, my Lord. My Lady, if you consent to this I will need to know your true name."

Eve licked her lips—suddenly feeling how dry they were—and briefly considered the possibilities. In 1816 she might pass as Lady Evelyn de Montfort—but that was a ruse dictated by Number Two, which would not do. Or she could proclaim herself Evelyn, Baroness Skaro, but only at risk of acknowledging Rupert's future claim on her—the very claim this ritual was intended to break, and which relied on a marriage license solemnized in the future. There was only one valid answer, it seemed.

"I was born Evelyn Michelle Starkey," she announced. She hated her middle name and tried to avoid using it: but the ceremony they were performing required her true and full name. Otherwise the contract, and any thaumaturgic side effects from it, would be invalid.

"George Ronald Philip Ruthven, sixth Earl of Marsden." The lamplight cast flickering shadows across his eye sockets.

". . . Starkey," said Richards, carefully penciling Eve's name in the appropriate gap on the document, matching the original's round hand script. "I have that. And your name is already here, my Lord. So, by order of this special license granted by the Archbishop of Canterbury, we are gathered here in the eyes of the Lord to join you in holy matrimony. Please repeat after me. . . ."

Eve spoke her lines with a dreamlike sense of distance, as if she was an external observer watching a woman swearing an oath to subsume her legal identity within that of another person. It barely seemed real until they reached the part with the subtly modified vows. But then the final words struck home: "I do," she said with a sense of finality and *rightness* as a ghostly touch of magic rippled up and down her arm. Then George slid a simple gold band over the tip of her ring finger and massaged it into place.

"I now pronounce you man and wife. You may kiss your bride, my Lord."

Richards took a step away as George leaned toward Eve. "My Lady," he said quietly as he gathered her close.

"My Lord." The relief was dizzying, and she savored it for a moment. There was no point in delaying the inevitable. Nor, Eve realized, did she want to. "Kiss me, George."

Sometime later the parson cleared his throat. In the dream roads a thousand voyeuristic demons cried out as one. "That was *most* irregular and I can't say I approve but you're not listening to me anymore so I'm going!" Richards complained. The door banged behind him, and the guards locked them in for the night. Eve barely noticed the querulous clergyman's departure, though. A wild and tumultuous urge had seized her, and she walked George backward toward the bed.

"Are you sure this is what you want?" George asked. "Because, my Lady, once I start, I won't want to stop—"

"Shut up and sit down." The let's-break-Rupert's-geas ritual wouldn't necessarily be bulletproof until the marriage was consummated—another detail, alongside the "from this day hence" that Rupert had neglected when he'd tricked her into the proxy marriage—but once she had her way with George any slimy residue of Rupert's claim on her would be shattered. And Eve had every intention of enjoying herself in the process. She shoved her newly captured husband down on the end of the bed, nudged his legs apart, and started to work on his buttons with growing self-confidence. "I am going to undress you, and then I will *permit* you to undress me"—his neckcloth would make an excellent wrist restraint, she thought as she untied it—"and then I will take you for a wild ride, and if you are *very* good I may even let you *come*—"

When George tried to sit up she scowled furiously and pushed him back down. "Stop that insubordinate behavior at once!"

"Do you always fuck like this?" he asked, eyes wide as she tied his arms to the top of the bed. "I know you were wed before, but—"

"Remember who's in charge here! Otherwise I'll have to gag you. Yes, I do, but not recently, to answer your other question." She sat back on her heels while she opened his fall and pulled his trousers down, leaving his legs trapped. Then she took him in hand and stroked his hot length. He gasped. Satisfied with his reaction, Eve shed her dress and underpinnings as fast as she could. "Do you want to serve me?" she demanded, climbing over him.

"I swore to love, honor, and obey you"—he gasped—"scandalizing the parson as you instructed—"

"Who am I to you?" she demanded.

"You are my wife." She slapped him lightly. "And *mistress*."

Suppressing a smile of delight, Eve slithered on top of her helpless (but, judging by the condition of his erection, extremely eager) husband and began to writhe against him. There'd be time to teach him about safe words and her preferred kinks once she'd broken him in: but first there was a timeless ritual to complete.

▸◂▸◂▸◂

Morning made itself known to Eve with a crash of breaking crockery and a tiny scandalized shriek. "Eek! I'm so sorry!"

Eve went from sleeping to sitting bolt upright instantly, clutching the bedding to her. The sounds of distress were coming from Mary, the maid, who stood backlit in the open doorway. She'd dropped her tray, spattering gruel halfway across the tiles. The draft blowing past her was icy on Eve's face. Also, George had sprawled across two thirds of the bed *again*, even though it was twice the width of the hanging bunk in the ship's cabin: she suspected he had feline ancestry.

She raised her ring finger and pointed it at Mary. "Married now." She pointed at George: "This is my husband." Then she smirked. "Now be off with you and let Number Two know!"

Mary shrieked again and scuttled away, slamming the door

behind her. "You shouldn't have done that," George chided her. He yawned. "It's cold." He dragged the bedding back over his chest and Eve was forced to admit that he was right: the fire had gone out overnight and the bedroom felt close to freezing.

"I'm going to set the fire," she said, and rolled onto the cold tiles before she could allow herself time for second thoughts. Today was going to be a busy day, she reasoned. It would be *very* interesting to see who—or what—their marital gambit brought crawling out of the woodwork. (Also, if she was right, they were going to have visitors sooner rather than later.) "Come on, time to get up." The allure of the bed was undeniable, but returning to it would only invite further, more embarrassing, interruptions.

She poked at the ashes in the fireplace then hefted a double handful of coals out of the scuttle by force of will (much cleaner than using the wrought-iron tongs). Then she focused on a chip of shiny black anthracite in the middle of the pile. Igniting coals was normally a lot harder than heating a candlewick, but the power came surprisingly easily this morning. After a couple of seconds she saw a thin spiral of bluish smoke, then a faint hiss as the coal outgassed and sprouted a flickering flame.

While she concentrated she heard George moving around behind her. There was some groaning and sighing as he gathered his discarded clothes and attempted to render himself presentable. Eve smiled to herself, then winced, and yawned. Neither of them had slept much, and she ached in unaccustomed places. The ring on her finger was buzzing with trapped *mana*: ritual sex was a *much* more agreeable source of power than human sacrifice, she decided, even though it took longer and yielded less. It was no wonder her ancestors had run to large families before the magical drought. And that was all part of the plan she had hatched aboard ship. If her supposition—an educated guess, but a plausible one—about Rupert's real objective was right, the rage-induced fireworks would start shortly, and she'd need all the accumulated magical mojo she could hoard.

"Do you suppose François will be all right?" she asked as she attended to her ablutions behind the screen.

George grunted. "He knows what is likely to happen to him if your—if Number One—gets his hands on him. That lad is *not* a fool. Remember he has a forty-seven-year-old mind in a twelve-year-old's head?"

"But the plan—"

"Eve. My Lady." She turned, and George met her gaze over the top of the screen. "He'd be a fool not to accept your offer," he said, and there was a trace of sadness in his voice that made her heart flutter. *I wish it could be you,* she thought wistfully, but she knew better than to say it aloud. They might be married for now, but there was no safe way for them to be together. She'd have to return to the future: George would grow old and go to his final rest alone. *I shall look for him in the records,* she resolved. Visit his graveside, wherever it was—Highgate Cemetery, most probably: she could imagine this older George interred in a grandiose early Victorian mausoleum in a hillside off Egyptian Avenue. She'd wear a black dress with a mourning veil and pine romantically beside the door to his crypt.

The fire was burning nicely and she was just about presentable, albeit wearing yesterday's traveling gown with her hair in a simple braid, when there was a hammering on the door. "Open up!" boomed an irate voice. "I know you're in there! You can't hide—"

Eve glanced at George. "Showtime," she mouthed. He walked to the door and pulled it open. The imprecations ceased as he scowled down at Number Two, who stood on the threshold with a face like a nightmare's blind spot, simultaneously unreadable and transparently angry.

"You!" Number Two quivered with rage. "Traitor!"

"I beg to differ," George drawled, and in that moment Eve thought he was magnificent. "She has nothing whatsoever to do with the conspiracy, as you would realize if you had the most meager pinch of common sense. Now go away and leave me to my wedding breakfast, why don't you."

"So it's true! You married the vixen!" Number Two bounced on his toes, working his way up into a fine rant. "She cozened you and—"

Eve, increasingly annoyed at simultaneously being scolded and ignored, stepped up close behind her *husband*—it was an uncanny realization, freighted with meaning—and pointed a sharp finger at Number Two's unface. "*I know your true name,*" she declared, the words of Old Enochian tearing stiff and sharp-edged through her larynx. "And if you don't bite your tongue, I'll. Tell. *Everyone.*"

Number Two shut up abruptly, visibly quivering with rage, but George put his hand out. "We will visit you in the town hall after we have broken our fast," he condescended, "and not a moment sooner. No breakfast meetings, sir! That is uncouth! Now begone." He reached for the door. Number Two didn't need to be told twice: the blur spread and he retreated with a wordless growl. Then the door shut, and it was as if he'd never darkened their threshold. Eve felt an almost unreal wave of relief as Two's cloud of free-floating anger receded. *It worked,* she told herself, still barely believing her own audacity. *Which means—*

"Well," George said, a note of uncertainty creeping in, "I don't suppose that's a meeting we can put off, is it?"

"Yes, but as you said, let's eat first," she proposed, taking her bonnet and stepping over the dropped tray. George took her arm, and they walked out together into the bright cold morning light.

Breakfast in the café was a strained affair. Fortunately the place was half-empty, for it was early and the Village residents of aristocratic birth kept late hours. Even so the constant twitter of whispered gossip kept Eve's hackles raised, and the occasional visitor gracefully approaching to offer their congratulations to

George (and a knowing smirk for the blushing bride) did nothing to smooth her feathers. "Should have stayed in bed," she whisper-grumped at George during a moment when they were blessedly free of attention.

"Yes, but I can't let you go hungry," he replied. "You might eat me."

If this was to set the tone of their relationship—Eve found it very strange to think of herself as being *married*: marriage sounded rather permanent, and if things worked out she would be back in her own time within hours, separated from George by a gulf of centuries—she could live with it. A solicitous partner whose vows had scandalized the curate was a much more tolerable option than a haughty, overbearing aristocrat who had the doctor in charge of an asylum for madwomen on speed dial—let alone a monster like Rupert.

George cleared his plate then waited for Eve to drain her second cup of tea. Finally she reluctantly admitted that there was no excuse for putting off the inevitable any longer. "I believe Number Two will be getting impatient," she said. "Should we put him out of his misery or look in on François first?"

"Trust the boy to do what his prototype does best—logistics and timing. He'll act when he's ready." George showed no sign of being ready to move. "Earlier, you said you thought you knew Number Two. From your own time?"

Eve carefully considered how much she could tell him. "I recognize his face, or one like it," she said. "The . . . person . . . wearing it directed what the Invisible College will become." *Careful,* she warned herself. "He put me on the course that brought me here, although I'm not *entirely* certain it was planned with intent. I can't be sure the person wearing the mask is the same: it seems unlikely, there being a gap of two centuries. But the resemblance is startling. Number Two could be his younger self, although that's impossible. . . ."

"Oh, I wouldn't say that," George said grimly. "What do you know of vampires?"

"Vampires?" Eve blinked in confusion. "Vampires don't ex—" she started to say, before a sudden urge to pinch herself stole over her, and she remembered. "They do?" There was an entire committee of them in the House of Lords in her own time. It almost felt as if another geas was subtly messing with her memory.

"They do. Immortal leeches that live in darkness and suck the life force from their victims, along with their blood. The idiot doctor from Edinburgh—Lord Byron's hanger-on—accused me in front of witnesses: I had to walk outside in daylight to shut him down, and let me tell you, finding daylight in Edinburgh in midwinter took some doing."

"I would have stabbed him," Eve said sympathetically. "Much simpler all round."

"Perhaps, but I was trying to prove that I was *not*—well." George finally rose, then moved to help her with her chair. "Vampires are very real. They're the consequence when a powerful sorcerer summons demonic helpers that refuse to return from whence they came after the blood rites are concluded." His shudder was palpable as Eve tucked her hand through the crook of his arm.

"Would Number Two be powerful enough to do that?" she asked as they left the café.

"Of course: *I* am powerful enough, as are you. It's just a matter of knowing how and then choosing to call on that—aid." He gave her an odd look. "I'm surprised you don't know how."

"My education was sadly truncated," Eve allowed. *Best to change the subject.* "Number Two knocked on the door this morning so obviously he hasn't turned yet," she mused aloud. At a guess, the blood rites George had mentioned were one of the topics her father hadn't seen fit to share before his sudden and unexpected death. "Anyway, the—man—I knew in my own time had no problem in daylight. How inconvenient."

George looked at her sharply. "Was your—was Rupert a blood-drinker?"

"Not the last time I saw him." It was her turn to shudder now. "He'd become something other than human, though, something worse. Something undead." Now her memory was working again she remembered that vampires, contrary to legend, were not animated corpses: they were just sorcerers who had accidentally acquired a hideous occult symbiote. Parasite. *Thing.* And for some reason they slipped out of mind easily. While George hugged her, she asked, "How did Number Two get this job, anyway? How long has he been running the Village?"

"I don't know. Longer than I've been working for Their Lordships. I don't even know *why* he got the job, whether it was a punishment or a reward. I've been engaged on their business since '05, so he's been in office for at least ten years. Why?" He pulled back, then took her arm and resumed walking.

"Rupert goes back further than that," Eve said slowly. "I'm just trying to put together a picture. . . . How old would you say Baron Von Franckenstein is, by the way?"

George gave her a look. "Thirty-two, I believe." He left the "why" unsaid, evidently sensitive to her mood. It struck Eve as oddly pleasing that some men became more, not less, solicitous after they'd shared a bed with you, and to learn that George was one of them.

"He would have been seven or eight when Rupert first arrived. Twenty-five when he, ah, created the boy," she continued. George was leading her around the Village gardens, presumably drawing out their discussion in order to pick her brain. "It's a name with a certain resonance in my time, remembered in fiction—a story by one of your annoying doctor's acquaintances, ostensibly about creating living beings by artificial means. Also about the moral consequences of doing so. The boys from Erfurt are a new twist, I admit."

(But if you were planning to conquer the world and change

the course of history, what better tool than an army led by an officer corps of Napoleon clones? A remake of *The Boys from Brazil,* starring the Corsican general instead of the Austrian corporal. Presumably the boys were leftovers from a War Office plan bankrolled by the Invisible College, to defeat Napoleon by turning his own tactical genius against him times a hundred. One that had come to fruition only after the big N was defeated at Waterloo and packed off to Elba, leaving a pool of precocious toddler warlords to someday threaten the stability of South America.)

She let George in on her current concerns. "I originally thought Rupert intended to return to my time—his time, too—in order to invite his ghastly god in. I mean, that's what he *said* he was doing, before I followed him here. But if he arrived six months before I did, and bankrolled Von Franckenstein's project as well as the Village, who's to say he's following his original plan? He's nothing if not arrogant, and I think he now intends to take over the here and now—"

"Why do you think that?" George asked, scrutinizing her expression.

They'd reached the front of the town hall. He paused while Eve collected herself and told him the sum of her fears—and, now she thought about it, the New Management's.

"In my own time, Number Two has achieved an occult apotheosis and ascended to become the Prime Minister—a Prime Minister with godlike power. Rupert had a plan to defeat him that relied on using me to incubate another clone." She wanted to spit, to get the taste of the words out of her mouth. She looked at George: he nodded, his expression one of deep disgust.

She took a deep breath and continued. "Number Twelve will have sent word to the bishop of her cult—Rupert—that I'm here. Knowing Rupert, his reaction will be that as I'm here now—and so is Von Franckenstein—his plan will work as well in 1816 as in 2017. After all, today's Number Two is easier to defeat than the Bl—the future time's Prime Minister. As an author I dare not name wrote, 'He who controls the past, controls the present; he who controls the present controls the future.' Which means Rupert will come for me. In fact, I'm getting a distinct feeling that this is exactly what the Prime Minister set me up for.

"I just hope Number Two is ready for him. . . ."

▸◂▸◂▸◂

Number Forty-Nine swung the doors open before George could ring the bell. He bowed deeply. "His Lordship is in the morning room," the butler announced. "I don't know what you said to 'im but he's in a frightful mood this morning," he told George, ignoring Eve. "Can't sit down lest the chair go up in flames."

Number Seven led Eve to Number Two's office. His hand in the small of her back was reassuringly gentle. Nevertheless, she could not avoid some trepidation. Number Two's palpable upset and anger when he'd doorstepped them earlier had been unsettling: he'd been frightened almost out of his boots, and not by her. (He clearly underestimated Eve.) Number Two was a powerful sorcerer in his own right: what could terrify him? Given the power hierarchy implicit in the numbered ranks, it could only be Number One. But Number One was—

"I told you to bring the woman back," Number Two snapped at George as the door swung shut. He stood by the fireplace, shifting his balance from leg to leg as if unconsciously resisting the urge to run. He stabbed an accusing finger. "I didn't expect you to marry her! My God, man, have you no decency? No respect for your family name? What would your father say?"

George's arm tightened, but Eve barely noticed in her indignation. "My father doesn't get a say," George said coldly. "Number One saw to that. And furthermore—"

"You can stop right there." Eve stepped between them, fed up with being spoken about as if she wasn't there. This kind of conversation reminded her of Rupert's more misogynistic old school chums, the kind who graduated straight from Eton to a dealer desk in the City and a membership at the Garrick Club without encountering the twenty-first century in any meaningful way. To them it was all CNN, fast cars, hookers, and blow, and a woman's place was on her knees.

"I am here because I am trying to prevent Rupert, Number One, from destroying you," she told Number Two. "If I'm right he'll turn up very soon, probably with the baron in tow, and he'll be looking for me." She glanced around at the circular room. "He has allies, but the hounds won't be able to get in here. He has a plot," she added, turning back to Number Two, "a conspiracy against the entire world, not just the Invisible College. For it to work he needs to enslave me, reinforcing an otherwise-weak geas he imposed when I first entered his employment, which is why"—she reached for Number Seven's arm—"our marriage was *essential.*"

"Your—" Number Two stopped talking, and Eve was certain that if she'd been able to see his face she might have seen him biting his tongue in an effort to hold his frustration. (Or his feeding palps, mandibles, or cyclostomic orifice, depending on what the glamour masked.) "You will explain. Please, have a seat," he said with heavy irony. "My house is yours. For as long as is necessary."

Eve laid it all out, or as much as she thought Number Two needed to know. "Von Franckenstein's boys are what the people in my age and Rupert's would call 'clones.' A simple clone is merely an artificial identical twin, like a graft from a sapling. The true innovation is Von Franckenstein's technique for copying memories and personality from the original into the—"

"*Do* proceed," Number Two interrupted heavily. "You may take this as read."

"Well, then, you may have noticed that Rupert is bodily deteriorating. He is a lich, a corpse kept moving by sorcerous intent.

If I stay here too long I'll go the same way." George seemed unaccountably displeased. "Anyway, previously Rupert intended to return to his own time and use Von Franckenstein's technique to clone himself, with me as the incubator." It was hard to keep a tremor out of her voice.

"To create a new body, regain his vitality, and attack his enemies, yes, I see." Number Two inclined his head. "By marrying Number Seven you broke his claim on you, hmm, yes, ingenious. I still fail to see how this affects me and why you expect me to help you."

"For starters, you've created the greatest concentration of captive sorcerers in England, and there's *mana* in human sacrifice," Eve said bluntly. "He'll have to start burning their *mana* soon in order to live long enough to turn me into a reproductive stump and clone himself." She licked her lips and swallowed, acid burning the back of her throat. "He'll need to keep my corpse alive, too. Neither of us belong in this time. And he'll attack you too, you mark my words."

Number Two scoffed. "Me? Why would he attack *me*? I am of no importance, a humble public servant," he said with exaggerated irony. "I rather think you are at greater risk from Number One than I, for I am a mere cog in the marvelous machinery of empire he has built for us."

"Yes, about that—how do you walk in daylight?" Eve asked, leaning forward. "Tell me that. Why doesn't sunlight burn you?"

"Because—" Number Two stood up. "Look at me!" he sneered. "The invisible man! Untouched by the very corpuscules of light, where it matters." His face was impossible to notice. "I held up a mirror to my soul once, and it stuck." He paced over to the deep bay window. "You would have me believe that Number One plots to create a clone of himself, using a powerful witch instead of the baron's beheaded whores, then attack the Invisible

College? Then take over the government and fly to the moon and drink all the tea in China, no doubt—"

"But he *will*, because it's all about you," Eve announced. "You're a lich, too, aren't you. And you will outlive any human. As you do so you will grow strange and powerful and invite something that isn't remotely human into your soul. You are the seed of the enemy Rupert intends to topple in his own time, and he'd be a fool not to attack you now where you are weaker. You—the being you became—sent me here to—"

Record scratch.

Motherfucker, Eve thought dizzily.

"What?" she asked, returning George's look of bafflement.

"I think I've heard enough," said Number Two, the faceless cypher who was the dream road's sketch of the undead sorcerer who—in her own time—was known as Fabian Everyman, before he began his ascent to the Throne of Skulls in Downing Street. He sounded shaken. "You should not have—"

A bell rang. Number Two crossed to a discreet speaking tube set in one wall. "What is it?" he demanded.

George touched Eve's shoulder. "We should go," he whispered.

But before they could move, Number Two turned on them, radiating fury. "A ship approaches!" he snarled. "You fools! You've doomed us all!"

The brig *Prince of Poets* sailed right up to the Village pier unseen. It was concealed by a deflection glamour so strong that it must have taken the combined power of an entire coven of the Silver Sisterhood to create—or perhaps a couple of discreet human sacrifices by Number One. But it was difficult to sustain such an enchantment when too many eyes were watching. As it came alongside the pier and dropped anchor, the sisters maintaining the glamour finally lost their grip: the vessel shimmered from mirage into reality as the crew swarmed onto the beach like angry hornets armed with cutlass and pistol.

Eve and George trailed Number Two, who dashed down the stairs to the panopticon observation chamber beneath his office. "Eyes on the beach!" he shouted at the frightened watch officer in charge of the observers. "Summon the key master! Summon the oath keeper! Ready Rover! Project, project! Is everyone around here asleep? Must I take personal control, lest we all be slaughtered in our cups?"

Eve swallowed, her throat dry. "Rover, that's the hunting—"

"Yes." George gripped her arm. In response to Number Two's barked orders, a view of the beach swam into view on one wall. The magical projection was upside down, dim, and lacked audio—it was severely limited compared to twenty-first-century electronics—but nevertheless painted a dismally clear picture. "We'll see them—"

Flickering sparks and a billowing cloud of smoke erupted from the gun deck. Number Two snorted angrily. "Good *luck* with that, sirrah!" Over his shoulder, in George's direction, he contemptuously added, "We're warded and besides, they couldn't hit a barn door at this—"

Crash. Everybody flinched.

"Sounds like they've got your range already." George produced a watch from his waistcoat pocket, flicked the lid open, and squinted. "Remind me where the cellar entrance is again?"

"Past the staircase, first door on the left." Number Two was distracted by one of the observers who seemed anxious to get his attention. "Why?"

"This is an obvious distraction. You should prepare for unfriendly visitors."

Eve straightened her back. "Where is François?"

"You should take your wife back to her—your—apartment."

Number Two spoke offhandedly as he picked up another speaking tube. "Unleash the shoggoth!" Shouting from the other end of the pipe suggested that his interlocutor was otherwise preoccupied.

"*Where. Is. François?*" Eve gritted her teeth. Number Two ignored her.

George stepped in. "You should answer the question."

"He's"—Number Two waved his left hand in an arcane gesture that apparently required hypermobile finger joints to avoid a painful dislocation—"somewhere upstairs," he said dismissively. "This is men's work, madam, you should seek shelter."

Crash. The walls and floor shook, and plaster dust puffed free of the ceiling, pattering down from cracks around the joists. The rocking viewing beam the watchers sat astride jolted, and one of them tumbled to the floor with a shout of pain.

"François is our best hope right now." Eve made for the door. "I'm going to fetch him."

George—Number Seven, she reminded herself: Number Two's subordinate, or coworker, or fellow employee of the Invisible College—followed her. "There is a door leading to the subbasement," he pitched his voice low, "where there is a ley-line end point. It leads to London, and you may find a branch that will lead you back through the dream roads to your home. I expect Number One has sent one or more of his minions, Number Twelve or Sir Lawrence or suchlike, along with hounds, to take us from behind—"

"Yes, I know, *do* try to keep up. Remember the plan? We should have reinforcements coming too. My brother and his friends by ley line, if he got my message." Eve bit her tongue. Now was not the time to pick a fight with her allies. "My point is, we need to find François—tactical genius, remember? With an army of toy soldiers?" She'd met a boy just like François before, one of the children of the head Home Office superheroes, although he'd been what, maybe five (or possibly six?) years old at the time. A toy animator called Ethan. François was infinitely more mature, a vast, cool battlemind grafted atop a young shoot that had inherited who-knew-what powers from its guillotined *maman*. She'd just have to pray that they were the *right* powers to deal with a pirate incursion and an attack through the dream roads by either the Silver Sisterhood or a ghastly groping fortune seeker or—

"Check the first-floor bedrooms." George took up a position by the stairs to the ground floor. "I'll hold the ley line for you while you search." He pulled a penknife and a draftsman's chalk from his pockets, then rolled up his sleeve and prepared to cut: blood was the best ink.

"Don't be an idiot! If you get yourself killed here I'll—"

"I'm not going to die." His smile was ghastly. "Remember the hounds? This time I'm prepared."

"Wait, what are you—"

"*Go,*" he said, the blood dripping from his forearm, and he began to chant something unspeakable that was almost drowned out by the sudden eager buzzing in her ears. *Hemovores,* she realized with a shudder of horror, and she moved to grab his arm, but before she could touch him he raised his other hand, and his fingers flicker-snapped and a shield sprang up between them. Eve was not the only practitioner here, nor yet alone in having macros a snicker-snack away. "I'll still be here when you get back."

But you'll be a vampire! she wailed silently as she turned and hurled herself up the stairs. Another shot rattled the wainscoting. She heard distant cries, and a muffled banging of musket fire that carried through the windows of the mayoral residence. A sound like thunder rattled the doorframes a couple of times a minute: the pier was well within carronade range of the village, and the gunnery crews had the range. The shore party could run all the way into town under cover of cannon fire before the Village guard could be mustered out to form a firing line.

She'd never visited the upper floor before, and now she found herself in the middle of a passage with doors in either direction. A worrying smell of wood smoke tickled her nostrils. "François!" she shouted until her throat was hoarse. "Where *are* you? We have to mount a defense!"

"I'm *coming*, mademoiselle." His sullen tones were behind her. The wood smoke was joined by a faint blue mist emerging from the skirting boards. In the distance, Eve sensed rather than heard the baying of hounds. "Dragoons, advance!"

Eve backed up against the wallpaper, then gathered up her skirts as a tide of two-inch-high Old Guard grenadiers double-timed past her, bayonet tips gleaming menacingly above their tall bearskin caps. They'd been crude lead figurines in Hamleys toy shop, thumb-high and roughly painted, but in the confines of a corridor perfused by the ghostly smoke from beyond the walls of the world they seemed somehow more substantial. François marched behind them, his chin tilted arrogantly high: he wore his bicorn hat *en bataille,* and as he neared her he tapped his brim with a swagger stick. "Mademoiselle. I would not linger here if I were you." He sniffed. The smell of wood smoke was stronger, joined by an acrid note of spent black powder. "Where are we to make our stand?"

"The road I mentioned is in the basement! George is guarding it." She urged him on frantically. "I'm right behind you! Remember the plan!"

François marched his tin troops downstairs with alacrity. They broke stride as they jumped down from one tread to the next, as if crossing a bridge: there was no hesitation or wavering, even though each step overtopped them by the height of an entire floor, had they been of human height. The smoke was thickening, and she heard shouts of dismay and more crashes of shot landing outside. It seemed the pirates were intent on bombarding the Village to splinters. The smoke suggested they were firing cannonballs heated by a shot furnace or a powerful pyrokinetic talent: *if his mission here is over, the Village is of no further use to Rupert save as a source of sacrifices,* Eve realized dizzily. Rupert would happily set his toy chest ablaze before he allowed it to fall into another's hands. And of course the real Portmeirion had been built in the 1920s—there had been no sign of its predecessor before the work began: it had to be destroyed.

As she reached the ground-floor passage the front doors flew open, eliciting a shriek of dismay from Number Forty-Nine. "Heh, I've got you now, missy!" Sir Lawrence strode forward, cutlass in one hand and pistol in the other. One of the men behind him gripped the choking Number Forty-Nine by the collar. Another leveled a bayonet-tipped musket at her. Hackmanworth looked positively gleeful, despite his smut-stained cheeks and a graze on his forehead that suggested he'd been lucky to keep his brains in their pan so far. "*And* the boy. Grab him," he shouted over his shoulder as he strode toward Eve. "*You* I've got a bone to pick with, 'cept the boss wants you for himself—"

More pirates boiled into the front hall as Eve dashed toward the basement staircase. "Men!" François shouted behind her. "Form up!"

"Remember the plan!" she repeated, and then she was skipping and almost tripping down the stairs, helter-skelter, straight into a wall of blood and death magic that caught her like a web of molten glass and deposited her at the threshold of Number Two's panopticon lair—

Record scratch.

By the time Eve blinked her way back to consciousness there had been some changes.

She wasn't in the observation room beneath the town hall anymore: this looked to be one of the side chambers of the Assembly Rooms. It was strewn with broken chairs and upended tables. Of George there was no sign. One of Number Two's watchmen stood with his back to a wall, hands raised and spine rigid with terror. Number Two was also present, as were—

As she shook her head and blinked blurry eyes to clear them, she felt herself being held ungently by rough male hands. *Hackmanworth,* she thought angrily, and lashed out. A man grunted in pain behind her.

"Enough of that." Rupert waved a skeletal hand lazily and Eve found herself released from one overbearing brute's clutches into the supernatural grip of another. Rupert's telekinesis was monstrously powerful, but his mastery didn't extend to directing it without hand gestures: he was like a child who had learned to speed-read but still had to move his lips to make the words come. As he gestured it felt as if bony claws gripped her at wrist and ankle, with a noose of finger bones drawn around her neck, not quite tight enough to choke, while he floated her halfway to the ceiling and across the room.

"Hello, *wife,*" Rupert gloated.

To Eve, it felt as if only weeks had passed since she had been ensnared in his web in London. But Rupert had been back in 1816 for many months, and they had not been kind.

Rupert floated in the middle of the room, his mummified feet dangling inches above the floor. He still had skin and eyes after a fashion, although whether the sickly green glow emanated from anything vitreous in the latter was beyond her ken. His lips and gums had shriveled, revealing yellowed fangs, and his hair was a nightmarish dandelion wisp. He bore the musty, foul odor of adipocere, the same corpse wax as a hand of glory: bathing had clearly not been among his priorities.

Eve felt nauseous, either from a blow to the head or an apprehension of her imminent death. Nevertheless, she decided she'd had enough. There was nothing now to be gained from cowering. She cocked her head to one side, covering her icy fear with a mask of studied insolence intended to enrage. "Did someone say something?" she asked. "Is there an echo in the room?"

Number Two spoke up: "Don't provoke him! He'll—"

With a negligent wave of one finger, Rupert slammed Number

Two into the wall. "*Silence, Fabian,*" he hissed. Power boiled off his bony frame in waves, like the heat haze around a reactor that had blown its containment dome apart and sent streams of red-hot corium flowing in all directions. To Eve: "Well, *wife*? What do you have to say to your lord and master?"

Come on *George, where* are *you?* She glanced at the doorway. Of poor, honorable George, of his determination to protect her, his defensive circle, his blood magic in the basement of the town hall, there was no sign. She was desperate to believe him still alive, but she had no memory of whatever had befallen her at the bottom of the stairs when she'd been fleeing Hackmanworth. *Fuck, on my own as usual, right when I most needed backup*. Just for once, she wished, she really, *really* wished, that she wasn't alone in the grip of an inscrutable alien nightmare.

"Pay attention to me!" Rupert screeched from across the room. He floated closer, clearly on the edge of losing his rag: if he wasn't a mummified revenant she swore he'd be spraying her with spittle.

"Must I?" Eve forced a hint of a smile onto her face, even though she ached with fear for George—curiously, less so for herself. It was too much to hope that the narrative pressure that had driven her into George's arms would give them a happy-ever-after, especially in the face of Rupert's human sacrifice–powered malice. But if she was going to go down hard, she nevertheless wasn't going to give Rupert any hint of fear. Fear was Rupert's catnip, and she was long past obliging her tormenter.

"You are my wife!" Rupert insisted. "We are of one flesh! You will obey!"

"I don't think so." *Now* she couldn't resist a grin. "I broke the geas. And *you* didn't read the contract."

For the first time Rupert looked perplexed. "What?"

"You didn't read the fine print. Marriage is time-bounded in one direction—right now the date on your proxy agreement is two centuries in the future, so it's invalid. Also, you never bothered consummating the marriage, so that's a second strike. Thirdly, I married someone else so you can't reimpose it. Your geas is a bust, so you can just find yourself another incubator and marry her instead. I'm *sure* Tiffy Ffoulkes-Ward would be happy to serve you except, oh no, I forgot, your cock shriveled up and fell off and wasps built a nest in your balls—"

Rupert's shriek of rage was interrupted as the door banged open to admit Baron Von Franckenstein, his hands held high, marching stiff-legged in front of a grim-faced François and his tin army. The stink of burning timber blew in behind him, almost strong enough to overpower the rank aroma of Rupert's decay.

"Help me, I implore you! He is out of control!" The baron had a tendency to whine when overtopped by setbacks, and bayonets and burning buildings were close enough to pitchforks and torches to constitute a crisis.

Rupert had not been calm before: now he positively howled. "What *is* this insolence? I was not to be interrupted! I am your superior within the Invisible College! You, child, you *will* obey me or I'll have you in the Star Chamber on Mahogany Row before—"

"I was never yours to command," François said coldly, "*never.*" Behind him, the Immortals raised their inch-long muskets and took aim.

Come on, *George,* Eve thought, clenching her fists. She glanced sidelong at Number Two, who seemed to be struggling to say something. *Come on, Your Majesty, Number Two . . .* But nobody answered, inside her head or outside. *Still on my own.* No help there, either. Or was there? The ghost of a memory nagged her for attention, a scrap of an email header glimpsed on her PC's screen—Subject: Inactive account reminder—and three hours neatly snipped out of her memory.

Three hours. Three hours after Rupert had returned but before he summoned her to his office. Three hours. Three—

Record scratch.

Something really important had happened, and it wasn't the three missing hours after Rupert's return, it was the three missing hours after her return from Lancaster House, the first gap in her memories from that night, a night when someone—not Rupert—had taken control of her hands—

Oh, she realized, *so* that's *what He wanted me to do here!*

She twitched her fingers in sequence, reaching deep into her reserves of *mana. Protect the boy.* The ghostly bone digits at her throat were a caution and a warning: Rupert might not control her mind, but if he realized what she was up to he could tighten his necromantic garrote in an instant. His power had grown bloated and terrible while he'd been squatting in this pocket universe, dining on the souls of his victims—most likely he'd run out of soul-stuff of his own when he came back to 1816. Power tended to run in sorcerous families, and judging from George's strength, his parents must have been pretty strong: no wonder Rupert had consumed their *mana* the instant he returned to this time via their town house. Even the near-immortal adept who would ultimately become Fabian Everyman was weaker than Rupert here, the Number Two to Rupert's Number One.

A vision came to Eve, of an instant, of Rupert standing triumphant in the wreckage of the Village, surrounded by burning buildings and corpses on every side. Of Rupert absorbing the souls and *mana* of dozens of captive practitioners of the art, of the lich-king's power, bloated by wholesale magical cannibalism, wedging open the door to the dream roads under the town hall. Of Rupert presiding over sacrificial ceremonies elsewhen in time and space, receiving an awful tribute from the worshippers of the Mute Poet at ghastly, blood-drenched step pyramid temples like the one she'd seen in her dreams.

This is where it all starts, she realized: *this is where he always* meant *to start.* By destroying the faceless cypher who would become the ruler of the New Management, Rupert intended to take his place. Rupert was bent on growing his underground church in the dream roads, where he would wait until the stars were right before taking on the mantle of the Mute Poet and emerging into the magical dawn of the twenty-first century—

Her focus narrowed to a laser-bright apprehension of tactical necessities.

Throwing her power at François was an essential defensive move. The boy held no love for the baron, whose willingness to prostitute his art for Rupert's cause could not appear anything less than insulting. Hopefully Rupert would attribute the boy's defensive ward—half the toy soldiers formed up into a pentacle around his feet, joining hands and melding together in a solid, uninterrupted circuit while the other half took aim at Rupert—to his own innate power. (Because if Rupert suspected it was Eve's work, it would all be over for her in a few choking seconds.)

The Immortals of the Old Guard—those not involved in the protective grid—formed a firing line, and it seemed to Eve that although they were only a palm's breadth tall, they were also much larger and very far away in some eye-warping perspective. They brought their muskets up and aimed at the specter hovering before them, and at François's shouted command they fired as one, with the shattering crash and billowing smoke of ghostly but full-sized guns—which should have come as no surprise to Eve, for enough of them had laid down their lives on the battlefield that *of course* an honor guard of his own hell-bound troops would rally to protect a clone infused with the emperor's fighting spirit.

Eve felt Rupert's attention shift of an instant. The musket balls hung in midair before him, buzzing like angry red-hot wasps, and she dumped another bolus of raw *mana* in François's direction (which he failed to acknowledge) as she slid one foot cautiously sideways, and then another, until she stood beside Number Two.

"We should be ready to run," she whispered in his ear. "François will only hold him for a minute—"

(Another crash of guns, beneath the distant brassy squeal of signaling bugles and the rhythmic pounding of drums beating time.)

"Can't," Number Two said hoarsely, "Rover's running wild—"

Who let the dogs out? Eve thought, then blinked. The narrative compulsion was still playing games with her. "Listen," she told him, "I have a message for you—no, *from* you. A seed—"

And Eve heard herself reciting, in a voice that was not her own: "*I was sent here by order of His Dread Majesty: I am here to retrieve a relic, and to plant the seeds of His Majesty's ascent to power in the new millennium; and I am here to water the bloody roots of the tree from which He will harvest a grisly crop when the season of skulls comes to fruition. This* won't *hurt a bit*—"

She leaned toward him, and with lips temporarily not her own placed an open-mouthed kiss in the void where Number Two's face should be, and her tenth finger crooked in a gesture so painful that the bright and shining pain of a dislocation bit into the edge of her right hand.

Something immaterial but ghastly lunged from the hidden recesses of Eve's mind to take root in Number Two's soul.

Seed delivered, Eve swooned.

▸◂▸◂▸◂

"How much farther is it?" Game Boy demanded. He sounded tired, as were they all. "I need something to drink."

"I don't know." Imp slowed.

"Where *are* we, anyway?" asked Wendy.

"About—" Imp consulted his twist of hair. "—oh, not far now! We're most of the way there."

"I hear you." Sergeant Gunderson kept her voice down. "Let

my people take point when we hit the end." She'd brought three of her security contractors along as backup. They wore pixelated battle-dress uniforms with body armor, and carried AR-15s: Bigge Organization had picked up a contract to provide strike-breaking services to the New Management at some point, and automatic-weapon licenses were part of the package. (The New Management took a libertarian approach to sunsetting laws that got in the way of business.)

A smell of wood smoke hung in the air. They'd left the familiar staircases and corridors of the dream mansion at least an hour ago, descending through lime-washed cellars to a rough-floored tunnel of roughly circular cross section, with stone walls bearing the marks of the hand tools that had dug it from the living rock. Imp was glad of the flashlights he and Wendy had brought—their experience of charting the tunnels under Skaro had taught him that much. Aside from their LED torches the only illumination down here came from a silvery thread of light that ran along the middle of the floor and made his skin crawl if he stepped too close to it. It was obviously sorcerous, and he had an inkling that every pace he took along this tunnel carried him farther than it had any right to. (He'd heard of ley lines: but he'd never walked one before, much less followed one through the dream roads.)

A kink in the tunnel ahead of them denied Imp a clear line of sight. He approached it, then paused just before the bend. "Nearly there. There's light—"

Sally stepped forward. "Please stand back." She waved a hand signal: two of her soldiers took up positions. "Stay behind me until we secure entry," she told the Lost Boys. Imp nodded. It wasn't their first time working with the Bigge Organization heavies—Eve had brought them along on her heliborn invasion of Castle Skaro—but their unusual powers didn't make them supersoldiers, or even bulletproof, with the possible exception of Game Boy. "Okay, go," she added quietly, and the heavies darted past the bend and disappeared from view.

Imp waited. "I hate this part," Game Boy whined quietly. "Why are we here again?"

"My sister's missing," Imp reminded him. "Only living relative, y'know?"

"I want to get paid," Wendy added, sotto voce. Her cynical excuse didn't fool anyone.

"This is stupid," Del opined. "We should—"

A helmeted silhouette appeared ahead. "Clear," it called, then ducked back. (A weird trick of perspective seemed to make the soldier shrink as if he'd stepped back ten meters instead of one.)

"Well, here goes," said Imp, sucking in a deep breath and moving forward.

The moment he turned the corner he was assailed by the sounds of fighting, of screams and swearing and the flat percussive banging of musketry, all muffled for having been filtered down a stairwell: by the sharp stink of gunpowder fireworks and acrid woodsmoke, by the light of oil lamps and the less familiar witch light of a sorcerer wasting precious *mana* on mere vision.

Sally Gunderson and her men (one of whom was a woman) had a thaumaturge at bay, their rifles leveled at him—he stood between the exit from the dream road and a more normal passageway, with an open door at the far end and a staircase leading up into the chaos overhead.

"Who the devil *are* you people?" the fellow demanded. His hands were raised, but not—Imp realized—in surrender: he was dressed as if he'd stepped out of a period drama, except no TV show would have let an actor appear so exhausted on camera. But seen through Imp's mind's eye he shone like a star, bloated with *mana* and surrounded by a peculiar buzzing halo of sorcerous darkness.

"Don't shoot!" Imp warned. "Who are *you*?"

The sorcerer did a double take at Imp. "I'm Number Seven.

You know, you're the spitting image of Number Six—are you by any chance related?"

"Who is Number Six?" demanded Sergeant Gunderson.

"She was born Evelyn Starkey, and also known hereabouts as Lady Evelyn de Montfort—"

"Where *is* she?" Imp demanded impatiently. "She's my sister."

Number Seven made to lower his hands. "Right!" One of the soldiers jerked his gun's muzzle, clearly fighting against Imp's hint. Number Seven made an odd gesture with his little finger: the soldier toppled sideways against the wall, gasping for breath. "Enough of that," Number Seven sniffed. "Your sister is known as Number Six here, and I happen to have the honor of being her husband. Also, *she's in trouble*. Do you mean to rescue her?"

"Yes, we do!" Sally Gunderson butted in while Imp stood slack-jawed, trying to process what he'd just heard: she nodded at Number Seven, then the stricken soldier. "Can you release him?"

"If you call your dogs off." Number Seven raised an eyebrow.

"Yes. Jim, Andrea, Pie-hole: he's with us, shooting the boss's squeeze is a career-limiting move. Right, you, take us to her. Chop-chop!"

"She *married* you?" Imp finally managed to squeeze out. He stared at Number Seven in disbelief. "Was she drunk or insane?"

"She had her reasons." Number Seven's cheek twitched rapidly. "She told me you'd be coming by ley line: I had to be sure." He was breathing rapidly, Imp saw, almost hyperventilating, as if in some distress. "Rupert's men took her—they're probably in the Assembly Rooms—he's there, with the others, the Baron Von Franckenstein and the boy from Saint Helena, and if we're lucky we may be in time—"

"Who else are we up against, and when and where are we?" Sergeant Gunderson asked urgently. "Quick description, please."

"You're in the basement of the town hall in the Village, it's the year 1816, and Rupert arrived here on board a pirate ship." George rapidly described what he'd seen of the crew. He turned to Imp. "And you will take her back to your own time, won't you." For a moment something ancient peered out of his eyes. "I shan't be able to follow you, but I trust you will take good care of her, sir. Now you need to come with me."

Eve did not remain unconscious for long—indeed, she began to come to as she collapsed to her knees, her vision gray, a sizzling chittering sound filling her ears as she gasped for breath at Number Two's feet.

It came to her that she was lucky to be alive. The PM had implanted something so deep inside her that it felt as if she had given birth, or donated a kidney, or been half eviscerated when it ripped free, like a worker bee relieved of its one and only barbed stinger. All she could do for now was sit and watch as François barked orders and the fog of battle spread through the room, the walls becoming indistinct and hazy. Distant cannons crashed and thundered as Rupert intoned sorcerous activation macros in a tongue that made her ears hurt.

She had no more power to push at François, and it appeared that everything would soon be over, but then Number Two stepped away from the wall and raised his inexplicably free hands.

He's not the Prime Minister, she thought dizzily, although it seemed not unthinkable that one day he might assume that mantle. She opened her inner eye to watch, even though the two of them were so bright they hurt to look at.

"Yield!" shrieked Rupert, throwing a pulse of distilled sorrow at François. (Mere brute force had failed to gain traction against the emperor's ghostly defense.)

"Perhaps you should pick on somebody your own size?" said

Number Two, his throat creaking like a gallows crossbar overloaded with strange fruit—clearly swallowing the Black Pharaoh's soul-seed had left him a trifle hoarse.

Rupert turned to face this new threat, and Eve's breath caught as she saw him in a new light.

Rupert and Fabian, Number Two, flickered like reflections half glimpsed in a distorting mirror. Neither of them appeared even remotely human, though one of them resembled a long-dead cadaver and the other might almost have passed (had he possessed a face). The room was filled with the deafening chitter of mindless eaters summoned from the void by their coruscating display of power, but like moths drawn to naked flames, any eaters that got too close to the duelists flashed into ash.

Eve's ward had grown burning hot from deflecting the overspill of the sorcerous duel, but Rupert had now lost his focus on her. His bony grip became tenuous as he directed his attention toward Number Two. Eve tried to move, experimentally stretching an arm, and found herself free to reach out and touch the wall. Heart pounding, she pushed off and stood unsteadily. Her vision briefly grayed again and she swayed as the overwhelming scrape and squeal of the eaters threatened her. *Can't stay here,* she realized. *Get François and go*—leave the two avatars to rip shreds of soul-stuff off one another—

"Eve?"

I must be hallucinating. "Jerm?" She blinked dizzily at her brother.

He raised a warning finger. "Can you walk?" he asked. Behind him she saw other faces: Sally Gunderson and three soldiers in twenty-first-century battle dress surrounding Doc Depression and Game Boy, Del standing in the doorway, Wendy beside her with a compound bow—*I* am *hallucinating*—and standing beside her brother—

"Come with me," George told her urgently, wrapping strong fingers around her upper arm and tugging.

"Hey, leave my sister alone!"

"It's all right," she told Imp. Eyes right: George. Eyes left: Imp. Both glaring at one another furiously. "I married him of my own free will," she told her brother. Blinking, she forced herself to focus. "The boy—" She rolled her head in the direction of François. "Get him out of here. The PM wants him. Hey Del, meet François. François! These people are friends of mine, you need to go with them."

François looked annoyed, but behind him Eve could barely see Rupert and Fabian anymore. The sorcerers were alight with power, surrounded by new swarms of eaters attracted by the release of raw *mana* as swirling trails of power funneled into the duelists—the stolen life force of worshippers and human sacrifices spiraling in from the dream roads. "But I have him under my guns!" the child prodigy protested. "Surely we should press our advantage—" He turned and looked at Rupert, a glowing saint of death floating in a nimbus of shredded souls, then turned back and swallowed. "And then, sometimes there is a time to retreat in good order. Let us go."

Del stared at him, then back at Eve. "Where do you find them?" she demanded.

"This one? In a toy shop in London. Go on, show him the dream roads. You, too, Doc, Game Boy." To Sally Gunderson: "I appreciate your diligence, I really do, but you should know better than to listen to my brother—"

"Sis, time to go." Imp scowled at her, then glanced sidelong at George and nodded slightly. Eve shivered with an intimation of betrayal as George released her arm. *Et tu, Brute?* she wondered.

"Yes." George nodded back at Imp. "Take her and go before it's too late."

"George!" She met his gaze and was briefly lost for words. Something had happened to him, something terrible, and now her sense of loss had a focus. Bargains with spectral horrors seemed to be all the rage among the Invisible College's prime-numbered agents, and Number Seven had inflicted a blood curse upon himself. "*Please* tell me you didn't—"

"Eve." He gathered her into a close embrace when she was fit to swoon again. "You can't stay here, and I can't go with you now. But this way, I *will* meet you on the other side. It'll be a long wait, but I'll see you again. Go now! And take the boy."

She met his lips and kissed him blindly, desperately, opening her lips to accept his tongue—and something else that flooded her with a dark and inhuman energy, virile and murderous. It was there and she swallowed it in a flash, felt it take root inside her, and then they were simply kissing, although it set her hair on end and her skin on fire—a kiss for the ages.

"I'm not leaving you," she began, with a warning glare at Imp, who was shifting anxiously from foot to foot and clearly planning something. "You can't achieve anything here. Come with me?"

George pulled back, smiled lopsidedly, and pointed one finger at the back of his head. He half turned to reveal angry red burns. "I got these dashing across the street to get here. I can't go outside in daylight without shelter, I'll catch fire. And you can't stay. There's a wine cellar: I shall take cover until dusk. You"—he addressed Imp—"please take my wife to safety."

With a thunderous crash the wall at one corner of the space that had been the ballroom collapsed, spraying bricks and timber and the joists of the upper floor everywhere. Choking smoke flooded into the room, far more real than the billowing powder fumes of the ghosts of the Imperial Guard.

"George!" Eve shouted. But George had disappeared in the haze. He'd cast an obfuscatory glamour around himself once again, she realized. Her indignation was a tenuous, appalled thing in the face of her despair.

Rupert shrieked a tongueless ululation, and Number Two responded with a chittering drone like a billion insects locked in mindless feeding frenzy. A storm of furious dreams washed overhead as Imp grabbed Eve and hustled her across the rubble toward Del, François, and the others. Flames rippled up the curtains on one wall.

"Ma'am." Sally Gunderson sounded tense. "We have to leave *now*. Mayor's cellar—ley line to London—"

Rupert's and Fabian's dream-road avatars were barely recognizable now: two sorcerer-shaped holes punched through the fabric of reality, windows onto a desiccated plain where a pair of malevolent immortal rivals stood atop opposing stepped temple pyramids, receiving an endless tribute of ghostly sacrifices as they threw the life energies of entire continents across the horizon at one another.

"But—"

"Lads, close protection protocol *now*, if you please. At the double."

Eve found herself picked up bodily and carried by a pair of guards. Behind her François emitted a hacking cough and spat on the parquet, then Del had him in a fireman's carry and was hustling impossibly far ahead of the party. The smoke was getting to her, and for a few seconds all she could do was choke. Game Boy was in the wind and a couple of Rupert's pirates had fallen on one another's shoulders, weeping piteously—Doc Depression's doing. *George*, she thought despairingly and, Orpheus-like, looked back.

The middle of the ballroom had collapsed into some sort of magical singularity, a knot of warped space surrounding the zone of high-intensity thaum flux where the emergent Black Pharaoh fought the nearly immanentized Mute Poet. There was no sign of George: he'd surrendered her to the custody of her brother's rescue party. Eve smelled ozone, saw blue sparks sizzle as her hair stood on end. She woozily summoned *mana* to reinforce her protective ward, stretching it as far as it would go around her escort while they skirted the death zone. For a while she grayed out, unable to see or hear anything but a dizzying chitter of eaters thronging around her. The next thing she was aware of was staring down at the gravel in front of the Assembly Rooms.

They'd emerged into a scene out of Goya. The Village was smoldering and shattered from the naval bombardment, the air rent by screams and groans from the not-yet-dead. A faint blue mist spread at ground level in all directions, lending the landscape an eerie luster and gradually damping the sounds of violence to either side. In the distance, a horrible gurgling moan was abruptly cut off as Rover engulfed some hapless soul: farther afield, Eve heard the iron-throated belling of the Silver Sisterhood's hunting hounds.

"We've got to leave before the hounds find us," she rasped, hoarse from the gunpowder smoke.

"Not a problem," called Del. "Hey, kid, can you walk?"

François moaned. "My head, he hurts." But he stumbled alongside them for a few steps before picking up the pace.

"I can walk, too," Eve told her porters.

"Yes, ma'am, but sarge said—"

"It's all right if she can walk," Sally interrupted.

"Put. Me. Down," Eve repeated. "I know where we're going."

"But, ma'am, we're to guard you—"

Eve gathered the tatters of her dignity around her, then stalked toward the town hall and the ley line back home. Behind her Imp was telling Doc and Wendy something—he sounded anxious—but she paid him no attention. *George, you magnificent idiot,* she thought despairingly. Self-sacrificing heroics did *not* amuse her, and suckering Imp into complicity with the protect-my-wife line was positively insulting: Imp's gallant fecklessness was the whole reason she was here in the first place, after all.

Two pirates, or bandits, or maybe Village guards who had shed their uniforms, came around the corner brandishing cutlasses. Eve tore a pair of pearls from her earrings and stabbed them at the pirates with her mind, venting her grief-fueled anger: they went down hard. She swept through the broken-down front doors of the town hall without checking whether they lived: François paused to retrieve one of their curved short swords. The flames had not reached the basement staircase. She led her people downstairs then turned toward the ley line.

I'll see you on the other side, George had said. He'd better have been telling the truth, because next time they met she was going to have some choice words for him.

EPILOGUE

Record scratch.

"I gather you brought me a gift," said the Prime Minister.

Eve blinked.

She was in the anteroom at Lancaster House, furnished as before with marble-topped occasional tables, spindly Louis XV chairs, and a bucolic eighteenth-century landscape by Stubbs. (Definitely Stubbs.) The Prime Minister, His Dread Majesty, arrayed in white tie and tails, inclined his head sardonically; beside him Baroness Hazard stood with hands clasped demurely before her. They appeared unchanged since her last visit, but—

As she took stock the fine details came into focus, like a spot-the-difference picture puzzle. She'd lost her gloves: her gown was stained with blood and worse, and her hair was a rat's nest. (Doubtless if she'd been male her fly would have been at half-mast.) Also, she was holding the hand of a twelve-year-old boy (or was he six?) who wore unfashionable breeches and a jacket that stank of gunpowder mischief and was haunted by the groans of dying soldiers. He held a cutlass that, now she considered it, was not *quite* dripping with blood . . . and they were in the presence of the Prime Minister.

"Excuse me?" she asked faintly: "what just happened?"

"Oh dear." Persephone swooped on François and gently relieved him of his sword: François merely swayed, his expression vacant. "They always do that," she told Eve apologetically.

"What?" Eve shook her head.

"My gift." Somewhere in some other dimension, the Prime Minister's face was smiling indulgently. "My boy." He extended a gloved finger toward François. "A most suitable tribute, his head."

Shock coursed through Eve's veins like ice water. "But you can't—I mean, he hasn't done anything!"

The PM chuckled indulgently. "Oh, I'm not going to *kill* him. Quite the opposite!"

"But what—"

"Events in the dream roads have consequences. Rupert, in one version of history, succeeds in cloning himself, and thereby—because Rupert is far more venal and less clever than he supposes—fell victim to the Royal Navy, who take an emphatically dim view of piracy in their home waters. In another version of history, he leaves the pillaging to the likes of Sir Lawrence Hackmanworth and instead focuses his efforts on building up his network of worshippers and inviting his patron to fill the gap left by his missing soul. And in a third cleft of the stick, you arrive in London and then disappear entirely from the historical record—presumably murdered."

The Prime Minister paused, apparently lost in contemplation. Baroness Hazard apologized on his behalf. "He *does* like to monologue, I'm afraid." (Rupert did it, too: it was a common weakness among evil deity–hosting sorcerers, Eve realized.)

"But in this new version of history you have gifted me with—well, well—I *thank* you for the veritable cornucopia of information! The letter under a floorboard that your wastrel of a scoundrel of a brother conveyed to Her Grace two weeks ago"—a tip of the head at Persephone to some extent explained his florid circumlocution—"most expediently made up for his negligence in signing away your *droit de seigneur.* After all, without it, who knows when you might have been summoned to court?"

"B-but—" Eve felt sick to her stomach. *I don't stutter!* she thought indignantly.

"Strange loops in the dream roads, sweetie," the baroness apologized. "They make my head hurt, too, if it helps."

"History: we do it over until we get it right." The Prime Minister sighed heavily. "Well, I shall thank you for your previous tribute"—he gestured at the gift-wrapped box containing the head of Rupert de Montfort Bigge from the wrong time line—"and consider the matter closed. This one's head"—his negligent nod took in François—"will do perfectly, as long as it stays on his shoulders: it's the contents that are valuable, after all! Lady Hazard, please arrange a suitable date for Countess Marsden's pledge of allegiance, not less than a month from now. My Lady—"

"Wait, who's this Countess Marsden?" Eve felt punch-drunk.

"You *did* marry George, didn't you?" She nodded. "Well, as the Earl of Marsden, that makes you his countess, a title which takes precedence over the Barony of Skaro."

"Oh my."

"Have a seat." Persephone moved in before Eve collapsed again. In doing so, she let go of François's hand.

The boy blinked and looked around, then saw the Prime Minister. "You! I saw you in the Village—"

"Yes, you *did*. And I look forward to getting to know you, monsieur." To Eve: "This boy I entrust to your guardianship: he needs a home where the owner is aware of his background and special needs. If there are any complications involving social services, schools, or his immigration status, Baroness Hazard will make them go away."

Eve shuddered. "Is that all—" After a moment, she remembered to add, "Your Majesty?" If the clock on the mantelpiece behind the PM was to be trusted, she hadn't even left the party yet: Sally and her car would still be waiting.

"Yes, it is—for now." The smiling faceless void raised a champagne flute to her. "Before you go, please do feel free to help yourselves to the buffet. And I shall see you again in, I suspect, no time at all!"

ACKNOWLEDGMENTS

No novel is ever written or published in a vacuum, even though it feels like it during the long, lonely process of writing.

This book in particular took a long time to germinate, partly because I was less productive than normal during the early years of COVID-19, and also because it was a background project. It started in 2020 as my NaNoWriMo project. During NaNoWriMo (National Novel Writing Month—better known as November), writers challenge themselves to try and write a book of at least fifty thousand words in a month. It's a productivity prompt, and I needed that in 2020. But it also turned into my 2021 NaNoWriMo exercise as well, and just barely missed stretching into late 2022.

There is a reason why writing it was so protracted: in *Season of Skulls* I was attempting to write outside my genre comfort zone.

Back in 2019 I got interested in romance. I've already messed around with the material of police procedurals, secondary-world fantasy, and various flavors of science fiction. In terms of raw numbers, romance sells more novels than all of them combined: were there any good ideas I could steal? It turns out that yes, there were. The Regency setting alone (roughly speaking the period from 1811 to 1820, although it can be extended to cover 1795 to 1837) is a huge secondary-world fantasy shared universe. It's a fascinating period that covers the Napoleonic Wars and a period of considerable turmoil in British social history, and the conventional genre distinctions we've grown accustomed to weren't recognized back then: it saw the first true science fiction and vampire novels (Mary Shelley's *Frankenstein, or: the Modern Prometheus* and John Polidori's *The Vampyre*) as well as the works of Jane Austen. What kind of smoothie, I wondered, might result if I ran them through a blender with the New Management?

Lord Ruthven, Earl of Marsden, was featured in Polidori's *The Vampyre.* Polidori was Lord Byron's doctor and attended the house party on Lake Constance where Mary Shelley wrote *Frankenstein.*

George, aka Lord Ruthven, Number Seven in the Village, also appears in the fifth book in the Laundry Files, *The Rhesus Chart,* as the ancient "Old George." (On her return, Eve has missed him by about five years—assuming he's actually dead.)

A good Regency gothic demands suitably gothic settings, and the Village is modeled on Portmeirion in Wales, the setting of Patrick McGoohan's avant-garde spy-drama *The Prisoner* (first broadcast in 1967). The construction of Portmeirion began in 1925 and is ongoing: it is a well-known tourist attraction. Its relative isolation and Italianate style would have made it an excellent detention centre for European sorcerers and aristocrats captured during the continental wars following the French Revolution, had it existed more than a century ahead of its time. The asylum (Saint Hilda of Grantham's Home for Disgruntled Waifs and Strays), is hopefully entirely fictional: it first appeared in the Laundry Files in the novelette *Down on the Farm* (*Tor.com,* 2008: bit.ly/StrossDownontheFarm).

Every genre I've dabbled in was harder to write than it looked from the outside. Regency gothic is no different—indeed, getting the historical details right takes a lot of research, and integrating it with the Laundry setting to fill in some of the historical gaps was a real challenge. Respect to anyone who writes Regency (or romance in general) for a living: it's not as easy as it looks.

And even if this book doesn't meet the specification for romance (it doesn't exactly have a happy ending), there's room for Eve's story to continue.

And now for the actual acknowledgments.

I'd like to thank my literary agent, Caitlin Blasdell, who has represented me tirelessly and been my number one test reader for twenty years. I'd also like to thank my editors (Patrick Nielsen Hayden at Tordotcom and Jenni Hill at Orbit in the UK) for their confidence in letting me plough a new furrow here. (It's the easiest thing in the world for an editor to say, "Why don't you write me a book just like the last one, only slightly different?" That's the commercially sensible move, after all. It's somewhat harder to say, "Sure, why don't you rip up the rule book and do something offbeat and weird instead.") I also want to mention my copy editor on this book, MaryAnn Johanson, who stepped in when my series copy editor Marty Halpern was unwell; production editor Dakota Griffin; editorial assistant Mal Frazier; and all the other folks at Tordotcom Publishing and Orbit who have worked on this book in the background—invisible to the author, but never forgotten.

Test readers provide invaluable audience feedback, spot snags before they get in front of the editors (to say nothing of the reading public), and provide an early sanity check. This book has been past a lot of test readers. I'd like to specifically mention some names here: Genevieve Cogman, Misha Snowball-Iddon, Birgit Gaiser, Stephen Harris, K. J. Charles, Martin Page, Ingvar, AJ, Graydon Saunders, Jamie Zawinski, Ursula Whitcher, Sherwood Smith, and Nile. There were many others: I apologize if I haven't listed you here.